FORGOTTEN KINGS

By:

MIGUEL BUSTOS

ISBN
978-1-954932-90-6 (Paperback)
978-1-954932-89-0 (eBook)

Prologue

Merlin stood in murky water along the shores of the lake as Nimue disappeared into the Mist, carrying with her the hopes of two worlds. Tears rolled down Merlin's weathered face and onto his gray beard. He shook his head in sorrow and with once proud shoulder hunched, he walked slowly to the shore. The spell had taken much more out of him than he had originally planned. He had stretched himself beyond the limits of his Vitality and like Arthur; he had once again paid a price beyond reckoning.

A war-horse thundered up to Merlin and pulled up rearing. The knight on its back balanced there before jumping down to Merlin's side. When Merlin saw who it was, his fury was kindled, and he drew up to his full height glaring at the knight.

"Merlin! I have found you!" the knight said with relief.

"You are too late, Lancelot," he growled, "Nimue has taken Arthur to Avalon and the damage is done. You have broken your oath and now you and your bloodline are twice cursed. Arthur will not survive this and you killed his only son. How many times will your family doom our world?"

"Merlin, I loved Arthur and it was not I that killed Mordred. I Arthur's hand stilled the boy's heart," Lancelot said reaching for Merlin.

"Bah! It matters not!" Merlin said pushing Lancelot's hand away. "It was your hand that set him on his path and it was you who abandoned your charge when he needed you most. You betrayed the confidence entrusted to you by your king. The bloodline is ended. You have doomed us, just like your father did."

"No! Not yet, there is still hope. The babe lives. When I heard rumors, I went searching and I found him. I have brought you a sample of his blood so that you could see it. We will guard this bloodline until Arthur's true heir arises," Lancelot said holding out a vail.

Merlin started at the news. He snatched the vial from Lancelot's fist delving into it, confirming that it was as Lancelot had spoken. He felt hope string in his chest once more while his mind raced at the news. He knew that there was hope now but it would take generations before the conditions were right again and another king rose up but that did not matter, he had to take the chance. He motioned Lancelot over to him. Lancelot walked up to Merlin and knelt. He remained kneeling before Merlin until Merlin placed his hand on Lancelot's head.

"Do you accept this charge? Will you and your bloodline bind yourselves to keeping this new oath? Do you have the strength and dedication to hold to this charge for the centuries it will take for the bloodline to strengthen and give us another Arthur?"

"I can and my sons after me will guard them, and we will not fail you," Lancelot vowed.

"And if the heir becomes as twisted and evil as Mordred? Will you kill the very charge you were sworn to protect and bear the curse?" Merlin asked.

"We will bear it. Seal the oath in our very blood, Merlin, before it is too late."

Lancelot drew a dagger and opened a vein in his arm and with the blood he drew and elaborate figure on his chest. Merlin's eyebrow rose at the power in the rune but he said nothing and made no move to stop Lancelot. A new oath like this one needed strong power attached to it.

Merlin gathered the energy necessary to carry out the spell. Tiny lightning crackled from his eyes and played down his arms.

"Merlin! No! Not like this!" Lancelot shouted panicking.

"You already killed me, there is nothing left for me but to do this," Merlin whispered his countenance softening slightly, "Do it, before I lose all control."

The large knight nodded numbly, but spoke with power, "By blood and honor I am bound. By blood and honor do I bind all that share my blood."

"By blood and honor are you bound," Merlin confirmed.

Merlin's eyes glowed golden as he chanted the words. Magic flowed from his body to cover Lancelot's causing the magic to dive deep into Lancelot and heal him. When it was finished Lancelot looked up at his charge and Merlin smiled back at him. Slowly Merlin's body faded into the mist and despite this, they held each other's gaze, hope shining in Merlin's eyes and steely determination emanating from Lancelot's. Tears flowed freely down Lancelot's face and a peaceful smile played on Merlin's. Even after Merlin had faded, Lancelot remained kneeling at that spot. His utter failure to his charge and his oath weighed on the great knight's soul. His hand tracing the soil where Merlin's feet had stood, still unable to believe what his choices wrought.

"We will not fail you Merlin," he vowed, "Not again. By our blood and our most sacred honor we will not. Until the king comes, we will stand. We will be the last shield of the light, guarding against the shadows of the night."

Table of Contents

Chapter

ONE

Gunnery Sergeant Travis Patton looked up at the man on top of the pole. He was dizzy just looking up at him and could not imagine what it would be like looking down. Add the sweltering heat of the desert base, the roar of jets taking off, the general chatter of the different men and women from the armed forces branches heckling each other, and it's a wonder he didn't collapse just standing there. He spared a glance at the obstacle course waiting for anyone foolish enough to jump and somehow survive the fall. At first glance, it looked complicated and at second glance it looked extremely complicated. There were handholds that tore off, trick platforms that looked solid yet were held up by nothing more than a single nail and the hope no one would breathe on it. Hidden razors and bits of sharp metal waiting to dig into unsuspecting flesh adorned it, along with an unnavigable labyrinth of moving parts ready to smash into anyone crazy enough to attempt crossing them. Travis shuddered at obstacle course and its nasty tricks. *I made the stupid thing, and it scares ME,* he thought, *I don't know if he'll survive this one.*

His eyes flickered back to the man on top of the post. He squinted against the glaring sun and fought for elbow room among the other servicemen and women gathered to watch the spectacle, like a bunch of semi-disciplined groupies. Despite pounding sun and the sweltering heat of the desert that surrounded them, dozens had come to watch today's exercise. Their upturned faces drank in the sun's rays as they waited for him to start.

Travis joined them in a sudden gasp as the man jumped from the post adopting a swimmer's graceful drive. He casually reached out and grabbed a bar and let his momentum swing him around two full rotations while the wood groaned audibly under the stress and the metal bar flexed to its maximum, threating to pull lose from its anchor. His form seemed to blur as he passed through the course, never standing still for more than a second. The gasps and squeals from the crowd rose and fell as whole sections crumbled and blades flashed within a hair's breadth from his skin.

Suddenly, he stumbled and slowed. One of the swinging sandbags came flying in and smashed into him with bone crushing force. The response from the crowd was instantaneous. They groaned with sympathy and disbelief with one army private losing her cool and fainting. The crowd mostly ignored her, except for a corpsman that was there to watch the show. Meanwhile, Travis allowed himself a smug smile. He had finally made a contraption to defeat the invincible Captain. The smug smile froze on his lips and he took in the scene before him.

The Captain hung on the bag like an overgrown burr, swinging back and forth with it, increasing its momentum. Borrowing the bag's momentum, he swung himself back on course. He punched a wall to weaken it and then jumped back on the bag once again borrowing its momentum but this time to smash through the wall. Once through wall, he flipped through the rest of the course with unnatural speed, and landed on the others side with a flourish. As the cheering crowd began to mob him, he scanned the faces. When his eyes met Travis's, he winked before the cheering masses swept him away as everyone simultaneously tried to slap him on the back and shake his hand.

"Um…sir?" a small voice squeaked and tugged on Travis' sleeve.

He turned and saw empty desert. At 6'7" this was a common occurrence, so he squashed a sighed and looked down. When he saw a tiny airman holding a slip of paper, a slight gleam entered Travis's eye and he grinned mentally. He knew full well the impact his large frame had on people.

"Did you call me 'sir', boy?" he growled putting on his best sergeant's face.

"Um, …yes sir…?"

"Was that a statement or a question Airman?"

"Uhh..."

"Never mind, see this?" he asked as he point to his sergeant's emblem, "That means sergeant, so don't you 'sir' me boy! I work for a living!"

"Sorry si...sergeant, it's just most soldiers..."

"Soldiers?! Do I look a soldier? I am a Marine, boy, a Marine!" He bellowed.

"Yes, Sergeant! Of course, sergeant but I, uh, um, have a message for you and the Captain, sir. From Colonel Rodgers, sir."

Travis put on his best glare and stared at the little Airman and ignored the proffered slip of paper. The Airman stared confused at him for a moment and then realization dawned on him. His eyes grew wider and his face pale as his mistake became clear.

"Sergeant! I meant Sergeant!"

Travis grunted and grabbed the paper from Airman. He started read it and realized the Airman was still there.

"Anything else Airman?" Travis asked calmly without looking up.

"Um...no?" the Airman asked unsure if that was the answer that Travis wanted.

"Well then, run along."

The little Airman scurried off and soon disappeared around the corner of the building. Travis allowed himself a small smile and a chuckle and returned to the note.

"Still finding tormenting the little ones amusing Gunny?"

"Sonofabitch!" Travis exclaimed.

He felt his heart race as the sudden shot of adrenaline coursed through his veins. It had been months since anyone had got the drop on him. He turned and stared at the blue eyes in front of him. Few men could stand toe to toe with Travis and look him in the eye and none of them could stare him down, except this one. He had always been faster and stronger than anyone around him. He could move much more gracefully than his bulk suggested but the Captain...

"Captain! Sir! We have orders."

"We were born to protect those weaker than us Travis. You were given strength and you chose to save people not hurt them," the Captain replied ignoring Travis. "You made me that promise when you joined my unit. What I just saw...that was disappointing, Gunny."

Travis nodded miserably as he felt the shame smother him and his cheeks reddening. It was true, and he had meant every word. The Captain led a very elite, hand-picked group of mixed men from all the armed forces. They were so deep into black ops their unit's name was never written down and rarely spoken, at least not to anyone outside their group. In fact, they technically didn't exist, and most of them had been declared dead or missing in action. They were people that one was looking for. The Captain didn't let just anyone in, and those he did were...special.

"Sorry, sir. There was no excuse for it," Travis said apologetically.

"You are my right hand Travis. I expected...expect, more from you. You gave me your word that you would protect those who needed your protection. Now I find you tormenting those who had done you no wrong and wanted nothing more than to do their job."

The Captain stared at him a moment but Travis couldn't bring himself to meet the Captain's eyes, but instead stood at attention staring into the desert. The Captain stared at him for several minutes before nodding and Travis could see the disapproval fade from his eyes.

"Very well. The orders?" the Captain asked.

"Right, Colonel Rodgers has our new mission ready for us. We're to report to him as of thirty minutes ago," Travis said handing over the slip of paper giving to him by the airman.

"I see," he sighed, "Purposely making me disobedient again."

Travis nodded. The Captain and the Colonel hated each other and because of this hatred or some reason he couldn't fathom, the Colonel loved and hated their little group, despite their perfect record. Every objective completed with zero fatalities. Sure, a few casualties along the way but so far, the Captain had gotten them all home alive.

The Captain read the terse orders then crumpled the paper and dropped it on the ground letting the breeze carry it off. He muttered something to himself and started walking toward the command tent. Travis followed next to him waving or saluting at the men who called out to them. The Captain said little and held a little frown as he started at the sand as they walked. To Travis, he didn't seem to notice anyone calling out to them or hear the congratulations on his success on Travis's obstacle course.

Colonel Rodgers leaned back in his chair. He stuck a cigar in his mouth and lit it. It was not something that was normally allowed, but the Colonel was allowed an enormous amount of leeway. It helped that he had "died" eight years ago and had reenlisted as Colonel Rodgers. No first name. He smiled at that. After all, it had been his idea to forgo the first name, and his genius still made him smile. It makes sense, he reasoned, groups with no name that don't exist should be led by a man that also doesn't exist and has no name. The only trouble with that was that it wreaked havoc when he tried to fill out forms that needed his first name, but that didn't bother him much, he had people that did that for him.

Rodgers played out his career in his head, a shining life and impeccable military career, a "tragic" accident, followed by a sound second career. His star had really started to climb when he began running the clandestine cells. That had put him in contact with the real wars. Wars today were rarely fought on any battle fields. The shadows were where real men fought and died, all without names or even a decent burial. It was a life of constantly hiding in the dark and striking at shadows and whispers. It was difficult to distinguish facts from rumors, but that was what he excelled at. So, as his skill in the shadow arts grew, so did his clearance and with it the best, brightest, and deadliest men and women in the world became his to command. Rodgers relished the power he wielded, the power over life and death. By his word, nations tumbled, and men disappeared.

Now, if his newfound power was his greatest blessing it was also his greatest curse. It had brought him the Captain and his brood. His good mood soured. That...thing was useful, too useful to just get rid of. What was worse, it had convinced the rest that it was just like them, better even. They were dedicated to it and followed it were ever it led them. If he were somehow able to place someone else at their head, his life would have been perfect but life isn't perfect so he dealt with it. Rodgers was too good of a commander to not use his tools wisely, but that didn't mean he had to like it.

The command tent flap opened and cast light into the tent. Rodgers looked up and saw a glimpse of the outside and enjoyed a little breeze. He went back to his paperwork, and drew a deep drag of his cigar.

"Sir?"

Rodgers' cigar smoke stopped half way down his throat. Two mountains disengaged themselves from the tent wall. *I see,* he thought, *they stepped in quickly while the light blinded me and trusted their camo to blend them into the walls where I would notice them, clever.* Rodgers stood casually and opened a small window to let in more light, no need to get blinded twice.

Rodgers eyed them as he walked back to his desk, specifically Sergeant Patton. Now there was an ideal Marine, tall, fast, ridiculously strong, smart and grandson of a General to boot. His eyes fell on the Captain and his lip curled a little, not that he really tried to stop it. He had made his feeling about the Captain clear, or at least as clear as anything got in their world.

"At ease. It's about time you made it. I sent for you hours ago. Well, now that you are done playing on your jungle gym, do you think you can spare some time for me, Captain?" he asked.

"Yes, sir," the Captain replied, "Though I would suggest you examine the quality of your help, they are constantly getting lost and can never seem to find me promptly. It might be time to court martial one or two of them to send a message."

"New orders came in this morning," Rodgers started ignoring the Captain's remark, "We have a situation in Thailand that requires our immediate attention. The Thai government has asked for a little off the books wet work in exchange for intel on other key ops we're running. So, here is the current situation. As of zero four thirty this morning, a group we had under surveillance, Sergeant you know them I believe, this… Sunan and the Good Word Revolution…and why are you dancing Sergeant? What is it?"

"If I may, sir," Travis responded, "I don't think that's the name of the group. At least not how you put it. You see Sunan means 'good word' in Thai. I think he's just arrogant and named it after himself, Sunan's Revolution, not The Good Word Revolution."

Rodgers took a drag of his cigar as he considered the new information and mentally cursed the egg heads that put the briefing together. With that the whole situation clicked in his mind and he realized what the end game was and how to stop it. That little bit of information from Travis was the sort of thing he needed. A good man that Travis, and a better Marine. Too bad he was enlisted and not an officer. He made a mental note to try and convince him again to go to Officer Candidate School so he could start his own cell.

"That makes more sense. It fits quite well with the information that is coming in from the CIA. They're the puppet masters in this one so we get to play with them this week. They may be pulling the strings but I'm still calling the shots. With that in mind, that changes the focus of his campaign from religious fanatic to megalomaniac. We need to move on this now. I am dispatching you to the area. As soon as we get the intel from the NSA I asked for I'll forward it on to you."

Out of the corner of his eye he saw the Captain's posture relax. He knew, somehow the ogre had figured it out before him and was happy to go. That made Rodgers uneasy, but he didn't let it show on his face or his posture. He would figure out why the Captain was so eager to go later. For now he would focus on the mission at hand and handle any deviances as they came.

"Gather your gear and your team. Wheels up in twenty minutes." Rodgers barked, "You'll get your final order in route."

The Captain's blue eyes widened slightly and then turned to ice as he stared at the Rogers, his face carefully blank. Everyone had been in enough scrapes to know when violence was just below the surface. The tension it tent skyrocketed and bodies adjusted and relaxed subtly as they went into battle mode, death was never far from these men.

"Something on your mind *Captain*?" Rodgers growled.

"I'm glad you asked, *Colonel*," the Captain spat, "Is this really the best solution?"

"I don't follow Captain. Decisions have yet to be made," Rodgers said innocently.

"No, they don't. You've already made them. All you need now is to ask for approval, which you'll get, and then we're off to cause another *forceful and permanent semi-voluntary retirement of the head of the organization and any others who wish to submit permanent resignation from human-kind*," the Captain retorted.

Travis snorted and quickly smothered his laugh. The Captain's mimic of Rodgers' voice was perfect and the wording of the future orders most likely exact.

"And what if that is what happens?" Rodgers demanded ignoring Travis. He needed his full attention on the Captain.

"Sir, it would just leave a power vacuum. Power like that doesn't just disappear. It gets redistributed or usurped. Killing him will only do so much and in reality not that much. Someone else will just fill his shoes, take over, and resume where he left off. We both know that the successor will most likely be even more brutal. We're better off creating a scandal, destroying him from within and break up his little kingdom. It's much neater, has more finesse and less likely to get our men killed. You used to have more tact, but now it's just kill, kill, kill. If I were to be inserted with a few trusted men…"

"Damn it Captain!" he roared, "I am your commanding officer and have with me the confidence of the President of the United States and the ear of its top generals. This is what I do for a living and will not be questioned by the likes of you. You exist only at my word and right now my word says get your giant, hairy ass on that plane!"

They stiffened at Rodgers verbal assault but didn't say anything. They shared a quick glance before returning their attention to the Coronel.

"I'm assigning Lieutenant Roberts to go with you as extra medical aid. He's got some little Corporal named Lambert tagging along," Rodgers said.

"Your nephew? Good man. We've been on plenty of missions through the years, he should be fine," the Captain asked, "Last I heard, he was hurt and I don't know this Lambert. Can they keep up? I won't have anyone that will slow us down. If we slow down, we die."

"Damn it Captain!" Rodger screamed, "How many times must I tell you?! I will NOT be second guessed in my orders! You *will* take the orders I give you and the personnel I deem fit *and* you'll do it with a smile! Of course they can keep up! I wouldn't have assigned them to you if they couldn't. Now get out of my tent and get this done. Dismissed!"

Travis and the Captain snapped to attention and saluted. Rodgers saluted was barely off his brow before they we out of his tent and on their way. Rodgers sat down heavily into his chair. He closed his eyes and willed his body to relax. He knew he was the Captain's commanding officer, but sometimes it was like trying to ride a lion. He could feel the raw power and death under him but knew it could also turn on him. And those eyes. Even after working with him all these years, those eyes could still pin him to his chair. He had seen what destruction was possible when the violence behind those eyes was unleashed and it sent a shiver went up his spine as he felt that sick pleasure at knowing his hand had caused that blood to run but he suppressed the feeling. He knew all too well the fate of those how bloodlust went uncheck because his own boot knife had ended his predecessor's lust. He knew the Captain would be more than willing to end his lust if he ever stepped off that ledge, and he held no illusions about who would win that fight if it ever came. He was definitely a lion, but for now it was his beast to command.

As his breathing return to normal, Rodgers returned to the papers on his desk, his mind already writing the op order. He shook his head to rid the last of his nerves and started making phone calls. So much to do, so many to kill, and so little time. Plus, he had to shred the current orders and find new wording. He couldn't use that one anymore.

Patrick liked his job. After all, there were only so many forms of employment a convicted arson could have. He had made a name for himself in Boston burning down old buildings, blowing things up and free-lancing for different organizations. When the law caught up to him the hammer had come down hard and poor Patty was shot during his capture. It wasn't his fault the police had tried to stop him. After all, who wouldn't defend themselves? Really, they were lucky he only beat three of them unconscious and then took off, when could have taken all five. In retrospect he should have, since the two he spared were the ones who shot him.

He was inspecting the cuffs that held him to the bed and planning a dashing escape, when he heard a polite cough coming from the window. To his shame, he squeaked and turned to the window in time to see a mountain of a man had let himself in.

"Hello Patty," he said.

"Hi...Have we met?" Patrick asked.

"So how are things?" he asked, ignoring the question.

"Oh you know. Things still burn and the world still turns," he replied with a debonair grin.

"Indeed. You have a problem, Patty."

"It's okay they make pills for it. It's no biggy. The Doc says it'll clear up soon."

"Yes, they do but you haven't taken them is a while. You should. Also, you missed your mother's birthday party yesterday. And to think you promised her a cake and everything. You don't need to worry about it though. She wasn't really expecting you to come. I took the liberty of sending her new pruning shears in your name. She loved them, by the way, along with the custom cake from her favorite bakery. I hope you don't mind, I charged it to your account," the giant informed him. Patrick could feel the eyes boring into him but he pretended to be busy studying the handcuffs.

Patrick blinked and felt his head swim. "I, uh, got kinda busy planning my last job. She's been saying she wanted new shears."

"Hmmm."

He met the giant's eyes for the first time. The blue eyes held him and he couldn't look away. He felt the weight of them judging him. They looked into his soul and started weighing his worth, and found it lacking. Patrick swallowed a lump that suddenly appeared. It's not like he was a bad guy he just had bad luck. He tore his eyes away and shook himself; no one could judge a man in one gaze, right? He looked back and then away quickly again. Well, then again, anything is possible.

"You have a set of unique skills my friend. I could use you," the giant said.

"Well, you see I'm a bit tied up at the moment. Lots to do, you know? I've got cuffs to slip out of, cops to avoid, and a rat that snitched me out to find. Besides when did we become such good friends?" Patrick asked.

"That 'rat' would be me and I shared cake with your mother which makes us friends. She's a charming woman, but she made me eat too much. How much closer can we get?"

For the second time that night, Patrick was at a loss for words, a truly uncommon occurrence.

"Ha ha! You ratted me out?" Patrick laughed. This really was too much.

"Yes."

Patrick's smile faded. This fellow looked dangerous, in truth more than dangerous. He was the kind that looked at you and knew exactly how to kill you without blinking. Patrick had been in the game a long time and knew something bad was brewing.

"You? Why? Do you for work the Family?" Patrick asked.

"No. The DiNassi family had a tragic accident tonight and most of the main family died when their gas main blew. Apparently, someone snuck in, cut the main gas line and ignited the gas using a faulty remote controlled helicopter. There was a spark and that was the end of their estate," the giant answered.

Patrick paled. That was his special signature for his bigger jobs. As a personal rule, he never killed anyone, just caused lots of property damage but he doubted the DiNassi family would care. Patrick realized he was wrong. This man wasn't deadly, he was lethal and clever. He owned him already and Patrick knew there was only two ways out. When the big man let him out or a quick dirt nap.

"What have you done?" Patrick whispered.

"Well, I have effectively stopped you. You are far too dangerous for this world. I cannot leave you to your own devices. I dare say, you cause far too much damage and chaos as it is now, and I think that it will only escalate. More so, as your…talents…develop," the giant explained.

"What?! Do you know what you've done?!" Dirt nap, definitely dirt nap.

"Not me, but friends of mine. And yes. I have put a price on your head. You will most likely not live through week on your own. Also, your trial is over. Guilty, seventy years, no parole," the giant informed him.

"Have I offended you? What was it I blew up? Boka? Miami? Bozeman?" Patrick cried.

"Bozeman was you? Montana is so far away you weren't even on the list of suspects. Interesting, but we'll circle back to that," the giant said thoughtfully.

"NO! No! This isn't happening," Patrick said shaking his head.

"I assure you it is," the giant said with a wicked smile.

"You've damned me," Patrick moaned burying his head in his hands.

"You did that just fine without me, but I am here to save you," the giant assured him.

"Nice my little angel," Patrick snorted.

"That is one of my names, though I've had few reasons to use it lately," the giant admitted.

Patrick shot him a glance. The giant was serious.

"I'm listening," Patrick said cautiously.

"Tonight, you will disappear and never return again," he informed him.

"Wow! The same deal the DiNassi will give me," Patrick grumbled, placing as much sarcasm in the statement as he could muster.

Surprisingly, the giant laughed. White teeth flashed at him and Patrick felt a grin spread on his own face despite the dread that had spread throughout his whole body.

"That's true Patty, but my offer has a better health plan. I will protect you and relocate your mother and set her up with a comparable house and new identity. In return you will testify against the DiNassi family."

"Fair enough. What's the catch, chief?"

"You may call me Captain or sir," the giant corrected. He leaned forward and gave Patrick another smile, but this one held no mirth. It was purely feral. "The catch is you belong to me. Where I go, you go. If I say jump, you say 'How high?' I need someone like you, and I happen to like you and while you are my first choice, always keep in mind you are *not* my only choice. So, what will it be?"

Patrick glared at the giant while weighed his options. How did this man know so much? Where did he come from? Why choose him? Could he really take the chance not to go with him?

"Very well Cap'in. Let's get this party started. I'm ready for my next adventure. Why not the…Army?" Patrick guessed.

"Marines actually. Let's get your things and go."

After that he had followed the Captain all over the world removing any object that needed removing. At first he had chaffed under the ridged rules of the Corps but somewhere along the way the Captain rubbed off on him. He was still Patty from Hell's Kitchen, but now he was part of something that he could actually put his mad genius mind to good use.

"Oye! Patty you still with us?" the Captain called to him from the barrack's doorway.

Patrick started out of his reverie. He saw the rest of the group scrambling for gear. He slipped off the bunk and started gathering his gear.

"What the word Cap'in?"

"Wheels up in fifteen Lance Corporal."

"Yes sir. So, anything need to go boom?"

The bunk laughed at that. Patrick always found a way to make it necessary for something to go boom but the Captain didn't laugh. He just looked thoughtful. The bunk's mirth faded as they all turned their attention to the Captain. Bodies and gear still flew around the bunk but he commanded their attention.

"This is a live one men. If this goes sideways, and I think it will, we'll want resources."

Patrick nodded along with everyone else in the room. If the Captain suspected it, it was a good bet that it was going to happen. As he packed and tried to decide between his extra "party favors", he felt a hand on his shoulder.

"Sir?" Patrick asked.

"All of them Corporal," the Captain ordered.

Patrick's good mood evaporated as he processed the order. All of it? The Captain only asked for all of it if there was a seriously bad situation ahead. The Captain knew something but wasn't saying. That was among worst omens Patrick knew of but at the same time he trusted the Captain. The man was legend. He never lost a man or a battle. Patrick just shoved his concerns to the side and packed as may party favors as his pack could hold. After all, it wasn't blind faith to follow a man who had proven himself so many times. If that Captain was leading them, they would accomplish their objectives, and they would get out alive. Of course, that didn't necessarily mean that they would enjoy the experience either.

Ten minutes later the squad was jogging out to the waiting plane. Patrick selected an empty seat and stowed his pack away while the rest of the squad adjusted their gear and buckled in for the ride. They all had jobs on what to bring to the plane, and normally one man would stow all their packs, but no one touched Patrick's besides him. He didn't trust them to handle it and none of them were dumb enough to try. As a result, Patrick's job was normally to stow his gear carefully and not get anyone killed.

Travis stood at the back door noting the men and yelling at them to hurry up. The Captain walked in and dropped his pack at the door and headed to the cockpit to brief the pilots and begin take-off procedures. Until they were actually in the air, the pilots were only given a general direction to fly in that way no one would know where they were really going and be able to stop them.

"Patty! Front and center!" Travis shouted.

Patrick jumped to his feet and walk over to see what was

needed.

"You remember Captain Roberts," Travis said pointing, "and this is his lackey, Corporal Lamberts." He motioned to a sleepy looking corporal. "Introduce him to the men while I bring Roberts up to speed."

"So how did you get into Spec Ops so fast? You're what? 20?" Patrick asked Lambert.

Lambert nodded, "I guess I'm just that high speed."

"I see. You're army so you can't be that high speed," Patrick countered with a grin.

Lambert didn't say anything, but a small smile played at the corner of his mouth.

Patrick nodded and dragged Lamberts over to the others saying, "These are the legendary Night Angels. Men from myth and legend come to bring down holy wrath on the heads of mongrels and tyrants alike. In descending order from ugliest to deadliest we got, Boomer, Contreras, the twins Anderson, and Anderson, we call them Left and Right, Porter but don't call him Porker, Peters, Weeks, Chuffels who we call Chuckles, Javier, Travis who you've met, and Asha."

"You said men. What about her?" Lamberts asked pointing at a slender woman with a mask covering the lower hald of her face.

"Uh, don't point and don't look. Just don't," Patrick warned.

Lamberts shrugged and moved on.

"Patrick!" Travis called.

"Sir!" Patrick called back grinning.

Travis grimaced but continued on, "Stow the Captain's gear. Heaven help you if it comes loose again! I swear if it does, I'll beat the crazy out of you and then right back in."

"That would be quite the trick Gunney."

Patrick grinned, grabbed the pack, dodged Travis's playful swing, and started to walk away. He jerked to a stopped and turned back to the pack. He grunted and pulled again. He staggered a little under the weight. He glanced back at Travis and saw a knowing smirk on his face. The pack had to be at least one hundred pounds.

"What's in this Gunney?"

"Just his usual stuff. Pretty standard pack I believe. One or two extra mags but I think that's it."

"This has to be over a hundred pounds! How does he run with this on?"

"One foot at a time Patty, one foot at a time," the Captain said from the doorway, "Buckle up. It's time for take-off. Get some shut eye men. We're gonna have a hot drop when we get there. They can't slow the plane this time."

"Yay!" a voice shouted from the back, "It's been a month since we did something crazy stupid!"

"Speak for yourself!" Patrick shouted back.

Laughter filled the plane, and the Captain nodded and head back up the hatch. The cargo doors closed and the plane started rolling. Patrick quickly stashed the gear and buckled in. He closed his eyes and tried not to think of hell that most likely waited for them. As sleep slowly claimed him, his mind distracted him from his fear by playing out all the fun things to blow up. There were endless things to blow up, and even more ways to blow them up.

Chapter

TWO

Javier had always hated jungles, even before he had ever had the misfortune of entering one. They were sweaty, sticky and it seemed like something wanted to kill him every five feet. His fatigues were already sticking to him and the sweat continued to roll down his back. He glanced at the Captain and envied how the man didn't even seem fazed by the sweltering jungle. Javier chided himself for his lack of focus and returned to scanning the jungle.

"Lieutenant!" The Captain called.

"Moving, sir!" Javier replied

"On my six. Let's go get our contact."

Javier gestured to Weeks and Boomer and together the trio followed the Captain into the jungle. Sure enough, eleven feet in, a bush seemed to reach out and grab his fatigues and snag on them. The Captain turned and frowned at the excess noise. Javier blushed slightly but otherwise pretended he didn't notice the gaze. Weeks' and Boomer's lips twitched but they said nothing nor did anything to draw attention to his mistake. Javier felt a little shame that he had made such a rookie move and redoubled his efforts to make less noise.

They continued on for about a mile until they came to a river. The Captain motioned for him to wait in the jungle while he found a spot in the sandy beach to wait. Javier found a bush he could hide in and still see the immediate jungle. He knew if he held still, no one would see him.

A few minutes passed, and Javier felt the jungle change around him. With his stillness the jungle came back to life and he heard the rustles and calls of the dozens of different animals and insects. He knew he would never see someone approaching until they were close, so he focused on his ears and the information they could provide. It didn't take long before he heard the jungle respond to a new intruder. The Captain had drilled stealth into all his men and so naturally Javier made no noise as he moved toward the disturbance but before he moved, he signaled to the others to hold their position. A small sweaty man stood in the foliage looking out at the Captain. He drew a gun and advanced slowly and quietly to the edge of the tree line.

"You're going lax, boy," he said to the Captain.

"I am not lax nor a boy, and neither am I unaware of your presence," the Captain replied not bothering to turn, "I taught you everything you know, but not everything I know. It is you who has grown soft and vain in a perceived victory."

As he finished speaking Javier struck. His leg swept the man's out from under him and brought an elbow crashing down on to the man's head. Javier stripped the gun from his hand while simultaneously with his other, brought his knife to the man's throat. Javier knelt on top of the man with one knee to keep him still and the other on the ground to preserve his balance. The man started to move and squirm but looked in Javier's eyes and saw cold determination in them. Javier's face showed no compassion and at that moment the foliage above them let just enough light down to them to let the sun's rays dance off the blade. A faint rustle announced Boomer exiting from the foliage, while Weeks remained hidden.

"Call your dog off," he commanded, "Now."

"Why? You drew first," the Captain replied turning and walking over.

"This is still my op you stinking…" He cut of quickly at Javier's growl and increased pressure from the knife.

"You've spent far too much time with the Colonel. You know me and you also know that while it may be your op on paper it's not really your op. It's mine. These are MY men and they are very good at what they do. I lead and you follow and give up any intel or we shall continue this conversation in private. And believe me. I am not as nice as my lieutenant."

The man roared in laughter and motioned for Javier to get off. Javier looked at the Captain and received a nod. The little man brushed himself off and mock saluted the Captain. The two walk toward each other and embraced.

"Damn, sir, you're more ornery than last time," the man said.

"Oh? You're twice as rude Barry," the Captain countered.

"Thank you, sir," Barry said with a grin.

The Captain grinned and shook his head. Javier blinked and didn't know how to react. The smile was so foreign on the Captain's face. The Captain noticed and sobering, he motioned for Javier to take point and lead back to camp. Javier walked ahead them taking point while Boomer and Weeks took the rear. Barry started in surprise when Weeks emerged. He obviously had not seen, heard, nor expected more back up. He raised an eyebrow at the Captain who gave no sign he noticed except for a smug smile that played on his lips.

Javier started back toward their camp, following parallel to the path they took getting there, to leave the least amount of wear on the jungle and make their passage less obvious. He heard the low conversation behind him but couldn't hear what was being said. He wasn't sure what was going on yet but he could feel the Captain's fury and frustration mounting. It seemed almost palpable and the jungle took notice. All around them the animals and insects stop calling and the very fauna seemed to get out of his way.

When they made it to camp the Captain's face was a thundercloud. The whole unit took notice of him and started easing weapons and limbering up for a fight. No one said anything. Everyone not watching the parameter stood watching the Captain waiting for him to speak.

"Men, this is Agent…"

"Green," Barry supplied.

The Captain shot him a look.

"Right. Green. Anyway, he has intel about our op. Basically, it's fubar and we got screwed in air support and any real or valuable assets. I'm scrubbing it," the Captain announced.

"You don't have a choice," Barry interrupted, "so I'm ordering you to continue. To refuse is treason and I will have you shot Captain. It's not like you haven't taken out bad guys before. There's no need to be a scared whiney little girl about it so shut up and nut up."

The Captain roared and quicker than most could follow he reached out grabbed Barry's throat. He lifted him off the ground and pulled him close to his face.

"I am many things," he growled, "but a coward and a fool are not among them. Your services are no longer required. You are dismissed."

The Captain dropped him on the ground and started to walk away.

"You don't have the authority," Barry coughed rubbing his throat. He stood up and sent a withering glare at the Captain, "Besides, you owe me."

"I owe you nothing. If anything, you owe me. As for authority, I'm making it and I *can* make it stick," the Captain replied turning on his heel.

"I'll have your hide for this," Barry threatened.

"Doubtful. What happened to you? When did you lose your soul? Have you become another CIA spook? A viper in the bushes?" the Captain asked.

"It's something a thing like you would never understand. I am in charge here," Barry said spitting at the Captain's feet.

The Captain's posture changed and his men translated his intentions perfectly. Everywhere Barry looked, the Captain's men adjusted their weapons and although none were pointed directly at him but he knew it wouldn't take much to turn them on him. Barry's hand started to casually drift toward his gun. Every eye was on him and they took notice. Hands griped weapons tighter, muscles tensed, and the whole jungle seemed to hold its breath when, suddenly, they relaxed ever so slightly. Barry froze and tried to understand what had changed. He was barely aware of something falling from above and started moving before he knew why. He made it half a step before he found himself in the dirt for the second time that day with a knife at him throat. He stared up at a pair of mismatched eyes, one blue and one green. Her lips were pulled back showing sparkling teeth and fangs. Barry didn't move, but he did start to quiver ever so slightly.

"Oye, Cap'in! The wee lil' lad seem 'bout to wet his'sef!" she called out.

All around him laughter burst out, while Barry did his best to not move. Of all of the Captain's team, this was that last one he wanted to be at the mercy of. How the Captain had tamed this assassin he had never found out. He tried looking towards the Captain, but the assassin was in the way, blocking his view.

"Are ya lookin' at me breasts?" she asked.

"Uh, no ma'am," he answered truthfully.

"Well, why not? Ain't they purty enuf for ya?" she asked with a hint of a pout on her lips.

"Well, it's hard to concentrate on the simple pleasures when there's knife at your throat," Barry explained.

"I got one on yer wee little marbles too," she informed him.

She grinned at him again and licked her fangs. So much like a cat. She bent down and sniffed his hair and slowed worked her way down to his neck. Even when he felt fangs tickle his throat, Barry held very still, so as to not give her an excuse to do something he would regret.

"Asha. Don't bite too deep. I would prefer him alive. He may still be useful," the Captain called.

"Is okay Cap'in. Just givin' him a wee nibble," she called back.

Barry felt a little pinch at his neck and then she sprang off of him and stowed her knifes back in their sheaths. He rose to one knee and brought his hand up to his neck and was greeted by wetness and he looked down at the redness that covered his fingers. He scanned the area looking for Asha and found her in a tree already, walking along a branch with unnerving ease. He held up his hand to her and she winked at him before disappearing into the foliage. He returned his eyes to his hand and let out a sigh of relief that she had decided to only take a little of his blood and not all of it or other of his precious commodities.

A shadow fell over him. Barry didn't have to look up to know the Captain stood over him. He waited for him to start talking but when he didn't; Barry was surprised to find Patty over standing over him. Barry looked over at the Captain and saw him conferring with Javier and Travis and made move to join them but stopped when Patty grabbed his arm.

"Don't," Patty warned.

"Why not," Barry demanded.

" 'Cus the Captain doesn't want you in the planning. If you insist, he'll just have Asha talk to you again," Patty warned.

Barry shuddered and walked off with Patty to settle in for the night. The team settled in for the night, melting into places where they could sleep and would be hidden yet easily escape from if they needed to. Anyone walking into their camp would never know there were so many bodies just feet away. The night slipped by quietly. While the rest slept and rotated watch, the Captain, Javier and Travis gathered around the map, their faces bathed in the red light of their flashlights. They discussed about the best way to deal the enemy encampment.

"I don't get it, sir. Why are we bothering with the base at all?" Javier asked, "Our orders are to neutralize Sunan."

"I have to agree, sir," Travis added, "Why not just have Asha slip in and kill him while he sleeps? We can cover her with the rifles from a distance and be gone in a few hours. You know they will never actually see her coming."

"Because it won't be enough," the Captain replied, "Sunan controls his men with an iron fist. They commit terrible atrocities but only so much bloodshed is allowed. He knows that he must sow fear for his power to be maintained. His men are willing and eager to sow that fear but he channels it to his benefit. Too much fear and people will just leave, not enough and they rise up and dispose him themselves. As bad as they are, they will only be much worse if there is no one at the head to keep them in check. No, I will not let this organization go without proper recompense. They have blood on their hands and their bill is due."

"Captain…" Javier started.

"I know what you're going to say Lieutenant, and I disagree. It is our problem. You've seen the pictures and read the reports of what they do to people. What's left of them anyway. Hundreds have already died because of them, and countless more will die if we do nothing," the Captain growled, not taking his eyes of the map.

"With respect sir, you're wrong," Javier replied.

"We are in a position to do something to help these people and we must. That is what the Night Angels do. We fight for those who cannot defend themselves. We right the wrongs; we defend freedom, and bring justice to those who are in need of justice, the good and the bad. We must deal with them," the Captain said unconsciously stroking his sidearm.

"Sir, you misunderstand what you're wrong about. These bastards need to pay, and with thirteen of us here, there are more than enough for the job," Javier stated with a hint of pride.

"Fifteen if you count Roberts and his apprentice," the Travis corrected, "They already said they'd fight. However, that much bloodshed will be impossible to cover up, even for us. That's not, strictly speaking, our mission and HQ will have your head for this. You know the CIA wants to place their own man at its head and rule this region. I'll bet that's why Barry is here. They will hate you if you mess with their plans, sir."

"The CIA already hates me and they would never admit their involvement, so they can't object. Even if what you say was true, so be it. The Colonel and his sycophants can shove their objectives. I have field command," the Captain said punctuating his remark by slamming his fist on the map. Travis immediately picked it up and started smoothing it out.

Javier smiled and said, "Well, if we're going to end our careers over this, we should do it to make a statement too. We'll let this be our legacy and go into the private sector with our honor intact and our heads held high. If we have to go out, then let it be with a bang, so that all will remember that the Night Angels were here and fought for those that could no longer fight for themselves. We'll leave our mark so deep here, that no one will dare attack this place again."

The Captain considered Javier's words for a moment before responding, "What did you have in mind?"

For the next several hours they hammered out the details and finer points of Javier's plans. Afterwards, Javier found a piece of ground that was surprisingly free of stones and roots and settled in for the night. He closed his eyes and started to dream of home.

He missed his native land of Barcelona. He hadn't been born there but he felt the pull in his blood. His grandfather had emigrated from Spain to Manson, Washington to raise apples, but he had always taken his family back to their native land every few years to breathe in the salt and breeze of the *madre tierra* that called to all of them. Javier had also spent time among the forges with his distant cousins in Toledo. He had played with them in the family smithies, and he had grown up on his grandfather's stories of heroes, *Las Ángeles de la Noche,* who had protected their family and aided them in the past. His grandfather even claimed to have known one and so Javier became infatuated with them and begged stories from his grandfather. Wanting to follow the footsteps of his idols, Javier could be found prowling the streets at night looking for trouble, not to start it, but to stop it. His escapades had varying degrees of success and more than once he came home scraped and bloody.

"Mijo, why do you do this?" his parents would ask.

"Because I am an *Ángel* like in abuelo's stories," he would respond.

"Mijo, they don't exist. They are just stories," his parents would insist.

At first he refused to believe that it was so, but eventually, he became convinced of his parent's words though he never gave up on the idea; the idea that there were some in the world that still fought for justice, and protected those that needed protecting. His decision to enlist had been devastating to his parents. His father felt betrayed that Javier would rather "risk his life helping strangers" than take over the family orchard. They tried to talk him out of it but failed and they had refused to talk to him after that. When Javier told his grandfather that he intended to join the Army his grandfather smiled.

"Esta bien mijo. Go and be a man. I will ask the *Ángeles* to take care of you," he said with a proud smile.

"Abuelo, the *Ángeles* aren't real."

"Have you ever seen one?"

Javier shook his head.

"I have and I will never forget it. He is my friend and my perhaps if you are lucky he will come to you and be your friend too. Go with my blessing and know they watch over you."

Javier had gone and soon after, his fists and prowess in combat had won him the special interest of many an officer. He quickly landed in special operations and it was there that he heard of a giant who fought deeper in the shadows. One who had never been defeated and held honor in high regard. He was always spoken of in whispers and held in awe, high regard and respect, even those who hated him and were jealous of his skill, or strength or whatever it was. Naturally, the stories of the *Ángeles* came to mind and he had to know if this giant was one. He went searching for him but like so many before, he learned that you don't find the Captain. He finds you.

Javier's op had not gone as promised. They inserted as planned but then quickly ran into opposition. It didn't take long to realize that they were getting ambushed in such a way that is only possible if the insurgents knew they were coming, so Javier ordered his men to return to base while he stayed behind to cover their retreat. He fought the enemy in hand-to-hand combat when his ammo ran out, and he battled on with no illusions that he was getting out of there alive but still he fought on. When the enemy bullet hit him in the back he didn't really feel it. He just felt the wind leave his lungs and dirt rush up to meet him.

As he lay bleeding and gasping in the dirt, he became dimly aware that a renewed gun battle had started and was blaring around him. *Those idiots,* he thought, *I told them to go but they came back anyway. Ha! Stubborn as I am.* As consciousness started to leave him, he felt himself being picked up off the ground and slung across broad shoulders.

"I got you lieutenant. We're headed back to base," Broad back said.

"Oh, okay. Have you ever met an *Ángel?* My abuelo says they guard the weak and stand with heroes. I was hoping one would come to my aid but maybe they only come after you're dead. You know, to ease you into the next life. Are you the *Ángel* that has come to get me?" why was head so light? And why was he talking?

"I have transport standing by to take you back to base," broad back said.

"My mission…" Javier whispered, struggling to stay conscious.

"I'll take care of it. You have my word," broad back promised.

"Thank you. Permission to pass out, sir."

"Carry on," the voice laughed.

"Thanks. I think I'll dream of *Ángeles.*"

"You made quite a stand, one to even make the Angels proud."

Javier passed out shortly thereafter but while recovering he found out that the Captain had found him. He also discovered that after saving him, the Captain remained true to his word and had finished out Javier's mission. When Javier was about to be discharged from the Army hospital, the Captain came to the medical facility and sought out Javier.

"Well Lieutenant, how do you feel?" the Captain asked.

"Good sir," Javier responded.

"Excellent. You did an impressive job holding up those insurgents."

Javier said nothing because he could feel the shame beginning to creep up. He had finally met his hero, and Javier had been lying in the dirt like an old lady. What's more he had lead his men head long into an ambush. His eyes remained down cast unable to look up and the Captain said nothing. Eventually Javier's curiosity overwhelmed his shame and he looked up from the sheets and met the Captain's eyes and found them clear of judgment and accusations. If anything, the Captain seemed to be proud of Javier.

"As promised, your mission was completed," the Captain said breaking the silence.

"No, thanks to me...what's with your eyes?"

"Lieutenant?"

"They see me. Like, really see me, more than anyone else's."

"You're observant. As for your mission, it was a success."

"Again, no thanks to me."

"Lieutenant," the Captain said with a softer voice, "It was only through you quick thinking and selfless sacrifice that anyone survived. None of your men died and they all saw you sacrifice yourself for them. That says more about a man than anything else. You should be proud of your success lieutenant." Javier still couldn't let the shame go. "It wasn't your fault, lieutenant. You and your men were sent to die. None of you were supposed to survive the ambush."

"I…uh…don't know how…I can't…what?" he stammered.

"You were betrayed. There was a play for power and a back-room deal was struck and you and your men were supposed to die," the Captain explained.

"Tell me who gets to die," Javier hissed, his shame forgotten. His blood felt like ice in his veins, "Who must die for this atrocity?"

"They are already dead, buried, and scrubbed."

"Gone?"

"All traces," the Captain assured him.

"Thank you," Javier said sighing with a mixture of satisfaction and relief.

The Captain grunted and handed him an envelope. Javier allowed himself a few calming breaths before he opened it and found papers belonging to a morgue but when Javier read the documents and couldn't make sense of them. Why was his name at the top of all of them?

"I think there has been a mistake, I'm still alive. I like being alive. Do you plan on changing that?" Javier asked.

"Maybe."

"Sir, I don't understand. You want to kill me? Now? Oh no, you told me and now you have to kill me?" Javier moaned.

"In a manner of speaking," the Captain laughed, "Consider this a one-time offer. If you agree, then officially, you died in that fire fight. You will be awarded a medal which your family will receive on your behalf which also means you can never go home. In exchange you join me and my team and make the world a better place. We will hunt those that need vengeance and bring to them the peace of the sword. There are many things that can be done if they are done by ghosts."

"I'm already dead to my family, so my actually dying will come as no surprise or blow to them," Javier said bitterly, "Except *abuelo*. They never liked my joining the military but he was always proud of me and my accomplishments. I suppose they will greet the news with lofty arrogance. I just wish I could tell *abuelo*, he would have loved this story."

While the Captain adjusted himself in the chair, Javier stared for a long time at his own death certificate. When he looked up the Captain was still watching him and they looked at each other as the minutes passes. Eventually, Javier nodded and the Captain gave him a small smiled in response.

"Welcome to the Night Angels Lieutenant."

Javier wasn't sure what the Captain said next. His words were swallowed up by the roaring in his ears and the blackness that claimed him.

Chapter

THREE

Patrick got up early. Something was in the air. He opened his gear and started assembling explosives. He had noticed the planning committee looking at him every so often throughout the planning session the night before, so he figured there was something important for him to do and had decided to get a head start on his party favors. When he heard someone walking up behind him, he turned to find the Captain watching him assemble his gear and get all of his party favors in order.

"Thank you for not sneaking up Captain," Patrick said with a grin.

"I have grown fond of living. I have no desire to make you drop anything that my potentially destroy us both," the Captain replied not taking his eyes off of the explosives assembled in a semi-circle around Patrick.

Patrick let out a small snort and nodded. The Captain did have a certain way with words that always made Patrick smile. The Captain watched for a while but eventually wandered off to other parts of the camp. Patrick remained focused on the job at hand and continued assembling his explosives and arranged them by the size of their volatility. Around them the others began preparing for the day ahead. Every one of them was a veteran and had been in countless fights but no matter how skilled you are, sometimes it just comes down to luck. Every one of them had developed nervous ticks and rituals that had amused Patrick when he had joined the group. He stopped assembling for a moment and grabbed the sniper bullet hanging on a chain around his neck. The bullet had come so close to hitting him it had nearly torn the end of his cigarette off. Coincidently, he had stopped smoking that day too. He let the bullet go when he noticed that the Captain was headed back his way.

"Are you taking special orders Patty?" the Captain asked.

"Sure, what do ya need, sir?" Patrick asked.

"Mayhem, chaos, ruin, destruction, death."

"So, Bozeman?" Patrick asked.

"Yes, but with more death," the Captain said somberly.

"So, it's not for show?" Patrick asked, excitement creeping into his voice.

"Make a statement. Make it your masterpiece. We clean up what's left. Just leave the command post intact. We believe there may be important intel in there. Besides, it will make the Agency happy if they have something they can poke around in," the Captain said with a bitter laugh.

Patrick started twitching at the beginning of the Captain's words and had missed the last part. He wouldn't help a smile rise to his lips while the Captain walked to where Javier and Travis were waiting for him. He started giggling and that quickly grew to a laugh which quickly morphed into an insane cackle. Asha dropped from the trees above and grabbed his head in both hands. The others turned their attention to them, concern showing on their faces, but not daring to get too close to where Patrick had set up shop just in case he really had gone insane this time.

"It's…hehe…okay Asha, hehe!" Patrick laughed.

"Are ya sure, Patty?" Asha asked.

"Yes! It's Christmas!"

"Oh, S'okay Patty," she crooned, "sit down an' breathe."

"What's wrong with the pyro?" Barry asked coming over to get a good look at Patrick

Asha hissed and the others glared at him. Patrick stopped laughing but kept the grin on his face and turned to Barry letting the crazy creep into his eyes. Barry took a small, unconscious step backward away from him suddenly not wanting to be nearby.

"Captain, why is the she-demon so concerned?" Barry asked turning to the Captain, who had returned to check on Patrick.

"'Cus, you lil' pecker, I'm a medic," Asha hissed.

"You? Roberts is the medic and how does a little butcher like you know anything about saving people when what you do for a living is to rob them of the life they hold so dear?" Barry said with a scoff.

"Ya don' think I don't know 'bout life and death and who ta..." Asha hissed.

"I think a lot and I've read your file. You know what I think of you?" Barry interrupted.

Asha didn't say anything to him. She just narrowed her eyes and waited. Barry smiled smugly at her before responding.

"I think you're little more than a whore and you know why," he smirked.

Patrick threw a jab at Barry's groin at the same moment the Captain slammed his fist into his throat. Barry crumpled onto the ground writhing and unable to move or breathe. The unit roared in laughter as Barry turned a brilliant shade of purple. Asha crouched next to him and pushed a pressure point on his back. As soon as she did, Barry found he was able to breathe once again.

"Aww, you should have left him," Boomer shouted.

"Yeah! He might have learned something!" Porter agreed high

fiving Chuffles.

Asha bent down over him and placed her mouth next to his ear so he could feel her breath on his face. She nipped his ear with her fangs before speaking again.

"Ya know what Mr. *Green*? You were a lil' right. I is a whore but the coin I be acceptin' aint money. It's blood. Care ta pay the fee?" Asha asked with a purr.

Barry shook his head.

"I didden think so. As fer yer other question, allow me ta finish. Ya see death and life, they be connected. Ya can't learn to keel without learnin' ta heal. Wet willie."

Asha licked her finger and rubbed it inside his ear before going back to checking on Patrick. Lambert came over and dragged Barry off to tend to him a safe distance away. As Asha crouched down in front of Patrick, he chuckled at her. She raised and eye brow at him and got a wink in return.

"It's okay Asha. Captain gave me an early Christmas," Patrick explained.

"Did he now? Do I need ta be jealous?" Asha asked.

"Ha ha! No, well, maybe…it is a good present," Patrick said bouncing up and down.

"Ya have my attention. Wat is it?"

"I have a green light for mayhem and mischief. I get to do what I want!"

"Patty…" she said paling, "Can ya handle somethin' like that?"

"Well, I'll have to borrow all the C4 from everyone, maybe

find some bats to make some party favors or…" Patrick said distractedly digging through his spare parts.

"That's not I meant Patty," she whispered, placing a hand on his arm.

Patrick grew quiet and his grin faded. He glanced over his shoulder to where the Captain wandered and was now with Travis pouring over the map. He looked down at the wires, casing, and explosives at his feet. Ever since he had been little, all the little pieces had spoken to him. In his mind he knew they didn't really talk, but his heart said they did. At times he had heard real voices telling him how to best attach what where to make the biggest and best explosions. It had been a long time since he had heard them. No one but Asha, the one who had helped him in the first place, knew about this. In his excitement he hadn't noticed the voices beginning to build.

Asha grabbed his chin and forced him to look at her. He looked into her eyes, took a deep breath and nodded slightly. He put his hand over hers and gave it a small squeeze, before pulling away. She looked at him a little while longer before nodding.

"How can I help?" she asked standing, "And why do ya need bats?

"Oh, bat guano is fabulous stuff. You see…you know what? Never mind the bats. Get me all the C4 you can get your hands on. Also ask for spare grenades and shotgun shells."

"Aight. Ya stay here and play with yer toys, lil' Patty."

"Not that little," he mumbled.

"What?"

"Nothing."

Asha wandered off to talk with the others and gather any C4 she could find. Patrick picked up his pliers, started striping wires and hummed a little tune. Around him the unit ate breakfast, joked with each other, checking and rechecking weapons and gear making Patrick to smile again at their nervous ticks. The Captain came over periodically to check on his progress, sometimes stooping down to help him assemble a few of the minor explosives.

It wasn't until night fall before he was satisfied with the work he had done. He stood and stretched, rubbing the knots out of his back. He went over to Captain to share an evening meal. This was the first real interaction he'd had all day since getting his assignment. For some reason he didn't really understand, the unit tended to stay away from him when he was building his toys. He knew they wouldn't blow until he wanted them to, and it really didn't matter how many times he explained this to them. They would simply nod and back up a little further.

At dusk, the Captain called them together to give the final briefing. Everyone learned the general plan and their specific parts in it. It didn't take long before it became apparent that the Captain had left out someone.

"Captain, you've forgotten your best man," Barry called out.

"Hmm, let's see, Travis, Javier, Patty, Contreras, Slappy, Weeks, nope got them all," the Captain muttered, just loud enough to be heard.

The Captain made a big show about studying the map and the battle plan. Barry grew more and more frustrated and was about to storm forward but checked himself. There were just too many people who didn't like him in this crowd. Asha lounged on a rock not too far away sharpening an already sharp knife, so he took a deep breath and tried again.

"Captain," he began, "I seem to be unutilized in this mission. You would be remiss not to use me."

"I'll tell you what Barry, if I need someone talked to death, I'll call you. Or maybe if I need someone to step on a mine."

"Captain," Barry said barely containing his fury, "This isn't a pissing match. I can help."

"Or you can stab us in the back, you honorless dog," Patrick said.

Everyone turned to him. Patrick shifted nervously. He didn't normally talk in the briefings except to crack a joke. He started to bring his thumb up to his mouth to nibble on a nail but refrained.

"Patty? Explain yourself," Barry demanded.

Patrick raised an eyebrow at him and then turned to the Captain. The Captain nodded to him. Patrick picked up a stick and twirled it in his hands before beginning. He considered his words carefully.

"Barry, you aren't one of us," Patrick started.

"You don't say," Barry snorted, "Earth shatteringly brilliant deduction Sherlock."

"I wasn't finished," Patrick snapped, "As I was saying, you aren't one of us. You assume that we are killers; that we live by the sword. That is where you are wrong. We live by a code of honor, courage, commitment, and peace."

"Please, you and yours have caused more blood and destruction than anyone I know," Barry said with a laugh.

"Yes, but for all the right reasons. Every life we take deserved far worse. We are not just knives in the dark. We are the Night

Angels. *We are children of the light sworn to fight in the night. We are the bane of darkness. Vengeance is our calling, justice is our charge, and mercy is our guide. As darkness gathers, the Angels stand firm, the last shield of the light, the shining bastion of strength against the darkness. By blood and honor we fight and by blood and honor we die. Sons of darkness, fear the Night for Justice is come."*

All around him, the unit had joined him in reciting their oath. Barry looked from one to another, unable to believe his eyes or ears. After a moment, he threw his head back and laughed.

"You're being serious!" he laughed, "You actually think you can live by a code of honor. Do you even hear yourselves? Who talks like that and who even thinks like that? You have no idea how ridiculous you all sound. I'm not sure what you all have been smoking but I want some of it 'cus it sounds like you get one hell of a trip!"

Patrick gave a strangled sound in his throat. He watched Barry laugh and felt something in himself go cold. He walk calmly up to Barry and wrapped his hands around his throat. Then he slammed Barry's head to the ground and started to pound his face with his firsts. He heard the Captain order him to stop, and so he stopped pounding Barry's face and switched to slamming his fists into various parts of Barry's body. The others came to pull him off, but Patrick got a hand around Barry's throat again before they could separate them completely.

"Patty, let him go," the Captain ordered again, "That's enough son."

Patrick snarled and held on, squeezing tighter. Travis came up from behind Patrick and picked him up off the ground and pulled while Asha and Javier pulled Barry away. They managed to pull them apart and soon as they did, Asha and Javier dropped Barry in the dirt gagging and trashing. Patrick roared a primal scream of frustration. The Captain gripped Patrick's head in his hands and looked him in the eyes.

"Patrick it's over. You won. Let him go," the Captain said, "Let him go Patty."

Patrick roared again in frustration and fury before willing his body to relax. He took a deep breath, closed his eyes and released his breath slowly, releasing his anger as he exhaled. He heard Barry's breath begin to come again with ragged, painful sounds. Travis set him back on the ground and released him. Saying nothing, Patrick turned on his heel, and walked off into the darkness of the jungle. Asha started to follow after him.

"Asha," the Captain called.

She turned and glared at the Captain. The Captain nodded toward Barry's limp form on the ground. She stared into the jungle after Patty before reluctantly heading back toward Barry but stole one last glance back toward the jungle. The Captain sighed but motioned to Contreras to follow Patty. The ex-Seal nodded and head into the jungle after him, taking Peters.

Asha knelt next to Barry to begin her assessment and treatment. All the while, her eyes kept wandering over the other men judging their reaction to Patty's outburst. A pair of large hands joined her. She looked at Captain and he met her gaze.

"Captain I think that mighta have been…" Asha said hesitantly.

"It was," the Captain said nodding.

"Then shouldn't…" Asha began.

"No," he replied flatly.

"But he deserves ta know tha…" Asha protested.

"No," the Captain repeated flatly.

"But sir!" she begged

"Asha my will remains unchanged. He can't handle it. Not yet."

"Sir, it's our duty! If we don't da shame…"

"ASHA!"

She recoiled at his shout. Everyone turned to watch them. Asha felt her cheeks turn red and the tears start to burn at her eyes. The Captain held her gaze until she nodded in submission. They finished treating Barry in silence and then propped him up on a tree. Asha stayed behind and dabbed ointment on a swollen eye. His good eye glared at her.

"Yer a lucky one, Barry. Ya don't mock a man like that. Mos' of us was lost till the Cap'in found us. He gave us somethin'. Now we tha Night Angels and we is proud of it. You mock a man for what he is an that's unforgivable. Mock the man that saved ya, and well that's unbearable. Ya mock the very thing he holds sacred in 'is heart and he'll rip out yer lungs. Yer lucky it was gentle lil' 'im and not someone else. If idda been meh I woulda killed ya. Still might," Asha said pleasantly.

She bared her fangs at him, while letting the blood lust rise into her eyes. She drew a long thin knife she used for stabbing men in the eye and licked it. Barry's good eye widened and sweat beaded on his forehead as she brought it close to his eye. Asha took a deep breath relishing the smell of fear. Casually she cut a small thread from the bandage around his head and started to walk away.

Barry let out a sigh of relief. Hearing him, Asha spun around throwing a dagger at the same time. Barry's frayed nerves failed him and he screamed. Small cuts on his cheek and ear, caused by the dagger, began to bleed. She walked back to him, retrieved her dagger, and leaned in close to him.

"A lil' payment in blood fer what ya owe meh," she whispered in his ear, "And also ya smell of piss and fear."

Barry realized his bladder had indeed failed him and did the only sensible thing a man can do at that point; he buried his head in his hands and started to cry. Barry waited for the men around him to start laughing but they never did. After a few minutes he regained composure and started breathing normally. A new man, Captain Roberts, came to check on him with a corporal shadowing him. His hands were gentle as they check the bandages and ointments on Barry's body.

"What are you doing?" Barry asked, "Asha did it already."

Roberts nodded and kept on working. Barry studied his face but was unable to read anything in it and few minutes later Roberts hands stopped over a laceration on Barry's shoulder. He removed the bandage and pulled a suture kit from his bag.

"What is that for?" Barry demanded.

"Stiches." Roberts replied.

"No! Really? I never woulda guessed. Why do I need stiches?"

Roberts said nothing as he prepared the site. Barry squirmed as the antimicrobials hit his wound and couldn't help the small groan that escaped his lips. Travis heard his moans and came over to lend a hand.

"Hold still Barry. Asha is a good field medic, but Roberts here is a real doctor. If he thinks it needs stiches, it does. Be glad he decided to check her work," Travis said.

"So, she's incompetent," Barry spat, "I knew she wasn't more than a butchering...ouch! What gives?!"

"You're lucky Slappy likes you," Travis commented.

"Ya, sure. How did you get a name like Slappy?" Barry asked Roberts.

Roberts only reaction was to slap Barry across the face with enough force to make Barry's head swim and spots wander across his vision.

"He slaps people who ask stupid question," Travis supplied.

Roberts smiled as he continued to suture more roughly than was necessary. Travis's large hands held Barry in place as Roberts worked. Barry glared at them both but held still. He swore that he wouldn't let a sound cross his lips no matter how painful it became. When he was finished, Roberts smiled and patted Barry on his freshly sutured shoulder before joining the others.

Travis shook his head and walked away. He joined the planning committee at the same time as Patty and Contreras came back from the jungle. Patty joined the Captain, Travis and Javier with the last of the planning and explained what explosives were available. None of them so much as glanced where Barry sat propped against the tree.

Barry changed his clothes, then returned to his tree. He closed his eyes and pretended to sleep but was really listening to the battle plans. He had to grudgingly admit that they had a better pan than anything he could have come up with. When they were all satisfied, the Captain rolled up his map and dismissed the group. Those not on watch, tried to get some sleep. They all knew the horrors that would meet them at moonrise.

Chapter

FOUR

Travis was having trouble standing still at his post. The moon was barely up and the air was still unbearably muggy. He stood in the dark recesses of the trees looking through the bushes at the encampment. The hill offered a good vantage point of the valley and the area surrounding the encampment, along with all the access roads. The Captain stood next to him looking through binoculars watching Asha's progress into the heart of the enemy camp below. Travis envied her ability to slip past the most attentive of guards.

"How long before the patrol is back, Travis?" the Captain asked.

"They should be back already. They're running late," he replied after checking his watch, "This is so like blood thirsty savages to show up late without even giving notice. Can you believe them, sir? They don't even have the proper manners to show up to their execution on time. The nerve of some people, I just don't get it."

The Captain grunted but otherwise said nothing. A small rustle in the bushes announced that Javier was back. He had made the rustle on purpose. It was never wise to sneak up on two elite soldiers in combat mode. They spared him a glance before returning their gazes back onto the base.

"Well, he's sleeping like a baby now and I've hidden him as well as I can, sir," Javier reported.

"Will he wake?" the Captain asked.

"Asha wanted me to give him extra sedative, but I only gave him enough to put him out for a couple of hours. It was tempting though," Javier admitted.

"Good. I hate to do that to Barry but he really didn't leave us a choice," the Captain said.

"I don't," Travis laughed.

"Ha ha! Me either," Javier laughed back.

The Captain shot them both a withering look. They stopped laughing but couldn't quite get rid of their smiles.

"Anyway. Is Asha in position?" Javier asked.

"Soon. She's over the wall but still needs to get to the ambush site. She'll radio when she's in place. Two clicks on the coms means we're a go," the Captain replied, "We'll attack as soon as the patrol gets back."

The waited in silence for several more minutes while Travis took stock of the scene below. Night had finally truly fallen and the enemy was just now starting to go to bed. A few could be seen wandering around eating stolen food and looking for distraction. He watched for Patty's movements but didn't see him anywhere despite the bright enemy spotlights lighting up the nearby jungle.

"Sir," Travis whispered, "I don't see Patty."

"Me either, sir," added Javier

"Well, he is good at sneaking around," the Captain answered.

They watched together, straining to catch a glimpse of Patty and a few moments later the Captain pointed to the last designated explosive site. Travis trained his night vision binoculars and caught a glimpse of fatigues before they disappear back into the bushes. Travis saw the Captain relax a little and mirrored his sentiment. The first phase of the plan was done.

A half hour later, light on the opposing hill drew their attention. Headlights lit up the road signaling the tardy patrol's return. Travis trained his binoculars on the car and involuntarily growled when he saw the jeep's lights illuminate the enemy's bodies, gear, and vehicle. They were all smeared in blood, the symbol of their group for fresh kills. There was far more blood than Travis had expected.

"Asha are we ready?" The Captain whispered into the coms.

A single click responded indicating that she wasn't ready. As the vehicle approached the compound and seconds ticked away, Travis felt the tension in his body rise and noted the same in his companions. The vehicle drove closer and closer but still no clicks from Asha.

"Sir…" Javier whisper.

"I know. Prepare to move to plan B," the Captain ordered.

Javier disappeared into the bushes towards his new position. He had just entered, when two clicks sounded on the coms. Travis's heart jumped as adrenaline flooded his system in preparation for the fight.

"Asha. Confirm ready status," the Captain ordered.

Two clicks answered him. When Travis heard the clicks he dropped to the ground and uncovered his sniper rifle. Javier returned from the bushes, picked up the spotter's scope and started feeding Travis information. The Captain paused long enough to make sure he still had his extra clips in his pack before heading down the hill towards the encampment.

"All right Angels, we are a go. Patty, prepare to dazzle us," the Captain ordered.

Contreras heard the Captain coming down the hill and met him. They ran toward the encampment following parallel to the road. The Captain stopped abruptly and pulled him to a stop as well, pointing toward the ground. Contreras followed his finger to the string attached to the grenade. He shook himself and pulled out a knife to cut the tripwire, chiding himself for his lack of focus. Afterwards he followed the Captain a little farther until they could see the road and the main gate of the encampment. They hid themselves among some ferns near the main gate while waiting for the car to appear, and the show to start.

As the jeep slowed in front of the gate, the earth beneath it tore upwards pummeling the car. The force of the blast threw the jeep into the air sending it flying end over end into the machinegun nest at the entrance. The impact killed nearly everyone in the jeep and the machinegun nest instantly. The unlucky survivors were ripped to shreds when the gas tank exploded sending shrapnel in all directions.

Instantly men all around the camp started yelling and running. Some towards the burning car, while others ran to take cover behind whatever shelter they could find, their guns pointed out into the night. Groggy men stumbled out of barracks, rubbing the sleep from their eyes. A few smarter ones, mostly officers, ran to the walls and franticly tried to get others to the wall with them. Those that made it to the walls and onto the catwalks were met by sniper fire from the hills. The survivors on the wall ducked down, hiding their exposed bodies from the snipers. They cowered in fear waiting for the next shot to ring out. Anyone foolish enough to peek over soon found themselves with a bullet.

Soon most of them were next to the wall or a building. Officers began restoring discipline, barking out orders, and preparing for a counterattack. They rose up as one and fired blindly into the hills about where they thought the shots were coming from. No sooner had they rested their weight on the wall, than more explosions rocked the compound. The very wall they thought would keep them safe betrayed them with jagged rocks and bits of debris flying in all directions.

Contreras and the Captain used the diversion to get even closer to the compound. As they approached, Contreras primed his detonator and he held up fingers, counting off for the Captain. On the count of three they ran the remaining distance to the entrance with the Captain in the lead and Contreras covering him from behind. They ran in silence toward the enemy at the gate and when they were getting close Contreras set off his explosives. More explosions blew out the back walls. The remaining guards at the gate turn toward the new noise and didn't see them coming. One guard heard their boots pounding on the ground and turned in time to see the Captain descend on him. The Captain grabbed the man's neck and snapped it before he could scream. He buried his knife in another. Contreras dispatched the remaining two guards with just as much brutal efficiency.

Contreras followed close behind the Captain picking off men at a distance. As a marksman, he didn't find it particularly difficult but he let the Captain handle all the close quarter combat. Contreras couldn't help but marvel at the Captain's deadly efficiency and grace. It almost seemed like a dance to him. He watched as the Captain kicked a man hard enough, that when he planted his boot in the man's face, it met with enough force to crush it, while he simultaneously used his knife to eviscerate another man. The Captain pulled two short swords from his back and truly began to dance.

Contreras jogged along behind him, occasionally stopping to shoot a straggler. He was having trouble keeping up and still wasn't sure after all this time how the Captain managed so much agility carrying that monstrous pack of his. Contreras considered himself a strong man, but the Captain didn't even seem to notice the added weight as he jumped around the battlefield dispatching rebel after rebel.

All around them other members of the squad descended into the camp dealing death and destruction on all those they could find. Contreras followed the Captain deeper into the compound and they were met with fire from a roof. Dropping to a knee he returned fire but the shooter pulled back behind the wall at the top of the building. The Captain threw a knife at the man but it bounced off the wall. He drew another knife and threw again, this time much higher.

"Drop," he whispered, "Come on drop!"

The knife seemed to hear him and dropped like a stone where the shooter was hiding. There was a scream and a figure jumped up with a knife buried in his back. Contreras finished him off and looked at the Captain out of the corner of his eye. The Captain took notice and shot him a smirk and a wink.

"Magic," the Captain said with a shrug.

Contreras half believed it but just shook his head and followed the Captain deeper towards the main structure at the middle of the camp, which just happened to be the headquarters of Sunan's operations. They continued to deliver death to anyone that crossed their path. Soon they met up with others assaulting the camp and head in further together.

The few lucky survivors fell back into the main structure and barricaded themselves in. Contreras left with Travis to clear out the stragglers they had missed in the initial assault, while the rest circled the main building. They created a perimeter and held position with every gun pointed toward the building, but no one was returning fire.

At first Sunan and his men fired out but soon screams filled the building. Guns that once pointed outward now pointed inward firing wildly in all directions. Small explosions could be heard going off in the building and occasionally blood splattered on a window.

Javier walked up to the Captain panting and wiping the blood from his face. The screams had mostly stopped but sounds of battle still raged in the building. Slappy appeared at their side and tried to treat a wound on the Captain's side.

"Leave it, Slappy. Others need you more," the Captain ordered.

"Negative Captain. You're the only casualty so far," Rodgers replied.

The Captain stared at him in disbelief. A small smile played on Javier's lips because he knew the Captain didn't get wounded often and the perceived shame of being the only one wounded didn't help. Slappy didn't say anything and didn't smile, as was his nature.

"There was a grenade and Contreras was too close," the Captain mumbled, a little pink gracing his cheeks. "Wait, what about you two?" he asked motioning to Peters and Boomer.

"Not our blood, sir," Peters said proudly.

The Captain grunted at that and let Slappy finish his work.

"Sir, should we breach?" Javier asked, changing the subject and rescuing him.

The Captain shook his head and kept his gaze on the building. It didn't take long before the screams stopped all together. Javier stood slowly and motioned his squad forward toward the building. Suddenly, a window shattered and a form came flying out. As Asha hit the dirt with terrifying speed, a giant Thai, as large as the Captain, jumped through the window after her. He grabbed her neck and pulled her close to his face. All around, the Captain's men surrounded them and vied for a clear shot but no one had it.

"You little woman," the giant growled, "You think you so

scary. You not demon. I am demon. You not so scary. You weak. I break you now!"

Asha punched what she could reach but her face was turning purple and blood ran from her mouth. All the while the giant just threw his head back and laughed. Asha stopped struggling and grinned at him, her fangs bloody but shining.

"Why you laugh?" the giant asked puzzled.

He relaxed his hand a little so that she would be able to answer him but Asha didn't answer. Instead she smiled even more broadly at him. As he opened his mouth to ask her again, she spit a mouth full of her blood into his mouth. The giant gagged in surprise and let her go. Asha seized his hand before he could pull away. She spun around, punching and kicking him in a dizzying display. Javier had seen Asha in action before but still marveled at her speed. She wasn't nearly as strong as the Captain or Travis, but she was faster and her slight frame made it impossible to hit. At the end of her attack the giant lay dead at her feet. She walked up to the Captain, lowered her mask, and saluted smartly.

"Sunan and his group 'ave been terminated with extreme prejudice, sir!" she said.

"Asha…" the Captain responded, "Did you just kill that man?"

"Yes, sir. That was my mission, sir. I was ta keel 'im or flush 'im out where you 'n the other could finish 'im off."

"Yes, I remember I gave you that assignment, but did you just kill that man with a thumb?"

"Um…more or less. The end bit there was with 'is thumb."

"With that man's own thumb?"

"Um, yes, sir."

"You killed that man with his own thumb?"

"Yessir."

One half of the squad looked at her scared while the other half looked at her with praise. Patty came over and slapped her on the back and she winced a little. Javier wasn't sure how he felt about it, so he kept his eyes on the Captain. The Captain studied her for a moment before roaring with laughter. For some, it was the first time they had heard the sound, so more than one of the squad stared open mouthed at the Captain.

"Well done Captain. I knew your group wasn't a total failure," a voice mocked.

They turned to find Barry standing nearby kicking a smoldering board. They glared at him and he didn't seem to care.

"A bit of an over kill if you ask me," Barry continued.

"No one did," Javier snapped.

"They would have been useful in the right hands," Barry continued unfazed, "but we'll make do with the best of this situation. I guess I can spin this in Langley and I won't insist on court martialing you after all. Asha a stunning display if I ever saw one," Barry finished ignoring Javier.

"I can reproduce it fer ya in private if ya like," she said sweetly.

"Ah, well, that um, will not be necessary," Barry stammered unable to look her in the eye.

"Alright cutie, but if ya ever change yur mind jus' let meh know," Asha said batting her eyes at him.

Travis and Contreras returned to the group, eyes shining and breathless. The Captain took notice of them.

"Report," he ordered.

"Captain, we found something," Travis replied, "I think you should come see it. It has the same mark as our tattoo. It's a funny looking prize Sunan was hiding."

The Captain grabbed his left shoulder where the tattoo of the Night Angels was on all of them and paled. This was another first for most of the squad. He locked eyes with Asha and her own eyes were wide with fright.

"Oooookay," Patty said, "Care to share with the rest of the class you two?"

"Is it green in the shape of a flame?" the Captain asked ignoring Patty.

"Uh, ya," Travis replied, "How did you…?"

"Did you touch it?" the Captain asked, worry in his voice.

"Just a little," Travis admitted sheepishly.

The Captain sagged with relief and Asha followed suit. Puzzled looks passed from one to another in the squad. This was becoming a strange day for all of them.

"Good. It's just a fake then," the Captain said.

"A fake, sir?" Travis asked frowning in confusion.

"I'll explain later. Just take me to it," the Captain orded.

Travis nodded and stared back toward the mystery stone. He led them toward the back of the compound where a little temple had been set up. A wizened old monk stood at the door. Travis had checked the monk earlier for weapons and any signs that this man was a fighter but he wasn't surprised to see the Captain eye the monk for threats. He knew the Captain would reach the same conclusion he had; this man was just a monk.

The monk bowed low to the Captain and to Asha, his blue robes billowing gently in the breeze. Both of them stopped in their tracks at the sight of the monk and shared another look. They looked back at the monk and bowed in return. The monk motion for them to follow him into the temple before going in. Travis held the door open as they filed in after the monk.

Once inside, the monk eyed their weapons casually but made no move to take their weapons or ask them to set them down. They followed the little monk into the secondary chamber further inside the temple.

"What is this place?" Javier asked.

The old monk started jabbering away in Thai.

"This is a sacred temple built to honor heroes and warriors who fight the darkness," Travis translated.

"Odd that Sunan would build such a place," Patty muttered.

"'Sunan did not build it. He felt that it was a place of power and built his army around it'," Travis translated, "'I and my order have kept this place in the name of those who would return. The candle is ever lit for' wait, what was that? I think he said, 'the Sons of Lancelot'. Odd. 'That they who are lost may find the way once more.'"

"May it ever burn," Asha whispered.

The monks wrinkled face split into a grin. He reached out and grabbed her hands. She tried to pull away but the monk held on to her. She relented and let him study her hands. He then reached for the Captain's and smiled broader and spoke some more.

"He says that he has waited a long time for the return of the sons. He didn't realize that one would be a daughter. He is glad you have come to claim your birthright," Travis translated.

"Chánshī, I am not he. I am not worthy," the Captain replied.

"He says, it is not for you to decide. That is his job. Yours is to accept or reject your duty."

"Chánshī, I beg you."

The little monk frowned. He reached up toward the Captain's face but couldn't reach. The Captain knelt before the little monk. The squad, minus Asha, unconsciously stepped back to the walls of the room and watched transfixed. Even Barry moved back and didn't make any inappropriate remarks or looks.

The monk walked in a circle around the Captain and looked over every inch of him. From a table he picked up a small ceremonial dagger. He held it out to the Captain, who took it and cut a pattern on his palm. The monk took the dagger back, licked the blood and smiled. The air around the monk rippled and he gave them another reassuring smile.

"Are these your champions?" he asked in English, drawing surprised murmurs from the group.

"They are," the Captain responded.

"Good. They are strong and they are many. Are you ready?" the monk asked.

"No, and I am not worthy," the Captain whispered.

"You fight for honor, for courage, for brotherhood, and for those who can't fight for themselves, do you not?"

"Yes."

"Your blood if full of purity and I have judged you. I find you worthy." The monk turned to the rest of them, "Which of you will stand for the Captains honor?"

To Travis's surprise, Barry stepped forward first. Travis and the others were half a step behind. The Captain looked at them all, longest at Barry. Travis couldn't be sure but he thought he some tears form in the Captains eyes. The Captain nodded in respect and gratitude to them before turn his attention back to the little monk.

"They too find you worthy, son of Lancelot. With so many before you standing witness to your character and judging you worthy, how can you still deny your birthright? We have waited a long, long time for you. Will you accept Merlin's blessing? Will you hold to your oath and see it fulfilled?"

The Captain looked them all in the eyes again and nodded. The monk smiled at him again and motioned for him to stand. He walked the Captain over to the statue and had him kneel in front of it. The monk leaned forward and kissed the Captain's head. The monk's eyes glossed over and a golden light shone from them. His voice deepened and grew.

"I give unto thee Merlin's blessing and bestow upon thee the key that is the portal. Mine charge is at an end and I say unto thee, remember your shame, remember your debt, remember your oath. I charge thee to seek honor, to seek peace, to seek love. Mayest thou find battle and blood, honor and glory, hope and happiness. Farwell chosen heir of Arthur, hope of the light."

The light in the monk's eyes burst out filling the room with dazzling golden light. Travis didn't feel a physical force lash out at him but something slammed into what felt like his soul. When he gathered his wits and looked around for the monk he found him on the ground. His tiny lifeless frame lay on the ground looking peaceful and content.

"Sir…what…what…was that?" Patty asked.

"Magic Patty," the Captain replied.

"It felt so…powerful but clean."

The Captain nodded. He stood facing the statute slowly reaching his hand toward it. He looked at the Travis and smiled. Travis had seen that look before. He gave it to Travis when he was doing something he didn't think he would live through. Travis's soldier's instinct told him something bad was about to happen, so his body eked out a little more adrenaline and he surged forward but he was too late.

The Captain lowered his hand onto the statue and screamed. It was a blood curling scream of purest agony. Travis grabbed a handful of clothing and tried to pull. He felt a tingling sensation creep up his arm. The sensation turned into pain that spread all over his body. All around him others tried to help the Captain at the same time and got stuck as well. Soon they were all screaming, unable to think, let alone move. Wind whipped around them pulling at their clothing and the world began to spin.

Travis felt like his body was dissolving and melting. Around him, he could hear fifteen other voices screaming in agony. The sky and the earth swirled together in unintelligible colors and shapes. He was spinning and contracting, and his mind began to unravel and even his very essence began to dissolve. When he thought he could take no more, a powerful force arrived to hold him together in the maelstrom and didn't allow him to dissipate.

Suddenly, it was over, and he smelled fresh grass. He stroked shiny, green blades gently with his finger, taking in their scent. He lifted his head just enough to see the others laying in the field around him. The effort to hold his head up was tremendous so he laid his head back down with a sigh and surrendered to the blackness.

Chapter

FIVE

Javier woke to find felt the sun warming his face and a long grass tickling his nose so he sat up and rubbed his temples. A metallic taste had filled his mouth while he slept. He looked round at their surroundings and couldn't figure out what was bothering him about the area. Then it hit him. Where was the jungle? Last thing he remembered was trying to pull the others off the statue before his bones turned to mush and the world started spinning. He stared looking around the field and noticed that all around him the squad still laid sprawled out in the long grass. Javier worked some of the stiffness out of his body before heading over to the Captain to check on him but tripped over Lamberts' body. He then heard a moan come from Slappy. Javier redirected his hobbling over to where Slappy lay groaning.

"Slappy?" he rasped.

Javier realized just how thirsty he was and pulled his canteen from his hip and took a long pull from it. Javier stooped over Slappy and brought the canteen to his lips and dribbled a little water between them into Slappy's mouth. He sputtered a little but drank his mouthful. Javier gently laid Slappy's head back down and moved onto the next person.

It didn't take long for him to go through the squad and realize that none of them were awake. He began an assessment of Asha when she grabbed his hand and twisted it. Javier gave a little yelp and Asha's eyes flew open.

"Ya need meh permission to be touchin' me sweet delicates. Ya know that," she said pulling down her mask and grinning.

"Asha," he said through gritted teeth, "I'm not interested in your delicates. You know that."

"Aww. Do be all hurtful like sayin' me delicates aint interestin' an' woman-like," she pouted.

"That's not what I meant. I meant that I was worried about you and not interested in touching your delicates."

"No need ta be hurtin' a girls feeling like that Javi."

"Please let go. Your delicates are very lovely but I know they are off limits. We need to check the others."

"Leave um' be Javi. They be needin' their sleep. Keep watch and let um rest. K?"

"Ow," he said grimacing, "But they could be hurt."

"They're fine. Leave um' be. Doctors' orders, understand? Let 'um sleep 'til they feel like wakin' up," she ordered showing off her fangs.

Javier nodded, eyes fixed on her fangs. Asha licked them before she let him go and replacing the mask. Javier rubbed his wrist absently as he scanned the area around them. They were somehow in a clearing of a temperate forest. The air was blessedly free of excess humidity but it still perplexed him where they were. People don't just disappear and then reappear in ramdom places. Okay, well, when their group was involved, people did, but it always happened to *other* people, not them. He dug out his binoculars from his pack and scanned the area but he didn't see anything of note until he looked up at the two moons hanging in the air above him. Neither was as large as the moon he was used to but one was definitely bigger than the other. The larger of the two moon was a light blue color. The smaller moon had and intricate pattern of purple, pink, and red. He sank to his knees staring up at the moons and attempted to process the information. Asha came up behind him and placed a gentle hand on his shoulder.

"The lil' one is called Asha. The big one is called Treshia," she said, "I have wanted ta see em both fer as long as I can remember."

"You just made that up," Javier accused.

"No," she replied dreamily, shaking her head, "Me da told me about Asha and that it was the name of the most beautiful of moons. That's why 'e named meh after her. Legend says that long ago there was this warrior princess who fought against her own father, a tyrant king, and keeled 'im 'for he could do more harm ta the people. In their death fight, her father's blade poisoned her before she keeled him. She freed her people an' they all wept with 'er 'cause she was dyin'. Da gods smiled on her and raised her to the heavens. On that night and everyone after that one Asha stands guard over all of Avalon."

"Avalon? Where's Avalon?" Patty asked joining them.

"She's under yer feet silly," she replied looking over her shoulder at him.

Javier looked down at the ground and saw only weeds. His eyes met Asha's mismatched ones, unable to understand what she was saying.

"I don't understand," he said.

"You. Are. In. Avalon," Asha said slowly, emphizing every word, "I don' have any crayons or puppets so I can't tell ya any simpler."

"Wait, like the resting place of King Arthur?" Patty asked.

Asha nodded. Javier still couldn't believe it, wouldn't believe it. He tore his eyes from sky and stared back across the field. The moons stood out in the sky above him mocking his denial. Javier pulled a weed from the ground and popped it into his mouth. He sat there chewing on the end thinking until he heard the others groaning. One by one they woke up and Asha checked them out. Javier sat on his heels, still thinking and chewing on the weed.

Its sweet juices filled his mouth with the comforting taste of his childhood home. It also brought back the feelings of security that he had felt when he was still a child growing up on the family orchard.

"What are ya thinkin', Javi?" Asha asked.

"Nice full flavor barley stalks. It should be ready in about a month or so. Not bad for a wild strain," he answered absently. He realized that he had finished the one in his mouth and picked another stalk and chewed on that one.

"I thought your folks grew apples," Patty said.

"They do," Javier agreed, "My uncle grew wheat and oats a few towns over. I helped him with the harvest in the summer and my parents in the fall."

"Ya okay Javi?" Asha asked concerned.

"Aye why wouldn't I be?" Javier asked absently.

Asha raised an eyebrow at Javier but when he said nothing else, she shrugged and went to her gear to check and see what had followed her here. Patty joined her and started a quiet conversation. Javier ignored them both and considered his options. If this really was where he was, how do they get back? Around them, as the others woke up they were treated by Slappy or Lambert.

Javier realized he needed to ask someone else if they he was going to find out what was going on. He also realized that the most logical person to ask would be the Captain. Even if he didn't have a more realistic idea than Asha at least he would know what to do. He looked around for the Captain and was shocked to find out that the Captain was the only one not up yet.

He found the Captain in the middle of their group still

unconscious and looking sallow. Javier dropped to his knees next to the Captain. Asha was there before he could speak or touch the Captain, her hand covering his mouth and a knife tickling his throat. This wasn't the first time she had pulled a knife on him and so far, no one had been brave enough to confront her or arrest her for disciplinary action.

"I said ta let um sleep Lieutenant. I meant every word of it," she whispered dangerously in his ear, "Don't make me have ta tell ya again. I'd hate ta have ta hurt ya Javi, but I will if I be needing ta in order ta keep the Cap'in safe."

Javier's eyes filled with defiance as he turned his head to meet her eyes. Asha's eyes filled with icy determination. Before he could blink another one of her daggers was at his eye and her fangs bared. Javier's resolve crumbled and he nodded to her. Asha's eyes narrowed as she considered him closely. Finally, she saw what she wanted to see so she released him. Javier returned his gaze to the Captain and remained transfixed on the Captain willing him to wake.

"But Asha, he's sick," Javier protested.

"Not sick, just tired. He used a lot o' mana ta keep us close tagether. Stretched his vitality to the limit really. The journey took a lot more out of him then it shoulda. I don't think he was plannin' on passengers. The best thing we can do fer him is ta let him sleep."

Javier didn't really follow the words that she said but figured it was better to let it be than to argue so he stood up and started issuing orders for camp. Today, (it was still today right?) had held more weird things than any other Javier could remember, and that was saying something for someone in the Night Angels. Javier ordered a stretcher pulled made to carry the Captain and his gear and moved their camp to the shelter of the trees.

Soon the day turned into night and there was still no change with the Captain. Javier decided to risk a fire. It could point them out to potential enemies but he figured the men needed the comfort of the flames. They sat around the fire all night long without anyone making much noise and hardly and talking. Their evening MREs were eaten in silence as they waited for the Captain to wake.

When the sun rose in the morning, the Captain rose with it. All around the camp men looked relieved and comforted to have their fearless leader back. He joined them at breakfast and laid to rest many of their questions and concerns.

"Asha tells the truth," he said gently, "This is Avalon. I know many of you are very confused about what is going on so let me explain or at least try to explain. The statue at the temple was not an ordinary statue. It was a key to a portal leading to a new land or perhaps an old one. This world is similar to ours and yes Patty that was done by magic."

Patty lowered his hand and adopted the same look of concentration that the rest of them had. Occasionally one acted like they were going to speak but didn't. The Captain let it sink in for a couple more minutes before continuing on.

"Sir?" Travis asked.

"Yes?" the Captain asked.

"Why didn't it do anything when I touched it?"

"Well, that's because it needed to be activated. The monk used his life force to prime the portal and get it started for me. You guys weren't supposed to come but here you are."

To that Barry snorted letting his anger show. The rest of the squad accepted the explanation and shot glares and silent threats at Barry.

"I know you didn't sign up for this when you came on this mission. I know I didn't, but here we are none the less. This is a strange new world for all of us and there will be many challenges ahead, but I promise you I will take care of you," the Captain promised.

"Captain, if I may. How are we going to get home?" Javier asked.

The Captain didn't say anything at first but rather stared into the flames for a while. When he finally met Javier's gaze, his eyes were grim. Javier felt his blood chill. A spark in the Captain's eye told him that he noticed.

"I don't know how to get you home Javi," the Captain admitted.

"Us, sir. You don't know how to get us home," Javier corrected.

"No, lieutenant. Not us. I am home. My real home. I don't know what the future holds but I will do my best to get you home," the Captain said.

Javier stood slowly. He looked each man in the eye expressionless and ended with Captain. He cleared his throat and took a deep breath before responding.

"Sir, I am already dead back home. I swore my service to you. You have never let me down and have always said that in life or in death I would follow you. I'm not sure what it is you have in store but if you say that you will do all you can to get us home, that's enough for now. I'm with you, wherever we end up."

Murmurs of accent echoed from around the fire. The Captain looked down at the dirt avoiding their eyes. He tried to casually wipe the moisture that appeared on his cheeks and everyone pretended to not notice. Well, almost everyone.

"Well, isn't this just a giant steaming pile of revolting brotherhood," Barry said dryly rising to his feet, "I know you all have a man crush on him, but really? That's it? No, why the hell did you trap us in an alternate reality? Is no one concerned that your precious 'Captain' is talking desertion?"

"I will remind you that you weren't precisely invite," Javier said, "I left your under a perfectly comfortable bush."

"There were ants," Barry said glaring.

"See? You even had something to eat!" Javier replied grinning.

A course of laughter surrounded Barry and his cheeks turned red but he stood his ground. He looked the Captain in the eye and waited for the laughter to end.

"Captain, we have a real problem here. Where are we? How do we get home? Why aren't we trying to get there?" Barry insisted.

"Captain as much as I hate to admit it and as much as it makes me want to shower," Javier said, faking a shudder, "I have to agree that Barry has a point. You are talking desertion. We need to be finding a way to get home."

"Barry, Javi," the Captain sighed wearily, "I know, I know. I will try to get you home but when Merlin built that gate it nearly killed him and he was the strongest magus in a millennium. The gate he built is dead. I burned it up bring you here. *Alive.*"

Barry nodded slowly and all around the circle the others nodded as well. The Captain took a deep breath and continued.

"As for desertion, it doesn't apply to me. I was never really part of the Marine Corp or any military branch. Not in the same way you were. When you guys joined my group you weren't part of the armed forces either. As a group we just…existed. As for going home, Javi, I already told you. I am home. I can never go back to Earth. There is nothing for me there anymore."

Javier rose to his feet headed into the jungle. Slappy made move to follow him but Javier shook his head.

"Javi, ya alright?" Asha asked.

"Ya, I just need to clear my head. I'll be back," Javier said not stopping.

He disappeared into the bushes muttering to himself. The others took his queue and wandered around the camp talking together in low voices or staring of into space. Patrick sat on a log they had pulled close to the fire and pulled his pack towards himself. He rooted around inside his pack taking inventory of his remaining supplies. Asha joined him and looked in his eyes before he broke the gaze and went back to his pack.

"Yur oddly calm Patty. Are ya feelin' okay?"

Patrick nodded and kept working. Asha squatted directly in front of him staring. Patrick pretended not to notice and fiddled away happily with a detonator. Asha pulled a hooked dagger she used for gutting people to casually cleaned under her nails. Patrick's forehead started to sweat but he continued to tinker. Asha gave up cleaning her nails and adopted a tactical grip while her eyes screamed violence.

"What?" Patrick asked innocently.

Asha responded pulling her lips back in a silent snarl. Patrick fell backwards off his log onto the dirt and leaves behind it. Asha took the opportunity to leap onto the log, landing in attack position with a dagger in each hand.

"Okay, okay! I'll talk," Patrick shouted.

Asha held still but kept her daggers and fangs out. Patrick picked himself up off the ground, dusted his pants off, and pulled leaves out of his hair. He pretended to reach for a detonator when Asha dagger plunged into the ground between his hand and the detonator.

"Fine!" he said feigning exasperation.

"Patty…" she warned.

"It's different here," he said turning serious, and sitting down next to her on the log. "It's like the world is full of energy and all that energy is clean. You know? Back home I could feel… something there but it seemed dirty and uninviting so I avoided touching it, except when I was angry. It sounds like the madness talking but that's what I felt. You know what I mean?"

"Aye," Asha said nodding, her fingers brushing his.

"It's like on earth it was like I was at an aunt's house, welcome but not really home, but now, here on Avalon, I'm home. Is that weird? That this feels like home?"

Asha shifted on her perch uncomfortably. Patrick's head snapped up when he noticed. He studied her face and she flustered even more.

"What is it? You know something. What is it?" he asked.

"Patty…" Asha said clearly torn.

"What?" Patrick demanded.

"Patrick she under orders," the Captain said from behind them, "She isn't allowed to say."

"WHAT?! Are you serious? TELL ME!" Patrick screamed.

"Patrick you may not be ready," the Captain warned.

"The hell I'm not! Tell me!"

The Captain sighed and rubbed his head. He looked over at Asha and she nodded to him. Patrick looked between the two of them bouncing from one foot to another. Asha motioned to the Captain again urging him on. The Captain sighed again and sat on the log while motioning Patrick to do the same. Patrick's heart was racing and he couldn't calm himself enough to sit.

The Captain took a deep breath before beginning, "While he was in the service of Arthur, Merlin fell in love with a woman. He didn't know it at the time but she was one that had magical talent born in her. Normally it isn't allowed but by the time Merlin discovered what she was he didn't care, instead he taught her his magical arts. Niviane was her name. She and Merlin married in secret with only Nimue, Niviane's twin sister, as a witness. Shortly after, Arthur was betrayed by Morgan la Fey and Mordred. In his attempts to save him, he tapped his magic too deeply and it killed him. His wife followed after him to the battlefield and got there just as he finished his magic. He had spent himself completely and was fading into oblivion but Niviane cast a spell to pull him together for a short while. They were able to share one last night together before he died and she bore him a child eleven months later."

"Eleven?" Patrick asked.

"Yes, that's the mark of a magus. Longer pregnancies," the Captain replied, "Anyway, after the child was born Nimue fear retribution from Morgan la Fey and went into hiding. She begged the help of Lancelot and his sons..." the Captain continued.

"Wait, that's what that monk called you! Are you one of

Lancelot's sons?" Patrick asked excitedly.

Asha and the Captain laughed. Patrick looked at them confused for a while until it dawned on him. That would make him hundreds of years old.

"No, Patty he ain't that old. Granted this ol' geezer is pushing eighty but he aint that old," Asha laughed shoving the Captain.

"Ha ha! True. Wait…eighty?" Patrick asked,

"Aye, Patty, we Sons of Lancelot are long lived," Asha replied.

"We?"

"Yes Patty."

"But you're not…."

"Not what Patty dear?" she asked batting her eyes.

"Old," he managed to choke out.

"Aw, thanks. But jus' so ya know, we age one year fer every three ya'all age," Asha said.

"Oh, so you're…you know what it doesn't matter," Patrick said.

"Wise choice Patty," the Captain said.

"Right, but what does this have to do with me?" Patrick asked.

"Yes, back to you then," the Captain said, "Lancelot pledged his help to his old friend's bloodline. We have watched it as closely as we could through the centuries, but we had our own oaths to fulfill and eventually we didn't have the manpower to shepherd two bloodlines. When I heard they had you in custody I came for you. If I didn't they most likely would have sent you to the chair or the mob or someone else you crossed would get to you and I couldn't let one of the last of Merlin's children die, or worse, become useless."

"One of Merlin's...me?" Patrick asked in disbelief.

"Yes. Haven't you noticed that things that should blow up don't? And some things that shouldn't do? That luck seems to be on your side more than it should? Remember choking Barry the other night?" the Captain asked.

"Ya...I just thought I was good..." Patrick stammered.

"Ya are good Patty. Ya jus' 'ave a little advantage is all," Asha said soothingly.

Patrick stood slowly and paced back and forth slowly. He struggled to assimilate all the new information. A realization struck him that shocked him to his core. He stopped mid-step, turned on his heel, and looked at them with wide eyes.

"Holy crap! I'm a bloody wizard!"

"Well, not exactly..." the Captain said.

"Yes I am! No, you're right! I'm a wizard Cap'in! Wow, what other stuff can I do?" Patty asked.

"Calm down, you need a lot more training first..." the Captain said, trying to get Patty under control.

Asha shook her head fondly at him as she walked off, leaving the Captain to explain the basics of how magic worked to Patty. She walked to the perimeter of the camp and scampered up a tree. She had always liked being higher than everyone else. Being up high gave her a perspective of the world she could handle, although, most of the time she preferred it simply because it was peaceful and solitary. She liked being free and alone, not like that cage Patty found her in. Being with the Captain was her responsibility now but it didn't mean she had to like it. It just made it easier that she did like it, but sometimes a girl just needed her space.

Later that night the Captain ordered a march deeper into the forest. Their MREs were almost gone and there was no water nearby. Contreras scouted ahead, heading in no particular direction. He was simply finding the easiest path through the forest. Part way into the day he ran across a herd of small deer grazing in a clearing near a small brook. He managed to get off a few shots before they scattered into the brush. In the end, three deer lay in the grass ready to be skinned and eaten. He had barely begun gutting the first when the Captain and Travis burst into the clearing, eyes wide ready for a fight. Contreras laughed at their alarm and motioned to the other two deer lying in the clearing waiting to be attended to.

"Dinner isn't going to prepare itself, Captain," Contreras teased. The Captain shot him a look causing the smile to wither on his lips. He cleared his throat and tried again, "But you know, I make a mean venison."

The Captain nodded while the rest of the group laughed at him. He pretended to ignore them while he finished with the deer but his pink cheeks alerted the rest of them that he had heard and felt their ribbing. The only one that didn't laugh was Roberts. He disappeared into the woods and return with an armful of wood. Patty took the wood as invitation to start a fire and promptly did so. Porter and Chuffles helped Contreras butchered the meat into steaks for dinner. Javier handed him a packet before heading to the brook to fill his canteen up. Inside the pack Contreras found some herbs and added them to their dinner.

When night fell, Contreras smoked the remaining venison

into a jerky while the rest settled in for the night. While he packed and divided up the meat, the Captain joined him. At first he said nothing to him and just helped him wrap the jerky. Contreras opened his mouth to ask him something but thought better of it.

"Spit it out," the Captain ordered.

"Sir?" Contreras asked.

"There's no need for secrets here, Corporal. What is it?"

"Well sir, I like a long march as much as the next grunt," he started. The Captain snorted and a small smile played on his lips. Contreras raised an eyebrow but continued on, "but what's the point? Where are we headed? Are we going home? What aren't you telling us?"

The Captain sighed and rubbed his forehead. He looked at Contreras for a little while. The rest of the group had slowed or stopped what they were doing to pay attention to them. He met their eyes before answering, "I don't know. This is uncharted territory. We need to find people, maybe a city, and get our bearings. There's lots I committed to and I have little information on how to go about it. Until we have more information, we must push on and stay alive. I will make you this promise though. Before this is all said and done you will all be grateful that you came with me. Here we will change the world."

Most of the group returned to what they were doing before. None of them like the idea of not going home but had accepted it. Only Asha was unsatisfied. She threw a glare at the Captain before stalking off into the woods. Contreras looked between the two and chuckled.

"Yes?" the Captain asked.

"Well, sir, that's one woman I wouldn't want mad at me,"

Contreras said shaking his head.

"She just needs time. She may not like me right now, but she trusts me. It took her awhile to find her place back home. Now that we have a new home, she has to start all over again," the Captain explained.

"Well, that's just crazy, sir. She's a Night Angel, she has her place," Contreras said firmly.

The Captain paused while wrapping, but continued on and said nothing.

Asha found a tree to sleep in but sleep came slowly her. She passes a fitful night in her tree but managed a few hours of sleep. The birds and sunshine greeted her in the morning and she allowed herself a small smile. The leaves rustled beneath her causing her to tense a little. She looked down and saw Barry pull an expensive looking phone from his pack. He glanced around him carefully checking his surroundings. After all her time working in the shadows, she still marveled at the fact that no one ever seemed to look up. Had humans really lost that much of their instincts? Regardless, she held still, careful to not attract attention to herself. Barry fiddled with the instruments on the phone and punched in a number. He held it to his ear a moment before frowning and trying new settings and trying again. He repeated this process several times, each time his frustration growing.

Asha kept an eye on him and an eye on her surroundings. She watched with great satisfaction when he finally threw the phone on the ground in disgust. Her mirth grew when he started jumping up and down on it like a two-year-old in a temper tantrum. Soon his frustrations brought out a string of curse words that even she found impressive. When he exhausted those, he began muttering to himself. Asha donned one of her masks and was about to jump down and scare him, when movement on the far side of the clearing attracted her attention.

A man stopped just before entering the clearing Barry was standing in. He was dressed in rough leathers with a strange armor on his arms and shoulders made of stranger material. It looked like shiny plastic but something about the way the light reflected off of it gave her concern. His bare chest boasted hard lines and large bulging muscles. A long sword poke out from behind his back and he had knifes at his belt and others, she could tell, were hidden in his clothing. He adjusted his position in the bushes and Asha noted the unusual grace with which he moved. Asha's instincts screamed that this was all wrong and blood was about to be spilled. They rarely failed her, so when the man drew a slim blade from his sleeve, she reacted.

Asha jumped from her tree at the same time as the would-be assassin charged from his hiding place. Asha landed on her toes and casually kicked Barry in the back sending him flying with a surprised grunt. Sparks flew as her knife met the stranger's mid-strike. She was vaguely aware of Barry's gasping for air while she circled her opponent. She adopted the cat stride that unnerved so many of her opponents before. The stranger took notice and adopted the same stride and stopped when she did giving Asha more goose bumps.

They eyed each other for a little while before some sparks between their eyes flew and they charged. She ducked low and surged upwards, while he jumped and brought his blade flashing down. His speed caught Asha unprepared and she narrowly missed his blades, deflecting one off of one of her own. Her other missed her intended target but still scored a hit on his chest. Asha jumped backwards, becoming painfully aware of a wound in her left arm. She realized she hadn't been quite quick enough. She gave the gash a cursory inspection and concluded that it wasn't that bad but it would slow her down and so she adjusted her tactics. Her opponent eyed her from a safe distance probing his own wound with one hand. He was much stronger than she first thought and much faster.

"You are fast little man," his deep voice rumbled.

"And yur a fat pig," she hissed.

His eyes widened at the sound of her voice and then narrowed as realization dawned on him. He looked her up and down judging her again making Asha's skin crawl at his gaze and she felt the need to bath. She adjusted her grip on her daggers and charged in again. She was ready for his speed and strength this time. She avoided taking blows directly and deflected them at angles away from her while she spun and danced around him. He kept up with her, barely. She threw herself completely into the fight moving even faster. She screamed her battle cry and contented herself with shallow non-mortal slashes at him.

"Stand still she-demon! You will not best a Son of Lancelot so easily!" he bellowed, "Women like you are not to be warriors! You are to be chained and used!"

Asha felt shock flash through her, closely followed but panic. Her momentary stumble was all her adversary needed. A hilt slammed into her face and she went flying. She hit the dirt blinking back black spots and spiting blood. She felt a shadow fall over her and she looked up to see him bringing his dagger down for a crippling blow. He knew what she was and wouldn't dare kill someone as valuable as her. Shots rang out and he lurched to the side crumpling onto the ground.

She looked to the side where the shots had come from. Barry stood with gun in hand, staring at the body on the ground. He gave her a weak smile before running to a bush and unceremoniously emptying his stomach. Asha picked herself off the ground and went to him to steady him.

"Was that yur first kill Barry?" she asked.

Barry wiped his mouth before nodding at her. He looked at the body again but Asha placed herself in his line of sight. He continued to stare through her, his mind's eye showing him the body. Asha cleared her throat drawing his eyes upwards.

"Me eyes are up here Barry. Ya may have rescued meh but that don' mean ya get ta keep lookin' at me like that," she warned him gently.

Barry flushed red when he realized his eye had been drilling a hole right through her chest and stammered some incomprehensible reply while slowly backing away. She kept in step with him, stunning him further when she laughed and wrapped her arms around him in a hug. Barry stiffened and then slowly relaxed. Just as he wrapped his arms around her, she pulled way.

"Ya know Barry, despite yur best efforts ya aren't a bad guy and if you weren't such an ass I might just like ya. It's not every day that I meet me a prince Charmin' an' 'ave 'em save meh and sweep me of my feet," she said.

Before he could reply she turned on her heel, leaving Barry muttering and thoroughly confused. Smiling to herself, she went to inspect the body. She had only pulled a few things from his clothing when the Captain, flanked by most of the squad burst into the clearing. Roberts went directly to her side to inspect her wound. She flinched and Roberts flinched in return, panic in his normally emotionless face. He met her eyes, and she lowered her mask and bared her bloody fangs in what could loosely be called a smile.

"Easy Slappy, be gentle. Ya know 'ow I like it," she whispered seductively.

He nodded before returning to the wound, albeit with much

more care.

"Now that's better. Yur so much more accommodatin' than that uncle of yurs," she purred.

"He's blood but that doesn't make the Colonel my family," Roberts replied.

"Nah, acourse not. It's that hatred that does," she laughed, "Is that why you changed yur name? Close to 'is but different enough to be yur own?"

He grunted his affirmation while he cleaned the wound, preparing it for stiches. Asha turned her attention back to the body. The Captain had squatted down across form her and had looked through some of the belongings on that side. He found a tattoo hidden under a bracer. He paused at the sited and his finger traced the symbol. He raised his eyes and met Asha's with eyes that held a question, and she nodded.

"He was one of us Cap'in. He attacked first. He gave Barry no choice," she said.

His eyes turned to Barry who was now being assessed by Lambert. His eyes were still a little unfocused but he kept asking about Asha, trying to get to her. Left and Right held him steady while Roberts finished his assessment.

"What were you two doing out here?" the Captain demanded.

"We? There was no 'we' Cap'in. I was watchin' da perimeter when this idjut shows up tryin' ta call on that shadow cursed phone fur help! It's like he was callin' me a liar!" she said, her voice gradually escalating until she was screaming remembering she was mad at Barry.

"I didn't think you were lying," Barry said slowly rising to his feet, "Besides I thought you liked me now."

"Ya may have saved me but that only goes so far in meh decidin' ta fergive ya," she retorted.

"Women," Barry muttered.

"Eh? Wat was that?" Asha demanded.

"I said I didn't call you a liar. I was just hoping you were delusional. I was trying to call to see if we really were where you said we were. I didn't want to come here with you. That wasn't my plan and I was hoping I could get back to day job. After all the general consensus at HQ is that the Son's stories are just that, stories. Your genetic code is very similar to humans..." Barry said defensively.

"Want to run that by me again?" the Captain whispered.

Barry licked his lips, and sweat appeared on his forehead. His eyes darted between Asha and the Captain as he considered his next words.

"The U.S. government never researched your DNA as per our agreement. Some of our enemies obtained your DNA and conducted research and experiments. When this was discovered we relieved them of their research and convinced their scientist to cease their research," Barry explained.

"So, you gave them my blood and let them research on it until they found out all they could and then stole it from them. You then captured or killed any scientist involved with the program right?" the Captain asked.

"Your words not mine Captain," Barry said grinning.

The Captain stood staring at Barry impassively. He remained

like that long enough that Barry started to feel awkward.

"Operation Contagion X," the Captain said suddenly.

"Yes," Barry said nodding, "I brought you in on that op hoping you would realize what the Pakistani were doing. I was forbidden under pain of death to reveal anything to you."

"We weren't at war with Pakistan. They're not our enemies."

"Yes, well, a splinter cell within the government was conducting secret and illegal experiments. They had heard about the American juggernaut and his angels…"

"You are a sneaky, conniving, low life, Agency goon *Barry*," the Captain spat.

"Yes, yes I am. That's what makes me so good," he said fiercely. He knew what he was and what he had done in the name of his country but it didn't mean he liked hearing it spoken out loud. Especially by the Captain.

The Captain pointedly turned his back on Barry and stared into the forest. Barry spared a glance around the clearing at the others. Once again there were no friendly faces staring at him. Travis walked over to the Captain to calm him down. Barry couldn't hear what they whispered but he tuned them out. Javier leaned casually against a tree staring very hard at Barry. Barry saw a light bulb go on in his head, followed by a sharp intake of breath.

"YOU!" Javier shouted storming across the clearing toward Barry, bloodlust and vengeance in his eyes, "You set this all up didn't you?! You said it wasn't your plan to come! You knew what would happen! You played us like fiddles! You sent us to die! If not by Sunan's hand then in the transfer here!"

Javier lunged at him but Barry slipped to the side and ran to the Captain. It wasn't his best choice but he figured the Captain would be more reasonable. He quickly realized his mistake when the Captain's large hands wrapped themselves around his throat. A strangled squeak of surprise escaped his lips as the Captain's powerful hands tightened around his throat and lifted him off the ground. The Captain brought Barry close his own face and Barry struggled in vain against him and could feel the Captain's breath on his face when he spoke.

"Barry, you get one word before I kill you. One word to convince me not to kill you. Say it, say it now," the Captain said sweetly.

"Shishkan," Barry managed to gasp out.

The Captain looked as shocked as Barry hoped and he felt the Captain's hand go limp, dropping him to the ground. As sweet oxygen filled his lungs, Barry took his time catching his breath. He used his coughing and to cover his subtle surveillance of the groups attitude and the Captain's contemplation. The Captain had turned his back on Barry while he thought on what he had heard. The rest of the group stood in a lopsided circle no longer certain what was next. Javier still had blood in his eyes but waited for the Captain.

"Barry, do ya know what that means? I mean, really means?" Asha asked.

Barry nodded at her. He knew all too well what that meant. He tried to tell her, but his throat had begun to swell and no words came out, just a weird croak.

"Good because if yur lying imma kill ya slowly and eat yur heart," she said. She locked eyes with him but Barry refused to look away. His life depended on the next few moments.

"Captain," Javier warned, "we can't trust him. He still set us up."

"No, Javi I don't think he did, at least not how you think he did," the Captain replied. He turned to Barry, his face set and grim, "Barry, choose your words carefully. When?"

Barry massaged his throat and used the delay to gather his thoughts. Once he was ready, he swallowed his nervousness and tried to explain himself, "Captain, the first part was in Pakistan. The second was in the Khyber pass."

While the Captain nodded slowly accepting his answer, no else was convinced. Javier descended on him in a flash grabbing Barry's shirt, unable to control himself. He shook Barry as he screamed, "Did you just say Khyber pass? Afghanistan? Was it you? Did you betray me and my men?! I should kill you!"

Javier was only able to get off one punch before the Captain pulled him off of Barry. Barry's head was swimming again and he could barely make out the Captain trying to calm down Javier. Barry's eyes drifted to Asha. She was holding a dagger, licking the blade all gratitude from before erased from her face look with a look in her eyes that Barry thought meant she had decided to kill someone. He had a sneaking suspicion that it was him. He realized the Captain was talking about him and switched his focus.

"…wasn't him Javi! He saved you!" the Captain explained. The revelation shocked Javier to silence. The Captain let him go and continued, "He tipped us off about what was happening. He sent us to you. Yes, he set up the op and all of that but when he realized his superiors had given you up, he reached out to me. He's one of us Javi. He's one of us."

Asha blinked, her dagger lowering and eventually she returned it to its sheath. Barry released a breath he didn't know he was holding and his body want limp. The day's events had completely over whelmed him. His frayed nerves finally gave out and merciful unconsciousness claimed him. His last thought was that he hoped no one would kill him in his sleep.

Travis was the first to notice that Barry was not awake anymore. He motioned to Slappy to check him out while Weeks and Boomer traded quiet jokes at Barry's expense. He turned his attention back to the Captain, who had his arm around a crouching and weeping Javier. He knew Javi had never really gotten over the loss of his men but he hadn't realized that he still blamed himself that much.

"How can he be one of us Captain? We're here because of him!" Javier shouted.

"Yes, Javi we are here because of him. In more ways than one."

"You're going to have to explain that one Captain."

"Of course but first, sit down Javi," the Captain insisted.

Javier looked at him in frustration but compiled. He dusted off a log and sat down carefully. His eyes drifted to Barry's limp form before meeting the Captain's eyes again.

"Javi, when we got wind of what Coronel Petersen had done to you and your men, Coronel Rodgers called me and we made for that pass as fast as we could. At that point we didn't have orders to interfere and actually broke our current orders to make it in time to save some of you. Coronel Rodgers stayed behind to gather evidence against Petersen while we did the dirty work. By the time we got back, we had enough to move on him. Travis and I took out Petersen's guards while Rodgers moved in to arrest him. He insisted on dying for his mad schemes so the Coronel obliged him. We never knew who tipped us off until now," the Captain said.

"Your mission was above top secret, as you know," Travis added, "and we weren't in the need to know, so Barry actually telling us anything was technically treason. Him setting up the mission was treason too, but he didn't know that at the time but if it had gone through he would have been a perfect scapegoat."

"So you protected his honor?" Javier asked.

"Yes, and I saved him in Pakistan. Twice. He led us to the lab that held my DNA, though we were told it was a new bioterror weapon. The raid on the lab went bad and I lost four men getting him out alive," the Captain continued, "He owes me a lot. It's a debt of blood and honor. He swore to repay me."

"And he betrayed us to Sunan," Travis spat.

"No," the Captain mused, "I don't think he did. He repaid his debt, his *shishkan*."

"What?" Travis and Javier said in unison.

The Captain laughed at their twin puzzled faces. Asha stepped up and explained for him, "*Shishkan* means that someone owes ya a debt of blood n' honor. It's an old Night Angel custom. If someone saves yur life and saves yur honor from becomin' ferever stained, 'e owes ya a life debt. Tha only way ta repay ya is ta do tha same fer ya or give ya somethin' of equal value."

The three of them looked at the Captain, who had regained his composure. He cleared his throat and nodded at their unasked question.

"How?" Travis inquired, "How is that possible? What could he have possibly given you that you needed? He almost got you killed. How did he save you?"

"Because," the Captain said matter of factly, "I was a slave and now I am not."

Chapter

SIX

Mud didn't want to move from his hiding spot. Not that he really could with these strangers hunting the area for more people. They were far too alert and dangerous. Even the *ariat* warriors seemed ready to kill. He was still trying to digest what had happened to Master. The little one that everyone hated had interfered with a pure blood fight, killed one, and no one seemed to care. They were so weird but so careful. Master had been following them since they had appeared in the clearing. Master had wanted to attack them then but Mud had held him back. They were too strong, even weakened. They would not have survived, not when they had at least two mages and a demon.

They were just so strange. Their clothes blended into the woods and even though they carried so much gear they made no noise. Why did they all share the duties? There were plenty of *ariat* to do all the work. Who would be powerful enough to enslave a pure blood? Where were their weapons? All they had were a few knives and those funny looking…clubs? No, they held them all wrong. What were they? The only one carrying a sword was the male pure blood and all he had were two small ones. That she-demon seemed to have endless knives and daggers but no swords. And why were they so frustratingly close knit?

It had taken patience and eventually one had come out alone and Master had attacked. But he hadn't been alone. The she-demon had been around. Mud wasn't surprised when Master overpowered her, but he was shocked that the little unmagical man *had* used magic and killed Master. Master had always been too overconfident and his arrogance had killed him just like Mud had always warned him it would. He started to sigh and realized his mistake quickly. It was only a small breath, barely more than a whisper, but the small, dark, angry *ariat* heard him. He motioned to the big blonde *ariat*, big as a pure blood, to follow him. That was another strange rule to their hierarchy. How was that small *ariat* making the big one differ to him?

As they approached his hiding spot, Mud tensed ready for flight. His orders had been to stay hidden and wait for Master to come back, but Master was dead. Mud saw no reason for him to die as well. He was almost about to blot when they stopped. They made little motions with their hands that Mud figured were directions. The little *ariat* wanted the big one to do something but the bigger one didn't want to. Eventually the little one won out and they turned away. Mud didn't need an invitation. He turned on his heel and exploded from his hiding place, making for the safety of camp. He made it three steps before they were on him. How? He knew he was fast. Apparently, so were they. Something to remember if they let him live.

They big one held him by the shoulders and lifted him to eye level. He smile, "Hello little rabbit," he rumbled, "Where might you be going?"

Mud squirmed a little but there was no fighting this giant *ariat.* He decided that pleading for his life would be the best or maybe a bluff. So he tried, "Take me to your leader. The one named Captain. I would speak with him."

"Lieutenant?" the big one asked.

"Might as well," the angry one said with a shrug.

He hoped they wouldn't see past his brave front. He had let them know he knew their leader's name. Let them stew on that! The big *ariat* didn't seem to notice or really care. He raised an eyebrow and looked at the little *ariat* who glared at Mud considering his request. He finally shrugged and walk back to the others with big *ariat* and Mud in tow. The pure blood looked up at their approach considering them. He looked at the crazy mage and the she demon and made a twirling motion with his fingers. They stood as one and disappeared into the foliage patrolling the perimeter. *Twirling finger means patrol,* Mud thought to himself making a mental note. The big guy dumped him on the ground roughly, but no more than Mud expected.

"A little rabbit for you Captain," the big *ariat* said.

Mud took his time arranging himself before meeting Captain's eyes. Captain hadn't said anything yet but instead, he took the time to gauge Mud, most likely deciding to kill him. Captain's eye pierced into Mud's soul. They were the startling purple of the main line of pure blood. A noble then. When Mud tried to look away, he found himself unable to, just like he had expected. Such a potent Mesmer. With difficulty Mud looked away. When he did, Captain grunted in surprise. Mud allowed himself a smile, even though he knew it would infuriate the pure blood. Why did he have to provoke them so much? They were just going to kill him one of these days.

"Well then my little rabbit friend, you broke free. Not many can do that," Captain mused.

"You may have purple eyes, my lord, but I am not impressed," Mud replied.

"Purple? You're colorblind little rabbit," one of the others laughed.

"Who's color blind?" the mage asked emerging into the clearing, "All's clear Captain. Asha is still patrolling."

Asha is the she-demon? Must be, Mud thought. He turned to the mage, "Of course they are purple. You're a mage, a druid I assume, you should be able to see through his Mesmer."

The mage blinked at him then turned a rosy color. He was obviously embarrassed about something. Did these people do anything normal?

"Patty, can you see my eyes?" Captain asked.

The mage, (Patty? What kind of name was that?) nodded. The others gathered around subtly to try and get a better look. Captain's face twisted in disgust and he gave Mud a dirty look. "I might as well show you all," he conceded.

Captain's eyes shimmered and the illusion broke. There was a collective gasp from the group. Now they all clambered up to get a better look. Mud found himself nearly trampled and pressed into the dirt. He didn't mind, after all it wasn't the first time and it wouldn't be the last time. *Atras* like him were below even *ariats* like them.

"They're just eyes people," Captain said.

"Ya, but freaking sweet!" someone called from the back.

Captain rolled his eyes but seemed pleased all the same. Why would he want to hide his eyes? Those purple orbs could get him just about anything he wanted. Captain seemed embarrassed by the attention but pleased at the same time. Who wouldn't like the attention? Nobility like him was bred and raised for it. Mud shrugged mentally. The behaviors of nobility were far too lofty for *atras*. He sat up, dusted off his clothes and cleared his throat politely to get Captain's attention again.

"Yes, little rabbit?" he asked.

"My lord, may this one inquire why you are here?" Mud asked.

"No. We captured you so it will be you who answers the questions. I will ask you and you will answer truthfully."

"And if I refuse?"

"Then I'll be askin' tha questions lil' rabbit," the she demon,

Asha, whispered in his ear.

Mud jumped a little at the sound of her voice. He hadn't heard her return. These people were more dangerous than he originally thought. Mud considered his options carefully. A small knife snaked its way across his throat and played down his sternum but Mud didn't spare it a glance. Instead he kept his eyes on Captain judging his reaction. Finally, Mud bowed his head in consent.

"You got balls, Rabbit, I'll give you that. Or maybe Asha is losing her touch," Captain said.

"I doubt that, Cap'in. This un' got a set of brass ones, sir," Asha countered.

"I fail to understand," Mud said confused, "I have neither balls nor brass. In fact, I carry nothing of worth. My master held all the wealth."

The group laughed at him. He wasn't sure why. Did he say something funny? Apparently. He refused to blush or blink. He had spent too much time under the heels of Master so this time he would not be so weak. A small smile played on Captain's lips but Mud doubted any of the others noticed it.

"What we meant was, you have unusually high courage and calm," Captain explained and Mud nodded slowly, "But to the point now. What is your name?"

"Mud," Mud replied. The Captain's eyes narrowed slightly. *He must think I'm lying. He doesn't know I'm an atras,* Mud thought. He mentally kicked himself for his mistake. There was no use but to explain himself now. "I did not choose it, Master did. I am a lowly *atras* my Lord," Mud explained lowering his eyes. Now his cheeks did pink up in shame.

Asha made a strangled noise in her throat. Captain looked

at her with eyebrow raised. She regained some composure before answering, "It's part of tha old customs, Cap'in. *Atras* were the lesser race who were enslaved ta pay some shame they or their fathers had created. Thisun' was that big oaf's slave I take it."

The Captain looked at Mud, who only nodded miserably. The Captain leaned back, a thoughtful expression on his face. "So who owns you now?" he asked.

"My Lord, surely you know?" Mud ventured.

"Our customs are different. What does your blood shame contract say?"

"I go to the man who killed my master," Mud replied even more miserably. He belonged to the one they all hated. Now he was lower than low. The only *atras,* belonging to the lower member of the clan.

"Well, by right of leadership I claim you as my own. I will be your new master," Captain declared.

"My Lord, I do not think it works that way," Mud said delicately.

"It works how I say it works *atras,*" the Captain said.

Mud bowed in submission and stayed bowed. Captain may be higher ranking but he had shamed him. He had taken Mud's name. Not that he had liked his name but it had still been a name. Tears burned in his eyes and threatened to flow but he refused to let them out. He would show them his strength and earn his name back.

"So tell me, where did you acquire a name like Mud?" Captain asked.

"This one earned his name be tilling the mud and feeding the clan in a time of famine, Master. It was given to this one as a reward."

Captain looked stunned. Horror filled the eyes of the others. So, even there they knew the shame of working the dirt. Feeding the clan had given him honor, but the mud had shamed him and given him a name of shame to carry, but it had still been a name.

"Do you like the name 'Mud'," Captain asked.

"This one did not, Master, but it was my shame and honor to hold it for as long as I did," he replied.

"As long as you…wait, did I take your name somehow?" Captain asked.

"Master claimed me and called me *atras*, this one is sorry to have offended you. How shall I chastise myself to pay for my sin, Master?"

"Chastise, sins? What?" Captain said confused.

"This shamed one did not tell his master that he was an *atras*. Losing my name is fitting and just, Master. What else can I do to lift my shame? Will a mortification of the flesh appease you, Master?"

"I think I am going to be sick," the mage said. *Atras* looked up and saw that the mage was indeed green.

"Would my Master's druid wish me to make him a remedy for him?" *astras* asked.

"No, I'm fine…I…think…wow. Just wow," the mage answered.

"Look at me," Captain said gently.

"I am not worthy Master," *atras* replied.

"Look at me," Captain repeated more firmly.

"Yes, Master," *atras* replied. He looked up into Captain's eye and found sympathy. It was the last thing that *atras* expected. Captain's gaze turned a little awkward and he turn eyes away, but *atras* saw the shame in them before he did. He threw himself on the ground again and plead, "Forgive me master, this one did not mean to shame you."

"The shame is mine alone. In the few moments I have…" Captain swallowed as if a bitter taste was in his mouth but continued, "…owned you, I have shamed you beyond words. I will give you back your name. What one do you want? What shall we call you?"

Atras could not believe what he was hearing. These people were so strange, trampling on custom, but right now he didn't care. Here was his new Master offering him the very thing he had been yearning for all his life. It was too good to be true and just like that his happiness deflated instantly. His body felt like it had been dropped in an icy river. Of course, it was too good to be true. Master was testing Mu…*atras*.

"You honor this one Master, but this one is not worthy. I… this one had not proved worthy of honor," he replied.

"It is not yours to judge. Do you think me a fool?" Captain asked.

"I do not doubt your greatness Master," *atras* said, "I meant no dishonor. Forgive this one's insolence."

Captain rose to his feet and adopted a posture that was worth of royalty, more than any other that *atras* had ever seen. From above he heard Captain, "We are the heir of Lancelot, the true king, and by sovereignty of our blood line, and by merit of our conquest we declare thee free of all shame. Let all who stand here, warriors and champions all, stand witness, that this man is cleansed of all dishonor. Let any who hold doubt stand forth and offer utterance."

Atras felt his heart stop. This wasn't just a noble, he was a prince! Not only that but he was removing his shame. All of it. *Atras* felt his breath stop and tears burn in his eyes but he didn't care. This was too much, it had to be a dream, but please, oh please let it be real. He strained his ears for any sign from the others. Maybe one of them knew something, maybe one would step forward. But no one did.

"Let the heaven's bear witness that in the presence of royalty and champions, there was no shame found in this man. We bid thee rise, receive thine name, and swear fealty unto your Lord," Captain declared, "What name shall we call you?"

"I…can't…" *atras*'s voice choked off. He couldn't do anything but shake his head.

"Would you like us to give thee thine name?" Captain asked.

Atras could only nod. This was it. After so long and after so many generations, the shame was gone. Honor could be gained now.

"In our youth we were saved by one named Pablo," Captain said. The angry *ariat* made a funny noise but Captain continued, "His is a name honored by our family. We bestow this name upon thee, and bid thee to honor it and bring more honor to it. Now rise Pablo, swear to us, and receive your accolades."

Pablo, such a powerful name. Pablo couldn't believe his ears. His fingers clawed the dirt that not so long ago had he had been named after. Tears streamed freely from his eyes. With a cry he rose up from the dirt with his knife in hand. He was aware of Captain's champions moving but he ignored them. He brought the knife down on his own hand. The knife slid easily through his skin and the blood flowed freely. He felt the she-demon press her own blade against his throat. Pablo didn't shy away from it but he didn't make sudden movements either and he let his knife slip through his fingers into the dirt. Slowly he brought his bleeding hand to his face, then across his stomach, and lastly placing his hand firmly over his heart. His blood decorated his face and flowed from his hand. Tears mixed with the blood but his eyes were clear when he met Captains.

"I swear my mind, my body and my heart to my new Lord and Master, Captain. I swear to uphold and honor the name Pablo and bring honor to my Lord. I so do swear by my life's blood and my sacred honor, such as it is," Pablo pledged.

"We do accept thine oath," Captain said and touched Pablo on the crown of his head. Light flashed and Pablo felt the magic flow from Captain, sealing the blood oath, "Now rise Pablo, and join your brothers."

Pablo stood and looked at the others. They gathered around his, some slapping him on the back, while others shook his hand. When he turned to the she demon she glared at him. Daggers drawn she stalked toward him hate burning in her eyes. He backed away right into a rock that caught his heel and sent him tumbling to the ground. She was on him instantly, straddling him, dagger filling the view in one eye. She leaned in close and whispered into his ear, "Welcome ta the Night Angels, but if ya so much as think about betrayin' us, I will take *days* in killin' ya."

With that she kissed him roughly on the mouth and laughed. The others laughed as well, but it wasn't the cruel laughter Pablo was so used to. This was the lighthearted laughter of brothers. Pablo stayed on the ground looking up at the sky, not trusting his legs to hold him. The mage came into view and looked down at him.

"She threated to kill you slowly?" he asked. Pablo nodded and the mage laughed, "Yeah, she does that to everyone. It means that she likes you. Normally she cuts people, but you got a kiss instead."

"I am not sure her affections are overly desirable," Pablo said dryly.

The mage laughed at him, "That wasn't affection. On earth, where we come from, some cultures kiss you right before they kill you. Also, careful, she has *really* good hearing."

"Oh my."

"Yup. I would sleep with one eye open."

"Yes…thank you."

"Mhmm."

"Pablo!" Captain called.

"Yes, Lord Captain?" Pablo called back standing and going to Captain's side, "How may I be of service."

Captain blinked. "My name isn't Captain. It's my rank. You know that right?" he asked.

"Then what is it my Lord?" Pablo asked.

"Let's talk about that and your duties. Come with me," Captain said putting his arm around Pablo and walked them to a nearby log, "Well for starts 'Captain' is a title you should address me by…"

Looking back on it, Pablo had found the gesture awkward,

but the Captain's arm on his shoulder was what eventually won his loyalty. When times were tough and his world was imploding, he remembered that moment. The moment when he, Pablo, made a friend.

Javier watched the Captain talk with "Pablo". *Who doesn't have a name?* Javier thought to himself, *I'm not so thrilled about this.*

"Worrying gives you wrinkles, Lieutenant," Patty said from behind him.

"Honestly, I never thought I'd live long enough to worry about that," Javier replied.

"Well, here we are Javi. So, what's got your panties in knot?"

Javier shot him a look but knew better than to try and get an apology from Patty. Considered his words before responding, "Pablo is my abuelo's name."

"Abuelo?" Patty asked.

"Grandfather," Javier explained.

"Oh, why not say that?" Patty asked frowning.

"I did Patty," Javier said, exasperation in his voice.

"Right. So, what's wrong about letting Pablo there borrow your grand pappy's name?" Patty inquired.

"Nothing. He should be honored. It's just…never mind," Javier said waving his hand.

"I've had lots of never mind in my time too," Patty said patting him on the back.

Javier grunted but considered Patty's words. They were stuck here and weren't going back so what did it hurt to open up a little? "My grandpa would tell me stories about Angeles de la Noche, the Night Angels, and claimed to have met one in his youth. I am wondering if the Captain knew him."

"It's possible," Patty said rubbing his chin, "After all the Captain is in his eighties. There's a good chance they know each other."

Javier didn't react at first, attributing Patty's babble to his randomness, but then reconsidered. "What do you mean he's in his eighties?"

"Well, the Captain is a Son of Lancelot or some such thing. They age one year for every three years we do, at least that's what Asha says."

"Hmmm," Javier replied. The wheels in his head were turning at the new revelation. "Thanks Patty. If you don't mind, I need to be alone."

"Ya, I would too Lieutenant," Patty said getting up and patting Javier on the shoulder again before walking away.

Chapter

SEVEN

Javier lost himself in thought for much of the day barely aware of those around him and completing all his work without thinking. Towards night fall his stomach reminded him that they hadn't eaten yet today. He gave Pablo a fleeting glance and Patty a word, before heading in the forest to look for food. Patty had offered to go with him but he had declined the offer, preferring the solitude that the forest offered him. He wandered aimlessly, not really sure what he was looking for, maybe a deer, and eventually gave up, heading back to camp empty handed as night truly fell.

As Javier approached camp, laughter filled his ears and the sweet smell of roasting meat filled his nose. He walked into camp to find the other gathered around a camp fire, eating and joking with Pablo the center of attention. Pablo gave him polite smile when he wandered in, but refrained from actually interacting with the others. His mind was on food and he filled his plate to the brim following the examples of the others.

"How is your meal lieutenant?" Pablo asked.

"Not bad," Javier grunted, "Where did it come from?"

"I gathered it from nearby and the beast I slew on my way back. This part of the forest teems with nutrients."

Javier stopped chewing and looked up to make sure Pablo was being serious. Pablo wasn't even looking at Javier, instead he was looking into the forest. His hands were fiddling with a small trinket that Javier recognized as one of the Captain's rings that he carried with him but rarely wore.

"You found food here?" Javier asked after swallowing.

"Yes, it was my responsibility to gather the evening food for Zemer, my former master. When the druid said he needed to eat before he killed someone and ate them, I went immediately into the forest before he carried through."

Javier choked on his mouthful drawing concerned looks from Pablo and the rest of the group. He held up his hands and waved them to show that he was fine and didn't need help. The rest were appeased but Pablo retained his concerned look and remained crouching nearby just in case Javier did need help.

"You thought he was going to kill someone?" Javier laughed.

"Yes. Druids don't lie and they are not someone you want to anger," Pablo replied completely calm like it was the most reasonable thing in the world.

"Wow Pablo, you really are that innocent, aren't you?" Javier asked.

"I do not understand…sir," Pablo said.

"Sir? Where did that come from?"

"That is the proper title for someone so esteemed as yourself, is it not lieutenant?"

"Yes, but that's normally only used by those in armed forces."

"Lord Captain said I was one of you. Should I not follow your customs and rules?" Pablo asked puzzled.

"Look, Pablo, you seem like a great guy and you're one hell of a cook, but I don't trust you. You haven't earned that yet, and I'm waiting for you to betray us," Javier said unable to keep an edge from his voice.

Pablo noticed it and shrunk back a little. "I have sworn a blood oath to follow Captain. Is that not enough?"

"The gesture was…dramatic but words and oaths do not hold men. I have learned the truth of this many times."

"Where you come from, men die rather than keep their word? What kind of place is that?" Pablo asked aghast.

"They only did it once. I found those that didn't and taught them the error of their ways. They kept their word after that, believe you me," Javier said, wicked smile playing on his lips.

"They did not die?"

"No, Pablo, I preferred to keep them alive, they were too useful to kill."

"But their blood oaths, how did that not kill them?" Pablo asked confused, sitting down at Javier's feet.

Javier adjusted himself nervously on the rock he had claimed as a perch. Having someone at his feet was an unnerving experience to him. "Why would that kill them? Like I said words don't hold men. Only the most honorable men."

Pablo's mouth worked opening and closing unable to work properly, words having fled him. Javier looked at him with curiosity trying to figure out what was so earth shattering to have left Pablo so speechless.

"You can't break blood oaths," Pablo said as though that explained everything.

"Maybe here they don't," Javier laughed, "But back home people break them all the time. There are few men who hold their word as their bond. Those you see around you are among the few that do, and I think that's part of the reason that the Captain picked us to join him."

"You just can't break a blood oath," Pablo repeated stubbornly.

"Okay little rabbit…"

"My name is Pablo," Pablo snapped.

"Okay, okay, fine. *Pablo*, I'll bite. Why can't anyone 'break an oath'?" Javier asked.

"Because it would kill them! That is the whole point. If you betray your word, your blood betrays you. You don't ever survive it!" Pablo said exasperated.

It was Javier's turn to be struck speechless, with a mouth opening and closing. He looked around trying to anchor himself and noticed that Asha was watching and listening to their conversation. His looked at her and back to Pablo with his eyes screaming the unasked question. Asha sighed but wander over to see what Javier wanted.

"Wats wrong Javi?" she asked.

"Is…is it true?" he managed to gasp out.

"Is what true Javi?" she asked flicking hair from her face.

"Is a blood oath unbreakable?" Javier clarified.

"Acourse its breakable silly," Asha said, and Javier relaxed but then she continued, "but it will cost ya yur life. There's magic in this realm Javi. Real magic an' most of it is strong, so blood oaths will hold all but the craziest. If ya hadn't been all butt hurt 'n hidin' in tha forest ya would have heard the Cap'in explain it 'n how Pabby here is of us. Pity though. I won't be able ta kill the cutie if he betrays us."

Pablo muttered something and then turned red.

"Oh I know what yur name is Pabby, but imma call ya Pabby. Is that all right with ya, cutie?" she asked grinning, showing off her fangs.

Pablo muttered something else unintelligible but nodded to her.

"There's a good boy," Asha said smiling. She blew Pablo a kiss before going back to her original seat by Patty and sharing a laugh with him.

"I do not believe that that woman's affections are what they appear to be at the surface," Pablo said frowning.

Javier threw his head back and laughed from deep within his stomach. He laughed long enough that he went past the hyena phase and into the silent laugh with tears running down his face. Once he got himself back under control, he noticed that everyone was once again looking at him and Pablo was once again pink.

"Feel that I am being mocked but I do not know why," Pablo said grumpily.

"Its fine Pabby," Javier teased earning himself a glare, "It's just so nice to laugh after so long. You seem to be bound to us then, and the Captain trusts you, so I will trust you. For now."

"Thank you Lieutenant. Your confidence is of importance to me. You are a man respected by all here. I think, now that you approve of me, the others will truly accept me as one of them," Pablo said.

"Of course, they do, the Captain likes you," Javier said with a small chuckle.

"Yes, that made part of the group, but your word makes me a brother. They respect you, Lieutenant. They would not trust me fully if you do not. For some reason they feel that you will protect them from harm. I am not sure why yet," Pablo explained with a pensive frown.

"What?" Javier whispered.

"Oh right, I forgot you don't know. I have a small magical gift. It helps me empathize with people. I can feel what they feel to a certain extent. It let me know that they hold your opinion almost to the same level as Lord Captain. I don't know what you did, but they feel safe with their lives in your hands. None will tell me. What did you do?" Pablo asked.

Javier pondered this revelation before responding, "I have laid down my life for my men before and I would do it again."

"Ah, I see. The bond of blood brothers," Pablo said nodding.

"We aren't related."

"No, but you have shed your own blood and the blood of your enemies to keep them save. Unless I miss my guest you have also risked your honor on more than one occasion to save them? Yes? Is there a stronger bond than that of brothers forged in blood and battle? Brothers who would risk all that are and all that they could be for each other? They love you and you love them. Blood may make you family, Lieutenant, but family isn't always blood."

Javier only nodded in response to Pablo. His eyes were too busy looking over the men around the fire who he held so dear to him. He had never thought of it like that but to his surprise he discovered that it was true, they were brothers. His family may have abandoned him just like so many of the others here, but they had made their own family, one of their own choosing.

"My grandfather said something like that once," Javier said absently, his eyes meeting the Captain's.

"He must have been a wise man."

"He was. You bring honor your name Pablo," Javier said rising.

"Thank you Lieutenant," Pablo said suddenly emotional. A question came to his mind as Javier walked toward the Captain, "Wait, what was his name? Your Grandfather's?"

"His name was Pablo," Javier replied over his shoulder.

Asha watched Javier and the Captain talk quietly at the edge of their campfire's light. A small tender smile crept up onto her lips as she heard their conversation.

"What are they talking about?" Patty asked.

"Javier made a connection ta'night and is apologizing fer bein' a tool to tha Cap'in," she replied absently.

"Oh, what did he learn?"

"If it was any 'o yur business, idda told ya Patty. Did I tell ya?"

"Uh…no ma'am."

"Then leave it be Patty."

Asha gave him her most dangerous and toothiest smile she could manage. It made Patty swallow nervously and sweat, just as she had hoped it would. Asha stretched out comfortably, leaning against him while she nibbled on a piece of meat off her knife that she had sliced off the pig-like animal Pablo had brought back. She listened to the pleasant conversation of the others until she felt drowsiness creeping up on her. She stretched and yawned before gliding off with her panther-like grace to find a tree for the night.

"Mistress?" Pablo asked stopping her.

"Yes, lil' Pabby?" she asked smiling inwardly when he grimaced at his new pet name.

"Why do you always sleep away from the others?"

"Why do ya care?"

"I…I am only trying to understand all of you. This clan can be very confusing. I would think you would seek the comfort of the fire and friends."

"Maybe, but fer now those things aren't reely fer me."

"Ah I see. You're not a Knight Angel. You're a Demon Bl…" Pablo said choking off as Asha grabbed his neck.

"Who told you?" she hissed.

"No one…I…figured it out…stories…" Pablo said gasping and clawing at her hand.

"What stories?" she demanded, letting him go.

"The ones my old master told," he coughed, "They were popular in our camp. The stories of the Knight Angels are still legendary. There were other Sons in the camp that like to hear of past glories. Aster, the clan leader, was gathering Sons to try and start up the Knights again."

"What? How?"

"He figured when he had enough men, he would storm the Druid Temple, and take it by force. He'd keep a few alive to teach him the old ways and force himself into the prophecy."

"Prophecy? Wait, we need ta get tha Cap'in."

Asha grabbed his arm and physically dragged him to the Captain. She dropped him in the dirt, missing the fact that Pablo was still rubbing his throat. Her mind was racing at the news that this man held and what it meant for all of them.

"Asha, I know you like to initiate the recruits," the Captain said wearily, "But I'm ninety percent sure he didn't try to fondle you no matter how much you goaded him. His just doesn't seem that stupid."

"No, Cap'in its…"

"Asha," he said with a small sigh, "can it wait till morning?"

"NO!"

The Captain started at her voice, and she knew it was because of the amount of panic and near hysteria that had found its way into her voice. Asha could feel those emotions rising in her and tried to contain them but found the task increasingly difficult. She closed her eyes and took a few calming breaths be for opening them and found the Captain considering her but waiting patiently.

"You have my attention Asha," he coaxed gently.

"Sir, he knows."

"Knows…?"

"That I'm not an Angel. He knows what I really am."

"Really?" The Captain asked, clearly impressed.

Asha saw the excitement creep into his eyes as he considered Pablo, who was shifting uncomfortably in the dirt at his feet.

"That's not all Cap'in," She continued, "He knows about the prophecy."

At that the Captain jumped to his feet, his dinner flying off into the darkness completely forgotten. He picked up Pablo by the front of shirt and shook him while asking, "The Prophecy? You know it? The druids? Do they live? Where are they? Do they know? What of Arthur? Did he make it?"

Pablo looked rattled and his eyes were dangerously unfocused. Asha placed a hand on the Captain's arm to remind him to calm down. The touch worked and the Captain noticed what he had done to poor Pablo. He set him gently on the ground but placed himself directly in front Pablo so he could see him clearly.

"Tell me, Pablo," the Captain demanded.

"My lord?" Pablo asked, still unfocused.

"Captain," he corrected, "What do you know?"

"I only know of the stories Zemer spoke of with Aster, my master's master. He didn't share much with me but I would listen at the edge of the fire light when he would tell his stories to the others. Sometimes they wouldn't chase me off. That's how I knew what Mistress Asha was."

"I like him. He's so polite," Asha whispered to Travis who had come over.

"What of Arthur?" the Captain asked shooting a glance at Asha.

"Arthur? I know no such man. I am sorry Lord Captain," Pablo replied.

"Tell 'im the other thing," Asha ordered.

"Mistress Asha?" Pablo asked.

"The druid thingy," Asha said impatiently.

"Ah, yes," Pablo replied remembering, "Aster is going to attack Druid Temple to capture some of the druids and reestablish the Knight Angels. With Knights at his side, he could be as unstoppable as he is unstable."

"Doesn't he have knights already? What kind of firepower does he have? Guns? Explosives? Aerial support? What kind of fortifications do they have?" Travis asked.

"They…who? I am sorry I do not understand your words," Pablo said.

"What weapons does he have?" Travis tried again.

"Oh that. Why did you not say so? He has a few swords, but mostly spears and clubs," Pablo said.

"Swords…wait do you people have *no* technology?" Travis asked incredulous.

"Again, I am sorry I do not know that word," Pablo said hanging his head.

"Let me ask this," the Captain tried, watching Travis shake his head, "What is the most powerful weapon Aster has?"

"His warlock," Pablo replied instantly.

"A warlock?" Asha asked.

"Can he summon demons?" Travis asked.

"Demons? Why would a warlock do that?" Pablo asked.

"Isn't that what warlocks do? What?" Travis asked as he saw the confused expression on Pablo's face and the smirk on Asha's face.

"Tha warlocks ain't like what ya think of. They are mages who can only do battle spells sweety. They are 'war' locked. War-lock. Get it?" Asha explained.

"Oh," Travis said frowning, "So a warlock is just a specialized magician?"

"What is a magician?" Pablo asked.

"Is an illusionist, Pabby an' no Travis 'es a mage," Asha clarified.

"Ooooooh. So a mage is just a term to describe anyone with the ability to do magic? And a warlock is just a type of mage." Travis asked.

"Yes," Pablo and Asha said simultaneously.

"So what about…," Travis began.

"Travis," the Captain interrupted gently, "we can discuss the ins and outs of the magi later, for now we need to focus."

When the Captain turned his attention back to Pablo, Asha kept her eyes on Travis and was the only one to notice the slightest hint of pink on his cheeks.

"Does he only have one warlock?" the Captain asked Pablo.

"Yes, that I know of," Pablo answered, "But his war-lock is powerful. I have seen spells that make the earth heave and tremble so there is little chance of a charge reaching the camp intact. Aster uses this tactic against his foe in both attacking and defending."

The Captain scratched his chin while he considered the dilemma of this new threat, while Asha thought of ways to sneak up on the man to stab him before he knew what happened.

"I may not know you well Mistress Asha, but I recognize that look in your eye. You cannot sneak up on this warlock. Your own gift will give your position away."

Travis's head whipped around to point at Asha, mouth hanging open. Asha felt naked with her secrets being exposed. "Ya, I'm a mage. How do ya think I always managed ta sneak past people so well?" she snapped, "I'm a special mage tho' ya see I'm what ya might call a Demon Blades."

"Do I want to know what that is?" Travis ventured.

"Sure sweety, I'll tell ya. It means I the best bloody assassin you'll ever meet. We Demons are specialized in shadow combat. We'll keel ya an' then disappear afore ya know what happened," Asha said sweetly.

"I see," Travis said clearly still confused.

An awkward silence filled the air between the four of them since none of them knew where to take the conversation from there. Pablo opened his mouth to talk but Asha was still fuming at him for revealing her secret and was making no attempts to hide her violent urges towards him, so he decided against speaking so as to not draw her anger out against him.

"Well, this is problematic. I need to get to the druids, but I can't have Aster there because he will most likely kill them but on the other hand he's the only one with the information about their where-abouts," the Captain mused.

"Well, sir, I might add that we have the advantage of technology on our side. A sniper rifle is an even match for a warlock I would imagine," Travis pointed out.

"Yes, it would, but I would prefer not to engage them if we don't have to," the Captain countered, "I still need those people."

"Lord Captain, if I may?" Pablo asked. The Captain nodded his permission, "I fear you will fail any assault on the camp."

"Explain," the Captain ordered.

"The warlock may be Aster greatest weapon but he is far from the only one. Aster has at his command twenty-one Sons of Lancelot, and another five hundred swords at the ready. We could not hope to overcome such odds," Pablo explained.

"Well, tha' will just make thins interestin', wont it?" Asha grinned.

"Yes, well," Pablo replied clearing his throat and trying not to sweating, "There is a better way of doing things."

"Pray do tell meh lil' rabbit. What brilliant scheme do ya have up yur sleeve?"

"Scheme mistress?"

"Plan, lil' rabbit."

"Oh. Your language and mannerisms are so different that I am unable to understand you sometimes. I find it fascinating the amount of time your speech says one thing but the meaning behind it is entirely different. It's if as though…I am babbling and off topic," Pablo said nervously when he noticed the increasingly impatient faces, "Yes well it has been a while since I was able to talk openly. My apologies. Now, back to the…scheme, was it?"

"Yes, Pabby," Asha purred.

"Well, Lord Captain," Pablo continued, "it may be easiest challenge Aster to a fight of honor and take his place as leader of the clan. The location of the druids is not a secret but it is not something I know."

"So yur sayin' I could just go up ta him and rip out his throat an' be a clan leader?"

"No, I did not say *you* could mistress. It must be a *Son* of

Lancelot not a daughter."

Asha felt an inferno of rage blossom in her chest and a growl erupt from her throat with blistering words coming out of her mouth, when the Captain put a calming hand on her shoulder.

"Let it go Asha, this is a different world with different customs. You will get your chance to prove them wrong in time. For now, I need to talk with Pablo about how challenges work. Go walk it off," he ordered. She started to protest but he cut her off, "Go. I need you clear headed now more than ever."

Asha stormed off from the meeting and headed into the woods to find something to vent her anger with. She saw Patty stand and say something, but she was so far gone in her anger that she blew past him without stopping or acknowledging him. She walked deep into the woods, far from the others, before looking around to make sure that she was truly alone. She let loose a feral and rage filled scream that silenced all forest life around her and even scared off a few birds. The scream did not come close to appeasing her rage, so she drew a pair of daggers to attack the nearest sapling. Her thrusts, swipes, punches, and fury soon reduced the poor tree to splinters that scattered in the wind. When the wooden adversary was not enough, she ran through all her fighting forms, one after another, each one faster than the last until she was a blur even to her own eyes. This reckless speed required all her concentration and that was what she was going for. After a while fatigue set in and she was forced to slow down to a more human speed.

She paused to wipe the sweat from her brow and noticed a figure in the shadows watching her practice and the figure noticed her noticing him. His shadowy form walked into the light and resolved into the Captain. He nodded to her in appreciation, and she inclined her head in return. The Captain walk up to her until he was a few steps away and adopted a ready position with his eyebrow raised, challenging her to a bout. Asha pretended to consider the offer but was waiting to strike when he wasn't expecting it. When she did strike the Captain was ready for her strike and did not back down from her ferocious assault. Asha found that having the real-life person in front of her to beat on greatly increased her pleasure and had an enormous calming effect, transforming her rage into focus. Asha knew that she was faster than the Captain, but not too much faster, and he had a longer reach and greater strength. The spun around each other jabbing, blocking, countering, kicking, and clawing for dominance. She threw herself in the match with fire and passion, willing her consciousness to become submerged and fusing it with gut instinct. At times she was pressed against him, feeling his body's heat and sweat, only to dance away half a heartbeat later, safely out of reach.

How long they danced and fought with blades flashing, she didn't know, but after a while a small twig threw her balance off just a little and provided the Captain with the gap he need to snake his fist past her guard and deliver a crushing blow. Asha found herself flying through the air, head over heels, until she smashed into a tree. As the wind left her lungs, she felt the tree's rough bark dig into her flesh and tear small gashes ranging from her shoulder blades to her lower back. She got her feet under her before she hit the ground, rolling to avoid the Captain's continued assault, which flew over her head, barely missing her. She countered with a jab to the kidneys, drawing a groan from the Captain, and received a blow to the ear. Her head was ringing but instinct, muscle memory, and sheer stubbornness kept her moving and fighting. Fury built up in her and escaped through her blades as they moved through the air humming and singing from the speed. Shouts and screams filled her ears and she matched them with her own to drown them out.

"Asha stop!" a figure in front of her shouted.

A mere distraction that held her from her prey. She snarled and jumped over him, using the back of his head as a secondary launching site. She threw all of her strength and fury into one last devastating strike that struck home, blades sinking deep on either side of his head. She pulled back her red hair from her eyes to look deep into his eyes. She felt his blade taping on her sternum but didn't look at it.

"I guess we'll call that a draw," the Captain said calmly. It was too calm, like the voice that he used on wounded soldiers that needed calming or comfort. A brief moment of annoyance was quickly buried by the soothing tones that represented most of the only comfort or happiness she had ever known.

"Asha?" he continued, "do you feel better?"

She pulled her daggers from the tree and turned so that he couldn't see the tears that threatened to spill from her eyes on the leaves under her feet. She nodded before fleeing into the woods only to discover that their sparring session had drawn a crowd, with the entire group staring at her. She realized they had never actually witnessed her sparring sessions with the Captain, which meant most of them hadn't been able to follow all the moves at the speed in which they had been executed. Their eyes were full of fear and awe. No one of them had ever taken the Captain to a draw, Asha included, and that meant she was *far* deadlier than any of them had given her credit for.

She only glanced at them for a moment, noticing Patty still rubbed his head from where her foot had hit him. She paused for a brief moment before she continued to flee, seeking the refuge of the woods. She heard boots following her so she picked up her speed, not that she could run that fast after such a draining match. Soon she collapsed again into some leaves with her back resting on a fallen tree, and waited for the boots to catch up to her again. The boots soon came into view, with the rest of Patty following suit.

"Leave me," she demanded.

"No," he replied.

"I…I…please," she whispered.

"No," he repeated.

"Patty…"

"Not this time, my fiery little demon."

"Patrick."

"Asha."

With that he sat next to her, placing his warm arm around her shoulders drawing her close. She resisted his embrace at first, but soon his scent and warmth called to her. She buried her face in his shirt, drawing in his scent, the scent of home, the scent of safety, the scent of freedom. There, she finally let her tears flow unashamed, knowing that he would say nothing, nor judge her. His calloused hands stroked her hair.

"Shhh, my little princess. Sleep, I'll protect you, just like I did last time," he murmured. His hands continued to stroke her hair and she let herself enjoy the touch, which lulled her to sleep, her first dreamless sleep in years. Neither of them saw Barry slink off into the woods.

Chapter

EIGHT

"Are you sure?" the Captain asked.

"Yes, my lord," Pablo replied.

Slappy sat nearby listing to their conversations but not saying anything. If you said things people noticed you and then they would want to talk and soon they were asking favors and dragging you off to parties. That was far too exhausting so it was much easier for him to remain silent. People forget you're there if you're quiet and silent, even men as accomplished as the Captain, who was more accomplished than Slappy's uncle.

Slappy's parents had died when he was young and his only relative, an uncle, came to the funeral and took him to a hidden base to be raise with soldiers. His Uncle Clarence had made Slappy call him Colonel Rodgers and in exchange had taught him all that he knew, which was really just combat. The base's soldiers adopted him as a mascot of sorts and became supplementary uncles, teaching him a variety of skills that any mother would have paled at seeing a boy learn. The tall gods that came to the base infrequently were always happy to play with him. That was until the meeting that changed everything, the night when even the skies cried with him.

Slappy blinked pulling himself back to the conversation at hand. There were too many dangers in this new world to be haunted by ghost of a dead past. This was a new world where he was as free as the birds that flew over his heads, with no one to tell him what to do besides himself, and he had chosen to follow the Captain.

"Explain why he won't just kill us on the spot?" The Captain asked.

"He wants you and possibly Travis," Pablo explained, "you two will be a huge boost to his military might. As I have mentioned in the past, Aster needs more Sons of Lancelot. Your group also contains a warlock, a druid, and a healer. These are also people in high demand that will not be turned away. If he kills you, he will lose the others, at least if he does it right away."

"So, we merge with his group and after a while I challenge him for leadership?" the Captain asked.

"Yes…no."

"Pablo," the Captain growled warningly.

"My apologies, Lord Captain, but the political structures of the camp are not well known by me. I was Mud then and no one talked to Mud."

The Captain growled in frustration and collapsed onto his stump staring into the fire. Most of the group was asleep with only the parameter guards awake and probably Asha. Slappy had never seen her sleep or relax for that matter. The doctor in him worried about that much stress on her system, even if her anatomy was not a typical human's, it was definitely close enough. The warrior in him applauded her ability to always be at the ready and always ready for a fight.

"This is not easy as I thought it would be," the Captain grumbled.

Slappy couldn't help a snort escape at the comment. The Captain was a great warrior but a terrible diplomat.

"Something funny lieutenant?" the Captain asked turning to him.

Slappy groaned inwardly but let none his annoyance float to the surface, but instead replied, "Yes, sir."

"Pray do tell," the Captain ordered.

"You, sir."

"Clarify."

"You are over complicating it, sir."

"And how is that?" the Captain coaxed.

"Just be yourself. Submit to his rule as you would any other superior officer. Unless I miss my guess, this Aster is cruel and strong, but not overly bright," Patty explained looking at Pablo for confirmation, which he received.

"He is smart for a Son of Lancelot and has a crude understanding of tactics, but I have heard the *ariats* complain of his lack of skill. His tactics tends to get them killed," Pablo said.

"So, you see, sir, it will only be a matter of time before you lose your temper and punch him through a wall," Slappy said with a small smile tugging at this lips.

"That only happened once…" the Captain started.

"It only takes once," Slappy interjected.

"…but I see your point," the Captain continued, "Pablo, will I have to kill him or will beating him be enough?"

"The combat continues until one cannot fight, there is no surrender," Pablo replied.

"So, yes," the Captain sighed, "So be it. If he forces my hand, I will do what I must. Will the other accept this?"

"They follow strength, Lord Captain."

The Captain motioned to Pablo dismissing him. Pablo saluted and went to his sleeping roll to settle down for the night. The Captain looked into the fire with a scowl that only meant he was accepting the fact that soon he would duel a man to the death for a claim on his clan.

"Slappy?" the Captain called.

"Sir?"

"Am I doing the right thing?"

"That depends, sir."

"On…?"

"You."

"Is it impossible for you to give me a straight answer?" he asked annoyed.

Slappy considered the question carefully before responding, "Not to such a complicated question, sir."

The Captain said nothing but kept his eyes on Slappy waiting for him to continue. Slappy rubbed his head, noting that he needed to get a haircut soon, and picked a perch closer to the Captain.

"I know you often bounce ethical questions off me when we've had intersecting missions, Captain, and I have in return, always answered you with the greatest honesty and wisdom that I can muster. I feel that this question is more than what you are asking. You are questioning all that we are doing here and all that we will have to do.

"All men are born with potential and each potential is a varied as the men themselves. Some men are born with greatness and seize it as their birthright. Other men are forged on the crucible of life and seize greatness and glory by right of conquest. Some deny themselves any path, finding them all too difficult and die in shame in misery. Then there are those few who fight their destiny and make a new path for themselves.

"You have gathered men that were born with greatness and destiny, but turn their back on their birthright and chose a new path. Javier would have been a master farmer, looked to and honored by other farmers, but chose the path of war and now stands a titan. Patty for all his quirks and crazy talk is a natural teacher, but chose a life of crime and then one of blood. I, myself, was born to be a warlord. I forsook that path and became a doctor only find that life…too tame. I have now found a balance. Sometimes I heal people and sometimes I kill them. I guess I just approach death from both sides. Travis is one who was born to be a warrior, a hero, a champion bathed in blood and battle and he is one that has embraced his birthright and now is one of the few people in the world that could match you. Asha is a prime example of one who would spit in the eye fate and forge her own path."

"I suppose she is, but how does that help me, Slappy?" the Captain asked wearily.

"I was getting to that, sir. You, sir, are a man who was born with greatness, with glory, with the rights *and* skills to be a ruler, a great ruler but you will not let yourself accept that. If you were to embrace your fate and tap that potential hidden deep within you, the very mountains would tremble at the deeds you would accomplish. Men like you are rare and when they do come along you destroy the world as we know it and build something new. It's for this reason I volunteer to go with you as often as I can. I know your family, and so I understand why you hesitate to become what you were born to do, but you are wrong. You ask me if it is right to kill this man who holds warriors and threatens the druids. I ask you, how is it right for you not to? You are twice royal, and yours is the crown if you just accept who you are and take it for yourself. I know of no other man that could take that power and not be corrupted. Aster holds what is rightfully yours. If he will not give it back and demands that you kill him instead, then do it. It's better that this one man die, than a whole world suffer and burn. Men like him get a taste of power and can never quench the thirst that arises. Hitler was tarnish enough on your father's name, don't let Aster be your Hitler."

"Hitler did not tarnish my father's name," the Captain snapped, "He did that on his own."

"So you say. Does that make you tarnished, too? Will you punish yourself for your father's sins? Will you punish us?" Slappy asked, earning himself a look from the Captain but he wasn't done yet, "How long have we been in this world? Three weeks? You claim to be Arthur's heir but your too much of a coward to do what you need to, and too weak to bow out as well. Make a choice. Any choice, we will follow, but make a choice."

The Captain recoiled at the verbal slap but after composing himself he stared at Slappy for a while saying nothing and his face betraying nothing as well. After several minutes he broke the eye contact and returned his gaze to the fire.

"Thank you," he said abruptly, to which Slappy only grunted. The Captain half turned as if realizing something, "You know what Slappy? I think that's the most I've heard you ever say at once. In fact, I bet that's as much as you said all year, last year."

Slappy grunted again, laying down on his own sleeping roll and turned his back on the Captain. He heard the Captain chuckle softly but Slappy paid him no mind. His mind was focused on more important things, like sleep. Any doctor would tell you that a good night's sleep is essential for any life style and prescribed himself just that. Slappy closed his eyes and drifted to sleep, doctor's orders.

Pablo woke before the new day was born as was his custom. The Captain had made it clear that he was one of the group and did not need to wait on them nor was he to let them take advantage of his willingness to serve but he had spent his whole life taking care of others and found the lack of chores disturbing. It surprised him how little they knew about living off the land and gathering the forest's bounty. Then again, they were warriors and were not raised learning the simple tasks that people like Pablo had done for them, though it did surprise him how eager they were to learn everything he had to teach. At first, he thought it was a game they were playing to humiliate him further, but it soon became clear that they really meant what they said, so he taught them with as much patience as he could. Other days, like today, he would sneak off early so that he could get the morning's breakfast quickly and not have to explain every edible plant he found.

Today he was lucky and found some lista berries for the morning's breakfast. He gathered them humming to himself, enjoying the songs of the birds that greeted the earliest morning rays. He heard a rustle in the tree above him but pretended he didn't and kept humming his song. He knew Asha liked to keep an eye on him but so far didn't have the heart, or the courage, to tell her that he knew she was following. He traveled farther into the forest gathering a few greens that, while bitter, were very filling, and would give them all the energy they would need for the day. A small rustling in the bushes in front of him, made him sigh again wishing Asha didn't play these games so much.

To Pablo's surprise and dismay a giant cat emerged from the bushes slowly, its yellow eyes watching Pablo hungrily and the morning's rays shining off the cat's shiny golden coat. Pablo recognized it as a wild *otorga,* the legendary riding cats of the ancient Sons. Pablo remained kneeling, not daring to move or meet the great cat's eyes, knowing from experience that it most likely would not eat or harm him if he held still. Most likely. The cat wandered closer towering over him, sniffing the air and then his hair and clothing when it got closer. It yawned casually like it was bored, giving him a perfect view of all of its teeth, some larger than Pablo's fingers. The cat noticed the berries that Pablo had in his satchel and nudged it trying to get at them. Pablo slowly tilted his satchel so that the berries fell out, and were hungrily eaten by the *otorga*. After its meager meal it eyed Pablo with renewed interest, once again circling him but this time with a lot more interest. After a few loops around him it retreated a little ways back and squatted, its tail and haunches wiggling in the air, making Pablo close his eyes, waiting for death. At least he would die a free man and not someone's slave.

As the *otorga* began its leap, a form fell from the trees landing on its back, dagger plunged deep into eat shoulder blade, screaming a war cry. The *otorga* was already in the air but its attention was taken by twin blades in her shoulders, allowing Pablo to drive out of the way. The cat landed spinning trying to get its attacker off her back and in range of her claws but the attacker was already retreating back into the trees, new daggers emerging. Pablo nodded toward Asha and she returned his nod with a brief wink before returning her attention to problem at hand.

The *otorga* pause briefly to pull the daggers from her shoulders, then charged Asha's tree, climbing it to get to her. She leapt from the tree flipping to keep the cat in view, throwing smaller blades at the cat. Pablo fumbled at his belt for the gun Captain had given him for emergencies, which he decided, this definitely counted as. Asha met the cat midfield trying to dodge the cat's pounce by leaping over it. The maneuver worked at first but the cat twisted with blurring speed and its enormous paw swiped Asha connecting with enough force to send her flying. Its four claws dug into her side when the *otorga* hit her, leaving furrows in her flesh and drawing a scream from Asha. Asha landed holding her side gritting her teeth against the pain with one dagger out trying to prepare for its next charge even though she knew that she wouldn't be able to dodge a second time.

The *otorga* knew that Asha could not run again, so it took its time calculating its next jump, not realizing it had two opponents. Pablo finally had his gun out and squeezed the trigger as fast as he could. The first few shots flew wildly in the general direction of the *otorga,* with only one of the bullets actually hitting the cat, which annoyed it more than anything, but the noise got its attention, allowing Asha to retreat a little. The cat slunk close to the ground, coming towards Pablo, who fired more shots at the cat, feeling his panic rise throwing off his aim.

"Breath Pablo, aim! Don' let the kitty scare ya'!" Asha called out to him.

The *otorga* glanced over at his shoulder toward Asha, giving Pablo time to set his feet, take a deep breath, and aim properly at his target. He looked down the barrel, just like Travis had shown him, too a deep breath like Javier had advised, emptied himself of emotion like Contreras had taught him, and squeezed the trigger just as the *otorga* turned its head toward him again. Somehow the bullet flew directly where he aimed, hitting the great cat in its right eye, blinding it. It didn't know how to react and responded by thrashing on the ground trying to rub its eye, hissing and screaming. Asha pulled her own pistol motioning for Pablo to prepare to fire together, which they did while circling the cat toward each other. Multiple bullets tore into the cat's flesh pushing her back towards the bushes she had emerged from but she stood her ground there. The two parties stood at facing each other, screaming but neither wanting to attack, retreat, or turn their backs on the enemy.

Pablo felt a bead of sweat roll down his temple, and felt it cooled by the light breeze that happened by at that moment. Asha let out a small groan, stumbling slightly, drawing Pablo's eyes towards her. Blood ran between her fingers, soaking her uniform and covering an alarming amount of her pant leg. The *otorga* noticed their distraction, and being a predator leapt into action, headed for Asha, who was seemed to be the weaker of the two. Pablo knew that she wouldn't be able to stand much longer, let alone dodge, so he threw himself at the cat in a feet-first kick the Captain had taught him, connecting with the *otorga's* side pushing the cat sideways. It twisted its body and got one claw on Pablo's shoe, tearing it off in the process.

The cat landed on its feet and Asha collapsed on the ground, no longer conscious. Pablo loaded a new clip into his gun and then scooped up one of Asha daggers while keeping his eyes on the cat, who was pacing a circle around them. The *otorga* squatted once more to pounce, and to Pablo was dimly aware somewhere in the back of his mind, that he was not afraid to face this cat, nor was he afraid of death. *Well,* he thought grimly, *this is what it feels like to be a warrior and have brothers, or sister in this case, that you loved more than yourself. I don't want to run at all, and I am not afraid.*

"Come devil cat! I am Pablo of the Knight Angels, and you will taste my steel before I die!" He bellowed.

The *otorga* looked mildly confused but seemed to give a mental shrug and resumed his attack. It charged a few steps and leapt into the air ready for the bullets that came, absorbing them with a snarl. Figures crashed through the bushes drawing its attention for a split second, but it continued towards it target, claws extended.

"NOOO!" Patty screamed, from the edge of the clearing, his hand extended before him making a grabbing motion trying to grab the *otorga* in his first.

The rest of the group came crossing into the clearing in time to see the *otorga* freeze in the air inches from Pablo. His blade swing missed the cats face and managed to only cut off a few whiskers. He backed way hurriedly, avoiding the cat's futile swipes and hisses of frustration, while Patty's scream escalated in pitch and force. Pablo turned to him as did the entire squad, all, besides the Captain, with mouths open.

Patty's hand remained extended, but his eyes had begun to glow golden. Everyone backed away from him as a small tempest started with Patty in the center, making debris circle him and his clothes whip in the wind. He flung his fingers open with a final yell. The *otorga's* scream changed from frustration and anger, to a single earsplitting yowl of pain. Pablo threw himself on top of Asha before the downpour hit them, sheltering her from the brunt of the flying gore and found himself splattered in cat pieces as the *otorga* exploded. Patty fell to ground, consciousness having fled him, and no one went to help.

Another *otorga*, the same golden color, jumped out snarling, which changed to cries of anguish when he saw what remained of his mate. He sniffed the blood, confirming that it was her, before turning it murderous yellow eyes on Pablo, who was the closest. It screamed again and leapt forward, but was met by a hail of bullets from rifles. It struggled forward a few more feet before collapsing on the ground mewing and bleeding from dozens of places. Pablo walked over to the beast, placed the muzzle of his gun on the creature's head and pulled the trigger ending its misery. After he shot it, Porter and Weeks poked the corpse with their rifles.

"What. Was. That?" Travis asked to no one in particular.

"They are *otorga*. A species of cat that can be ridden, though they do not normally inhabit this area," Pablo answered.

"Not that," Travis clarified. "*That,*" he said pointing at Patty's unconscious form.

"Patty?" Pablo asked, "Surely you've seen a druid work, yes?"

For his question he got blank stares until Javier blurted out, "Like that monk at the monastery."

"That's right! His eyes glowed like that too," Contreras said.

"Yes, all druids' eyes glow when they work complex magic. I would conclude from his disposition," Pablo said nodding toward Patty, "that this is the first time he attempted anything difficult at all, which is strange because most druid begin casting magic at a very young age."

"Where we come from there is little mana," the Captain explained, "The old ways died and the mana with it."

"Then how do you wage war? Or heal the sick?" Pablo asked.

"We make new weapons of war," he said lifting his gun, "and we make better healers with much better medicine," gesturing toward Slappy who was busy working on Asha.

"Oh," Pablo said.

"Our old world didn't hold the same blood lust as this one, but we were more…elegant, so we created better ways of killing each other," the Captain explained.

"I suppose you didn't have the Purge of Light either?" Pablo asked.

"No, we…"the Captain started when he heard mewing sounds coming from two golden *otorga* kittens pawing their dead father.

"Oh no," Javier said, "They had…oh no."

"It was them or us," Contreras said putting a hand on his shoulder.

"Well, they won't make it, we might as well kill them so they don't suffer," Barry said drawing his weapon.

"No!" Pablo said throwing himself in front of the kittens glaring at Barry, "These are riding cats. We can raise them and train them to carry one of us."

"Like horses?" Javier asked.

"Yes and no," Pablo replied, "They are ridden much like horses, if you were foolish enough to do so, but they are faster and can climb up trees and cliffs, so they require much more skill."

"Well, I figured that," Javier grumbled.

"If you are crazy enough to ride one, yes, they could be ridden" Pablo elaborated with a smile, "but they also choose their rider. No one else is stupid enough to ride them. When their master is killed, they avenge them or die trying, and take no other rider."

"Oh."

Pablo picked up the kittens and handed one to Javier, who grunted at the deceptively heavy cat. He cradled the kitten and talked softly to it, making a few of them laugh softly at him. The Captain scratched behind the ears of Pablo's while he considered the fearsome cats.

"Uh, Captain..." Travis called hesitantly.

The Captain looked at where Travis was pointing and saw another kitten in the bushes looking at them, watching the scene. It stepped out hesitantly from under the log he had been hiding under, his black coat drawing a sharp intake of breath from Pablo. It walked slowly and hesitantly toward Asha and Slappy. As it approached, Slappy hissed at it baring his teeth, making the kitten pause half a step, but then it slunk a little closer to the ground and continued onward them. It stopped by Asha face and licked her hesitantly, before turning his red eyes on Slappy.

"My I continue, your majesty?" Slappy asked. The kitten meowed before laying his head on Asha's shoulder where it could watch Slappy work.

"Lord Captain," Pablo whispered.

"What is it?" the Captain asked alarmed.

"It's black. These other *otorga* are hard to find, but that black one is sacred to many people," He said still whispering.

"I see, interesting," the Captain grunted relaxing.

"No, you do not," Pablo countered.

"Explain," the Captain said.

"Such cats are only seen once every hundred years at best and are said to only bond with the most ferocious and deadly of warriors. This cat has bonded with Asha already and that can only mean that she is destined for great and terrible things. My lord, legends will be sung about this woman now. There is no resthouse that will not offer her free drink and a bed for the night. People will flock just to get a glimpse of this creature."

"Well, congratulations, Captain," Barry drawled, "You now have the single most important weapon in your unification efforts."

"Barry," the Captain groaned wearily, "Not now."

"No, you misunderstand," Barry objected.

"That's not hard to do with you," Travis muttered to which Contreras chuckled.

"What I mean is," Barry continued ignoring them, "if Asha will be, by all intents and purposes, worshiped by these people, what will that make you as her commanding officer? If she is so fearsome, why does she follow you? Unless I am mistaken, most people here follow strength."

"Of course we follow strength, what else would we follow?" Pablo asked.

"A valid point, Barry," the Captain mused.

"Sir, this all well and good but let's ponder this back at camp," Javier urged, "Slappy says Asha is safe to move and Patty seems to be fine, just out cold."

"He will sleep through the night," Pablo interjected.

"Very well, let's move out, bring the *otangas*," the Captain ordered.

"*Otorgas*," Pablo corrected.

"Yes, those," the Captain replied.

Pablo sighed but followed orders.

Chapter

NINE

Javier scratched at the ears of his new cat. He wasn't sure what to make of the little fur ball but it sure seemed happy enough to sit on his lap and purr. He stopped rubbing its head to clean his gun and was rewarded my sharp teeth in his hand and a small growl. He bopped the cat on the nose and it yowled at him. He wasn't sure if she was complaining about the pain or if its feeling were hurt, but either way he immediately regretted having hit his new friend. He wrapped his arms around his cat and whispered comforting words to her, pointedly ignoring the snickers coming from the squad, trying to comfort her and assure her that he still loved her.

It had been two weeks since they had gotten the *otorgas*, and it was hard to imagine life without them. Javier hadn't named his yet but felt the name would come to him eventually. Asha had recovered slowly and was constantly guarded by her cat, which she named Bubbles. Strangely Bubbles the cat seemed to like the name and responded when called. He only let people near Asha if she was awake and then rarely let them stay long, always watching them with his red eyes. The third cat, Breeze, had taken to Pablo and was constantly romping through the camp playing with anything he could find. The three cats had already grown visibly in the two weeks they had been with the group and had an appetite to match.

Javier set down his cat to get some breakfast for them only to find his feet tangled up by his cat. He rolled his eyes a little but just stepped over his friend and went to the fire where the morning's meal was roasting. He carved a piece of meat off the spit and divided it in two, a piece for him and a piece for the cat, and added some berries he had picked yesterday, all the while listening to the cries coming from his feet. When Javier set his plate on the ground, his cat pounced on it and consumed everything that was there and proceeded to lick the plate clean. Her large golden eyes looked at him hungrily, begging for more.

"Meow?" she asked Javier.

"Sorry sweetheart, you ate both of our rations. I'm afraid there won't be more until later," Javier apologized.

"Here, lieutenant," the Captain interjected offering Javier another portion of rations.

"It's okay sir, I can wait until lunch," Javier said.

"Take it lieutenant, don't make me order you, I will if I have to," the Captain warned, "These cats will be a great asset later on and we must take care of them. We'll just hunt more and teach them to hunt as well. Eat. We're going hunting soon anyway so there will be opportunities to get fresh game."

"Thank you, sir," Javier relpied accepting the food and sharing it, "Where are we headed?"

"Pablo says that Aster's camp should be a day or two away from here or at least it was three weeks ago. I was expecting to stay here for a few more days until the *otorga* bonded with us, but it seems that they already have," the Captain commented motioning to Javier's *otorga* who burped and laid her head on Javier's lap for a nap, "so now we're just waiting on Asha to heal."

Javier laughed softly at the snores that were coming from his cat. He put his coat under her head, careful not to wake her. Together they stood and nodded to each other before going their separate ways, the Captain for more food and Javier on his rounds. He made his way over to where Asha was resting, nodding at Bubbles, who considered him for a moment before returning to his bath. Asha was picking at her breakfast, not really eating any of it.

"How are you Asha?" Javier inquired.

"Well, sir, I feel like tha south end of a north bound mule," she snapped.

"Well, that's an improvement then," he laughed.

"Aye. A lil' one. If Slappy don't let me up soon imma sic Bubbles on 'im," she threatened.

"No, you're not. You know he's only got your best intentions in mind. We nearly lost you a couple of times from that *otorga* attack. You're luck you're as tough as you are or you might have died," he soothed.

"That's true I suppose. But still, I don' like sittin' around like a lil' baby. I'm a warrior and I wanna fight an' train!" she whined.

"You will, just as soon as you're back to full strength," Javier explained, "Bubbles, you make sure she stays put." Bubbles gave him a look that was clearly not impressed by Javier and pointedly started cleaning a paw.

"He don' listen ta no one but meh," Asha giggled, "Ya should know that by now Javi."

"Bah!" Javier grumbled as he walked away, listening to Asha giggles at his back.

He wandered over to where Patty was sitting on a log meditating, breakfast all but forgotten on the ground in front of him. Breeze bounded by and stopped when he noticed unclaimed food. He glanced at Patty and saw that his eyes were closed, so he slunk a little closer. A small branch lifted from behind Breeze sneaking up behind him. As Breeze got close to the food the branch smacked him on the tail, making him jump and retreat to where Pablo was arranging some supplies. Pablo soothed his cat and shot a glare at Patty who cracked open an eye wide enough to wink at Pablo before returning to his mediation.

"I see you're putting your gift to good use," Javier muttered drily watching the twins coax Breeze over with some of their own breakfast.

"Yes, sir," Patty grinned not opening his eyes, "I am getting the hang of this. The Captain has been very helpful but he only knows a little magic so I'm having to learn this on my own. I bet by the time we get to the druids they won't have much to teach me."

"Maybe, but I wouldn't count on it. Hitting kittens with sticks is hardly masterful magic," Javier said annoyed. He watched the floating stick for a moment before continuing, "So, is it exhausting?"

"Eh, kinda. It's…like a muscle I didn't know I had. It does make me tired but it's like how thinking too much makes you tired. Training my vitality and fortitude is like exercising. The more I use it the more I have," Patty explained.

"What do you mean?" Javier asked.

"Well, it's like there is this pool that fills with magic, well mana, and then when I meditate I stretch it out so next time it fills there's a bigger reservoir. Then there's this other part, like a spigot in a bathtub, called vitality, that lets in the mana. The more I work that the faster my pool, the fortitude, fills. Captain says to be careful because if I stretch either one too far or too fast it can break and once it breaks, you can't fix it," Patty said, waving his hands to elaborate.

"I see. Well, keep at it. I suspect that we'll need you a lot before this is all through," Javier said clapping him on the back.

Patty nodded and went back to his meditation. Javier when over to where the Captain was eating to talk to him. The Captain looked up as Javier approached and motioned for him to sit down. Together they watched Breeze chase a rather large rat through the camp and eventually catch it. He took it over to Bubbles who swallowed it in one bite.

"They're very watchful of each other," the Captain mused, "More than I would have expected from cats."

"Well Pablo assured us that they are much smarter and reliable than the cats we're used to. It's strange they don't have house cats here, just those monsters," Javier replied.

"Yes, they will be quite the sight when they grow up," the Captain agreed. Javier nodded but didn't reply. Awkwardness filled the air between them. Questions burned at him and the Captain noticed, "What is it Lieutenant?"

"Sir, it's just that…well how do you know my grandfather?" Javier blurted out.

"Ah, finally. I was wondering how long you would wait before that question would come out. I suppose you deserve to know about your grandfather," the Captain started. He took a moment to gather his thoughts before taking a deep breath and continuing on, "After the Second World War, my father was allowed to join the U.S. military, and the Brotherhood eventually assigned him to guard a foreign diplomat in Spain. They allowed him to keep me at his side, not that he gave them much choice, so I went with him. For the most part I was left to my own devices and wandered the streets most days looking for things to entertain me.

"One day I came upon a woman that was getting mugged and possibly worse, when a passerby heard her calls for help and rushed to aid her. That man was your grandfather, though at the time his was little more than a boy himself, he stood against two men to give that woman some reprieve. Unfortunately, your grandfather was never a good fighter, and frankly was losing badly. I may have been only boy at the time, but I was already the size of a man and had been training with my father for many years, so I stepped in to rescue your grandfather and the woman. Your grandfather a took bullet meant for me shot from the ally where I hadn't noticed a gunman hiding. Together we finished them off and got the woman to safety. Afterwards, I took your grandfather back to the hospital and was adopted in by your family. We spent a lot of time together that year and they taught me how to make swords and other blades in their shops.

"My father sent me to an uncle to train in martial arts and in magic for a while and I didn't see your grandfather for a few years. When I came back to visit, I just happened to be by when the local mob was shaking down your great grandfather for 'protection' money he didn't have. It was getting violent and your grandfather tried to stop them but was struck hard enough that it left him with a scar. At that point I jumped down from the roof and ended up having to kill most of the thugs, but I let a few go with instructions to never bother that family again, that I was the Night Angel guarding them.

"Your family didn't recognize me because I was wearing my Night Angel uniform, but your grandfather recognized me somehow. While your family respected me, they feared me at the same time, but your grandfather never did."

"That's why they set a place for the 'Guardian'!" Javier exclaimed.

"Yes, your family in Spain still saves a place for me and I come by every couple of years and eat with them, normally only when the older ones are alone. I also stop by the head mobster's house while I'm in town. It does them good to know that I am watching them," the Captain continued with a small self-satisfied smile.

"My grandfather spoke of you a lot," Javier nudged.

"Yes, we're still good friends and I try…tried, to stop by every year to say hi to him," the Captain said with a smile.

"How did he take my death?" Javier asked.

"He didn't, I told him the truth. I needed you and I took you under my wing," the Captain admitted.

"What did he say?" Javier asked eagerly.

"'*Mijo* is an Angel?' I told him you were and I've never seen him happier. I explained that everyone needed to believe you were dead, so he agreed to keep it a secret."

"Thank you, sir," Javier whispered.

"You're welcome," the Captain said nodding.

"But, sir?" Javier asked.

"Yes?"

"Is your friendship with my grandfather the reason why you picked me?" Javier asked.

"No," the Captain answered shaking his head, "You earned that on your own. When I led my strike team to support your team in the Kyber Pass I knew what kind of man you had become and chose to raise you to the Night Angels."

"Thank you, sir," Javier said.

"No need to thank me, lieutenant. You earned it on your own," the Captain replied.

Javier stood and saluted the Captain who returned the salute. Returning to his cat, Javier considered everything the Captain had told him. Feeling his mood, his cat woke up and rubbed her head on his chin. She crawled onto his lap and demanded his attention. Javier scratched behind her ears and she licked a tear that had worked its way onto his cheek. Her mewings drew Javier's mind back to the present.

"Don't worry, I'm not sad…just…happy. I'm feeling proud of myself," Javier soothed. His cat sat up purring at his comment making Javier consider her. "I think it's time to find you a name. What about Arete? The goddess of virtue?"

The cat perked up and put on her best regal pose drawing a laugh from Javier. Later that night, the squad cheered and toasted to Arete, who sat on a stump, looking for the entire world, like the queen she knew she was.

A week later, Asha would not sit still and refuse to be restrained to bed rest and did in fact sic Bubbles on Slappy. Slappy only received a few scratches before relenting to Asha's demands and letting her walk around the camp at first, then two weeks later gave her a clean bill of health and let her go back into regular training. Three days later they packed up their camp and head towards Aster's camp. Asha set the pace for their journey through the forest, with the three cats bring in small game every night. The second day in the forest they managed to corner a deer and kill it, bringing their human companions to the kill so that they could skin it for them. Bubbles had stayed behind to guard their kill and was found sitting on it proud as a conqueror.

The next day they came to a clearing next to a lake that had been Aster's camp only to find it empty, its occupants long gone. Luckily five thousand people don't march along without leaving a mark. They set up camp beside the water, while Javier and Pablo went out to find more game and provisions for the long march ahead.

"Lieutenant Javier, you are learning the plants very quickly,"

Pablo commented.

"Thanks," Javier grunted.

Arete brought him a bird that he tied to his belt along with a rabbit she had found earlier. Breeze was not the hunter his sister was, but had managed a rabbit of his own, that hung on Pablo's belt. They moved through the forest gathering plants and found themselves back at the camp in short order with enough food for a couple of days. Upon their return, the Captain motioned them over.

"Sir?" Javier asked.

"Lord Captain?" Pablo echoed.

"Sit you two," the Captain ordered, "We need to discuss the next few days. Right now, we get to play catch up to Aster's band and who knows how many weeks ahead of us they are. Pablo do you know how fast they move?"

"They are very slow Lord Captain. They only move a fraction of what we do, even slowed as we are. I would estimate that what we move in one day is what they will move in four days. They have women and children and number in the thousands," Pablo answered.

"Good. That means we will catch up to them in no time. Now, Javier, this next part will be hard for you but you will have to defer to Travis for a while. At least in the beginning until they are able to learn how skilled you are in the arts of war," the Captain said.

"I figured as much, sir. I would suggest that we train with hand to hand combat every night until we catch up to them. We are running low on munitions and its best we learn to use the local weapons," Javier added.

"Agreed. You're the best after me and Asha so I'll let you lead the practice," the Captain consented.

"Sir, I would prefer if you did," Javier said.

"Why is that lieutenant?" the Captain asked.

"Sir, we will be facing many more people like you, just as strong and fast," Javier replied, "We need practice fighting people like that."

"I don't think that Aster will have too many Sons my size but they will be plenty strong and fast. Very well, Asha and I will whip you into shape," the Captain conceded.

"My lord, if I may?" Pablo asked.

"What is it?" the Captain asked.

"Patty may be a druid but he is untrained. He has gained much fortitude and vitality, but he has little mastery in magic and I know your training is limited in that area, but he will need to train in magic more than he will his skill of armed combat. When he is fully trained, he will be worth more than a hundred swords," Pablo urged.

"What do you suggest? That I train him?" the Captain asked.

"Yes, my lord. If you teach him to control the basics of magical forces, then he will be able to safely experiment. You know he will not leave it alone now that he is able to channel mana at will and will pose a threat to us if he is left unchecked," Pablo cautioned.

"For a man who was a slave, you sure seem to know a lot," Javier pointed out.

"Yes, a slave is below notice and as such I was around many conversations that no one else should have been. *I* kept my mouth shut and listened and learned," Pablo retorted.

"Look at you, all full of spit and vinegar. A few weeks ago, you wouldn't even lift up your eyes," Javier taunted.

"All men learn and grow, you of all people should know that," Pablo shot back.

"Boys, enough. But he is right Pablo, you do seem to know a lot. Who did you hear this from?" the Captain inquired.

"Meem, Aster's warlock, often spoke of it. Aster wanted to know the methods of the druids and the mechanics of magic to find any weaknesses he could exploit," Pablo answered.

Javier noticed the respect and change of tone in Pablo's voice when he talked to the Captain. He pursed his lips but otherwise did not say anything about Pablo's behavior. Truth was, he wasn't sure how he felt about Pablo anymore. He knew some of it was jealousy that the Captain was relying on Pablo as much as he was on him these days and some of it was Pablo's popularity with the men.

"I see," the Captain continued, "I also see your point with Patty. I will teach him what I can so he doesn't blow us up on accident."

"Can he do that?" Javier asked shocked.

"I think so," the Captain replied, "He'll soon be stronger than me but he will need to learn control. I have no idea how strong he will eventually be, but I suspect it will be as large as his ancestor's."

"Merlin?" Javier asked.

The Captain nodded but Pablo interrupted, "Merlin? THE Merlin?"

"Yes, didn't we tell you?" Javier asked smugly, "Patty is a direct decedent of Merlin the Magnificent."

"THAT Merlin was a genius with-out equal. He was the one who constructed the Purge, and the only druid to survive it," Pablo replied clearly awed, looking at Patty.

"How many Merlins do you know?" the Captain asked.

"Merlin is the name taken by the Master Archdruid. I don't know how many there have been but if Patty is truly the descendent of Merlin the Magnificent and carries his gift…he will be an Archdruid in a very short while, and maybe even the Master Archdruid," Pablo answered absently.

"Oh," Javier and the Captain said simultaneously.

They all watched Patty sitting on a stone with little rock floating and marching neat circles around him. With little flicking motions he sent the rocks one by one skipping across the pond's surface with blind speed. Grinning, Patty scanned around to see if anyone had watched his latest display of power and grinned even wider when he saw the trio looking at him.

"I'll teach him fire tomorrow," the Captain decided.

"Is that wise, sir?" Javier asked.

"It is. I would rather he understands the ins and outs of fire magic than let him discover it on his own and possibly get us all killed," the Captain explained.

"Sound thinking, sir," Javier agreed nervously.

The next morning, Patty walked alongside the Captain listening intently to everything that the Captain said. Occasionally they would stop and practice a new spell or some technique. By the time the Captain called a stop for the night, Patty was able to light the wood on fire. He was showing off and managed to consume all the wood in a scalding whoosh of fire. Breeze and Arete screamed and hid behind their humans but Bubbles only yawned and went back to sleep.

A few days later, they noticed a change in the forest. Every now and then they would catch the smell of rotting meat. At first, they ignored it and tried not to breathe deeply but the *otorgas* made them change their minds. They disappeared for a few hours sending their owners into a frenzy looking for them. The cats were eventually found in the middle of a battle field. Both sides had apparently killed each other off.

The group stood shoulder to shoulder looking in on the carnage. Hundreds of bodies lay on the moss quietly rotting away. While everyone was a little green at the sight, only Chuffels threw up but Boomer did gag when Chuffels lost his breakfast. They group looked at the Captain, whose face betrayed nothing. He stared at the field for a while before turning on his heel and started to head back into the forest.

Pablo was at the end of the line and bent over one of the bodies to search it for valuables. He paused when the Captain stood over him. He returned to the body for a moment and then thought better of it.

"What are you doing?" the Captain demanded.

"Just what is expect, Lord Captain," Pablo answered understanding the Captain's real question, "It is the custom of the forest. If the victors do not take it, and the forest doesn't claim it, it is for whoever wants it and can take it."

"Looting the dead is acceptable then?" the Captain asked.

"Why would I let these things go to waste? These men have no use for it, and we do. They will have gold, weapons, and armor. Those are all things we will need," Pablo replied, "If it is against my Lords wishes, I will stop but even if I do, someone else will take it."

The Captain considered Pablo for a long while. He then turned to the men laying in the field and considered them for a while longer. Then, without a word, he bent over the nearest body, and went through his pockets. Wordlessly, the rest of the squad followed suit, gathering anything of worth and piling it on a hand wagon the twins found.

"Sir, may I talk to you?" Javier whispered.

"I don't like it either Javier, but these are the customs of the land, and we need weapons, we need to survive," the Captain replied.

"Not like this, sir, let the dead rest," Javier begged.

"They are resting Javier. What we do to them now, won't affect them at all, only us and how we view ourselves. In another time, and another place, I would have agreed with you, but this is our new home and it has new rules," the Captain explained patiently, "We must adapt or die lieutenant. The dead rare haunt the living, it's the living that haunt themselves. Like I said, we need these things, or we will not survive this world, and I for one want to live."

Javier didn't like what he heard but he had to agree with what the Captain said, so he took a deep breath, which he immediately regretted, and started searching the bodies like the rest of them. At the end of the day they divided up the gold and weapons, piling the extras in the wagon. As they traveled through the forest, everyone took a turn pulling the wagon.

Chapter

TEN

Contreras stood with his back against the steam and the glare of the morning's rays. His hands gripping his new spear were sweating slightly. Blood pounded in his ears and his breath sounded thunderous as he scanned the tree line looking for what he knew he would never see coming. Realizing that he was getting too excited and nervous he adjusted tactics. *Easy,* he thought to himself, *this is nothing new. You've done this before. Deep breath, that's it, in and out.* With his breathing under control, his heart slowed its frantic pace. Training his ears to the sounds of the forest, he closed his eyes and drank in the sounds, listening for the faintest betraying sound.

There! He thought, eyes flying open. A faint rustle to his right was all the warning he had to react. Spinning on his heel, he lowered his spear toward the sound screaming his battle cry. A black streak leaped from the bushes swatting his spear to one side, as it pounced toward his head. By letting his instincts and reflexes guide him, Contreras was already gone and to the side. He used the momentum from the spear to spin it into another attack. The black streak hissed at him when he scored a hit on its flank but managed to snake its way inside Contreras' guard. Prepared for this, Contreras kicked it in the face full force, interrupting its attack and knocking it head over heels.

Sweat ran down his forehead but ignored it for the moment, keeping his eyes on his opponent. Bubbles paused long enough to lick his wound briefly before turning his attention back to Contreras. Contreras knew he couldn't hold a fight with such a fast opponent for too long. Switching to offense, he bellowed again and charged Bubbles, who in turn charged at him. Contreras held the spear half way down the shaft and gave his spear a sweeping swing at Bubbles, who dodged it. The momentum carried the spear around as Contreras planned. The butt of the spear connected with Bubbles sending him flying once again with Contreras hot in pursuit. Bubbles' feet had barely hit the ground, when Contreras was upon him sending in a flurry of jabs, making Bubbles dance. Bubbles laid his ears back against his skull and matched Contreras's scream. Reversing the grip on his spear, Contreras connected with Bubbles again, sending him flying for the third time that day.

"Stop! He's had 'nough fer one day," Asha shouted. She beckoned to Bubbles to summon him, "come 'ere Bubbles. Mama is gonna take care of ya."

The black *otorga* considered Contreras for a long while. Contreras returned the gaze meeting the red eyes without blinking. The *otorga* finally found what it was looking for, so it returned to Asha. Contreras dropped his battle stance and saluted the cat as it followed Asha in the woods, disappearing quickly and flipping its tail at him.

"That was most impressive Sergeant Contreras," Pablo praised, "A fine display of weapons skill. Both you and Bubbles have grown in skill and strength, though I think Bubbles' skill has grown much faster than yours has."

"Thanks Pablo, I hadn't noticed I was about to get my butt kick by some cat," Contreras said drily.

"Excellent, I am glad I was able to be of assistance to you," Pablo replied, completely missing the sarcasm attached to the comment.

Contreras couldn't help but laugh at Pablo's oblivious nature, not that he blamed Pablo's lack of understanding. Spying Pablo's look of confusion, Contreras laughed harder earning himself a glare at first, but Pablo succumbed to infectious laughter. Sunlight flashed off of Breeze's fur as he joined them, drawn by the laughter. He bumped his head against each of them trying to get their attention, which he received along with a generous amount of scratching behind the ears.

"I worry about this one," Pablo confessed, "His siblings take up the training with ease and grace, but this one insists on playing."

"Well, who says he has to be a fighter?" Contreras asked. Pablo blinked in response, so Contreras continued, "You're not much of a fighter either."

"I can fight!" Pablo said indignantly.

"I know you can, but that doesn't make you a fighter, not like the rest of us. You approach fighting as a chore, something you have to do but not something you want to."

"This is true," Pablo admitted.

"I know," Contreras replied nodding, "The thing is, not everyone can be a warrior, nor does everyone need to be a warrior."

"I don't understand," Pablo said frowning and concentrating.

Contreras sighed, "These cats seem to follow the traits of those they bonded to. Breeze will fight when he needs to, he has on many occasions, but that doesn't mean that's what he has to do. It's just like humans, not all of us were born to be warriors, although we could all be if we wanted to or were pressured into it."

"So, you think he will fight when the time comes?" Pablo asked.

"Yes, if there is something worth protecting, he will. He hunts with his siblings easily, working with them as needed. He is a lot like you Pablo, carefree on the outside but tough as nails on the inside," Contreras replied.

Pablo inspected his nails, trying to understand Contreras's analogy, "I think I understand. You are suggesting I not worry about his training as much as Lieutenant Javier and Mistress

Asha?"

"Correct. Train him as much as you can, but don't worry about it. They way these cats are growing they will be intimidating people out of fighting in no time."

Contreras eyed Breeze who had stopped to clean himself when he realized they were talking about him. He paused briefly and met Contreras's eyes with his own golden eyes before returning to his bath. In the three months they had the *otorgas* they had quadrupled in size, putting their shoulders just shy of Contreras's waist when standing. The cats' appetite grew to match their growing frames making it difficult to have enough food on hand. Luckily, they were natural born hunters and were able to hunt for and kill game on their own. They would often drag a fresh kill into the group's camp to let the humans skin their dinner for them.

They walked to camp together, splitting when they got there. Contreras headed over to where Javier was talking with the Captain. They both looked up at him when he approached them.

"What is it sergeant?" the Captain asked.

"I was hoping to speak to the lieutenant," Contreras replied.

"Very well. Lieutenant, we'll finish our conversation later," the Captain grunted, rising to his feet.

"What is it sergeant?" Javier asked.

"Did you still want me to train that cat with you?" Contreras asked.

"Was that today?" Javier asked.

"Yes, sir. I already finished with Bubbles, and now I am here waiting to see if you and Arete are interested."

"Of course we are, here we go," Javier said.

A short while later, they wiped the sweat from their foreheads and started back towards the fire. No sooner had they taken their seats, than the Captain walked up wanting to talk to them. He waived off the tradition standing salute and indicated they were to remain sitting.

"The cats are getting quite large. Do either of you know how large they will be when they'll be done growing?" the Captain asked.

"Um sorry sir, I don't know," Contreras said. "All I know about them is what I have been told by Pablo."

"Ah, well, I suppose that when you two are done eating and have cleaned your nasty bodies, get ready to move out. We're headed out at soon as you two are done," the Captain ordered.

While they bathed in the stream, the rest of the group broke camp and prepared to leave. Upon their return the Captain sent Contreras ahead to follow the trail that had been left by Aster's clan and to mark which way they should go. Bits of refuse and crushed plants littered the ground leaving a path that any novice tracker could have followed, so Contreras focused on trying to figure out what other information he could glean from the tracks.

Towards late evening he came to a man-made clearing. On the far end of the field he spotted a large structure, nestled next to a cliff, with a copious amount of chicken running around on the front lawn. Contreras stayed in the shelter of the trees and pulled out a pair of binoculars to get a closer look. Men in rough leathers sat on the front porch drinking from clay mugs while laughing and shouting at one another. He spotted one man leaving with his mule, piled high with supplies, heading up a dirt path toward the mountains. Contreras retreated without making himself known and head back to the others to report in.

"It's a resthouse," Pablo explained after he heard the description, "We have a small enough group they should let us all stay inside. It would be wonderful to sleep in a real bed and eat at a table again."

"I wouldn't be a bad place to spend the night, Captain," Contreras agreed.

"How far out of the way will it take us from Aster's path?" the Captain asked.

"It won't. As far as I could tell, they spent a day or two there in the field," Contreras answered.

"Interesting. I wonder why they did loot the place," the Captain mused.

"Why would they do that? It's a resthouse," Pablo asked puzzled.

"Probably because it would be easy picking," Javier supplied.

"But it's a resthouse," Pablo repeated.

"Yes, it is but that doesn't mean there isn't something worth taking from there," Javier retorted.

"But it's a resthouse," Pablo repeated again.

"Okay, why wouldn't they do it than Pablo?" Javier asked, struggling to keep the annoyance out of his voice.

"Because it's a resthouse," Pablo explained.

"Yes, we established that already. I still don't see the reason," Javier snapped.

"You…you…you just don't do that to resthouses. The leaders will sleep in the house and the rest in the field up front. No leader would want to jeopardize a good resthouse if he could help it. They are just too useful to ransack and too much work to claim it as your own. Resthouses are places of peace and if you get thrown out of one, no one will want anything to do with you. They will often throw out the whole group, so you would have some explaining to do. Men have been killed for less," Pablo explained.

"Okay, note to self, don't let them talk to Barry," Javier muttered.

"Well, do they have real beds? With mattresses?" the Captain asked Pablo.

"Yes they do, Lord Captain, and if we're lucky a hot bath as well."

"Well, I'm convinced. Let's go get ourselves a hotel room," the Captain announced.

They approached the resthouse together with Pablo in the lead to secure them the rooms. The lure of a warm bed and hot bath had them all practically skipping across the field. Barry brought up the rear keeping his eyes out for signs of trouble and taking note of the body languages of everyone that he could see. Once they reached the resthouse itself, the house master came out to meet them.

"Hello, honored house master…" Pablo started.

"Rahn," house master Rahn supplied.

"Rahn. We have traveled the forest for two months now and are seeking lodging for the night, possibly the next night as well," Pablo continued.

"Ah, I am sad to say that I have no room. There was a time that I would have gladly taken you in but my humble body betrays me and in my delicate stated, I can no longer host as many as I once could, though I do on occasion make exceptions," Rahn said with exaggerated sorrow, his eyes flickering to where Asha stood.

"Understandable honorable house master, but perhaps…" Pablo said.

"Great Mother Asha, what are *those* doing here?!" Rahn exclaimed interrupting Pablo.

Rahn pallor shifted to chalky white, while he tried to back pedal into his house. Around them scream rose and fingers pointed behind them. The group turned, weapons drawn, to see what had scared everyone into near panic. Across the grass came bounding the two *otorga* each with a rabbit in its mouth. They came up to respective humans and proffered the rabbits for skinning.

All around them the screams turned into mummers and excited whispers. Fingers point to each of the great cats in turn and speculations about the humans began to surface like wild fire. Just as quickly as the screams started, silence fell on the occupants of the rest house. Many of them fell to their knees and left their mouths hanging open unashamed.

Once again the group turned to see what the commotion was, though Barry was sure he knew what was causing all the excitement. Walking calmly across the field came Bubbles, pausing briefly every now and then to inspect something that caught his interest. Once he made his way to Asha, he sat quietly next to her while Asha rubbed his head.

"House Master Rahn, if I may be so bold," Barry called out. Rahn tore his eyes away from Asha and turned them to Barry. Barry took this as his cue to continue, "May I present to you, the great Asha Poisonfang, great daughter of Asha the Blessed, and Night Rider of the black *otorga* Bubbles. The great Asha is twice as deadly as she is beautiful, and she is a beauty without equal among all the Sons of Lancelot."

Rahn's eyes bulged out, and he wiped his hand repeatedly on his pants. He opened his mouth to speak but found his throat too dry for the task and tried swallowing to loosen it up. Barry noticed his flustered composure and pushed onward.

"And if I may also present, Pablo the Humble with his cat Breeze, and Javier the Cunning, with his cat Arete," Barry introduced pointing, "Now that brings us to our leader."

Rahn passed flustered, skipped nervous, and went straight to panicked. His eyes showed white all around. He finally managed to swallow and forced a polite smile.

"It is my honor to present Lord Captain…"Barry started.

"Captain," the Captain interrupted hurriedly, "will suffice for now. You may call me Captain."

"Of course, Lord Captain," Rahn murmured faintly, "I did not see that you were such esteemed guests. I will prepare rooms for you and your companions immediately."

"Much appreciated, Master Rahn," the Captain said, "My Riders will need larger beds so that may share them with their *otorga*."

"Of course, of course, I will see to it right away. If you need anything at all let me know. Me and my house are at your disposal," Rahn assured them hurriedly.

"Thank you Master Rahn," the Captain said

"And you my Lord? Will your man servant sleep in your room or shall I prepare him a servant's room?" Rahn asked motioning to Barry.

"Don't worry about him Master Rahn, he can fend for himself."

"Very good, my Lord. Would you care to eat now or would you prefer to rest first?"

"I will take my meal, a hot bath, and then my bed, in that order if you please, Master Rahn."

"I will see to it personally, my Lord."

Barry fumed inside but said nothing to contradict the Captain nor made any move that might undercut his authority but instead adopted a humble servant's posture behind the Captain. They followed the house master into the resthouse to a large room on the second floor. The room had a balcony that face towards the field, giving him a perfect view of the surrounding area.

"Master Rahn?" the Captain called out.

"My Lord, how may I serve?" Rahn replied.

"Did a man named Aster pass through here with his clan?"

"Why yes, as a matter of fact there was a man by that name. There was a large amount of people with him but they stayed in the field."

"Good, good, when did they pass through here?"

"About ten days ago, my Lord."

"Good then they are still with-in reach," the Captain muttered softly.

"I beg your pardon, my lord?" Rahn asked.

"My Lord is tired. If something is needed, we will let you know, Master Rahn," Barry answered.

"Of course, I will inform you when your meal is ready," Rahn informed them smoothly.

Neither said anything until the door closed behind Rahn. Barry counted to ten then opened the door to make sure that no one was listening on the other side. When he turned back to the bed he saw the Captain looking at him.

"What is it Captain?" Barry asked.

"I have never really seen you in your element," the Captain replied, "That's real smooth how you got them to take us in. I've never seen a CIA spook work his magic."

"It's hardly magic, Captain," Barry winced.

"Oh, I don't know about that. The way he was looking at Asha I was afraid we would find pieces of him in the morning, or maybe spend a ridiculous amount on this place," the Captain laughed flopping onto the bed.

"You saw that too? Well I thought he would feign some ailments for a higher price, so short circuiting that conversation seemed in favor of his health and our discretion."

"Discretion?"

"Well, I assume you still hold to the notion that you need to remain anonymous for a while," Barry started, and the Captain nodded his assent, "So for now I think that keeping you even more mysterious than usual would be better. The less they see and know of you the better. Let's keep the *otorgas* front and center and keep all attention on them."

"Okay…"

"People should see them and see how they fight. I would suggest staging a fight between two of the men. Whichever two people crowd around to see fight would be the best. Then while the fight is starting to heat up you stop it with a single word. They cower just a little but otherwise obey immediately."

"Making me look like a badass," the Captain finished.

"Correct," Barry confirmed.

"That's all fine but I'm getting a bath first."

"That should be just fine, Captain," Barry laughed.

"You know Barry, I'm not sure if I should like you right now or not."

"Captain, this is what I do, let me help you," Barry begged unable to keep some of the hurt out of his voice.

"I will Barry," The Captain sighed rubbing his eyes, "I know doing what you do is necessary but I that doesn't mean that it I will enjoy it. Your job has always been so…underhanded."

"Oh and yours hasn't?"

"It has, but it always seemed more honorable."

Barry winced, "I agree, but no one likes the sewers but they are still necessary."

The Captain grunted, "I told you that one."

"Yes, you did but the most important things is…" Barry

started when a knock sounded on the door. Barry walked to the door to who it was. He opened the door to reveal a small boy in the door way.

"Hello, my name is Tobus and my granda sent me to tell ya that the Lord Captain's dinner is ready. Will he take his meal in here?" Tobus asked.

"He will indeed. Have it brought to these rooms," Barry replied.

"Right away," Tobus said before scampering off.

After the Captain had eaten and bathed, he nestled into his bed for the night. Barry left the room as quietly as he could, so he would not wake the Captain. He had plots to weave and plans to set in motion. As much as his body cried out for sleep and a warm bed, he ignored them for now.

Chapter

ELEVEN

"Wench! You'll pay for that!" Javier spat.

"Bite meh, ya dirty lil' pig kisser!" Asha hissed back, "Yer not good enough ta even look at meh and yer ancestors weep just looking at your pathetic frame."

With a wordless snarl, they ran at each other launching into a ferocious salvo of kicks and punches. Javier moved closer to rob her of her speed and force the fight into a grapple on the ground where he would have the advantage. He managed grab a wrist and pull her off balance but she quickly recovered and landed a kick on his chest breaking his grip. Clutching his chest, he began a rhythmic breathing to clear his head and ease his pain. Asha danced back and adopted a new ready position.

Javier couldn't help letting his eyes flicker to the crowd their brief match had already drawn. He turned his full attention back to Asha. A knowing smirk graced her lips as she waited for Javier to make his move. It was a trap the he knew he had no choice but to spring, but knowing it was a trap gave him an edge in the next round.

Roaring his rage, he launched into another attack and Asha met him halfway, but was not prepared for him. Flipping backwards, Javier landed a kick to Asha's chin, snapping it backwards, laying her out on the dirt. Dizzy from the impact, she shook her head trying to clear it but Javier was already there. Before he could land a blow, Bubbles was there hissing and swiping at him. Trying desperately to get away from his claws, Javier backpedaled and landed on the ground. A golden blur appeared before Javier hissing and spitting at Bubbles, Arete had come to save him. The two *otorgas* glared at each other for a brief moment before launching into their own fight.

The distraction served Asha well! She wiped the blood from her mouth and prepared for a renew assault on Javier. Smiling wickedly, she braced for his attack, dodging his initial swings. Javier growled as his blows met nothing but air the first couple of seconds. The speed advantage was Asha's but the strength advantage was his. Like so many before him, Javier learned that it doesn't matter how strong you are if you can't hit your target.

Finally, Asha slipped a little allowing Javier to land a blow and then grab a new hand hold on her. In seconds they were back on the ground, rolling through the dirt trying to assert dominance. Move by move, he managed to slowly control the fight and wear Asha down. Asha wasn't done with her tricks. She thrust her hips toward Javier's crotch and then her head back when he tried to twist away. Asha's head connected with his nose, breaking it and releasing pools of blood. Undeterred, Javier continued to attack Asha.

"ENOUGH! You are warriors, not resthouse drunks or common bloods with ill tempers!" the Captain roared from the fence, "And you too! You flea bitten fuzz balls!"

The two cats looked at him briefly before pointedly turning their backs to him with their tails twitching. They started to bathe themselves and the Captain ignored them after that. Their owners had the courtesy to looking abashed. They disentangled themselves but remained kneeling in the dirt as the Captain approached them. His back was to the sun and his enormous shadow fell on both of them.

"What is the meaning of this?" the Captain demanded, "What makes you think you can make a fool of yourselves?"

"Captain, sir, I must be honest, sir," Javier started drawing a raised eyebrow from the Captain, "It was all Asha's fault, sir."

"Lies!" Asha shrieked, "You were tha one who abandoned honor, ya shadow blasted troll!"

They launched themselves at each other but the Captain was there in a flash. Grabbing them both by the scruff of their necks, he pulled them apart only to slam their heads together and throw them both back in the dirt. They sat there rubbing their head sullenly but not saying anything, nor giving any reason for the Captain to turn his fury toward them.

"You two are a disgrace to our walk of life. Silence!" he roared cutting off their objections, "you will attend to your *otorgas* and for every scratch on them you will run a lap around this field."

Javier opened his mouth to protest but closed it when he saw no remorse or pity in the Captain's eyes. Squaring his shoulders and lifting his chin, he walked over to where his cat was licking herself and keeping an eye on her brother. A small growl escaped her throat but Bubbles gave her no more than a cursory glance. As much as Javier hated to admit it, Bubbles had definitely won the fight.

He carefully counted the cuts on Arete and listened to Asha do the same thing with her cat. Normally, Javier would go about his business without any more thought to Asha or their squabble but today's performance needed to be sold. Slappy stopped by briefly to set Javier's nose and make sure neither had permanent injuries. Javier's biggest consolation was the large bruise forming on Asha's jaw.

He turned his attention back to the task at hand. While he counted each claw mark, he pretended that his anger grew with each cut. Occasionally he would throw Bubbles and Asha a withering glare but both of them pointedly ignored him. Asha finished attending to her cat first and set off in a jog around the field. A few minutes later Javier started after her determined to catch up.

The sun was setting by the time he finished running around

the field. Sweat ran down his face and chest. He had long since shed his saturated shirt in order to take advantage of the breeze blowing through the meadow. One of the house maids brought him a cup of water to quench his thirst. Javier gratefully accepted the drink and didn't fail to notice the smoky look she was giving him. A nervous cough escaped his lips and it only served to excite her more. She stepped closer to him and traced a finger down his chest stopping occasional to play with his scars.

"M'lord has a warrior's chest," she breathed huskily.

"Uh…" Javier said.

"Shhh. I have something for you m'Lord," she breathed holding out a scroll.

Javier took it automatically, "What is it?" He asked.

"I guest wanted you to have it. 'Tis a map to the druid temple. A gift for such brave and valuable men."

"Um, thank you?" Javier stammered not sure if it was something he should thank her for. Her sent wafted up his nose and clouded his thoughts.

"I have something else for you, m'lord."

"Another map?"

She laughed gently stepping up and pressing against him, her green eyes drinking in his face and paralyzing him, "Nothing so mundane, m'Lord."

All of his time in the Army had given Javier many skills, but none of them helped him now. He shifted from on foot to the other and even took a step back but the maid boldly kept up with him. She reached up and grabbed a handful of his hair and pulled his head down roughly to her soft lips. Javier froze in place unable to move or breathe. His eyes had shut when she had started pulling his head down, but then flew open and seemed to be widening by the second.

The maid finally let him go but Javier still did not move. She looked at his flared nostrils, and wide eyes and realized her advances had not been what was expected. She paled before gathering her skirt up and disappearing around the corner of the resthouse, all the while screaming that she didn't do it.

"Well Javi, you sure do have a way with words," Barry drawled from the fence. Javier's eyes were locked where the maid had disappeared around the corner and did not respond to Barry. "It's like you've never kissed a girl."

Pink graced Javier's cheeks, "I, uh…"

"Holy crap, you haven't, have you?" Barry asked incredulous.

"Who hasn't done what?" Travis asked coming up from behind with Contreras.

"Javier hasn't…" Barry started.

"Don't," Javier begged.

"…kissed a girl before," Barry finished, barely suppressing his laughter.

"Really?" Travis and Contreras asked together.

"Nope," Barry smirked.

The trio looked at each other exchanging glances before bursting into laughter. Javier could do nothing but stare intently at the dirt feeling like his ears were on fire. His legs were watery but he wasn't sure if that was from the run, the embarrassment, or the shock of his first kiss.

"What's this?" the Captain asked materializing at their side.

"Javi…had his first kiss," Travis wheezed.

"Ya, and she ran off screaming!" Contreras finished.

The trio burst out laughing anew. Travis laughed so hard he had to bend over and support himself on his knees, while Contreras fell to the dirt in mirth. A small smile twitched on the Captain's lips but he managed to keep his composure.

A small but threating hiss came from behind them. Barry was the first to react to Arete and immediately dove behind the Captain. She flowed between the men and placed herself between them and Javier, all the while glowering at them and hissing softly. Travis and Contreras stopped laughing quickly and stood slowly. She crouched down into the attack position Contreras had taught her. The men adopted similar stances, ready to move at a moment's notice.

"Shhh, Arete," Javier soothed, "Daddy's okay. They are just teasing me. You don't need to hurt them this time."

Arete glanced over her shoulder at him before relaxing her stance. She walked off casually back towards the resthouse where the patrons were giving the cats all the food they could eat. As she walked by Barry she made a short jump at him, like she was about to attack. Barry fell backwards into the dirt, while the Captain jumped in front of him to protect him. Arete spared the Captain a look before looking back at Barry pointedly licking her teeth. She then stretched and walked casually back to the throngs of adoring admirers.

Dusting himself off Barry muttered, "That would make a nice throw rug. I could wipe my feet on it every night."

A knife snaked its way around his neck and rested on his throat. Not even daring to swallow Barry raised a hand slowly toward the hand that held the knife. A gently increase in pressure stopped him.

"You will not make that joke again," the Captain whispered softly so no one else could hear, but with a dangerous tone, "I don't care how sarcastic it is, never threaten a member of my team again."

Barry nodded slowly and then the knife disappeared up the Captain's sleeve. The team squared up for the evening training sessions. Left and Right started to pair up like they normally did and launched into their katas attempting to gain ground on one another.

"It's stupid the way you fight," Barry said.

The twins froze and turned on him. Their matching glares bore holes through him and in unison they came at him.

"Right there, do you see what you're doing?" Barry asked. The twins slowed but didn't stop their approach. "The way you have been fighting is no longer safe. As we switch to lesser weapons, you two are better off as a fighting pair. You already read each other's minds and in any sword fight, how nice is it to have someone at your back you can trust."

The twins stopped and shared a look before turning on their heels and walking to where Boomer and Weeks where practicing. A brief hushed conversation ensued before the pairs squared off and went at each other with vigor.

"Smart Barry," Javier drawled from behind him, "I didn't think you were that smart."

"I assure, you my little Spaniard, there are entire depths of me you haven't so much as glanced at," Barry retorted.

"I'm not sure I want to explore your depths," Javier smirked.

"Cute but the fact remains you don't know me," Barry smiled.

"Well then, let's get to know each other, shall we?" Javier asked smiling back.

The two men squared off smiling at each other. They bowed and assumed their ready positions but before they could start, Asha landed with a puff of dust between them.

"If anyone gets ta smack him around, it's gonna be meh Javi," Asha breathed, eyes sparkling in anticipation, looking over her shoulder at him, "Barry still owes me some blood and I'm here ta collect."

Javier threw his head back laughing and bowed to Asha letting her take the ring. Around them the squad gathered around and placed bet on how long Barry would last. Even the Captain came to the fence to watch. A group from the resthouse detached themselves from their tables and came to watch the spectacle but kept a respectable distance from the Captain and his group.

Asha danced around Barry grinning like a maniac and giggling. She threw a few jabs at him, giggling every time he flinched. His blocks were too slow and she would have hit him if she had tried. Asha stopped moving and put her hand behind her back and presented her chin to Barry. He knew it was a trap but he went for it anyway. Sure enough, she danced to the side and shoved his shoulder, driving him into the dirt.

"I got five he doesn't land a blow," Porter said.

"Five she lets him," Javier countered, "To make him feel good about himself before she beats him into a gooey puddle."

"Five he wets himself again," Contreras said.

"We'll take that action," Left and Right replied excitedly in unison.

"I thought I ordered you never to do that again," the Captain grunted.

"Sorry, sir," they apologized without sincerity.

He looked at them sideways before asking, "What are we betting on and what are we betting with?"

"Asha and Barry's fight. Close!" Javier replied moaning at another miss by Barry, "And we're betting the gold coins we found in that clearing. That's the only thing we have left of worth."

The Captain grunted before smiling at them. He reached into his pocket and pulled out ten rounds, "Does brass play? If so, ten he hits her twice before she freaks out and we have to pull her off of him."

Stunned silence gripped the men as they looked between the Captain and the rounds. They had all run out of ammo and carried their weapons as a habit. Their swords and spears were their main weapons now. A gasp from the crowd drew their attention to the fight in time to see Barry pull himself from off the ground again.

"Captain, are you sure?" Contreras asked. When the Captain nodded, Contreras said, "Brass plays."

"You men forget," the Captain said while Barry assumed a ready position and grinned winningly at Asha, "Barry has been with us the whole time. He's never slowed us down, and always pulled his own weight. "

As he spoke Asha charged him, this time swinging for real.

Barry skipped to the side, slapping Asha on the posterior as she passed him. A collective gasp rose from the crowd and whispering erupted around the ring, while the Captain's men stood with open mouths. The Captain stood with a knowing smile.

"The thing you men have overlooked is that I trained Barry myself. Who could walk away from that without learning a thing or two?" the Captain smirked.

Asha stood with her back strait and cheeks bright red staring at the field in front of her. She slowly turned to Barry with death in her eyes. Barry in turn, kept his winning smile and seemed unfazed.

"This is it, after this pass be ready to move in," the Captain ordered. The men didn't question him but prepared themselves.

Asha charged at him again ready for Barry to skip to the side but he held his ground instead, slipping a fist past Asha's guard and connecting with her chest. She stumbled backward clutching her offended beast, shock written on every line of her face. The look lasted a moment before she shrieked and pounced on Barry. Thanks to the Captain's warning, Asha only managed a few blows before they restrained her. The Captain wrapped her in a bear hug and dragged her back to the resthouse.

"Tell me that wasn't cool," Barry demanded spitting blood, looking at them through one eye.

"Its fine," Roberts announced after checking out Barry's bruised face.

"Yes, very stupid of you Barry," Javier replied drily.

"You're just mad you lost your bet," Barry taunted.

Javier's eyes flashed but a grin spread across his face, "It was worth it to pay that much to see you get your ass handed to you by a girl."

The men laughed at him as they walked back to the resthouse for dinner. Javier shot one last look at him before following the Captain. As he walked by Arete he called to her and she reluctantly came over to him. One of the little girls had tied a ribbon around her neck. Undoubtedly, the ribbon had been her most precious possession, but she had wanted Arete to have it. Javier locked eyes with the child before entering the house. Her green eyes were startlingly clear and wise. He blinked in surprise and found himself looking back at normal little girl eyes. Shaking his head, he heeded his stomach's rumbling and he went inside for the meal.

Once they were seated, Rahn brought them steaming platters of vegetables and tubers. Several roasted pheasants followed with warm flaky bread. Jars of honey and fruit marmalades were already at the table.

"Would my lord care for some wine? Or perhaps some ale?" Rahn asked.

"No thank you. I will have water," the Captain answered.

"Are you sure my lord? My resthouse is famous for its flavored ales. There are few who haven't heard of…" Rahn started.

"Water, will be fine," the Captain interrupted.

"Of course, my lord," Rahn conceded bowing.

"House master!" Contreras called.

"Yes, good sir?" Rahn asked.

"Me and my mate here will take a mug!" Contreras called pointing to Travis.

"Of course. Will you have some as well Rider?" Rahn asked Javier.

Javier glanced at the Captain who shrugged in return. He nodded to Rahn and reached for the bread. He stopped and turned to Rahn, "Bring us all a mug, except for my Lord of course. Make it a double for my fellow Riders."

"Right away," Rahn said bowing with a flourish.

Javier glanced at Pablo who looked decidedly green. Everyone knew he had never tried alcohol. Contreras launched into instructions on how to best drink the booze and how to avoid the dreaded hangovers. Pablo listened intensely nodding frequently and asking no questions.

Soon, Rahn returned with several mugs held tightly in his fists with Tobus and the green-eyed maid behind him carrying more. They all soon started quaffing their mugs, jeering at Javier's rosy cheeks and tearing off large chunks of meat from the fowls to stuff them in their mouths. The air grew thick with laughter and jokes, each more brazen than the last. The twins each grabbed two mugs and started a drinking race while Porter, Peters, Weeks and Boomer placed bets. Left finished first with a flourish and burped loudly.

Asha sipped her mug politely and then passed it on to Pablo, who looked at it cross eyed and took three tries to grasp the mug. He drank part of the mug and shared the rest with Breeze who drank happily as well.

"Thish drink ish really good," Pablo slurred before throwing up and passing out in the mess.

The table roared in laughter. The Captain laughed as well but picked him up and took him to his room, Breeze trailing behind staggering slightly mewing in concern. The rest of the party stayed behind laughing at the drunken duo and finished their own meals before staggering to their beds.

Asha shook her head at them. She had found the ale quite good, but like the Captain, she did not believe in getting drunk. She was the master of her body, and her body did not rule her. She had gotten drunk once just to see what it was like and found the experience left her distressingly vulnerable. Since then, she had only taken drinks sparingly and never more than one.

Asha reached down and scratched Bubbles between the ears where he liked it. His content purring rumbled through her hand and up her arm. She liked the sensation as much as Bubbles liked the attention. She saw Rahn headed toward her and she put a drunken grin on her face as he approached.

"Mistress Poisenfang! I think you have had too many of my family's drinks. Allow me to escort you to your room. Tobus!" he called bring the boy in from the other room, "Clean this mess up. Get help if you need."

While the boy scampered off to find help, Rahn wrapped one of Asha's arms over his shoulders and wrapped another hand around her chest and headed up the stairs with her.

"Master Rahn?"

"Yes, my dear?"

"If ya don' take yer hand of me delicates, imma have Bubbles eat yur hand an' then yur manhood," she giggled.

His hand moved instantly, and he turned his wide eyes to Bubbles, whose red eyes seemed to glow. Bubbles gave him a toothy silent snarl. Rahn helped her to her room without incident and deposited her in her bed gently. He turned to leave only to find Bubbles stretching across the doorway. He yawned, opening his mouth wide enough to show off all his teeth while stretching his legs extending all his claws. They sunk into the wooden floor tearing huge gouges into the wood.

Rahn said nothing about the damage as he left the room. He didn't run but the tremor in his hands betrayed his fear. He turned to Asha before leaving, "Anything else mistress?"

"Nah, I'll be alright. Jus' don't be sendin' anyone else in. Bubbles don't like it when people interrupt me beauty sleep and tends ta eat them if they do," she yawned.

"Of course, mistress. I will see that you are not disturbed," Rahn assured her.

He hurriedly closed the door and headed back downstairs. Bubbles sniffed the door for a moment before heading to Asha's bed. They shared a look and Asha burst into laughter. Bubbles purred in contentment, not really understanding but enjoying the mood all the same.

"Ya were perfect, Bubbles. Pure gold," she giggled.

Chapter

TWELVE

Late that night a knock sounded on their door, startling Bubbles. Asha glided over to the door, slipping a knife from its hiding place as she approached the door. Bubbles crouched low ready to spring and Asha threw open the door. Barry looked drunkenly at both of them wearing a huge grin on his face. Asha blinked in surprise and Bubbles hissed before returning to the bed.

"There's a good kitty," Barry laughed, then turning to Asha, "Hi there gorgeous, how are you doin'?"

"I think yur drunk Barry," Asha said.

"Aye!" Barry said happily, "A little liquid courage ta help me out."

"Help ya out with wat?"

"With this," Barry said leaning in and grabbing Asha around the waist and behind the head.

Asha whipped her knife up to Barry's throat and Bubbles leapt across the room and was at her side in a flash. Barry ignored them both, smothering Asha protest in a kiss. Asha remained frozen in the doorway unable to react.

"There that wasn't so bad, right? I dunno about you, but that was good for me," Barry murmured.

Asha still did not respond and watched Barry stagger toward his room. Tobus stood at on the stairs staring at them wide eyed. Asha raised an eyebrow at him, sending the lad scurrying down the stairs toward his uncle. Asha watched him go before slamming the door and spinning to look for Bubbles. He sat back on the bed washing his tail.

"Some help ya were!" she shouted.

Bubbles stopped cleaning his tail to look at her. He blinked slowly holding her gaze.

"NO! It wasn't that good fer me," she snarled.

Bubbles kept staring at her. "Ya don't know what yur talkin' about," she insisted. Bubbles still made no move, holding her gaze. "I'm tellin' you. He's an okay kisser but that was uninvited. He's lucky he was drunk or idda cut him good."

Bubbles cocked his head at her. Her eyes narrowed at him, "I hope 'e enjoyed that 'cus that's the last time he gets ta touch me."

Bubbles blinked again and cocked his head the other way. "I'm serious! No more touchin' fer Barry!" she promised loudly.

Bubbles responded by purring at her. Asha growled and threw a pillow at him. Bubbles ducked casually, letting the pillow fly over his head and returned to cleaning his tail. Asha walked over to the bed and curled up next to Bubbles. He nuzzled her hair while she drifted off to sleep.

"Seriously Bubbles, imma hurt him next time," she whispered, "Probably."

Javier staggered towards his room but found the journey difficult. The hallway swam in dizzying waves, throwing off his balance. He sat down heavily on a bench and stared, mesmerized, at a torch on the wall. Arete sat by his side gently prodding him with a paw, mewing in concern.

"Ish okay shweety. I'm jusht a little drunk," Javier slurred, "That was shome good beer."

Arete growled suddenly drawing Javier's attention toward the far end of the hallway. A pair of green eyes peeked from around the corner.

"Ish that the little girl who gave you your ribbon?" he asked.

Arete kept staring at the eyes growling. The maid from the field slowly edged out from behind the corner and advanced on them. Javier stared at her drunkenly, unable to decided how to react to his biggest fan.

"My uncle sent me ta check on ya, M'lord," She purred still coming at them slowly.

"Ah, thatsh really thoughtful of him," Javier soothed patting Arete, "Ish okay sweetheart, she's a friend. I think."

The maid drew up close and helped him up to his feet. She supported one side and Arete walked on Javier's other side. Javier found his feet unusually unsteady but Arete and the maid held him up. When they reached his room, they fell into his bed giggling together. She gave him a quick peck on the cheek, drawing a blush and a laugh from Javier. The maid pulled of his boots and reached for his belt.

"Whoa the shweety. Thatsh all you gettin' offa me tanight," Javier protested, "Listen, mishtress…um…"

"Fawn. M'lord can call me Fawn," she cooed.

"Fawn…right," Javier said sleepily.

From the floor Arete's yellow eyes burned bright, from hate or envy, Javier wasn't sure, but he was too drunk and enjoying himself too much to really care. Fawn was too intent on Javier to giveArette more than a cursory glance.

"Shhh, m'Lord," she whispered in his ear, "I'll take care of you."

Pablo lay in his bed unable to make the world stop spinning

in circles. He closed his eyes but that only made it worse. Next to him Breeze seemed to be in no better shape and was making weird noises. Pablo tried to reach out to him but found himself unable to move. He heard noises from the hallway.

"Are you sure they are in there?" A voice asked.

"Yes! I told you they would be," another voice answered. This one seemed familiar for some reason.

"And this one is the weakest? What of his beast?" the first one asked.

"Yes, yes, and the beast drank my ale as well and it should also be drugged," the second voice replied.

"Don't worry master. Rahn and I have an understanding. He won't betray us," a third voice interjected.

"Alright but pray for a quick death if either of you lied to me," the first voice said, "Too bad you couldn't have gotten the Night Rider to drink. A woman would have been easier to best."

"Not that one m'lord," Rahn objected. Wait. Rahn? The house master had betrayed them? Pablo tried to shake his head but couldn't move. "That one is a demon. She is the deadliest woman I have ever met."

"You should meet some of my master's warlocks," the first voice snorted.

"Begging m'lord's pardon, but I have, and I stand by what I said," Rahn corrected.

"I see," the first voice mused interested.

Asha felt nervous. There was something wrong in the air and it wouldn't let her sleep. She looked over at Bubbles and saw that he was nervous too. His red eyes bounced around the room and his tail twitched nonstop. Unable to stand the confining room any longer, Asha climbed out the window onto the eves of the first floor, and Bubbles flowed out after her.

A dark patch of shadow detached itself from the wall and walked toward her. Bubbles started to growl softly but cut off when the shadows fell away and the shape resolved into the Captain.

"A shadow cloak, sir?" Asha asked.

"Yes, something is off," the Captain replied.

"I feel it too," Asha said.

Javier struggled against the thick ropes of drowsiness that seemed to be gripping at him. Fawn continued to remove his clothes at random. His sluggish brain tried to tell him something but he couldn't tell what. Arete stared from the ground with a silent snarl on her face but she didn't move against Fawn. Fawn gave Arete, her most winning smile.

Like thunderbolt it hit Javier what she was doing. His weapons lay useless on the floor, not far out of reach, but in his weakened condition, they may as well have been on the other side of the room. Adrenaline flooded his system but was no match for Rahn's ale. Javier's breath became ragged as he struggled to gain control of his body.

"Shhh my warrior, I will take good care of you," Fawn whispered.

A gurgling noise was all Javier could muster. Panic rose in his chest and he couldn't do anything to help himself and watched helplessly as Fawn pulled a thin blade from the curls in her hair.

"Why can we just kill them?" the third voice said.

"Because, the cat will just try to kill us if we do. We will have to turn this one to make it join us," the first voice answered contemptuously, "If he won't join us voluntarily, then we will have Meem turn him for us."

"Meem can't do that," the third voice reminded.

Pablo heard a smack through the door and a body hit the ground. "If I want your opinion *ariat*, I will beat it out of you. Until then, keep silent or I will rip out your tongue and make you eat it."

"As you say," the third grumbled quietly.

The door hinges squeaked slightly as they entered the room. The light of a single candle flooded the room bathing Pablo and Breeze in its light. Pablo still struggled with nauseating spinning but Breeze had given into sleep and was snoring softly next to him. The floorboards creaked as the men crossed the floor. Strong arms pick Pablo up and slung him over broad shoulders next to a sword then carried him towards the door.

Breeze! He thought with a panic. Where was his cat? Behind him he heard two men grunt as they picked up Breeze and followed them out the door and down the stairs. The rug on the stairs muffled and protests from the wood and the foot falls of the men. Soon, the cool night air hit Pablo's face and filled his lungs. Despair and helplessness filled Pablo and he couldn't help the tears that fell from his eyes to soak the shirt of his abductor.

"Patty," the Captain whispered shaking Patrick.

Patrick groaned before rolling to the edge of his bed and emptying his stomach onto the floor. When he was finished, he wiped his mouth and looked blurrily at the Captain.

"Sir?" he asked.

"Patty you've been drugged. You need to flare your Vitality. It will purify your blood and cleanse the poison," the Captain urged.

"Sir, I can't focus," Patrick moaned.

"You have to try," the Captain ordered.

"Sir, I can't. Please let me sleep," Patrick begged.

"Patty, listen ta meh," Asha said gripping his head in her hands drawing his face close to hers, "Listen ta my voice."

"Okay," he whimpered.

"Focus now. Listen ta me. Ya have to flare your vitality. Can ya do that fer meh?" she asked.

Her breath thrilled Patrick so he nodded and did as he was bid. At first there was blinding pain but Asha held his head and stroked his hair. Slowly the pain receded and his vision cleared showing Asha's face in front of his. On impulse, he reached out and stroked her cheek. When she leaned into it, he grew bolder and drew her close and kissed her quickly on the lips. Her eyes widened in shock. The Captain jumped forward and put a hand on her shoulder but it wasn't necessary, she was still in shock.

"Again? Really?" She muttered as Bubbles bumped his head against her purring. "Shut up, you," she snapped at him.

The Captain cleared his throat, "Patty you good to go? We need to get to the other men."

"Help me up. I can clear the rest as we walk," Patrick answered. He turned to Asha, "Sorry about that. Not sure where that came from. Again? What's that supposed to mean?"

In response Bubbles hissed at him and snapped his jaws. Patrick jumped back with his hands up, giving up on the question.

The Captain grabbed the cat by the scruff of the neck, lifting him up off the ground, no small feat, and brought him up to his face snarling. Bubbles averted his eyes in submission, so the Captain set him down.

"Come, the night is young. Patrick, I have time to teach you one spell so learn quickly," the Captain ordered.

They head into the hallway, Asha trailing behind them muttering to herself with Bubbles by her side purring like thunder. Asha drew her daggers and hushed him. Bubbles sensed her tension and stopped purring abruptly.

"It's okay, m'lord," Fawn soothed, "We don't want to kill you. Not yet anyway. We still need to get the bond from you so your *otorga* can bond with a more worthy Rider. *Ariats* are not worthy of such gifts."

Javier's fingers twitched uncontrollably as he tried to reach for his knives. They were just too far away, he couldn't reach them. He tried to communicate his will to Arete, but she remained where she was like he had asked her, to which Javier was now regretting.

Fawn pulled his face towards her again. She bent down close, her warm breath tickling his mouth, before she gently placed her lips on his. Arete watched them with angry eyes. Fawn smiled down at Javier while she tickled his ribs with her knife where Arete couldn't see. Triumph shined in her face as she relished the power she held over him, infuriating Javier. He gathered his strength and hissed at her or what was a fair approximation of a hiss. Arete was on her feet in flash, growling at Fawn. Fawn's eyes widened and she licked her lips nervously.

"Shhh, Arete, we are just having fun," she soothed.

Javier hissed again, this time with more force and managed a floppy, limp armed strike at her face. Fawn swatted it away loudly, making the slap sound meaty and harder than it really was. The sound was Arete's cue to attack. The *otorga* screamed as she leaped at Fawn.

Fawn turned to meet the attack, knife raised. Seeing that the knife was pointed at Arete's heart, Javier grabbed the naked blade in his hand. Fawn pulled it out of his hand easily, slicing the skin on his palm and fingers, but the delay was enough for Arete to close the gap between them. Fawn shrieked once before it Arete's jaws clamped shut on her throat cutting of the scream and reducing it to a gurgling moan.

The door blew apart inward into the room, spraying them all with debris and littering the room with door fragments. Arete jumped off the bed screaming defiance at the doorway, jaws dripping with blood. Patrick, Left, Right, Lambert, Bubbles and Asha poured into the room looking for a threat. Arete looked frantically at them, bloodlust still in her eyes. Bubbles placed himself between them and Arete hissing softly at her. She crouched low, growling softly but didn't attack them.

Patty strode across the room toward Javier ignoring Arete completely. Arete, still confused, misread his intentions and jump towards him and Bubbles moved to tackle her.

"No," Patty said calmly holding his hand out at the *otorgas*. Both cats froze in the air thrashing. Patty released Bubbles but kept Arete suspended in the air. "I got you Javi, don't fight me," he instructed Javier.

Patty grabbed Javier's hand sent magic coursing through him. Javier felt the poison's effect lessen on his body, and his strength return. A few seconds later he was on his feet calming his otorga. When she was sufficiently calm, Patty let her go and she dropped to the floor.

"Report. What happened?" Javier demanded, "This doesn't seem random. What about this?" Javier asked showing Patty his hand, which was still bleeding.

"Nothin' I can do about that. I'm not good with flesh wounds yet," Patty answered.

Javier started to sigh but Lambert rushed forward and started pulling gauze and glue from his med kit, "Good to know the old ways still work," Javier commented dryly, "As I was saying this wasn't an accident or am I missing something?"

"It ain't," Asha replied, "Somethun' is goin' on 'ere. Tha Cap'in left with Travis an' the others after Pablo 'n Breeze."

"What?" Javier asked.

"Someone kidnapped them. They drugged us so we wouldn't be able to follow," Patty explained.

"How?" Javier demanded.

"The ale," Left started, "Someone added extra flavoring to it."

"And then tried to kill us," Right finished.

"Where are they now?" Javier asked.

"They are past the meadow, into the woods," Patty replied.

"Let's go. They are going to need our help," Javier ordered, shouldering past them into the hall.

He paused briefly when he saw the bodies of his would be abductors outside his door, but shrugged it off, continuing on. There was time to dwell on them later, he had things to attend to right now.

Pablo's teeth clicked together gently as he was jostled around on his captor's shoulder. He snagged a leaf off a bush as they passed by it quickly stuffing it in his mouth before anyone noticed. The effort left him faint and dizzy but he chewed doggedly on his leaf. The leaf's juices filled his mouth and he swallowed the goopy concoction. He felt the poisons effects begin to ebb and used his new found strength to grab leaves off another bush as they passed. This time his ride noticed.

"What are you doing back there?" He demanded.

Instead of saying anything, Pablo made a lot of retching sounds. It had the results he had been looking for. The giant carrying him, dumped him on the ground in disgust.

"If you are going to shame yourself do so under that bush *atras*," the giant growled, "I am Kint of Aster's Sons, and I will not be sullied by you."

Pablo's mind raced as he considered his options. He racked his brain trying to figure out if he knew Kint. His leaves were clearing the fog in his head, but they had a long way to go before they cleared him completely.

"On your feet *atras*," Kint sneered.

That's it! Javier thought to himself, *He thinks I'm still Mud. Of course! Kint! He was Aster's strongest scout and gatherer. He's the one that got sent to pick up Sons that Aster heard about.*

"I said get up!" he yelled accentuating with a kick at Pablo's ribs.

Pablo groaned and curled up into a ball whimpering pitifully. Kint spit on him in disgust but threw him over his shoulder again. Pablo allowed himself to go limp while he let the leaves do their work on his body. He only hoped that they would stop soon and he could somehow get to Breeze and give him some of the leaves as well.

"Where did they go?" the Captain asked.

Contreras scanned the ground frantically looking for clues. "Sorry, sir," he apologized, "They covered their tracks well."

"Well uncover them! This is supposed to be your specialty," the Captain snapped.

"Sir! Yes, sir!" Contreras shouted.

He shrugged off his pack and tossed it to Porter. He dropped to his knees and scanned closer to the ground. Finally, he found a cat hair and from there faint boot prints. In a flash he was on his feet crashing through the brush with the others hot on his heels. A few dozen yards deeper into the forest it became apparent to him that his quarry had given up hiding their trail. Contreras would have done the same thing in their position. If someone could follow their trail this far, there was no point in trying to hide it and speed was of the essence now.

"They picked up speed here, sir," He shouted over his shoulder.

"Let's move people, they have a head start on us and they have our people! We are the Night Angels, such a thing cannot be allowed!" the Captain roared, and the group roared with him.

Contreras's heart pounded in his chest as he followed the trail as fast as he could stopping only briefly to pick up the trail to head out again faster and faster. The forest blurred around him and his lungs burned, but he kept on determined to regain his friend.

Hang on Pablo, he thought, *Don't do anything stupid until we get there to help you do it.*

Chapter

THIRTEEN

"Sir, your orders?" Patty asked.

Javier considered his options. Their forces were divided by an unknown enemy, and they had tried to kill some of them outright instead of attempting to capturing him and sneaking off, so that meant they weren't too much stronger than his group. At least the group as a whole. With their forces divided who knew which side would come out on top. Then again, any side with the Captain held the advantage.

"We will have to follow. I don't know if we can catch up but, we will try. Hopefully we can get to them before they get too far away," Javier decided.

"We still have ta take care of da mole, Javi," Asha insisted.

"We will Asha but there are more important things to do right now," Javier replied.

"Ta hell with them, they tried ta kill ya an' Patty, I demand blood!" she screamed angrily.

"That's not how we do things," Javier reminded her, "Besides they wanted me alive, at least for now."

"No, that's how we *used* ta do it. Now we's in a new place. Blood is the only thing they understand," Asha countered.

"I don't care how they…" Javier started.

"She's right," Barry interjected coming into the room. He was unfocused and staggering but determined. Patty grabbed his hand cleansing him of the poison.

"Yes, your endorsement is a huge bonus," Javier scoffed, his voice dripping sarcasm.

"It should be, you arrogant little man," Barry spat, "Of the two of us who has more experience dealing with new cultures and customs?"

"Well…"Javier stalled.

"Me. Who has more experience as a diplomat? Who has brokered more power deals? Or peace proposals? Gained the trust of countless tribes?" Barry pressed.

"Irrelevant."

"No lieutenant, not irrelevant, inconvenient. Who do you think the Captain will turn to for guidance on this topic?"

"Oh, and you're so sure that it will be you?"

"Yes, he doesn't keep me around for good my good looks. Well, kinda, that and my charm, wit, and ability to win people over."

"Hmmm."

"Have you forgotten yours and Asha's fight? You think the Captain put *that* together? It's not his style. He has kept me close because he needs me for these kinds of things. It's dirty, it's low, it's what I was born and trained to do. I can do these kinds of things in my sleep."

"Well, you think killing Rahn will even the scales? I don't think killing a resthouse owner will give us reputation that we want," Javier pouted.

"Ha! Don't be ridiculous," Barry scoffed, "Nothing so extreme. So far, no one has died so there's no death debt, just a blood debt. He did offer safety and hospitality, but betrayed us and you were bleeding."

"Okay, I follow so far," Javier agreed hesitantly.

"So glad ya do," Asha said dryly.

"Asha," Patty warned, putting a hand on her shoulder.

"What would be best," Barry proposed, eyes flickering toward Asha, "would be to extract something from him."

"Like…?" Javier prompted.

"I was thinking a hand," Barry announced with a flourish, "And a stern warning that if any ill befalls your party we will be back for the other hand. That and if any of us die…"

"I see," Javier interrupted hurriedly looking sallow.

"Brilliant," Left commented excitedly.

"Ya, Arete should eat it," Right agreed.

"Wicked," They said in unison.

"You're not helping," Javier moaned.

"I will make sure he doesn't die, sir," Lambert assured him.

"Great even the medic thinks this is a good idea," Javier muttered exasperated.

"Lieutenant," Patty prodded gently.

"What?" Javier snapped.

"Sir, this is no different than the Kyber Pass," Patty reminded him.

"Don't you dare bring that up," Javier warned softly but dripping with menace.

"I must, sir. A man had a sacred duty to protect you and yours, then betrayed you and left you for dead. We don't know what will happen to Pablo or Breeze. You have the chance to avenge your own. We are the Night Angels, vengeance is our calling."

"And mercy is our guide," Javier snapped.

"By blood and honor we fight. By blood and honor we die," Patty recited.

"All they understand is the law of da sword, Javi. Fer now we will have ta follow that. Once the Cap'in claims his birthright we can change things, but till then, we'll have ta do it this way," Asha coaxed gently.

Javier turned to the window, considering his options. A fat figure waddled across the yard towards the barn where the goats were kept. Javier recognized Rahn plump frame. Arete put her paws on the window and gave a feral noise from deep in her throat. She turned her eyes and he felt her demand retribution and was begging for permission. He turned his eyes back to the figure and saw three others with swords handing a sack to Rahn whispering urgently.

"So be it. Vengeance will be ours. Bubbles, Arete, go! Slow them down. The rest of you, for our brothers, for our honor, for justice, let's get them," Javier roared, pulling his sword from his back.

Beast and man alike howled with him and poured from the window, down the roof, and onto the yard towards the figures. Two of the swords men pulled their swords and squared to meet them. A third tore across the field towards the woods. Rahn in turn scurried towards his resthouse.

"Patty!" Javier shouted.

"I got him!" Patty shouted back adopting a look of

concentration.

As they got closer to the swordsmen it became apparent that at least one of them was a Son. Bubbles and Arete reached them first hissing and snarling. Bubble went for the larger of the two and Arete for the smaller one. Bubbles danced around the giant hissing and scoring shallow but painful hits. Half a field away, Javier could only watch as Arete failed to hurt her target. The smaller swordsman was fast, faster than he should be so he stepped to the side casually as Arete jumped at him, landing a kick on her ribs as she passed.

"NO!" Javier screamed, but it didn't matter.

The smaller swordsman brought his sword down for the killing blow. Then, suddenly, Bubbles was there biting at his neck drawing both swordsman against him but he danced away slightly out of reach, darting in for a swipe or two and then dancing away, each time drawing them a little father from Arete.

Javier reached Arete just as she gained her feet. Asha and the others went to help Bubbles. Patty fell to his knees next to them, sweat rolling down his face.

"I got him Lieutenant but…it's so hard…from so far away. Bring him to me…please," Patty panted.

"BARRY!" Javier bellowed in his battlefield voice.

When Barry spun around to see what Javier wanted, Javier pointed toward the last swordsman, now held aloft by Patty's spell. Barry nodded and dashed towards his target. Arete rolled her shoulders and locked gazes with Javier. He nodded to her, and they moved in unison towards the battle ahead.

Left and Right harassed the giant swordsman stabbing him in the back every time he turned his attention away to attack the other one. Lambert stood a ways away throwing rocks with startling accuracy and force. The giant roared as a rock tore a gash above his eye. He started toward Lambert but the twins harassed him from behind. Suddenly he spun, catching them off guard, landing blows on both of them, making them spit out blood. Lambert unleashed a hailstorm of stones from his pouch to draw the giant's attention.

Nearby Asha and Bubbles blurred as they attempted to subdue the smaller swordsman. Javier watched in fascination as parts of him seemed to disappear into the night. He landed a kick on Asha but before he could take advantage of it, Bubbles pressed him, giving Asha time to recover. After she shook off the kick, she attacked in earnest, angered by the blow.

Javier looked at Arete and nodded towards Asha and Bubbles, "Help them, you're faster than I am and they need your help. Left and Right need mine," he ordered. She grumbled but ran towards her fight. Javier shook his arms to limber them up and headed into fray to try and save Lambert.

Javier turned the blade before it hit Lambert, and aimed a kick at the giant's crotch as he did so. The giant saw the move coming and took the blow to the hip. He spun delivering a blow to Left's face, who had been trying to sneak up on him. There was a crunching noise as Left's nose crumpled and his eyes rolled into his head as he fell to the ground. Javier and Right cried out and rushed the giant but the giant reached out, grabbing Javier's shirt and threw him bodily into Right. They fell into the dirt stunned by the force of the throw. Right whimpered as he tried to stagger towards his brother, holding an arm that bent where it wasn't supposed to bend.

Not wasting any time, Javier scrambled to his feet, running towards the giant who had renewed his attack on Lambert. He had a large hand wrapped around Lambert's throat and had started squeezing. Javier spared a glance and saw that Asha and the cats had the other swordsman well in hand, so he continued on towards Lambert.

By the time he got to them Lambert was already purple, and the giant was laughing in glee. He held the helpless Lambert in the air with one hand and a naked sword in the other. Javier drew back his sword but stopped abruptly when a shot rang out in the air. Brain matter and blood splattered on his face making him flinch.

On the other side of the giant, Barry stood, holding the foot of the floating third swordsman and a faintly smoking gun. He grunted and looked at his gun, "Huh, hot load. Better be careful repacking these."

Javier wiped goo from his face and turned to face the last swordsman. A strange sight met his gaze. The swordsman was kneeling humbly on the ground, bleeding from several shallow but nonlife threatening cuts, flanked by the two *otorgas* and Asha with dagger at his neck. Javier turned to the floating swordsman, listening to the twins whisper to each other, and Lambert cough and gasp as air filled his lungs once again.

"Do you yield as well?" he asked the floating swordsman.

"I do m'lord," the swordsman replied through gritted teeth.

"Swear it," Javier demanded.

"I swear, by my honor and by my blood, that I yield to you m'Lord," the swordsman swore.

"Your name," Javier asked.

"Si Swiftfoot, m'Lord," he replied.

"'Sir' will suffice," Javier snapped, "Patty, let him go."

"Yes, m'Lord," Patty replied with a grin.

Si hit the ground with a grunt but said nothing about his treatment. He merely kneeled and waited for Javier to say something. Javier glanced towards Lambert who had made his way to where the twins were moaning.

"How are they Corporal?" Javier asked still considering Si.

"Left has a broken nose but is fine. Right's arm is a bad break. Internal bleeding most likely," Lambert rasped pursing his lips, "He needs surgery, but I don't know how to do it out here."

"Great," Javier groaned, "How are you holding up?"

"Fine, sir," Lambert replied.

"You sure? You were awfully purple and you sound like crap."

"I'll be fine just a bruised larynx at most. I will be fine in a few minutes, though as a precaution I won't talk as much as I normally do."

"Ha! You talk almost as much as Slappy and he doesn't talk at all but I see your point," Javier laughed raising a hand stalling the reply.

Patty walked over to them and whispered with Lambert, but Javier ignored them. He turned his attention back to his captives. He considered the other swordsman.

"I can only assume you are a Demon Blades like Asha," he started. The man nodded so Javier continued on, "What shall we call you?"

"Drink blood and die," the swordsman hissed spitting.

"Now that wasn't nice," Asha purred, "I'm thinkin' imma have ta teach ya some manners."

"Now, now Asha, he's a crude second class warrior. Maybe that's his name," Javier reasoned.

"Aye, that's true, 'e was easy ta beat," Asha agreed.

"Is that your name, son?" Javier asked.

"I will not talk," he said defiantly.

"Oh that's alright cutie," she grinned, "We're gonna have us some fun. Can I 'ave a few moments alone with him, Javi?"

"Carry on," Javier consented turning his back on them.

Javier looked at Barry who's eyes grew to round saucers. "What?" Javier asked.

"They're gone! One second they were there then the next a blackness took them and they were gone," Barry gasped.

Javier glanced over his shoulder and confirmed that they were indeed gone but just shrugged his shoulders, "I guess they are."

"That's it? No awe?" Barry asked mystified.

"Nah, getting used to magic. Unless there is a dragon nearby, I'm not going to get excited," Javier replied.

"There are dragons?"

"Captain said there were at one point but they were hunted to extinction so he's not sure if there are any left."

"Oh, bummer."

"Ya. Patty! What are you two whispering about?" Javier called out.

"I think Lambert and I can link and fix his arm. We need to get him to a bed and sedated though. It's going to hurt. You got any ideas on how to knock him out? I was considering a rock," Patty called back. Left grunted as Lambert popped his nose back in place.

Javier was considered options when Barry leaned in whispering, "I think Master Rahn can help us there."

Javier blinked and realized what Barry was referring to. He nodded motioning to Right, "Let's get him back."

At that moment Asha, the *otorgas,* and the swordsman appeared back in the field. The swordsman was on his feet in an instant and fell at Javier's feet clutching his ankles.

"My name is Rashta the Knife, and I am Aster's chief assassin, you know my apprentice Fawn, and since you're alive I can only imagine you killed her. You have already met Si and the other you killed was named Pice. Ask me anything I will tell you anything, just keep her away," Rashta blurted out, his eyes rolling in panic.

Asha gave a toothy grin and slowly swaggered up to where Rashta lay trembling. She drew a finger down his cheek and he flinched.

"What did you do?" Javier asked.

"Tsk, tsk, Javi," she purred, "Ya shouldn't be askin' a girl ta reveal her secrets. Ya might not be able to ta handle meh."

"Sure, whatever," Javier sighed, "Let's just get Right back to the resthouse. You and Bubbles run ahead and find Master Rahn. We have questions for him. Keep him whole for now, we will need his help."

"Aww you take all tha fun outta it," Asha pouted.

"Well, if he resists, convince him not to. Just don't kill him," Javier instructed.

Asha brightened and dashed off with Bubbles trailing behind. Rashta blew a sigh of relief but had it cut short when Javier's sword touched his throat. He looked up and met Javier's eyes.

"I will have an oath from you as well, assassin," Javier demanded, his eyes steely and dangerous.

The assassin drew a tiny dagger and cut his palm letting the blood hit the ground, "I swear by my blood and honor, that I will not attack you or you comrades, and do hereby surrender to you and any else you would have me surrender to."

"Good," Javier said, "Time to move."

They helped the twins to their feet and head back the resthouse. Lights shone through most of the windows showing that many patrons where now up.

Rahn scrambled around the room as fast as his bulk would let him. His hands were trembling so bad that it took him four tries to get the key into the lock of his trunk. The last time he had open the trunk was so long ago that a thick layer of dust covered the top, hiding the wood beneath. He was too old and fat to wear the armor that was in it, but the daggers were things of beauty and magical as well.

"I told you it was a bad idea. I told you a thousand times not to trust that man or any of his men but noooo, 'Trust me' you said. 'This is the great Aster, he will make us rich' you said. I told you were a fool then and I'm telling you again," his wife Shara nagged from the corner where she was knitting.

"Quiet Shara, I'm trying not to get us killed here," Rahn begged.

"Oh, sure, now you believe we will get killed. I told you not to take the job. I *begged* you not to. I told you that betraying our duty to protect our guests would only bring despair. I begged you. Begged! But no, you had to take the money. Now they will most likely kill us both. Ugh, I should have listened to father. Life would be better if I hadn't married such a fat fool," Shara said, refusing to look at him.

"Don't say that, my flower," Rahn sobbed.

"Bah, you shadow blasted fool!" she said scornfully.

"I'm not shadow blasted," Rahn muttered.

"Yes, you are, this was your fault and now we *both* have to pay the price for your failures. Again," she snapped spitting at Rahn's feet, "If they give us a chance to talk, I will tell them everything."

"Why thank ya Mistress Shara. I think I will be takin' yur offer ta talk," a voice said behind her.

Shara squeaked in surprise, and turned to find the mismatched eyes of the she demon staring at her. She began trembling, which only doubled when two red yes emerged from the dark. The black *otorga* walk by her and started circling her husband. Rahn was weeping freely now, moaning and muttering to himself. She felt a brief amount of fear for him but it was quickly replaced by contempt.

She whirled back around to the she demon and said, "Very well, Mistress Asha, it started when that eel, Aster came through. He promised my fat, stupid, shadow spawned husband gold…"

Patrick laid Right on the bed and pushed a spell into his head forcing him to sleep. "It's only temporary Lieutenant. It won't work as an anesthetic. It only induces a natural sleep," he explained, answering Javier's question before he could ask.

"Fair enough. Where is Asha?" Javier wondered.

A knock on the door answered him, and without waiting for a response, Tobus opened it letting in his uncle and aunt followed by Bubbles and Asha.

"Success I see," Javier commented.

"Aye," Asha agreed nodding towards Shara, "This one is singin' like a canary and her husband is lil' more than sobbin' squalin' babeh." She left them at the door then went to stand behind Si and Rashta, both of whom cringed in her presence.

Javier grunted but Patty laughed for a moment before turning serious. He placed himself in front of Rahn but reconsidered and stood in front of Shara. Barry looked from Asha to Rahn's family considering them all. Asha met his gaze with an eyebrow raised, then winked at Patty.

"Do you know what I am?" Patty asked.

"Yes, m'Lord. You are Captain's druid," she answered.

"Yes I am. Do you know what I can do?"

"Many painful and humiliating things I imagine."

"Indeed, so do not lie to me, I will know and will punish accordingly," Patty warned. Shara nodded dropping her eyes to the floor. "Where does your husband keep the poisoned ale?"

"I don't know m'Lord," she lied.

Patty frowned at her and she yelped and grabbed the offended area, her bottom. Judging from her blush and Patty's smug look, Barry figured out what Patty had done to get his point across.

"How could you dare to do that?" she demanded.

"Mistress Shara, you fail to comprehend," Barry interjected, rising from the chair he had taken. He leaned forward into her face, "We own your life. We own your husband's life. A small spank on the bottom for a rebellious child is appropriate right now. If you prefer, we can make an example on your flesh. Or perhaps that of you nephew."

"No! It's in the cellar under a false bottom," she cried, "Don't hurt him, I will do anything."

"Indeed you will," Barry agreed, grinning evilly, "The Night Angels make no empty promises."

Both Rahn's family and their captives gasped at his words. The two captives looked at each other not saying a word but both sharing a look of dread.

"I see you have heard of us," Barry noted.

"M'Lord, every child has heard of the Knight Angels. We thought you were all dead," Si replied.

Patty started to open his mouth, but Barry cut him off with a small gesture. He got it immediately but obviously didn't like the fact that Barry was in charge, but Barry didn't care. For the good of them all, this was his show. For now at least.

"I assure you, what you heard was wrong," Barry started and the captives relaxed until they saw Barry's eyes glint, "We are much more than your stories said."

Si nodded accepting Barry's story, while Rashta looked skeptical.

"Asha," Barry asked turning, "Could you have beaten Rashta here alone?"

"Aye, 'e's not nearly as tough as what's 'is name, ya know Pablo's old master?" Asha answered.

"Zemer," Javier supplied.

"Aye that oaf. Still mad ya stole that kill too," Asha pouted.

"Zemer? The Champion?" Si gasped.

"Oh, you know him?" Barry asked.

"Yes, he set out with his *atras* and we never heard from him," Si replied.

"Well now 'e's just feed fer da birds," Asha gloated.

"But that's impossible!" Rashta shouted, "Only Aster could have beaten him!"

Asha dangled a medallion between them. Rashta recognized it and truly started fearing Asha.

"The lost Kings' medallion," Rahn whispered.

"Enough," Barry ordered, "To business. You know who we are and what we can do now. Listen and obey or face our wrath."

"I will be attempting to heal my friend here. If something goes wrong, your family will bear the shame together," Patty said, "Tobus will stay here while you go and retrieve the ale. I get bored easily. Hopefully I wont have to entertain myself."

Shara bowed her head in submission and scurried to get the ale. Rahn sat in the corner crying, ignoring the snot running from his nose. Bubbles and Arete flowed around him alternating licking their teeth and sniffing him. Tobus went to a chair and sat quietly looking at his hands.

Javier edged closer to Barry, "You think threating that child is a good idea? What would you do if they called our bluff?"

Barry was silent for a moment then met Javier's eyes, "I wasn't bluffing. If it comes down to them or us, I will choose us every time. Perhaps I have twisted morals, but I will always choose the life of my comrades to the comfort of a few traitors."

"Comrades, huh?" Javier asked.

"Oh shut up," Barry muttered.

"And the boy? You would do that to him?"

"He may be young lieutenant but don't assume he is a child. Look how he sits, he makes himself look small and vulnerable but sees everything," Barry whispered. Javier turned casually to look and caught the spark in the boy's eyes. Barry continued, "No, Javier, this one is no child."

Javier grunted but didn't argue. His time in Afghanistan, Africa, and China had taught him how fast children could grow up. He walked over to where Patty was kneeling next to Right. A small glow came from his hand as he moved it slowly above Right's arm.

"What are…?" Javier asked.

"I'm delving," Patty answered impatiently, "I am seeing how closely I can attune to his body. When Lambert and I link, I will use Lambert's knowledge on how the arm is supposed to look, and the body's own knowledge to fix his arm."

"The body's knowledge?" Left asked.

"Yes, the body knows what it's supposed to be like. I can tap into that some to return it to its original state, but it's not perfect,"

Patty explained.

"So, you use Lambert to fill the gaps?" Javier guessed.

"Yup, that's about right," Patty smiled.

"Aw, an' I thought ya were just really smart. Too bad ya had ta go an' ruin it fer me," Asha purred.

"Hey! I am smart. I can already heal better than you or the Captain. I'm into uncharted territory here," Patty retorted defensively.

Asha blew him a kiss and laughed while Patty grumbled and returned to delving Right.

Chapter

FOURTEEN

Patrick sat back rubbing his back against the pain and released the mana and Lambert at the same time. Lambert fell to the carpet sweating and gasping for breath. In a flash, Asha was there assessing him.

"What's wrong?" Patrick asked alarmed.

"I…may have over done it," Lambert gasped.

"Oh, why didn't you say anything?" Patrick demanded.

"He'll be fine, but I wouldn't recommend movin' 'im any time soon," Asha announced.

Lambert gave him a weak smile before answering, "I could see how bad it was, and I had to save my patient."

"You're an idiot," Right moaned.

"Leave him be brother," Left urged gently, "He just saved you."

"Right is correct, you are too valuable to let die, Lambert," Barry reminded him.

"Agreed," Javier agreed, "Yes, I agreed with Barry, don't die from shock."

The group shared a laugh. After a moment Asha ushered them all from the room so Lambert and the twins could get some rest. Patrick followed them out assuring Asha that he was fine and hadn't exceeded his limits. Once out in the hallway he confronted Javier.

"Sir, the Captain left orders," Patrick informed him.

"Now you tell me?!" Javier cried.

"Well, sir, we were supposed to clean up here and then follow as we could. We cleaned up here and now we are ready to catch up," Patrick replied.

Javier shot him an annoyed look, "How long do you think they've been gone?"

Patrick consulted his watch, "About three hours, sir."

"Your watch still works?"

"Ya, it's a wind up, no battery needed here."

"Okay, so how are we supposed to catch up? Man, what I wouldn't give for a truck right now."

"Ha! I'd settle for horses."

"Wait, Rahn has some in the back. We should take those."

"Do you know how to ride, sir" Patrick asked.

"Of course I do, don't you?" Javier asked.

Patrick had no idea how, nor had he even been near a horse but he nodded anyway. "Sir, we should interrogate the prisoners while we wait for Right and Lambert to recover," he suggested.

Javier nodded and walked to the next open door and looked the prisoners in the eye while pointing inside the room. They immediately took the hint and went in meekly kneeling on the floor. Javier started to go in but Barry grabbed his arm, stopping him from going in.

"Sir, it will be best that you don't sully your hands with ones as unworthy of you as these two," Barry warned carefully.

"Very well," Javier conceded grudgingly, "but if they give you no information, I will have words with them."

"It should be fine, sir. If I accidently kill one in interrogation, I'll have a second one to try on," Barry grinned.

Patrick paled a little and turned his back to them considering Rahn and his family. "What of these, sir?"

"Bubbles, Arete, escort them to the dining room, Asha and I will join you shortly. If they try to run you may eat them," Javier ordered.

Bubbles licked his lips and turned his red eyes on Tobus. Rahn paled while his wife wrapped the boy in her arms and glared at her husband. Patrick hid his smile, he knew that neither cat would eat the family but the threat was scary enough that they probably wouldn't even think about running.

"Patty, I'm going to need you in here," Barry said.

"Me?" Patrick asked.

"Yes, I may need you to…persuade them," Barry explained.

Patrick sighed and went in after him. The duo was kneeling on the floor and didn't move or respond as Patrick and Barry entered the room and shut the door. Barry pulled a chair to the middle of the room where he could sit and stare at the both of them, while Patrick took the bed and leaned against the wall.

"What were you doing here?" Barry asked.

"We must respectfully decline to answer," Rashta said.

"You were awfully chatty when Asha was around. Shall I have her come and ask the questions for me? Because if that's what needs to happen, I can make that happen," Barry threatened.

"It does not matter who asks. Aster will do worse if we talk to Knights," Rashta replied.

"Nights?" Barry asked.

"You are Knight Angels, aren't you?" Rashta asked.

"Well, yes, but we're Angels not nights," Barry explained.

"I think he means knights, with a 'k'" Patrick guessed.

"Ah, yes, the old name," Barry said covering, "No matter. Why would Aster care about that?"

"Because…you don't know?" Rashta asked, incredulous.

"We have not been in these parts in a very long time. I am not sure which stories were handed down accurately and which were corrupted by time," Barry said.

"Oh," Rashta replied, "Well here we know of a prophecy that says that the Knight Angels will come from the world beyond ours that shares our love of war and will shepherd with them the King that will be."

"Go on," Barry coaxed when Rashta hesitated.

"I will say no more. Do what you will," Rashta declared, twisting suddenly and snapping Si's neck.

"Don't!" Barry shouted as Patrick wrapped him in air.

It was too late for Si. His glassy eyes stared at Patrick in silent accusation cursing his slow reaction. Patrick used magic to close the eyes before they became engrained in his mind and started haunting his dreams. He turned his eyes to Rashta, fire building in him. He stood slowly, not paying attention to the amount of mana building up in his body.

"Patty…" Barry whispered.

Patrick didn't need to look to see that the mana was seeping from his pores lighting him up like a beacon. He trained his eyes on Rashta daring him to look away but he knew that he couldn't look away. In fact, he knew that Rashta could only see and hear what Patrick wanted him to see.

At first Rashta said nothing just, remained kneeling on the floor his mouth twitching every now and then. Patrick pressed harder forcing smells and sensations into Rashta's mind. He also reached into Rashta's body and manipulated his hormones to increase his fear response.

"What are you doing?" Barry asked.

"Persuading," Patrick answered, "Now hush, I'm concentrating. I don't want to scramble his brains."

Barry opened his mouth, then reconsidered, closing it. Patrick turned his full attention back to Rashta, showing him image after image.

"These could all be you Rashta," Patrick warned, "With my medic, we could heal you and start over every day."

"No," Rashta whispered, then with more force, "No, no, no, NO, NO, NOOOOOOOOOOOOO!"

Patrick ignored him and pressed even harder, his eyes beginning to glow. He cut Rashta off from reality and submerged him completely in the horrors that Patrick chose. Soon Rashta was screaming unable to form words, the fear also forcing him to lose control of his bowels.

"Patrick!" Barry said grabbing Patrick.

Patrick whipped his head toward Barry and doused Barry in the same imagery and reality that he had trapped Rashta in. Slowly

Patrick forced back his rage and magic. Once he was in control of himself, he released both Barry and Rashta at the same time. Rashta lay sobbing on the floor, while Barry threw up on the floor.

"Was that Deathbash 2000?" Barry asked, referencing a popular new horror film.

Patrick blushed as he felt the embarrassment flow through his body. He hadn't meant drag Barry into the magical reality but what was done, was done.

"Ya, the part you saw was," Patrick answered.

There was a polite tap on the door.

"So, you guys getting ahead of yourselves in there? Everyone still alive?" Javier asked.

"No, but that wasn't our fault," Barry answered.

Javier threw open the door, his eyes wide with either shock or anger, Patrick couldn't tell.

"This is not okay, Barry," Javier growled.

"It was Rashta, sir," Patrick countered quickly, coming to Barry defense.

"Please go Lieutenant," Barry urged, "We do not need you right now. Please go interview Rahn and his family, before you ruin our progress here."

Javier's eyes shot daggers at him, but he left. Once the door had shut behind him, Barry looked at Patrick, "What did you show him?"

"The highlights of the goriest, bloodiest, most twisted horror films I could think of. I trapped him in a world where it seemed like he was really there, or it was happening to him."

"That's brilliant," Barry grinned, then returned his focus to Rashta. "Well then, my little assassin, will you talk now, or shall the druid fulfill all those horrors?"

"No! I beg you, in the name of the sun, and all things of the light, do not do it again," Rashta begged, "I will talk. Just…please."

"Speak," Barry demanded.

"You are more frightening than the she-demon," Rashta whispered to Patrick.

While Patrick beamed at the compliment, Barry punched Rashta full force in the mouth. While Rashta picked himself off the floor, Barry settled himself back in his chair.

"You will speak of our members with respect," Barry said.

"You would protect the brood mare? I'm…" Rashta said.

This time it was Patrick that punched him in the face. He followed up the punch with a kick in the stomach. After that, he picked up Rashta with his magic and stretched his limbs to their limits. Sweat rolled down Rashta's face as his mouth opened in a silent scream.

"Let him go Patty," Barry ordered, "No need to tear anything off."

"Just an arm?" Patrick begged.

"No," Barry said firmly.

"A finger? Oh! How about his pinky toe, he won't need that," Patrick argued.

Barry appeared to consider it. "Denied," he decided finally, "Let him go."

Patrick sighed but let him go. Barry adjusted himself on the chair and cleaned under his nails with his knife while Rashta composed himself.

"I hope I don't have to repeat this lesson to you again," Barry said slowly, pointedly looking at Rashta.

In return, Barry received an enthusiastic nod. Patrick snorted but didn't say anything to contradict either one. Barry eased himself to the edge of his seat and changed his intonation.

"Rashta," he said gently, "Rashta look at me."

Rashta looked for a moment then got a panicked look on his face when he glanced at Patrick, who was grinning evilly.

"It's okay, you safe as long as you keep talking to me. I promise you I won't let Patrick hurt you," Barry promised.

Rashta glance up again and nodded slightly to Barry. In return, Barry gave him a beaming smile. Patrick knew his role. He threw his hands up in frustration and walked grumbling to the window to go pout. He felt he milked it a little but he figured that's what Rashta needed. Sure enough, as soon as he was out of Rashta's line of sight, he relaxed visibly.

"Now, back to the Knight Angels, what can you tell me?" Barry asked.

"When Merlin the Magnificent left Avalon, he prophesied that he would return with a king worthy of this realm. A man who would once again be worthy to lead the armies of the light and bring balance back to the world. He said that the king would return, claim the swords and relics, and pick his champions from among the Knight Angels and men, and with them they would rebuild what the world had lost."

"So why would Aster care?" Barry asked.

"If the people knew that the real Knight Angels were here and that Merlin's Chosen was here, they would never follow him," Rashta said.

Patrick considered his words carefully. If what Rashta was saying was true, the Captain was more than simple leader. The world would change soon, and Patrick needed to be at his side.

"When did my grandsire prophesy this?" Patrick asked.

"Gra…grandsire?" Rashta stuttered.

"Yes, Merlin, my grandsire. I am his heir. When. Did. He. Prophesy. That?" Patrick asked biting off every word with frustration.

"Forgive me, holy one; I did not know you were one so esteemed. You did not seem skilled enough, if I may be so bold," Rashta said.

"Yes, well I haven't had any training, I'm just figuring this out on my own right now," Patrick retorted defensively. He felt his cheeks heating up but squashed the embarrassment down.

"You have no training? You are truly Merlin's heir. I have never heard of anyone, not even full druids, healing without training. The works you will do when you reach your prime…," Rashta whispered.

"Yes, we can fawn over him later. Where did your master take my people?" Barry asked.

"He is not my master," Rashta sneered.

"You will answer respectfully," Patrick whispered in his ear, sneaking up on him. Rashta flinched but nodded.

"Kint is not my master, Aster is," Rashta said.

"I see. Kint being the one behind this little kidnapping?" Barry asked.

"In a manner of speaking. Kint is strong and fast, but he is a poor leader. His *atras* manipulates him into making his more brilliant decisions. The kidnapping was his *atras's* idea; he just worded it with small enough words so Kint could understand. Truth is, my master does not trust Kint, so he gave him the *atras* to keep him in line and spy on him," Rashta answered.

"Interesting," Barry mused.

"Where did they take our people?" Patrick asked.

"I imagine they will take them to Kint's 'secret' fortress and then to the wilderness mage," Rashta guessed.

"Wilderness mage? Why?" Barry asked.

"Breeze, Pablo's *otorga*," Patrick guessed.

"Correct. Kint plans on forcing the bond to him," Rashta confirmed.

"How far is the fortress?" Patrick asked.

"I don't know, maybe a day or two of urgent marching into the forest," Rashta answered.

"Let's debrief the Lieutenant," Patrick suggested, "He needs to know this, and we need to get a move on before the Captain gets too far ahead."

"Agreed. What shall we do about him?" Barry asked nodding toward Rashta, "He stinks."

"Allow me," Patrick volunteered grinning. He snapped his fingers and Rashta yelp, turning slightly red. "That should take care of it."

"What did you do?" Barry asked.

"I used a fire spell and burned it out. I may have singed a few hairs," Patrick answered quite proud of himself.

"You have been overzealous, your holiness, but I thank you none the less," Rashta grimaced, sitting tenderly on his heels.

Barry and Patrick looked at each other and laughed. Rashta said nothing until they were done laughing.

"If I may, your holiness, I would bind myself to you," Rashta announced bowing to the floor.

"Eh…what?" Patrick asked elegantly.

"The Demon Blades are assassins and unseen guards. We may not be the same as a Champion, but we have always assigned one of our numbers to guard those of noble birth when Champions are scarce. If you do not have a Demon Blades to guard you yet, I would ask you consider me," Rashta replied humbly.

"Help," Patrick whispered out of his mouth to Barry.

"How are the Demon Blades organized here? How do you decide who goes where?" Barry asked.

"We are not organized; we only use the ancient names that were used to describe the different classes of Sons. I know I am not trained officially, but we have rediscovered many of the old ways," Rashta answered.

"Tell me the classes and abilities of the classes of the Sons of Lancelot, as you understand them or had them explained," Barry ordered.

"Yes, m'Lord. The Sons had five orders, the Soldiers, the Knights, the Champions, and the Demon Blades. The Soldiers protected the cities and up held the laws. The Knights patrolled the borders defending against enemies. Both Soldiers and Knights were lesser Sons," Rashta explained.

"Wait, lesser Sons?" Patrick asked.

"Yes, ones like Si. They are long lived but have none of the magical enhancements like Champions and Demon Blades have," Rashta clarified.

"Got it, carry on," Patrick ordered.

"Where was I," Rashta asked.

"Lesser Sons," Barry supplied dryly.

"Ah yes. The Champions were of the higher Sons. They are blessed with large stature, enormous strength, and speed. They are capable of taking several wounds and not dying thanks to the magic that flows through them naturally. Sadly, they can't cast magic with purpose. They can only cast defensive spells on an unconscious level. They were assigned to take care of someone very important," Rashta continued.

"Why someone important?" Barry asked.

"Both Demon Blades and Champions are fearsome warriors but small in number, so there are not enough to guard everyone. The person they guard usually magically binds them," Rashta explained.

"Interesting, go on," Barry urged.

"The Demon Blades served multiple purposes. We are the best assassins that you could ever find, and we blend into the dark, just like demons do," Rashta continued.

"Ah, hell. Demons? They're real?" Patrick asked.

"Yes, this is what the Knight Angels were formed to protect against. How do you not know about demons," Rashta asked.

"There are no more demons where we come from," Barry explained, "They've faded into legends."

"Oh. It is a blessed place where you need not fear demons. Anyway, the Demon Blades also act as guardians when there aren't enough Champions. We are also the great check against the Sons' power," Rashta said.

"You stopped them if they ever grew too powerful. If they ever became corrupt," Barry guessed.

"Yes, and without Champions around I wish to be your guard. I can think of no one worthier than Merlin's heir," Rashta said.

"Hold it," Barry ordered, "You said there was five classes. What's the last one?"

"The Guardians of the Light, or just Guardians," Rashta whispered reverently.

"And they are...?" Patrick asked.

"They are a combination of all three. There is at most only one every few generations, and usually not even that," Rashta continued, still whispering reverently.

"And if there is more than one?" Patrick asked.

"War. There cannot be two. There can never be two," Rashta whispered, "A Guardian always changes the world. They cannot help it, it's in their blood. When there are two, they kill eachother or tear the world apart."

"That sounds a lot the Captain," Barry murmured to Patrick.

"The Champion you follow is really a Guardian?" Rashta asked excitedly.

"Well, he casts magic, and is really strong, and I've seen him disappear in the shadows," Patrick supplied.

"Then he must be one. Perhaps I will bind myself to him," Rashta muttered loudly.

"Never," A voice from the door declared.

They all turned to the now open door to find Asha standing in the doorway looking like a thunder cloud. She glared at Rashta with purpose.

"The Cap'in is my mark. That's my job," Asha hissed.

"Begging your pardon, why are you here then?" Rashta inquired.

"Because he ordered me to do it," Asha snapped.

"Enough we must find the Lieutenant and tell him all of this, and catch up to the Captain before he's fully ready," Barry decided.

"And my request?" Rashta asked.

Asha had her daggers drawn advancing on Rashta before Patrick stopped her. "He wants to guard me Asha. It might not be bad," he explained.

"Fine but he will vow in blood," Asha declared.

Before they could speak, Rashta had a slim blade pulling through the soft skin of hand. He drew an intricate pattern on his chest chanting something the whole time. No one said anything while he worked. When he was done he went and knelt before Patrick.

"I vow under the Sun, and by the light, that I, Rashta the Knife, will spend my days in the service and protection of Patrick, heir of Merlin, until I breath my last and return to the light, or my Lord release me. I swear to be the breath of my master, the blade of his might, guardian of his desires, and champion of his cause. I so do swear by my blood and my honor," Rashta swore making the blood runes glow.

Patrick summoned his mana and touched Rashta on the head, "I accept your oath and take you as my protector and as my knife."

Light flashed, and the runes soaked into Rashta, save one that traveled up Patrick's hand and sunk in there. As soon as the light had faded, Asha tackled Rashta and started whispering in his ear. She cut him on the cheek and licked the blood off her dagger.

"Welcome to the club," Patrick laughed, "You're not one of us until Asha bleeds you!"

After Rashta picked himself off the floor they went downstairs to explain things to Javier and fill him on the information that they had learned from Rashta. At first, he was furious that Patrick would accept Rashta's protection, but eventually he shrugged and accepted it as part of Avalonean life. By the time Javier was up to speed, the twins and Lambert emerged from their rooms and had to be filled in as well.

"So how will we catch up to the Captain?" Javier asked.

"The horses are the only way. We'll have to ride them there," Barry supplied.

"You would ride a horse? Why?" Rashta asked.

"Because they are fast," Barry replied.

"So are goats, or pigs but I wouldn't ride those either. Horses are for eating not gallivanting into the woods with," Rashta snorted.

"You're getting awfully disrespectful of your betters," Barry warned.

Rashta shrugged at him, "I am the Demon of a powerful druid. You are merely a ley man. I have no fear of you, so long as I serve Lord Patrick."

Javier laughed, "He's got a point, but so does Barry. The horses will give us the edge we need if we can ride them. Patrick?"

"If linked with you, I could teach the horses what they need to know. We will be going bare back which will be awful but doable," Patrick said.

"Let's do it and show our new friend what we can do," Javier decided, "Oh and Master Rahn?"

Rahn turned toward him from where he was cowering in the corner trembling. He swallowed but responded, "Yes m'Lord?"

"You caused bodily harm to come to those under your roof and under my command. I think you owe me a debt. Some among us think you owe us your life. I think a hand might suffice for yours and your family's failings. What do you think?" Javier asked.

Rahn held up a hand considering it. He glanced at his wife begging her for some clue about what to do. She held out a hand to him which he clutched on to. Faster than he could blink, she pulled a knife from her skirt and separated his hand from his wrist. Rahn stared at the stump for a few seconds before he started screaming.

Lambert was there as fast as he could stumble over, binding the new wound to keep it from bleeding. He motioned for Patrick to join him, and together they healed the stump. Shara threw the hand at Javier's feet staring him in the eyes. Javier didn't spare the hand a look.

"If his hand will keep us and the boy safe, then it's a small price to pay," she said.

"Your actions are accepted. So long as none of our companions die, our debt is settled. We will also be taking your horses for our personal use," Javier informed her.

"They are yours with our blessing," Shara replied.

"Patrick, you done there?" Javier asked. When Patrick nodded to him, he continued, "Good let's go teach some horses and get out of this light forsaken place. We have a Captain to catch."

Chapter

FIFTHTEEN

All around him the lesser warriors panted and had sweat saturating all their clothes. More than one of them staggering in exhaustion. Kint curled his lip in a sneer and considered for a moment carrying on so that the weak *ariats* would get some more exercise and maybe harden their pathetic little bodies. The moment passed and he called for a rest break. Without bothering to look, he dropped his captive on the ground and shouted for food.

One of the *ariats* brought him some bread while others rustled in the bushes looking for food. The *atras*, moaned pathetically from dirt. Kint still couldn't believe the little mud troll had managed to get himself an *otorga*. Not that he cared all that much, because soon they would be to the wilderness mage's cabin and he would force the bond to himself. Then Kint would be a Rider and even Aster wouldn't be able to challenge him. He could almost see all the mugs lifted in his name and hear all the songs that would be sung about him for generations to come. And the women! Oh, there would be plenty of them too.

"Someone give the mud flea a drink," Kint roared.

Three of the *ariats* tried to give him water at the same time and ended up spilling most of the water on the *atras*. Mud formed under him drawing a laugh from Kint.

"M'lord? What amuses you?" one of the *ariats* asked. Kint had never bothered to learn their names. They were all lesser creatures, not worthy of his notice.

"This animal is Zemer's *atras*, Mud, and now Mud is lying in mud!" Kint said roaring in laughter. The *ariats* stood around dumbly, not reacting to his joke. He glared at them waiting for them to get the joke. Slowly one of them laughed and then the others fell over themselves to join in laughter.

Kint laughed with them for a little while longer then lost interest in his joke. The *ariats* continued to laugh and the ruckus grated on his ears. He glared at them again and only the closest ones noticed he had stopped. *Ariats* were always unobservant but this lot seemed slower and more unobservant than usual.

"Enough! Back to work," He roared cuffing the closest of *ariats*. The little rodents scattered doing whatever task they did, preparing the noon meal.

They rested briefly, only taking enough time to eat their midday meal and replenish their water supplies from the river. When he went down to splash his face with water, he noted fish swimming by. He held still for moment, then, faster than any of the *ariats* could follow, his hand flashed out and snagged one of the fish from the stream.

Laughing he bit the head off the wiggling fish. He threw the remaining body to one of the *ariats*. Chewing and then swallowing, he returned to his pack and prisoner. He placed both back on his back and continued on into the forest. The *ariats* scrambled to gather their own gear and follow him into the woods. They had all learned the hard way, that Kint did not tolerate laziness or even perceived laziness.

The forest was comfortable to him. He had grown up in one and had been left by his father in a different one with only a knife and sword to test himself with. He had met up with another Son undergoing the same crucible, and together they had fashioned a truce of survival. They had worked together and triumphed over the savage wilds. He regretted leaving Pice behind, but he had to make sure he wasn't being followed.

He led them over the river and into the wilderness. They rushed through the bushes making enough noise to be heard for, what seemed like, miles around. Normally, Kint liked to take as many men as possible but he was glad that he had only brought a few this time around. There were far too many making noise right now, as it was.

They continued on for several more hours until they came to the bulk of Kint's army stashed away in his wilderness fort. Aster wouldn't let him gather Sons to his banner but couldn't deny him the right to gather his own men. Aster may have been his superior and clan leader but Kint was a noble too and had the right to Arms. While he gathered Sons to his master's banner, he gathered the *ariats* to his own banner.

He looked around the camp they had constructed in the few days he was gone. He had left all his new recruits under the supervision of his veterans. He may not have Sons, but with this wilderness fort helping him train *ariats*, their combined might would over power Aster's Sons and make Kint the new warchief. That was Aster's greatest weakness, underestimating the strength of the *ariats*. Sure, alone they were next to useless, but get a group of them and they will destroy the strongest of the Sons.

Kint inspected the work they had done in his absence and found that they hadn't been nearly as lazy as he had expected. The wall was mostly finished with only a few places needing help. Many of the *araits* had moved away from wall construction and were working on other structures in the camp.

Those not actively working on fortifications, were on the parade ground. Drill sergeants shouted orders, and drilled lessons in the thick *ariat* skulls. One burly armed sergeant's only job was to walk around with a whip and strike any *ariat* that was going too slow, or that tried to rest outside of the rest periods.

At first the *ariats* had been slow to learn their lessons, so Kint had whipping post erected. It had only taken one day of whippings before the *ariats* learned their lessons and started paying attention.

There had been a few in his army that had tried to run away, but those had been captured quickly. Kint had his entire force stand at attentions while he personally put them all to death.

Now that he was back, he could see them marching in uniform rows, and moving much more like warriors. He smiled at the progress and headed into the heart of his new warcamp. A familiar figure met him with a smile.

"Welcome back, master," his *atras* said meeting him at the central cooking fire where the camp cooks were preparing dinner.

"What are those *ariats* working on?" Kint asked pointing towards a group around a smaller building.

"I believe that is a dwelling place. The finished it this morning and are making it habitable now," his *atras* replied, "It may be a nice place for you m'Lord, I helped them make a bed."

"Hmm. It just might. Keep up this kind of work and I might just give you a name one of these day *atras*," Kint said absently.

"If that is you wish, m'Lord," his *atras* murmured, "but service to you is its own reward."

Kint dumped the Mud in dirt near the fire and threw his pack on top of him. "Take care of those *atras*," he called over his shoulder.

At first, none of the *ariats* working on his new house noticed him, but when did, they quickly point him out to their friends. There were a few inside the dwelling and they came out to greet him.

"Welcome back, m'Lord," their leader said.

"What do we have here?" Kint asked.

"This is the first of the dwellings we are planning, m'Lord," their leader said, "It's just a little something we made during our free time, after we were done with our shifts on the wall."

"It's very nice," Kint praised.

"Thank you, m'Lord," the leader said beaming.

Kint grinned on the inside at the leader's stupidity. The poor shadow blasted fool still didn't know what was about to happen. Kint stepped inside the hut. The building showed signs for care that would not have been present if he had asked them to build it for him. The leader followed behind him proud of what he and his men had done.

"What's your rank soldier?" Kint asked.

"I am a sergeant first tier, m'Lord," he replied.

"Well, done sergeant. I applaud you and your men's initiative. Not many other squads had the presence of mind to build their Lord such a spacious and comfortable lodging. For that I promote you to second tier," Kint said smiling.

The sergeant eyes bugged out as he took his promotion and eviction at the same time. He cast a side long look at the bed he had no doubt been looking forward to sleeping on that night. The sergeant hesitated, acknowledging Kint's words. While he hesitated, Kint's *atras* arrived with Kint's pack and began unpacking it and placing furs on the bed.

"Thank you, m'Lord. I hope you enjoy the lodging," the Sergeant said bowing.

"You sound as if you are done here," Kint mused.

"M'lord?" the sergeant asked.

"No, this will not do. You still have some learning to do it seems. *Atras!*" Kint barked.

"Yes, m'Lord?" his *atras* replied.

"Would you say that my new house could use some improvement?" Kint asked.

"I do m'Lord," his *atras* agreed.

"See sergeant, even my *atras* knows this. I suppose he will have to show you what to do. You will follow his every instruction until he is satisfied with my lodgings." Kint ordered walking back outside.

"I am to take orders from an *atras?*" the sergeant asked in unbelief, following him outside.

"Yes, you are. Which of you is the second in command?" Kint asked.

As the second in command stepped forward the sergeant sputtered, "An *atras?* That can't be."

"Your sergeant has been promoted to second tier for having the initiative of having you men build me a house to live in," Kint said smiling, ignoring the sergeant's sputtering and outright rage playing itself out behind his back.

"I will not take orders from an *atras*! I would rather die first!" the sergeant declared.

Kint grinned wider and spun to face the sergeant. The sergeant tried to move to the side but Kint was too fast for him. He latched on to an arm and pulled the sergeant toward him. When the sergeant tried to punch him, Kint knocked the blow aside as absently as he would a fly or a mosquito. He then grabbed the sergeant's forearm and casually snapped the bone. The sergeant looked at the bone sticking out from the skin in shock before screaming in agony.

The squad stepped forward to help their sergeant but Kint looked at them and they stopped staring at the second in command, waiting for instructions. Kint also looked at him, daring him to make a move, but the man wisely averted his eyes in submission.

"You. You are now promoted to sergeant in place of this corpse," Kint said.

"Begging your pardon, m'Lord, but he isn't dead," the new sergeant said.

"Oh, it would appear your right. Your old sergeant still has life in him," Kint replied.

Without taking his eyes off the new sergeant, he pulled the old sergeant's sword from his scabbard and buried it in its owner's chest. Kint then let the sergeant drop to the ground. The sergeant held the hilt of the sword with his good arm, eyes wide uncomprehending what had just happened. He locked eyes with Kint and gasped once before dying.

The squad stood silently and woodenly as they watched their former sergeant's blood soak and disappear into the ground. The new sergeant stepped forward and gently closed his eyes and pointedly ignored Kint's gaze and removing the sword from his chest. His unhooked the scabbard from the belt and attached it his own. He then tossed his own sword to another man in the squad. The man missed he toss and dropped it in the dirt. He bent down slowly and retrieved it.

"Drop it again *ariat* and I will cut off your hand and make you an *atras,*" Kint warned.

"Yes, m'Lord," the *ariat* said trembling.

"M'lord?" the new sergeant interjected.

"What?" Kint asked still glaring at the other soldier.

"Permission to bury this man," the sergeant asked.

Kint sighed and turned toward the fire where stew was simmering, "Do what you will with that, and then report to my *atras*. You and your squad are his command until he says otherwise. He will instruct you in making it habitable. You will not join the regular army until he sees fit."

Kint left them to stare at his *atras* in disbelief while he went to go find himself some dinner. The captured *atras* was tied to a stake near the stew where he could see and smell it, but would never taste so much as a drop of it. The stew was a combination of deer and rabbit, with root vegetables. His grandmother had made him a similar stew and when he sampled it, it reminded him of her, and he realized it probably was his grandmother's recipe. She had served briefly as the camp cook when the camp first started, but had succumbed to illness shortly after arriving. He would never admit it to his men, but he missed her. The cook served him a bowl and he accepted it and went to go eat it.

Finding no comfortable resting place, Kint picked up a rock and carried it to a tree to use as back rest. Once it was set down, he grabbed an *ariat* that was running but and tore off his cloak before shoving him away. The *ariat* had the audacity to glare at him to which Kint responded by kicking the arrogant worm in the stomach. The *ariat* flew through the air and smashed into a tree. He twitched once and did not move again. Kint shrugged and placed the cloak on the rock and sat down on his new throne while two *ariats* appeared to rub the fatigue from his legs.

Humming to himself, he ate the fruit and honey his *ariats* had found for him along with his stew. After finishing his meal, he had his men bring the *otorga* over to him so he could admire his future mount. The creature was far too untamed from what he saw while scouting the group back at the resthouse but that could be remedied easily. On impulse Kint lifted it by the scuff of its neck to look it in the face. The creature opened his eyes and stared at him. They looked at each other curiously for a moment until the *otorga* broke the gaze to look around and take in its surroundings.

Its eyes fell on its current master. From there the *otorga* lost its self-control. It struggled against Kint's hand, but its blood was still full of the drugs that Rahn had fed it. That resthouse keeper's wife had known her poisons; she had even taught Kint a thing or two about them. Kint let the *otorga* struggle a little before calling for someone to bring him the special flask he had taken from the resthouse.

The *atras* raised his head to look at his…no Kint's, *otorga*, but he too was full of drugs. Kint spat in the *atras's* general area. One of the *ariats* brought the flask and gave it to Kint. Kint forced the *otorga's* mouth open with his knife and dumped half of the concoction down its throat. It didn't take long for the thrashing to slow and eventually stop. He tied it to a post adjacent to its soon to be former master. Let them spend one more night together.

That night, Kint spent a glorious night on his new bed, which his *atras* had scented with fresh grass to bring the smell of the forest into his new home. The next morning, he awoke refreshed and ready to get the camp finished.

He whipped the *ariats* into a working frenzy finishing the wall. They were all dripping sweat when he called a halt for the midday meal. The afternoon held no reprieve for them, as he ordered more buildings built and trees cut for lumber.

That evening he settled himself in a proper throne his *ariats* had carved for him. The evening stew was even better the previous night's. While he ate the *otorga* woke up again and started thrashing against the ropes the held it bound. Kint laughed and poked at the creature with a stick, laughing at its attempts to reach him.

"Shhh, Breeze," the captive *atras* said, "it's going to be all right."

"Ha!" Kint laughed mildly surprised the *atras* was even awake, "Don't lie Mud. This isn't one of your happy little stories you tell to children. This is the land of truth and here the strong rule and take what is theirs from those who don't deserve it."

The little *atras* looked him in the eye smiling, "Truth is a finicky mistress. You think you understand her but then she shows you her other side and you realized the side you were looking at is nothing but smoke and myth, and her true face is terrible to behold."

"Huh?" Kint asked.

"You have no idea who I am now, nor how powerful my new master is. The Lord Captain will tear out your lungs and the world will see you for the monster that you are. Vengeance is coming for you Kint, and your actions will reap their rewards," the *atras* said ignoring Kint's most fearsome glares.

"Ha! And what reward is that? I have already received glory and an *otorga*. What more could I receive?" Kint asked.

"A glorious battle and a death," the *atras* said still meeting his eyes.

"Ah, could use kill right now. It's been a while since I killed someone," Kint laughed nodding to the lifeless form he had taken his new cloak from.

"You poor fool. It is *your* life that will be claimed. The Captain is coming," the *atras* said calmly from his pole. He glared at the rest of the *ariats* that had gathered to hear his bold words. He raised his voice and continued, "As for the rest of you, don't think that you will be spared. There is blood on your hands, the blood of so many innocents you have killed. Your clothes are stained with the tears of the orphans who you stripped of their innocence."

"Be quite, *atras*," Kint demanded.

The *atras* ignored him, "You should have listened to your mothers when they told you the Knight Angels tolerated no such acts."

"The Knights? They died off generations ago," someone shouted.

"No, you poor fools, they did not. They can never die. And you know what? They are following your trail right now bringing with them the vengeance that you all so desperately deserve. Before this is over you will envy your friend there," he said motioning to their dead companion still by the tree, "that he was able to pass so peacefully."

"I SAID SILENCE *ATRAS*!" Kint bellowed.

The *atras* turned to him slowly, a faintly amused smile on his lips. "I am no *atras*," he said to which Kint blinked in surprise. The *atras* continued, "I have a new master, and he lifted from me the curse of my fathers. I have shed the shackles of an *atras* and have been given a true name."

Kint looked into his eyes and saw the warrior's fire burning there and nodded his head in acceptance of his statement so he asked, "What is your name then, *ariat*?"

Turning back to the *ariats* crowed around and raising his

voice, "I am no mere mortal! I stand as a witness to the world. I am Pablo of the Knight Angels, and in full face of the sun and under the Light I condemn you all! I have beheld your many acts of unspeakable shame, and have seen the lives you have shattered."

"I have done what the strong do and take what is mine!" a particularly large *ariat* said stepping up to Pablo, "You think that you are better than me because of that?"

Pablo grinned at him, "You, I remember. You have killed many who did not deserve killing. You kill for the pleasure of it."

"What is you point *Knight?*" the *ariat* spat.

"All of you!" Pablo shouted, "Look to this man and witness the terrible might of the Knight Angels and the fate of all those who would presume themselves entitled to rape, murder and steal!"

As soon as he finished speaking, everyone held their breath waiting to see what would happen. When nothing did the big *ariat* spoke out again, "Well? I feel nothing."

Pablo smiled at him as a round hole appeared where the *ariat's* eye used to be. The *ariat* was dead before he fell to the ground. A stunned silence filled the camp. There had never been this much silence or this many still bodies around Kint before.

"You! *Ariat* where is his mage?" Kint asked pointing at the *ariat* that had some magical abilities in tracking.

"I'm sorry m'Lord, there was no magic used. I cannot even feel anyone holding mana besides you. At least no one within a mile," the *ariat* said.

Kint spun looking for a source of danger but couldn't pinpoint it exactly. His gut told him that there was something else going on that he just hadn't gotten a hold of. His eyes fell on Pablo and he realized that there was someone who did know exactly what was going on and could explain to him what was going on.

"Well, my little Knight," Kint growled, "I'll play along. What is going on here?"

"I have already told you. The Knight Angels have come, bringing justice and vengeance upon you all," Pablo replied solemnly.

"Why? I have done nothing wrong."

"In that, you are mistaken."

"Me? Wrong? Watch yourself Pablo, you may not be *atras* any longer, but you are still an *ariat* and not my equal."

"I am not trying to be your equal. I am your warning. You have twisted and abandoned the precious oaths of the Sons of Lancelot. Now the Knight Angels have come in all their glory and wrath to lay waste to all that you have built."

"I doubt that."

"They have bested Zemer without taking casualties. They have *otorgas* and demons. They have a mighty druid and magical weapons. You were defeated and dead before this battle started."

"Ha ha ha! Let them come. Zemer was an arrogant fool. I will not be taken so easily. Come then Knights Angels! Take your best shot! The Kint the Powerful is ready for you!"

Kint stood arms wide staring into the forest waiting for something to happen. A moment later he saw a flash in the forest and a split second later, he felt something slam into his skin. He had only ever been cut by magic, but whatever hit him threw him to the ground and left his chest sore and bruised. He sat up a little clutching his chest. In his hand he held a small bit of metal. How had they thrown that with such force to hurt him? He looked up into the forest in time to see another flash.

The force of the metal slamming into his forehead left him dizzy beyond anything he had ever felt. Another bit of metal fell from his forehead into his hand. Any mere *ariat* would have died from a blow like that but he was no *ariat* and no ordinary Son for that matter.

"Rally the forces! Muster shields! We're under attack," he thundered, still trying to clear the dizziness from his head.

He stood and headed to a group of captains to give them their orders. He turned to the forest to point to them where the metal was coming from so he could send a force to wipe them out. There was another flash and this time it found a softer mark.

At first the captains weren't sure what happened, but they heard a faint pop coming from the forest and turned to see what the noise was. Their leader sank to the ground clutching his very bruised manhood. He lay on the ground mouth open, gasping like a fish. Kint hadn't chosen his captains for their initiative, so they weren't sure what to do.

"M'Lord, what are your orders?" the senior captain asked.

"Nuuugh," was all he could moan.

They leaned closer thinking he was giving orders to them. "I am sorry m'lord. I didn't catch that," a particularly bold captain asked delicately.

"It hurts. Why does it hurt?" he moaned.

The captains stood scratching their heads trying to figure out what to do. Eventually one gave the order to drag him inside a building and the sent the rest to secure and man the walls. Kint heard the orders being given and could find it in himself to care those orders were being issued that he himself had not given.

I'll kill them, Kint thought, *this will not stand. I will kill them all slowly. I don't know who you are but I will find you, you will the regret having humiliated me.*

Chapter

SIXTEEN

Travis looked up from his scope grinning at Boomer. Boomer scowled but handed him the two gold coins.

"And think Boomer, all those times you laughed at me for spending so much time at the firing range. Snipers have a lot of fun," Travis laughed.

"You wasted one of my bullets," the Captain censured lightly.

"Well, sir, you saw me hit him in the chest and the head. If those wouldn't kill him, I figured I'd see if there was anything softer," Travis replied grinning.

The Captain held his composure for a moment but then grinned back, "Okay that's fair enough. Keep your eyes on the scope though. I don't want anyone touching Pablo or Breeze."

Travis nodded his approval. He kept his eye on the scope but asked, "Captain? Did that make you feel as good as it did me?"

"Yes, as a matter of fact it did. I'm just glad they haven't noticed the spell Patty and I put on the radios," the Captain replied.

"Me too. Nefty spell. Using the magic to convert the sun's power into a charge the batteries could hold. Lets us keep coms open. Why do you think they haven't taken it away yet?" Travis asked.

"They have no technology here. They would have no idea what a radio was. Just stop looking a gift horse in the mouth and be glad we can keep talking to Pablo," the Captain ordered.

"Yes, sir! Keeping happy thoughts in my head, sir!" Travis said smartly.

"Don't do that, you can't pull off insubordinate like Patty can. You're too much of a Marine to make it funny," the Captain said wincing.

"Sorry, sir."

"Let me know if anything develops down there. Shoot anyone with a whip you can find and the occasional grunt. Let's keep them on their toes and cowering," the Captain ordered.

"Mmm, cowering. That's how I like my bad guys," Chuffles hummed.

"Oorah," Travis agreed.

"Agreed. Anything that takes their focus off Pablo and keeps them in the camp. I don't want them going and getting away from under our noses. They are far too interested in Breeze and not enough on Pablo. I don't like it," the Captain said.

"You think Pablo will be okay, Captain?" Boomer asked.

"He'll be fine. He's toughened up since he met up with us," the Captain replied.

"You know it," Chuffles agreed.

"Porter, Boomer, you're on over watch with Travis, the rest of us are pulling back for now. Let's keep it tight, let keep it neat," the Captain ordered.

"Sir!" they said in unison.

"Also, let's keep the chatter to the minimum. They know we're here so there should be a counterattack soon. We'll give Javier and his group time to get here, and it will be bad for us if they decide to come up here sooner than we want," the Captain warned.

With that, their brief moment of levity was over and they were all business. Travis switched to a night scope and took shots at men who stuck their heads up. He didn't like killing so many, but if what Pablo said was true, these men needed a little thinning out. Boomer picked up the spotters scope and found a group headed out of the camp and pointed them out to Travis. A few well places shots had them headed back to the safety of their camp, down a few members. The fact they didn't try to help their comrades told Travis that these men had given up their honor long ago. No true warrior leaves his comrades behind.

A few hours of this had the bugs out and about nibbling on exposed skin. When Travis didn't think he could take any more of the little critters, Left and Right came to get them.

"Hey! Nice of you to make it," Travis said, "Left! Your nose! Now you're uglier that your brother."

"Told you," Right muttered.

"Don't be jealous, girls dig the dangerous look," Left muttered back.

"What's up?" Travis asked.

"Captain wants us to take over watch," Right said.

"So you guys can hear the plan," Left finished.

"How long have you been here?" Travis asked.

"About three hours," Right replied.

"Aye, and my butt's sore," Left added.

"Why?" Boomer asked grinning.

"Horses," the twins answered in unison.

"Where did you guys get horses?" Travis asked.

"Rahn was…how would you put it?" Left asked.

"Eagerly cooperative," Right answered.

"Yeah, after he lost his hand," Left continued.

"Okay, I'll need that story, but for now, Boomer, Porter, let's go," Travis ordered.

Down the hill they came across the famous horses, all standing quietly grazing on the grass. On the other side of the horses, the group sat in a circle around a map the Captain had drawn in the dirt, pointing to different parts of the camp. Travis pulled up short at the sight of a slim tattooed warrior standing protectively behind Patty. They locked eyes and Travis knew this man was no stranger to battle and had seen his share of kills. He approached carefully not taking his eyes off the man. When he reached the circle the man nodded his head in deference and mutual respect.

"I am Rashta the knife, Lord Patrick's Demon," Rashta said by way of greeting.

"I am Travis, of the Devil Dog clan," Travis replied.

"You are no Son of Lancelot," Rashta said slowly, "I do not think I have ever met a more imposing *ariat*," Rashta mused.

"Thank you," Travis responded.

"Are all members of the Devil Dog clan as large and imposing as you?" Rashta asked.

"Of course," Travis lied. He then turned to the Captain, "What is he doing here?"

"Later, for now just know he has my trust," the Captain answered.

"Yes, sir," Travis said relaxing. Rashta blinked in surprise at the amount of trust Travis had in the Captain's words, and reconsidered the Captain thoughtfully.

"Sir!" Boomer exclaimed.

"What?! What is it?" the Captain asked looking around for the danger.

"Your eyes are purple again," Boomer breathed.

"Oh, that," the Captain grunted relaxing, "Yes, I let them go purple again. It's time to let the world know who I am."

"Hmmmm," Barry hummed smugly.

"Yes, Barry, shut up," the Captain ordered.

"The Captain has decided that he is done running from his fate and wants the world to know that Merlin's mission did not fail. The Guardian of the Light has returned again to Avalon," Barry clarified with a flourish.

"Back to the matter at hand. So, we have Pablo here with Breeze next to him," the Captain cut in ignoring the puzzled looks he was getting. He indicating on the dirt map, "The walls are too thick for us to blast through effectively. Furthermore, they out number us a lot to a little. I wish I knew how many they had or even what weapons they had."

"Captain, we do have a spy in the camp. He could give us the details we need," Javier pointed out.

"Negative," the Captain countered shaking his head, "His coms are now stuck on transmit and reception is shotty at best. He may give us the intel we want, but it would be pure luck, so we can't count on it."

"Great," Javier muttered.

The Captain turned considering Rashta, "Do you know about this camp? Does he have counter measures? How many bowmen? Catapults?"

Rashta blinked in surprise, "I…I do not know this camp. My master, excuse me, my former master knew that Kint was building a fort but nothing more."

"Hrm, I just wish I knew how many arrows we would have to dodge," the Captain grumbled.

"What are arrows?" Rashta asked.

Everyone turned to look at him. Rashta blushed at his own arrogance.

"Arrows, the things shot from bows," Javier explained.

"I do not understand," Rashta said.

"Like this," Patty said making an apparition of one in the air with a wave of his hand, "They shoot arrows killing people from a distance."

Rashta considered the bow and arrows for a moment before replying, "I see the advantage of such a weapon, but I have never seen or heard of such a weapon. Are they more powerful than your…rifles is it?"

Again they all stared at Rashta not believing what they heard. Rashta squirmed, and turned his eyes to study his boots.

"No," the Captain answered finally, "They are inferior weapons but they are much easier to make. We assumed that such a weapon existed here. My father's spoke of such weapons, and they are standard weapons in our training."

"Perhaps before the purge such marvels existed, but they no longer do," Rashta explained.

"They are still ignoring me," Pablo whispered over the coms, "Kint has yet to appear from him hiding place. They sent in a soldier, and he came out missing his eyes. No one else has dared go inside."

"Okay let me rephrase my question, does Kint have weapons that will attack from a distance?" the Captain asked not showing if he heard Pablo.

"He will have spears to throw, and some stone slingers, but what other distance weapons are there?" Rashta asked.

In response the Captain laughed from deep in his belly, "Well, that makes things so much easier."

"Captain?" Left interrupted over the coms, "I'm down to ten bullets. You still want me to hold?"

"Yes," the Captain replied, "Save the last of them. Shoot one person an hour. Only take a shot if you can guarantee a hit."

"Yes, sir," Left said.

The Captain turned back to the group. He looked each of them in the eyes, "I don't know that we can do this one and come out in one piece."

Travis felt himself deflate like he had been slapped by the Captain's words. He had always been honest with them, and this was the first time he had said he didn't think they could do it.

"Breeze isn't moving. I'm beginning to worry for him," Pablo updated over the radio.

Travis cleared his throat, "He's one of us, sir. You know he would come for us himself if he could. We are the Night Angels, we do not leave our people behind and we do not tolerate the evil of this world, or any world, to dictate the course of our actions."

All around them the group murmured their agreement. Rashta shifted on his feet but did not add anything to the conversation.

"Sir," Javier said, "I accepted long ago that I would not die an old man in my bed peaceful and quiet. I am a Night Angel. I suffer so that other can have peace; I die so that other can live. If I my time comes today saving my comrade and brother, well, hell, that's all I ever wanted."

"That's not what I want for my Angels," the Captain said.

"What about what we want, sir?" Travis asked, "We want to help him, we want to tear these men apart, we are not afraid of death. We are meant to end corruption in the world, and this is corruption. So, let's go down in our vengeance and wrath and destroy this encampment."

The Captain stared at the map not speaking or giving any indication that he had heard. He looked up at Rashta, "What do you think? Is it reckless to save one man in the middle of a foreign army?"

"Yes," Rashta answered. The Captain grunted when he heard but Rashta wasn't done, "but that is what I would expect from the Knights of old. I don't know if you are everything you claim to be, but you actions have been in accordance with what the stories say. Doing this may be reckless, but it is also brave."

"My Demon is right Captain," Patty said, "Let's blow something up and bring down fire and brimstone on their hairy butts." Rashta shifted again rubbing his own posterior.

The Captain snapped his head up and gave them all a savage

grin. The group grinned back ready for action, ready for anything.

"Well, we all know that look," Travis said, "We're about to do something crazy stupid."

"Surely you mean brilliant," Rashta asked.

"Meh, same thing," Patty said.

They all roared in laughter at Rashta's alarmed and confused face. The Captain, Travis and Javier immediately start patching together a new plan. While they haggled of different points, Patty stood and motioned Rashta to follow him.

"Where are we going m'Lord?" Rashta asked.

"To hunt bats," Patty replied laughing.

"M'Lord?"

"Come on, it will be fun," Patty assured him, still laughing.

Contreras climbed up to where the twins sat on top of the hill looking into the enemy camp. He squinted and was able to make Pablo and Breeze by the fire. Right looked up from the spotters scope grinning while Left kept his gaze on the camp scanning for trouble.

"What's the word?" Left asked.

"Captain, Travis and the Lieutenant are hashing out the details while Patty looks for bats with that Rashta fellow," Contreras replied.

"Yay, poo bullets," Right grumbled.

"I wouldn't laugh. They have good results," Contreras said dropping a handful of sniper shells on the ground next to them.

"Score!" Right said diving on them.

"Was that more ammo I heard?" Left asked not looking up from his scope.

"Yup, Patty put together another fifteen rounds for us," Right said.

"So, with you shooting that should be about eight dead bad guys," Contreras teased.

"Really? I miss one shot, just one shot in my entire career, and no one ever lets me live it down," Left pouted.

"Well, bro, you nearly blew the op. You're just lucky he jumped in a jeep Patty had already rigged to blow," Right teased poking his twin in the ribs.

"Stop that I'm trying to bring down righteous vengence on our enemies here," Left protested.

They laughed at him but they kept their hands off of him. Contreras watched him take careful aim with the sniper rifle wishing it was him shooting. Not that he wanted to shoot people; it's just that he missed the feel of the recoil and the smell of spent gun powder. Before they had come to Avalon, he had gone to the target range every chance he got, honing his skills and trying out new ones.

The night passed slowly, with only the occasional shot being fired. Left switched out with Contreras and let him take over sniper duty. It took him about three seconds on the freezing ground to realize why Left had been willing to trade with him. An hour into his turn he got the consolation prize he had wanted. The big guy Rashta had said was Kint stuck his head out and Contreras had scored a hit on his neck. Kint coughed up a little blood and retreated back into his hut.

"One to the neck of the bad guy number one, Captain," Contreras said into his mike.

"Kint?" the Captain asked, "Result?"

"He coughed some blood, non-lethal though," Contreras answered.

"I hate you so much right now," Left grumbled.

"My turn!" Right announced.

Contreras grinned at Left as he relinquished his spot to the twin. A few minutes later Patty and Rashta came to their hiding place and chatted idly for a few minutes. When Patty found a comfortable spot, he sat on the ground placing both hands on the dirt.

"Watch over me, Demon," Patty ordered, "I'm delving for metal and when I find it I'm going to summon it. I don't always see what's going on around me."

"Yes, Lord Patrick," Rashta said.

No sooner had he closed his eyes, when his frame started to glow slightly. Rashta frowned at the light and went over to a bush to cut down some shrubbery. Contreras saw what he was doing and joined him gathering limbs and using them to build a screen around Patty. They worked together listening to the twins joke and rib each other.

"Quiet," Rashta ordered.

Out of reflex everyone stopped moving and speaking, except Patty, who was too far into his delving to notice them. Contreras opened his mouth to remind him that he had no authority here, but Rashta silenced him with a motion. After burying his pride, he listened to see if he could hear what Rashta heard. Even if Rashta's hearing was only half as good as Asha was, that was still better than his hearing.

At first, he heard nothing, but after a little while he heard the faint rustling in the bushes. Contreras grabbed his spear from the tree where it was resting and prepared while the twins packed up the rifle and scooped up their empty shell casings.

"Captain," Contreras whispered into the coms, "We have…"

He cut off as a figure burst through the bushes, screaming at him. Contreras leveled a spear at him, but Rashta was there cutting him down. The brush spat out more and more figures at them. The twins pulled out their swords and joined them in front of where Patty was sitting, oblivious to what was going on.

Rashta snarled and disappeared. Contreras swore and stepped over to fill the gap. Together with the twins they held off the attackers the best they could. Eventually, one broke through their line and made a bee line for Patty's enclosure. Before he could even separate the branches, he fell to his knees clutching his throat. Rashta flickered into view above him before disappearing again. The attackers noticed and faltered, so Contreras used the distraction to jump into the middle of them stabbing and punching anyone he could reach. The twins stood back-to-back fighting ferociously. The occasional body dropped, stabbed or hamstrung by Rashta.

All this happened in a few minutes, but all three were already covered in cuts. Contreras knew that they wouldn't last much longer, but they fought on grimly. Then, a knife got buried his hand, and he knew it was over. His numb fingers dropped his spear and all Contreras had was his knife, so he fought on with that. He pushed through and found that all his enemies were dead. He breathed in relief and his legs buckled.

Travis caught him before he fell to the ground. Contreras's head flopped over and he could see the Captain, who had one of his punch dagger buried in the belly of one of the attackers. Rashta flickered into view next to the Captain and almost got a dagger to the neck. Only his agile feet spared him from having his throat slit.

"It is only me, your highness," Rashta assured him.

"Captain, will do," the Captain corrected.

"As you wish, your…Captain," Rashta conceded bowing his head.

"Captain…" Barry started.

"Baby steps, Barry," the Captain replied.

"Well done Contreras. You may be an *ariat*, but you fight like a Son. You are all that I expected from Knight Angel," Rashta praised, to which Contreras nodded his thanks.

"This location is compromised. Wake Patty, we're moving," the Captain ordered, "Travis, take Boomer and find a new sniper's nest. The rest of us are moving now. We can't wait to take the camp. They must have snuck men out, and they are crawling all over these hills. That means the camp is weaker with less forces guarding it."

Slappy succeeded in bringing Patty back and together they healed Contreras and the twins. The Captain ordered the twins to find Travis and Boomer and relive them. They did not like it.

"I know how much healing takes out of you," the Captain said silencing their protests, "I need them for the close quarter combat, and you two don't have the energy for it. Take the last of my sniper shells and kill as many as you can as soon as we attack. Give me your grenades too."

The twins grumbled but obeyed. Contreras remained silent hoping the Captain didn't notice he had also been healed.

"Oh I remember you, Contreras," the Captain called out, "You will climb the wall once we're in and pick off as many as you can from there. Avoid close combat if possible. I'm sending Barry with you to watch your back."

Contreras groaned but otherwise offered no objections to his orders. He didn't want to risk getting left behind.

"Sir, we haven't heard from Pablo in a while," Javier reminded him, "We will be going in blind."

"We'll deal with it as we go," the Captain replied, "Just watch your line of fire, remember Pablo is in the middle of this hornet's nest."

Half an hour later they were lined up outside the camp's wall, just inside the tree line. The Captain motioned them forward and they moved up quietly. Contreras felt his blood pounding in his ears, and adrenaline coursing through his veins. They lined up against the wall on both sides of the gate, the Captain leading one side and Javier leading the other. Contreras checked to make sure his full clip was in place. The Captain had exhausted his supply making sure they all had at least one full clip of ammo. Since he was going to the wall, the Captain had given him an extra half clip.

"They still in the same place?" the Captain whispered to the twins over the radio.

"Affirmative, all bogeys holding position," Right replied.

"Good, commence shooting, use all of your remaining

ammunition then meet up with us down here," the Captain ordered.

A sniper rifle crack rang from the hill and a yell met them from inside the camp. Patty blew the doors open with his last C4 charge, and they all poured through the breach. The door had blown inwards killing most of the first row. They rest of the formation held, lined up perfectly for the spray of bullets that flew from their rifles. Row after row fell screaming and Patty let loose a huge fire ball burning a hole through the middle of their formation. It was too much for the survivors, and they broke and ran.

Asha winked out of sight and hurried on to her own assignment. Bubbles growled in agitation, but stayed near the Captain, like Asha had asked him to. The Captain went left with his group, while Javier and his group went right with his group. Patty peeled off and went his own way with Rashta, hovering protectively. Contreras scrambled up the wall and up to the catwalk. Barry went a little ways down the wall and used the ladder to get up to the catwalk. He came over to where the Contreras was standing and smirked at him. Contreras grinned at him and turned his attention to the battle.

Travis followed as close as he dared to the Captain. Boomer and Chuckles tagged behind him bringing up the rear. They could hear enemy sergeants and captains trying to organize the resistance. Every now and then the shouting was cut short followed closely by the rifle crack that silenced the voice.

"Captain that's the last of my ammo," Left reported, "Most of the officers are down, but there doesn't appear to be any left in your area. Javi, watch your six, you got a group coming at you. Captain! Two large groups are converging on you now."

"Good," the Captain said, "How's Pablo?"

"Asha has him free they are working on Breeze right now," Left answered.

"Excellent, pack up and get down here," the Captain ordered.

The group that Left had warned them about appeared from around on of the larger buildings. Travis lined up with the others and formed a firing line. He emptied his bullets and then dropped his rifle. After lobbing a few grenades, he drew his sword, preparing for hand-to-hand combat. The Captain had chosen a choke point between two buildings to make their stand. As discussed beforehand, Travis and Chuckles stood on the Captain's right, while Boomer, Peters and Bubbles held the left side. The enemy's front line clashed with them and fell just as quickly. Bubbles howled like a demon and slaughter men faster than they could attack. He ran back and forth killing and tearing anyone he could reach. The group scattered faster than Travis had expected.

In a rare moment of quiet, that happens occasionally on the battlefield, Travis noticed that his enemies were either dead or running. On closer inspection he saw that only part of them were running. A good half of the men had not run. Travis could only assume this was the second group Left had warned them about.

The Captain's blade was pressed at the throat of a trembling soldier who had both hands up. Behind him the second group stood motionless waiting to see what the Captain would do. Every one of the members of the second group had their chest piece painted blue.

"Um…m'Lord," the soldier stammered, "We are loyal sons of the Light. We would ally ourselves with the Knight Angels."

The Captain studied him for a moment, "You are…?"

"Cricket, m'Lord, Cricket son of Reft," the soldier replied with a rush, licking his lips, "We have painted our armor so that we could fight with you. Most of the army is loyal to Kint, but we have decided to join you against him."

"Very well," the Captain decided, then into coms, "Lieutenant, we have friendlies mixed in. Identifiable by blue on the armor."

"Copy that, sir. We found some of our own," Javier replied.

"Asha, how's the rescue coming?" The Captain asked.

"M'Lord?" Cricket asked.

"I am speaking to my men, with this," the Captain answered, pointing to his throat mike.

"All clear, head back to the gate," Asha reported.

"Lieutenant, objective complete, head back to the gate," the Captain ordered, then pointing to Cricket and his men, "You men follow us out."

They filed behind the Captain, keeping a respectable distance from Bubbles, who was eyeing them like a tasty snack. They marched as quickly as they could to the gate, meeting no resistance. Travis didn't like how easy the exit was, considering their entrance. Sure enough, his fear was confirmed when they reached the open space in front of the gate. Kint was there with the rest of his army blocking their way. Javier and Asha reached the clearing at the same time. Even with the addition of their new allies, it didn't look good for them. A second army filed in behind them closing off their retreat.

"Welcome, pretenders," Kint greeted them with a smile, "I see you brought me more *otorgas*. I also thank you for weeding out the weaklings in my but I'd hate to have to kill you all. I'd lose a lot of men that way and so would you. As you can see, even as strong as you are now, we would still overpower you."

With that, his men threw the unconscious bodies of the twins on the ground in front of him. Boomer and Chuckles exchanged a glance then broke ranks and charged him.

"Get back here!" the Captain bellowed.

The two ignored him and threw themselves at Kint. He laughed and caught their swords in his bare hands. They looked at him in shock even as he ripped the swords from numb hands and ran them through with their own swords. For good measure, snapped their necks, letting their limp bodies fall to the ground. Travis froze in shock at the casual brutality of the monster in front of him. He looked over at the Captain who had his eyes closed, but had grief written all over his face.

"I declare, *ramwa*. You and I will fight to the death," Kint declared pointing to the Captain, "Winner takes control of both armies."

"I accept," the Captain replied, opening his eyes.

The whites of his eyes had turned red and tears of blood ran down his face.

Chapter

SEVENTEEN

Kint felt his confidence evaporate like the morning dew. He was beginning to realize that the Son in front of him was no Champion like he had assumed. Sure enough, mana began leaking from his opponent's skin and flames burst from his sword. Even as strong and invincible as he was, he was no match for a Guardian. He knew that wasn't even the worst part. The red eyes and bloody tears told him this "Captain" had his blood boiling. Once, a long time ago, he had seen Aster's father go into a Bloodrage. He had destroyed an entire *army* by himself. The carnage that had resulted, still hadn't been matched to this day.

He heard his grandmother's stories float up from his mind, "There is no force greater than the Bloodrage. Any Son of Lancelot can achieve this transformation, but the stronger they are, the more powerful the Bloodrage. Lancelot the First was a Guardian and said to be able to do it at will. Entire goblin hordes would flee at the sight of him. Others would surrender rather than face him. Even dragons would not dare attack him."

So, here he was, facing a creature of legend. A Guardian in full Bloodrage, the deadliest thing to ever walk the earth, stood opposite him and he had mocked, taunted it and been foolish enough to challenge it to *ramwa*.

Oh, nana, I'm sorry. I've killed myself, and challenged the man born to change the world, he thought.

"I am waiting, Kint," the Guardian said.

Kint noticed the sword in the Guardian's hand. Kint sword was still on his back, and *ramwa* required that both sides be armed before the battle started. He moved slowly to unsheathe his sword and bring it to his side in a weak grip.

"The Knight Angels were the soul of the light. Anyone who fought them was no better than a shadow spawned troll. Even thieves and murders wouldn't harm the Knights of old," his nana's voice frail voice chided him, "When they come again, you will know them, and all the armies of the Light under the sun, will rally to them. Make sure you're on the right side, fool boy. If you're not I will rise from my grave and beat you silly."

Kint slowly pulled his sword strait up in a ready position from his side. He knew he was stalling the fight but he didn't feel the least amount of guilt for it. Fiercely, he racked his brain trying to think of a way to back out of the fight and submit to the Guardian, but could think of none. Too many people had heard his challenge and *ramwa's* rules were clear, two leaders fought to the death and the winner took both armies. There was no surrender, no quarter, no mercy allowed, for the winner had to be the winner by an unquestionable result. Only someone's death would ensure complete victory. It had been his plan for Aster, after he had the *otorga*, to declare *ramwa* and seize control of the army and the clan.

"I am sorry," Kint whispered.

"Not yet," the Guardian replied.

"Glory to the Knight Angels," Kint whispered straitening his back and saluting as was required by tradition.

"Knight Angels bring their own glory, they do not need yours," the Guardian snapped, saluting back.

Kint nodded resigned. He knew the Guardian spoke the truth. There was nothing left for him to do than embrace death. He raised his chin and looked straight ahead but there was no fire in his eyes, no fight in his heart. In truth, his soul ached.

The Guarding charged, but Kint did not. When the Guardian came, he put up no defense and let the sword pierce his chest. The Guardian pulled out his sword and placed his hand on the wound.

Kint's sword fell to the ground and he let his magical defenses drop. He felt the Guardian enter his mind and heart roughly but still offered no resistance.

The Guardian shifted through his memories, all of them, from his childhood, to the present. When he thought the Guardian missed something he pointed it out to him, like Aster's plans, or as much as he knew of them. The Guardian paused when he came across the memories of his Nana. Kint had spent years building walls around every memory of her and her tender ministrations. By reflex he blocked the Guardian, but it did little to stop him. Kint's struggle was brief and then he submitted once again.

An eternity later, though in reality only a few seconds, the Guardian let him go. Kint clutched his wound and fell to his knees. All around him his army gasped in horror and shock. His remaining captains started issuing orders, but Kint glared at them, cutting their orders off mid-sentence. With that done, he turned his eyes to the Bloodraged eyes of the Guardian.

"I have seen your soul, Kint son of Kint. You have betrayed the sacred duties giving to the Sons of Lancelot. You were taught the ways true ways of the Sons of Lancelot, and of the Knight Angels, by your grandmother, and you chose to ignore them. I find your soul tainted and name you Fallen," the Guardian rumbled.

Tears streamed down Kint's face as he nodded his acknowledgement of the Guardian's words. The Guardian put his hand on Kint's head and Kint surrendered completely to him. The darkness came for him, and Kint went towards it. He heard himself say the last words.

"I, Kint son of Kint, do surrender. I relinquish my army and give my final command. Follow this man, and swear to him. This is a true Guardian and champion of the Light, the last hope of man. I condemn myself and my master, Aster."

Javier heard the words Kint said but could not believe that he was hearing them. The fight, if it could be called that, was over before it began. He adjusted his grip on his sword while he scanned the faces of parts of Kint's army that were still loyal to him. Surprisingly, they were all watching solemn faced, with their weapons either sheathed, or in rested positions.

The Captain glowed brighter, and so did Kint. A blue substance flowed from Kint to a sphere of blue light which filled the night with its light. When the blue substance stopped flowing from Kint, he gave a pleased hum, and then fell on his face on the ground, dead. The light drifted over to where the Captain stood with his eyes closed, and seeped into him. The Captain's glow grew brighter and brighter, then he flashed once and was back to his normal self.

Javier started forward to check on the Captain, but Travis grabbed him, clearly frightened. Javier looked at the hand on his arm and back to Travis; annoyed the Sergeant would hold him back. Travis was unfazed by his look, and his own eyes were still wide. Then his brain processed what his eyes were trying to tell him. Travis was *afraid.*

"What?" Javier asked a hint of fear touching his voice.

"I have seen the Captain like this before, sir," Travis whispered.

"When?" Javier asked.

"Remember the op in Pakistan we told you about?"

"Yes, so?"

"Do you remember how it went sideways?" Javier nodded. "Well, we got ambushed on the way out and lost three men instantly, and Barry got hit and the Captain took shrapnel to the arm. He wasn't able to really use it until we got back to base. Well, when that happened, the Captain lost it and his eyes went red like that. When he was done, we just walked out of there, sir."

"You walked out? How? They just let you go without any resistance?"

Travis shook his head. "Dead. Almost three hundred of Pakistan's finest, died that day. The Captain went at them with one good arm and a knife. They all died, to the man. When I tried to calm him, he didn't really know me, in fact he almost killed me, sir."

"The scar on your chest," Javier guessed.

Travis nodded, "Yes, sir. Until his eyes clear, he can't tell friend from foe all that well."

Javier's attention was captured by a commotion from one of Kint's groups. One of the captains stepped forward saying, "He's no Knight. Let's get him men!"

The captain's men surged forward and surrounded him. When they stepped back, the bleeding mess that used to be their captain lay dead on the ground. Javier shook his head at the eagerness of the men to exact their vengeance on the man. Only a terrible leader could inspire such hate and resentment.

Barry stepped forward until he was close to the Captain but not too close, "I am Barry, and all of you who wish to live, lay down your arms now, or face the wrath of the Night Angels and the full might of a true Guardian! Anyone of you still holding steel will die."

There was an instant cacophony of clanging metal, as every single enemy soldier couldn't let go of their steel fast enough. Behind him, Javier could hear his new allies dropping their weapons as well, not daring to press their luck. The enemy captains made their way to Barry who shook his head and motioned to were Javier was standing. They turned and went over to surrender to him, giving the Captain a wide berth. Together they handed over their swords, officially surrendering themselves and their troops.

The Captain stirred from his position and walked over to the assembled captains. He eyes were still red, but the mindless rage was no longer burning there. Instead, a contained rage hid behind his eyes, which made him no less frightening to his newest prisoners. The closer he got, the lower they got to the ground. By the time he reached them, they were on their knees with their faces in the dirt. One by one he pulled them off the ground and looked them each in the eye. Without saying a word, they all meekly separated themselves into two groups.

"Captain, sir, what are you doing?" Javier asked.

"Justice, Lieutenant. I have looked into the souls of each of these men and judged them. They have felt my judgment, and in their hearts and in their minds they know which are worthy of death and which are not. None of them are innocent, but only some deserve to live," the Captain rumbled.

"Captain, this isn't the Night Angel way," Javier protested.

"Javier, I know this, but that is not what this world needs," the Captain replied.

"We don't kill prisoners, sir. These men all surrendered to us," Javier argued.

"Javier, I am no mere Marine captain anymore. I have assumed a role that is rightfully mine. Here, I am royalty, a prince, and one day a king. I was born and bred to rule this land and its entire people. It is my responsibility to judge these men and execute the law accordingly. Or maybe even write new laws," the Captain explained.

Javier felt slapped. Not by the Captain exactly, but rather by what the Captain was explaining to him. He had forgotten who and what the Captain really was, and reconsidered what was being done here.

"You're correct, sir. I had forgotten that but is this how you really want to start your rule? As an executioner?" Javier asked.

"Javi, look into my eyes," the Captain whispered.

Hesitantly, Javier looked into the Captain's red eyes, and saw what the Captain had seen. He saw the lives of the men before him and all the acts they had done. More than that, he also saw and felt the Captain's pain at sentencing these men to die. The Captain was a man who had sent many men to the bosom of whatever god they believed in, but had never once enjoyed it, even when they had more than deserved it.

"Do I want to start my rule as an executioner? No, but I will because that is what is needed. If the price of freedom and peace is that I am branded a tyrant and a warmonger, so be it. I will pay that price. These men are like children, they have no clue what they are doing, but we do. We were brought from our world precisely for this reason. Right now, these men only know the law of the sword, and I will teach them that way. These men are expecting bloodshed, they need it, and so I will give it to them. Eventually that will change, but for now I will do what I must." The Captain looked at Slappy who gave him a small smile. "I will lead these people Javi, I will guide them."

"I see, sir, but I am not sure if I agree," Javier said.

The Captain nodded, "There are natural laws, Javi, laws that every man, and every culture embraces. They are written deep into the souls of men, and no matter how much you justify it to yourself, or how often others tell you it's okay, you can feel that it's wrong, and one day, the moment comes when you can no longer hide behind such lies. You come face to face with the monster that you have become, just like these men did, and the stain on your soul is too great, and all you want to do is die. These men go willingly to their deaths, let them have this last honor; let them pay the only restitution they can for their crimes.

"Besides, who am I to ignore their laws? No monarch, no president, no *leader* is immune from answering to those beneath him. To ignore the will of the people, and impose my own ideals and plans on them is tyranny. I will *not* be a tyrant. I will love my people, teach them, and when they have grown, I will do away with the unjust laws.

"Until that day comes, I will subject myself to the laws of the land, no matter how I feel about it, because that is what is right. I am a King, Javi, or at least I will be. I do not have the luxury of dealing with things how I want to, or how it's easiest. I must act in accordance with what is right, no matter the personal cost. That is my lot in life, that is my burden, and I take this solemn responsibility with pride. I will bear the cost and shoulder the responsibility. Will you stand by me?"

Javier turned to face the men kneeling in the dust. The ones the Captain had marked for life stood behind them holding naked swords waiting for the signal. Javier called for all the men to stand in rank and at attention. Without hesitation, everyone filed into rows as ordered and waited silently. The Captain looked at each of the condemned men, his eyes clearing of the Bloodrage. Javier turned to the Captain and nodded slightly.

The Captain nodded to the spared captains, and they carried out the sentence.

That evening they built a large pyre for the dead soldiers. Their friends took turns coming to the flames to offer words, or bits of food to the dead. Late that night, the Night Angels assembled to give Boomer and Chuffles their own private pyres. They had dressed the bodies in the newly washed uniforms and laid their swords across their chests.

They stood back, shoulder to shoulder facing the pyres. The Captain signaled to Patty, and he lit the fire with magic, stoking the flames hot enough to consume man and steel alike. When the fires were hot and high the Captain saluted them and the others did the same.

Patty cleared his throat and sang an old Celtic funeral song. To his surprise, Asha joined in with a surprisingly sweet voice, but he didn't falter, together they sang the song, their voices intertwining and creating a new and richer sound. By the end, none of them had dry eyes, and even Barry was wiping away tears. Rashta stood a respectful distance back, and felt his master's pain, and made it his own.

Rashta walked up behind Asha to whisper in her ear. She listened intently to what he was asking her to do. She nodded to him, and Rashta turned to go, but Asha grabbed his arm stopping him. When he looked to see what she wanted, she handed him her favorite dagger. He reverently took the blade and nodded to her. The two held each other's eyes for a moment, then the moment was gone, and Rashta headed into the night.

That night, the Avaloneans showed the Night Angels their tradition of honoring the dead. In retrospect, Javier didn't find it that different than that of the Marines or the Army. Mostly they got really, really drunk, and told rude stories about the dead and laughed until they passed out. Even the Captain gave in and raised a cup to honor the dead.

Contreras woke up with a pounding headache. Someone had thrown up on his shirt and he wasn't entirely sure that it wasn't him. Whoever managed to pee on his pants was much less of a guess. He extracted himself from the mess and went towards the stream, just outside the wall to wash his face and the worst of last night's revelry. The night before, Kint's men had shown them where the back wall hid a door that led to the water.

While he waited for his clothes to dry, he took the opportunity to swim in the man-made pool. Kint had expected his men to live here for many years and had ordered the stream dammed so that a small lake would form. The result was really more of a pond than a lake, but it still allowed for enough room for him to actually swim laps.

Kint's men slowly staggered from there sleeping areas and each made their way down to the pond and bathed themselves. At first, Contreras was confused at their actions until he realized he liked bathing too, so why wouldn't they? The trickle turned into a flood of men and the camp came to life with its well engraved routines showing the discipline that Kint had managed to instill. There was no wasted movement, with everyone doing all the tasks needed. Contreras wasn't sure where he would fit in with them, so he stayed by the shore, not wanting to disrupt the machine.

Contreras was watching a bird, so at first he didn't notice Pablo literally drag himself to the water's edge and plunge his whole head in the water. He didn't notice that his head remained under for longer than was wise. If Breeze hadn't made a fuss trying to lift his head out of the water, Contreras wasn't sure Pablo would have come up for air. When Contreras finally came over and pulled Pablo's head from the water, there wasn't a more relieved cat in the world.

Breeze spared Contreras a grateful look, and then proceeded to lick every square inch of Pablo he could reach. At first, Pablo didn't move, he just laid still trying to squeeze his eyes shut against the sun. When the rough tongue made its way to his face, he couldn't ignore it anymore.

"Nghhhh," he moaned, feebly pushing at Breeze. "I'm alive. Just…leave, let me die in peace."

Breeze mewed miserably and looked to Contreras for help. Contreras shook his head and squatted next to the miserable man.

"How's the head?" he asked louder than he normally would.

Pablo flinched, "I think I suffered a grievous wound I was not aware of in the heat of battle last night. The night has proven me for the next world."

"Oh, don't be so dramatic. It's nothing more than a hangover. Haven't you ever been drunk before?" Contreras asked laughing.

"No, I have never partaken of strong spirits before and the ale at Rahn's resthouse was drugged. Strong spirits were not shared with *atras*. Now that I am no longer an *atras*, I am sampling the pleasures denied to me," Pablo said, keeping his eyes closed against the glaring sun.

"How is it going?" Contreras asked.

"It may yet kill me. Is this normal?"

"Indeed, but most people don't get hammered and sing bawdy from the top of stumps for the whole camp to hear. If your mother had been there, she might have had a few words for you."

"That is…regrettable; I was hoping that it was nothing more than a bad dream but it would appear that it was not."

"Nope, you are quite the dancer too."

Pablo just groaned and covered his face with both hands. Having never seen his rider like this caused Breeze even more distress. Pablo spared one hand to pet his *otorga* to calm him down.

"So, this group is surprisingly loyal in a very short amount of time. Any reason for that?" Contreras asked.

Pablo cracked an eye open to look and make sure Contreras wasn't joking before answering, "Yes, there is. Lord Captain and Kint preformed *ramwa,* so Kint's men are Lord Captain's men now. The blue light from last night?" Contreras nodded. "Well, that was Kint's essence. When he surrendered, he gave all of himself to Lord Captain, including any blood contracts he owned. Most of this army is sworn to the Lord Captain."

"Oh, I see. What else did he get?" Contreras asked.

"Everything that Kint had is now his, including his magical abilities. I am not sure why, but he gave him everything even though it was not required," Pablo answered.

"So, what happens now?" Contreras wanted to know.

"Well, traditionally, the conquered army swears formal allegiance to their new master, and the officers swear in blood," Pablo replied.

Two of Kint's men came to them at the shore with breakfast for the two men. A third followed close behind with an entire deer for Breeze. When Breeze pounced on the deer all three jumped back and started to run.

"Stop!" Pablo ordered.

They froze in their tracks, clearly frightened of Breeze but for some reason, more afraid of Pablo. Contreras looked at them and back at Pablo with his eyebrow raised but Pablo wasn't looking at him and missed the eyebrow.

"What is this?" Pablo asked.

"Breakfast, Rider Pablo," one of them answered.

"Why do you bring me this?" Pablo asked.

"And why does his plate have more food than mine?" Contreras demanded.

The men were hesitant, clearly not sure if they had made a fatal mistake. "M'Lord, a rider need not scurry for his food like a common soldier. You are above such things, and your prowess in battle proves you are above mere *ariats* like us. As for you m'Lord," he said turning to Contreras, "We brought you food in respect to your master. Are you an officer as well?"

As Pablo shifted uncomfortably looking at his food Contreras answered, "Well, no, but I am one of the Lord Captain's most trusted soldiers."

"Our apologies, m'Lord, we did not know. Where do you rank in comparison to the Rider?" the soldier asked.

"Uhhh, right below," Contreras guessed.

"We will remember, m'Lord," he said bowing.

They left Pablo and Contreras to eat in peace. Contreras left Pablo to eat, or rather pick at his food awkwardly, in peace for a little while before he started asking questions.

"So...your prowess in battle? Did you and Asha hit some resistance on the way back?" Contreras asked.

"No. There was no one left alive by the time she arrived," Pablo whispered.

"What? Where did they go?" Contreras wondered, confused.

"I killed them. I killed them all," Pablo murmured miserably staring at his food.

Contreras stopped eating and waited patiently for Pablo to continue. Breeze noticed his rider's discomfort and dragged his deer over so he could lean against Pablo while he gorged himself. Pablo reached out and took a handful of the cat's coarse fur.

"Last night, I did not hear from you. I knew you were out there and I waited for hours for you to come for me but as the hours passed it seemed like you would never come. The men set to guard us, hid close by taunting me with lewd gestures and obscene words. They taunted my Breeze with spears and rocks. When I heard the gates explode and the screams start, I knew you would not reach us in time. I had figured you would come in the night and steal us away quietly. When I realized your plan was to kill as many men as you could, I decided it was time for me to act as a Knight Angel would and join you in bringing justice to these men.

"I had freed my hands hours ago, but I was waiting for the right time to act. They had figured I was still an *atras* and had treated me as such, so they never checked me for weapons. When I cast off my bindings, only one of them came to restrain me, which made it easy for me. When he got close enough, I twisted him around and onto his knees like you showed me. I killed him with my knife before any of his comrades knew what had happened.

"They all came at me, at this point, but I was armed with the sword I took from the soldier and I fought all five of them in close quarters. They had seen me kill one of their own so they took me seriously now, but it was not enough. They too fell to my blades, with the last one fleeing from me. I had my fill of killing so I let him go. Shortly after dispatching them, Asha arrived and helped me free Breeze from his magical and temporal bindings. Together we made it back to the rest of you."

"How do you feel now?" Contreras asked gently. Five was more than Contreras thought him capable of, but Pablo was not one for exaggeration, in fact he was almost positive Pablo didn't know how to exaggerate.

"I don't know. At Asters camp, many of the men would speak of the pleasure they had from killing while others spoke quietly of the guilt they felt. I feel nothing. I took no pleasure from those deaths, but I do not feel guilt either. If I had to do it over, I would change nothing," Pablo answered miserably.

"You told me what you don't feel, but what *do* you feel."

"Sorrow. Sorrow at the waste of life. Sorrow that these men could be so misguided. What is wrong with me?"

Contreras laughed softly, "Nothing Pablo, you are fine. What you feel means you are more of a warrior than we originally thought. Your soul can bear the burden of war. It's a rare gift that one can take lives without losing his soul to the bloodlust or succumbing to the guilt."

"Me? A warrior?" Pablo asked in disbelief.

"Of course, you told me how you were always antagonizing you masters. You are no gentle sheep, Pablo, you were born for this life as much as I was. You were born to lead men as well, that's why Breeze chose you," Contreras assured him.

"What do I do now?" Pablo asked unsure of what to do.

"Take the day off. Think about it. Come to me a new man. Come back the warrior this world needs you to be, and the man I know you really are," the Captain answered from behind them.

Both men turned to look at him. The Captain smiled gently at Pablo, his purple eyes full of pride in his subordinates.

"Contreras, come with me, I need you. Pablo, take all the time you need. We'll be here for a while, just make sure you eat something every now and then. Breeze you keep an eye on him," the Captain ordered.

Breeze meowed at the Captain and rubbed his head against Pablo's chest. Pablo scratched behind Breeze's ears and smiled weakly at the Captain.

"Don't make a problem where there isn't one Pablo. You're too important for me to lose you. I don't have many friends, and I'd hate to lose you," the Captain said, turning and walking back to the camp.

Pablo nodded at the words, not grasping their full meaning until the Captain was well out of ear shot. Contreras glanced back at him in time to see the realization spread on his face and smiled his him too.

Chapter

EIGHTEEN

The Night Angels sat around the fire assembled at night fall, just as the Captain had requested. The past three days had been a huge adjustment for all of Kint's men. Even the group that had painted their chests blue didn't get the Captain's new rules right away. At first, Kint's captains had tried to order the Captain's men around and establish themselves as their officers as well. Two bloody fist fights, and a curt word from the Captain, and they accepted the Captain's men as their superiors in both combat and in hierarchy.

"Hey LT, why are we here?" Right asked Javier.

"We're still here because the part of Aster's army that we were following went to join his main army. Whatever the Captain saw in Kint's made him change his mind. He won't be challenging Kint like we had originally planned; instead, we're going to train up this army and stop them before they reach the temple. His current army has a ton of women and children, so they travel slow and we'll be able to pass them and get to the temple long before Aster does. The map we got at the resthouse also shows a shortcut that Aster doesn't seem to know about."

"Well, we all know that," Right scoffed.

"What we meant was, why are we here? As in tonight?" Left asked

"You know as much as I do. If the Captain wanted us to know why we are here, then he would have told us," Javier replied curtly.

"You noticed how he's gotten grumpier now that he has more people to boss around?" Left whispered to his twin.

"I know, I would have thought the idea of more people to kiss his butt would have made him happier," Right whispered back.

"So strange, he even has groupies, and he still isn't happy," Left commented.

"I saw that! A powerful man like LT would love groupies normally," Right said.

"True, but there's no chicks."

"What about Kush? She has a thing for him."

"Kush? The cook?"

"Ya."

"Dude, that's no chick, bro."

"Ya it is. She washed Asha's back yesterday."

"Really? Is that why Asha broke her arm?"

"Uhhh, well you know how Asha is with the whole touching thing."

"Point. We could ask her," Right said looking at Asha, who pulled a gutting knife from her belt and played with it. "You should ask her."

"No way, it was your idea," Left protested.

"Enough," Javier snapped.

"Sir!" the twins coursed.

"She's a gurl," Asha purred, "Though I don't think she's really tha girly type. But she might make an exception fer Javi."

"Asha…" Javier warned.

"Just sayin', Javi. Ya might consider yerself a gurl that aint tryin' ta kill ya. Fawn had 'er charms but thisun' aint gonna gut ya," Asha teased.

"Asha," Javier moaned.

"And she can cook," Asha laughed, "An' if ya asked her she'd kiss ya too!"

The group burst into laughter, enjoying Javier's extreme discomfort. He turned bright red and tried to act unfazed but eventually gave in and laughed with them.

They were still chuckling when Breeze and Pablo wandered into the group. The group's mirth died down a little as they check to see what kind of mood Pablo was in. Breeze walked with more confidence, losing some of his playful walk. Javier tried to catch Pablo's eye and managed to do it. The look in Pablo's eye told him everything.

"How are you Pablo?" the Captain asked, appearing from thin air.

"Cap'in!" Asha gasped.

"I mastered shadow walking before you knew what it was Asha," the Captain said dismissively.

"I am myself, your Highness," Pablo answered the Captain fiercely, "For the first time in my life, I am myself."

"So you are," the Captain said, meeting Pablo's gaze, "Just in time, I need you and you can finally grow into what I need you to be. I need you all to grow into more than you are now."

"Sir?" Javier asked, "What are you saying?"

The Captain took a deep breath, "As of now I am dissolving the Night Angels."

There was an immediate uproar from all sides as everyone tried to ask questions and protest at the same time. Everyone but Barry, anyway, who looked on with a self-satisfied smile.

"This was your doing wasn't Barry?" Travis demanded.

There was an instant and deadly silence that came from the group. Barry smile faltered and disappeared, while he licked his lips.

"Barry did counsel me," the Captain answered for him, "but the decision was mine. I have been considering this for some time now, but it wasn't until we took this camp that I was able to reach the conclusion that I needed to."

"Why? Tell meh why, sir," Asha begged, "What did we do?"

"Oh Asha," the Captain said gently, "You were everything you needed to be. Now I need more from all of you. The Night Angels were a force of nature, a force of justice…back on earth, but this is Avalon and Avalon needs more than a group of assassins. We must bring back this world's heroes."

"The Knight Angels," Pablo whispered.

"Yes, the Knights of old have returned and I would like to ask all of you to join," the Captain said looking at them each I turn.

"He means Knights with a 'k'," Left explained to his brother.

"Oooh," Right said understanding dawning on him.

"Sir, what are you asking us to do?" Javier asked, "I swore myself to God and country. Now I am supposed to do what? Abandon those oaths?"

"Javi," the Captain said, "Yours was the last service commitment to expire. I have been honestly looking for a gate home, but no such gate exists. All of your military contracts are over."

Javier blinked in surprise. He counted the months in his head and realized the Captain was right. They were supposed to have signed new ones after the Thailand job, but they obviously never made it home. A small laugh started in his belly and worked its way up his throat and out into open air.

"Well, when you put it that way, where do I sign up?" Javier asked.

"It's not that simple Javier," the Captain warned, "With this type of commitment is a life-time commitment."

"Will I stand for all that I have stood for when I joined the Night Angels on earth?" Javier asked.

"Well, yes, I took the oath from the original Knight Angels," the Captain started.

"Then I accept," Javier interrupted, "I always planned to stay at your side in the Night Angels, until I died or I could no longer fight. Though I suspect they will be one and the same."

A heavy silence penetrated the group while the Captain considered Javier's words carefully. Javier in turn held the Captain's gaze the whole time daring him to give another lame excuse why he couldn't swear to him already.

"You would follow me in blind faith into this?" the Captain asked.

"With respect, sir, you have proven yourself many times over, so it is not blind faith to trust a man how has earned it without reservation. I trust you with my life, my soul, and my honor. Every time I have second guessed you, you have shown me how I was wrong and you were right. I will swear because you need me, and you will not abuse my trust," Javier said and murmurs of agreement flowed from around the fire.

The Captain nodded his acceptance of Javier speech. He drew a small knife from under his bracer and held it out to Javier who took it, waiting for instruction. The Captain motioned for Javier to kneel and stepped close when he did so.

"Cut your hand and draw the symbol of the Knight Angels on your chest. Once you have done that repeat our oath. Be warned though, this time, if you break your oath, you will die," the Captain instructed.

Javier hissed a little when he drew the blade across his hand. It was sharper than he expected so it didn't hurt as much, but it also cut deeper than he had want it to. The others rose to their feet and stood around him while Javier drew the symbol.

Javier took a deep breath and looked the Captain in the eyes. "I am a child of the light sworn to fight in the night. I am the bane of darkness. Vengeance is my calling, justice is my charge, and mercy is my guide. As darkness gathers, I stand firm, the last shield of the light, the shining bastion of strength against the darkness. By blood and honor I fight and by blood and honor I die. Sons of darkness, fear the Night, Justice is come."

The Captain's eye glowed gold as he reached out and touched Javier on the crown of the head. Using Javier's blood, he placed an intricate blood rune on Javier's forehead. When he spoke, his voice rumbled and seemed to shake the ground.

"I am the Guardian of the Light, a Lord of Avalon, King of men and Commander of the forces of the Light. By right of my birth and the sovereignty of my crown, I accept your oath, and name you High Commander of the Knight Angels, until such time as you die or one worthier arises. Stand, Javier, High Commander of the Knight Angels and be recognized."

The group roared in approval to Javier's new position and Patty shot fireworks into the air in a flurry of colors and explosions. Javier pulled his two swords from his back and threw his head back roaring back at them. Unexpectedly, two wings of golden light extended from Javier's back, and stretched out. Everyone but Asha and the Captain, stepped back not expecting the wings. The crowd that had gathered around, drawn by the magic and fireworks fell to their knees in difference to Javier and his wings.

"Angel wings," Contreras said awed.

"Knight *Angels*," Travis said, "Of course."

"Me next," the twins said in unison.

The Captain laughed in joy and obliged them. That night he accepted them all as Knight Angels and named them each captains. He explained as time went on there would be many more Knights and they would command them in his name and in defense of the light. All except Barry, Asha and Patty.

The Avaloneans cheered each new Knight and after the last one was done they broke open more spirits and partied into the night again. The Captain raised a single glass in celebration to his men, but didn't get drunk. Halfway through the party Patrick came up to him.

"Shir, why didn't you have me swear?" he asked.

"Well, Patty, you're a druid, you can't be a Knight but you do have a more important job. My plan for you is that you will train with the druids and act as my personal druid when you're training is complete. You'll be at my side most of my life and hopefully in time, assume your grandfather's mantle and become the Arch druid," the Captain answered.

"Oh. Okay. I guess thatsh okay," Patrick slurred, "Hey, what about Barry?"

"I would not fare well with the Knights, I fear," Barry said from his perch in the shadows.

"Eh?" Patrick asked drunkenly.

"The Knights require certain…moral fortitude that prohibits me from using my most useful…talents," Barry explained.

"You can't be a sneak," Patrick giggled.

"I will be more useful as a politician, and spy, yes," Barry admitted grudgingly.

"Not everyone is cut out to be a Knight Angel Patty," the Captain said.

"Hey, Cap'in, how come on earth we were Night Angels without a 'k'?" Patrick asked suddenly distracted.

The Captain's ears turned a little pink and he cleared his throat, "Ah, well, when I submitted the idea of putting together an elite group, it was a spoken request. The upper brass thought I meant night not knight, with a 'k', so, it gotten written up as Night Angels without a 'k'. I didn't care to jeopardize my new unit, which meant I never corrected them. You know how touchy higher ups can be about their giant egos. Plus, it kept my grandfather from blowing a fuse and trying to kill me."

"Your grandfather, sir?"

"Yes, he was the leader of the Sons of Lancelot on earth. They didn't take kindly to my assembling the group, but they couldn't stop me either. It was just different enough that they let it slide, without a fuss."

"Oh, tough family."

"Ya have no idea," Asha chimed in, slipping an arm around Patty.

"Sir, have you seen my Demon? He's been gone a while. I'm worried," Patrick said.

"Oh, I bet 'e's fine," Asha said hurriedly.

The Captain's eyes narrowed slightly, "I haven't seen him."

"I've tried summoning him but he won't come," Patty pouted.

"Look! More beer fer everyone!" Asha cried beckoning a server.

The Captain held up a finger stopping the server in his tacks, "There is only one reason I know of that would send a Demon from his mark's side and not answer his summons. Asha, why would he leave Patty alone?"

"'E asked me ta watch over Patty till 'e got back," Asha confessed.

"And he is where?" the Captain demanded.

"'E's doin' what needs doin' Cap'in. We swore there would be repercussions if sumthin' happened an' sumthin' did. 'E's protectin' our honor an' after that speech ya gave ta Javi, ya best not be blowin' no fuse at me, *sir*."

The Captain pulled himself to his full height and turned eyes burning with fury at her. His jaw worked as he kept his rage in check and considered her words. At last, he closed his eyes and gave her a new look.

"I do not condone your actions, but I do not condemn them either. It was not what I would have wanted done, but it is the way of this land. The eye for an eye is an attitude that I want to change. Be willing to accept that, Asha, change is coming," he said.

"Yes, sir," Asha said.

The Captain turned on his heel and walked deep into the camp and its festivities.

"That was close," Patty said drunkenly sitting down.

"Aye," Asha said easing him gently to the ground and leaning against him, "Can I ask ya a question Patty?"

"Hmmm?"

"Did I do tha right thing?"

Patty's only reply was a snore. Asha sighed in exasperation but didn't try to wake him nor did she move off. A pair of boots invaded her view of the dirt.

"You did the right thing, Asha," Barry assured her from above.

"That's not really a very good assurance Barry," she retorted.

Barry squatted down and held her chin gently tilting her head to make her look in his eyes. She glared at him be he didn't move his hand from her face.

"You did the right thing Asha," he repeated.

He leaned in closer and she had a knife at his sternum. He spared it a glance but no fear showed in eyes.

"Worth it," he whispered brushing her lips with his.

Asha froze at the touch, and the knife slipped from her fingers. Barry pulled back and smiled a little, gently stroking her cheek.

He held her gaze a moment longer, then stood and walked away. Asha slowly picked up her knife from the dirt and placed it in its sheath while she replayed the moment in her mind. Whiskers tickled her cheek announcing Bubble's return.

"I suppose ya saw that?" she asked.

A cold wet nose touched her ear and his purring thundered in her ear. Asha giggled softly while she pushed him back. She sighed and looked at her *otorga*.

"What am I gonna do about 'im?" she asked herself.

Bubbles sniffed the sleeping Patty. Asha looked at his sleeping form.

"That Barry is so…infuriatin'. I suppose Patty can be too, but 'e's just so…solid, even when 'e's jokin' I can trust 'im. I don't think I could trust Barry. Which would you pick?" she asked Bubbles.

He gave her a level look.

"Assumin' they was both girl *otorga*," she revised.

Bubbles yawned and settled around Asha and Patty.

"Ya, I figured you'd say that."

Rahn read the latest property letter by candlelight while he reached absently for his wine. The stump on his arm did nothing to hold the cup and ended up spilling the contents on to the table. He hissed in pain as he scrambled to save the papers from the staining wine.

His wife sat next to the fire, knitting, and laughed at him, then proceeded to hum a jolly tune to herself. Rahn gathered his paper and gave her a mournful look. He didn't deserve this kind of treatment. She had help Aster just as much, but she just hadn't gotten caught. Wait, was *that* her plan all along?

He sat up and rubbed at his sore back, trying to ease some of the knots that had developed there. He glanced at his wife who was far too interested in the blanket she was making.

"Dearest flower…" he cooed.

"No," she interrupted.

"You have no idea…"

"I am not doing anything for you. Whatever it is, the answer is no."

"Now see here woman…" she raised an eyebrow and he changed tactic, "Now, sweetness, what can I do for you?"

"Grow a spine, and a pair. I should have left you long ago when father suggested I did. You had your charms, but you are not nearly handsome enough and far too poor to interest me anymore. Go and eat something. That makes you feel better."

Stung by her remarks, he fled before the tears started falling from his eyes. He wandered toward the kitchen, deciding that he did want some food. The dogs were not by the fire, so they didn't give him away as he snuck into the cakes. They liked the cooks more than they did him, well, recently everyone like someone else better than they did him. Even the rats stopped bothering him.

He stuffed cake in his mouth and realized this one tasted vaguely like meat. He pulled his hand back to where he could see the cake and stared at it in horror. He hadn't noticed, in his self-absorbed pity party, that his hand and cake was covered in blood. He turned to flee through the door, but a dog carcass fell with a meaty splat in front of him. He turned to the other door and found more dogs raining form the ceiling.

"I did what you wanted! What do you want now?" he screamed at the ceiling.

"You," a voice whispered, sliding a blade next to his throat.

"Please," he begged sobbing and soiling himself.

"Coward," the voice whispered.

"Wait, you're Aster's creature. Right? Take the gold; tell your master I'm sorry."

"I have no interest in gold. I belong to the druid now and the Knight Angels make no idle threats. We lost two of our number, but rest assured we got our comrade free and Kint is dead. His men now belong to the Lord Captain."

"That's good though. You won. No need to do anything rash."

"You were warned. The Knights make no idle threats. A debt is due."

Rahn didn't have time to scream before the darkness claimed him. Rashta let the body slide to the floor, giving it no more thought than the dogs. Rahn wife though, did interest him. She stood teary eyed in the door way holding a sheathed dagger.

"He was a fat arrogant fool," she whispered.

"But you loved him," Rashta guessed.

"But I loved him. He died thinking I didn't. Have you come to kill us all Demon?"

"Perhaps. What did you know of this plot?"

"As much as my husband told me."

"Is that to kill me?" he asked nodding at the dagger.

She barked a short laugh. "Nothing so reckless. This is to appease you and your masters," she said tossing him the sheathed dagger.

Rashta caught it. As soon as his hand touched the dagger, his eyes widened in both shock and surprise. His looked wide eyed at the resthouse matron.

"Do have any idea what this is?!" he asked sounding strangled to his own ears.

"An heirloom. A relic of an age long past and an age yet to come. The treasure of this resthouse, but it was never really ours to keep. Take it, let our business be concluded. Let me burn my husband and return to my work in peace."

Rashta nodded slowly and turn toward the door. He paused there but didn't look back at her. "Walk in the Light, wife of Rahn the Betrayer. We do not want to have to return. For now, your debt is cleared."

"Thank you. Tell you master's master, he may wish to go to the village north of Kint's fort. It's nestled next to a clear lake. This dagger rested there for some time. He may find some of what he's looking for there."

"Are you one of *her* daughters?" he asked urgently over his shoulder partially turn to face her.

"My name is Shara, like my mother before me. Maybe we once were, but not anymore. My family's power faded long ago."

Rashta said nothing. There was nothing left to say, so he melded into the night and disappeared. Shara pulled her husband's head onto her lap and closed his eyes. Only then did she let the tears flow, and they flowed deep into the night.

Chapter

NINETEEN

The training grounds were full of grunting and sweaty bodies, as Contreras cursed and shouted at them. Pablo stood on a tower in the middle watching the different groups go through the forms, his face impassive. The drill sergeants that Contreras and Travis trained at night were shouting and cursing louder trying to get their smaller groups to master things they themselves had mastered the night before.

Pablo turned his eyes to the far side of the camp where workshops had been erected and where others were being built. The Captain had gone through all of his new men that first week and removed anyone skilled in other professions from the army. The result was in front of Pablo's eyes. Two weeks after taking over Kint's fortress, it now held blacksmiths, potters, carpenters, engineers, armorers, and a few other professions. A small group tended animals outside the walls led by a newly found wilderness mage. A pen was being erected to corral them at night and a barn to harbor them in rough weather.

He grunted in satisfaction at the changes but didn't let a smile reach his lips. Javier had assured him that a leader can still smile, but judging by how infrequently the Lord Captain and Javier smiled, they did not do it very often. He had studied both of them extensively and was trying to emulate them. While the skilled labors were no longer trained, the majority of the army remained in training. The Lord Captain had placed Pablo and Contreras in charge of training them.

At first, Pablo wasn't sure why such a task would be left to him. He hadn't believed that he possessed the knowledge to train these men. Once he started training them, he realized that he did possess such knowledge, and possessed it in abundance. The time in the wilderness had not been wasted, so now he passed on the knowledge that had been passed to him.

Once he had relaxed in his position, he turned his thoughts

to the others. It became apparent that most of the Lord Captain's men possessed a wealth of knowledge. The Lord Captain was insistent that everyone learn to read and write. As it turned out, it was a skill they had all learned as children but had not passed on to Pablo, so he sat at night with all the recruits learning his letters.

At first, the Lord Captain's men had been unable to grasp the concept that every man in the world spoke and wrote the same language, and had since the Purge. Merlin had figured that many wars could have been avoided if people could have just talked to each other so had tied a communication spell to the purge. Since then, every language looked and sounded like their native tongue. They had tried speaking other languages, but they all came out sounding like Common. Javier assured them that he could still *think* in Spanish, he just couldn't speak it.

The others of the squad imparted what other knowledge they could to the men who wanted to learn. Left and Right taught the engineers new ways to make buildings and weapons of war, while Patty taught what appeared to be alchemy. Roberts and Lambert taught medicine to what they kept calling medics. This group was always huddled together and rarely slept, and they all listened with rapt attention whenever one of them was talking. More than one student carried a palm mark on their face, but despite this, none left nor seemed inclined to want to leave. They just took their chastisement and tried even harder.

Pablo noticed one of them walking through the camp. Pablo wasn't familiar with him, but that wasn't saying much, there were almost three thousand people in the camp. Something about him seemed off, so Pablo jumped down from his tower and headed toward the man.

"You there," Pablo barked in his best commander's voice, pointing at him, "What's your unit? Why aren't you with them? This isn't free time."

The man turned a tattooed face to him and casually waved his hand. Pablo felt a wave of energy crash into him, throwing him into the air. The air in lungs left abruptly, and he crashed into the ground with equal brutality.

He struggled to his feet spitting gravel and trying to fill his lungs. Whatever this mage was, he was skilled. Pablo hadn't seen the magic until it had been released. It took skill and discipline to hide the weave, and few were capable of it. Pablo wiped the blood from his mouth and tried stalling for time so others could get there.

The first ones there was a squad of recruits led by Peters, who saw the naked blade in Pablo's hand and the fire in his eye, and decided to charge the mage. Pablo panicked and tried to choke out some words but could get his throat to squeeze out the words. He could only watch as the mage brushed Peters aside and blew the rest apart as casually as he had brushed Pablo to the side. Once he was done with them, the mage walked up to Pablo and grabbed his head between both hands.

Pablo felt the mental attack but he was prepared for it. He smiled grimly as he fended off the mage, barely. The attack stopped for a moment and the mage reconsidered him.

"You are strong little one, but it will not save you. Kint thought me a wilderness mage, but I am in truth, a fully trained druid. You may have some training, but it will not stop me," the druid murmured softly.

The attack came again, building in pressure, and Pablo know it was only a moment of time before he caved and the druid held all his secrets. He felt his defenses crumbling, and then vanish. The druid took a moment to relish his victory before he started picking through s few of his memories. He started at the beginning of his life and worked his way forward. Pablo saw what he saw, and watched his childhood again. Before they left it, something stopped the druid cold.

Pablo came to his senses and smelled burned fur. The druid's cloak smoldered from Patty's fireball. He held a second ball between his hands.

"There's plenty more where that came from so you can go ahead and surrender now," Patty said.

"You will have to do better than that pup," the druid replied throwing his own ball.

The two fire balls hit each other and exploded. The heat and sound hit Pablo at the same time and threw him on the ground. Breeze jumped over him and placed himself between the druid and Pablo and started hissing and screaming at the latest threat.

The druid considered him with interest and didn't bother stopping Patty's next fire ball. The ball hit his cloak and did nothing. Patty's jaw dropped in surprise and he threw another and got the same result.

The druid looked Pablo again, "So you are the one that Kint was going to have me relieve of the *otorga*. I am not sure I approve of men bonding these beasts, but it would appear that this one has claimed you. For that alone, I will not kill you just yet. As for you, little annoying pup," he said not turning to Patty, "I will kill."

"Ya, that will be the day," Patty snorted.

Pablo saw Patty gather a massive amount of mana for his next spell and decided to run. He grabbed a handful of Breeze's fur and pulled himself to his feet. The druid wasn't done with him and attacked his mind again. Pablo had to stop moving or be invaded again.

The druid held him but felt the power in the spell as well. He turned to meet a molded jet of fire. The flame was shaped like a serpent, but it had legs and wings. It flew a circle around Patty before crashing down on the druid.

"I am impressed," the druid said from the smoke, "Not many have the energy for Dragon's Breath, but it wasn't wise to use all your mana on a single attack."

"Who said that was all I got, punk? I got lots more where that came from!" Patty shouted back at him.

The druid shook his head at him in mock sadness, "Your attacks are powerful but you are still untrained and undisciplined. You should have stayed at the temple."

"What temple?" Patty asked launching another attack.

"Don't be insolent child; I am still your superior as a druid. You young ones are so pert. You think raw power is everything and do nothing to shield your mind. You will not last my attack I think," the druid replied.

Patty froze as the mental attack came. If he hadn't been so focused on saving his own mind, Pablo would have felt sympathy for Patty. Breeze launched himself at the druid in hopes of saving his rider. The druid stopped him with a wave of his hand. The *otorga* was held immobile in the air by a single spell.

The druid stroked the fur and it made Pablo burn with rage at the sight. He threw his mind at the druid trying to fight him off. The only thing this succeeded in doing was drawing an amused look from the druid.

The Lord Captain strode from the shadows of a nearby building. "You have made many mistakes today druid."

"Ah, you must be the one that killed Kint. I have come for you and all those in this camp. I have already beaten two of you champions and I do not think you will do any good against me either. I had hoped to kill Kint when he came with the *otorga* so I could free the beast and the world from him, but it would appear that you did that for me," the druid said smiling.

"Why have you come for me then? I have not harmed Breeze nor am I Kint," the Lord Captain asked.

"No? Then why do you still run a war camp? Why are you making weapons of war and training warriors? You may not be Kint, but you are much better at war than he was. A few moments in this fortress let me know that," the druid said looking around some more.

"You know nothing about me and you will find me harder to kill than you think," the Lord Captain snarled.

Pablo watched as the Lord Captain's charge stopped as he fended off the druid's attack. Deep in himself, Pablo smiled when the Lord Captain took a step forward, and then another. Sweat beaded on the druid's head as he strained to hold him.

A fireball formed in his hand and he threw it at the Lord Captain, who raised his sword, but slowly. A moment of panic filled Pablo, but the flame hit the Lord Captain and seemed to have done no damage.

"Ah, I see you took Kint's defenses. I am surprised he gave you his Talents. No matter, this next one will not be stopped by that skin of yours," the druid warned.

This time, Pablo could feel the mana being gathered by the druid. Pablo tried to strain against the mental attack, but he couldn't fend it off. His eyes rolled in their sockets and that's what allowed him to spot Javier jumping from the building above them, sword out. As he fell he screamed and his Knight's wings unfurled and magic ran up his sword.

Pablo was the only that could see Javier cut the magical strings that showed the druid's attack, but they all felt the effects. They severed and snapped back like the strings on one of the Lord Captain's new bows.

"ENOUGH!" Javier roar, "We are the Knight Angels and to attack us is to attack the Light. If you do not submit now, we will kill you."

The druid picked himself off the ground and whirled around to face Javier. "The Knight Angels have…" He cut off looking at the wings poking out from Javier's back. The druid's mouth fell open and he dropped to his knees.

Javier's wings folded back into his back and disappeared. He walked up slowly to the druid with his sword out but at his side. He stopped a little ways from the druid and drove his sword into the dirt between them.

"A wise choice, mage," Javier said.

"It is you. Are you him? The one I have waited for?" the druid asked.

"Doubtful, I think you want him," Javier said motioning to the Lord Captain.

"Him? Are you sure? Yours are the only wings I see," the druid asked doubtful.

"I am a Guardian. I do not use wings," the Lord Captain replied walking up to them. His form crackled as he gathered his power.

"You must forgive me, m'Lord. There have been a lot of imposters. Most of the druids consider them a myth for children. The current Archdruid claims they are dead and gone. When I suggested otherwise, I was cast out and cursed," the druid said.

"Well, the Knight Angels have return. I am High Commander Javier," Javier said holding out his hand.

"Javi, you sure you want to tell him anything?" the Lord Captain asked.

"Yes, sir. Since you gave me this position, I have felt…odd. I think I am a mage now. I don't know, it's like I can feel what people are feeling. I can't read their minds, but I can read their hearts. Anyway, he's no threat to us anymore," Javier replied.

Javier helped the druid to his feet but the Lord Captain didn't relax. The druid rolled his eyes and held his hand out to the Lord Captain. He grabbed the hand hesitantly then delved into the druids mind. Pablo watched the glow around the Lord Captain while he rubbed Breeze's head to calm him down. While the Lord Captain delved, Bubbles and Arete showed up at his side, with Asha hiding in the shadows.

The Lord Captain let the druid go with a grunt. The druid blinked his eyes and noticed the other *otorga*. He gasped and fell to his knees in front of Bubbles. He grabbed Bubbles paw and looked at it closely, then moved on to his teeth. By the time he got to the tail, Bubbles had had enough and took a halfhearted swipe at him, to warn him away.

Out of reflex the druid caught his paw up with magic. Bubbles hissed and his siblings were there in a flash, teeth out, and Asha was there too, knife out and on his throat. He druid froze and didn't move.

"You are very good, Shadow Rider. Can you do that with your

otorgarash yet?" he asked gently trying to move her blade.

"Ya do not touch me kitty without my permission. Ya do it again, an' I'll eat yur liver," she hissed.

"Of course, I wouldn't dream of it," turning so he could see her face, "You are quite the specimen yourself. A Demon Blades no less. It has been a while since one of those bonded an *otorgarash*. I hope to see you become legend."

"Why are ya callin' my Bubbles a rash?" she demanded.

The druid looked at her shocked. "You don't know about *otorgas*?"

"Aye, I do. Pablo told us all about 'um," she answered slowly pulling her dagger back but not into its sheath.

"Ah, an *atras* wouldn't really know much about *otorgas*," he laughed.

Breeze snarled and bit his arm and the other two *otorgas* jumped on top of him, pushing him into the ground. The Lord Captain and Javier grabbed the cats and pulled them off. The druid pulled at his sleeve and looked at the bite.

"This will leave scars, but I should know better than to mock an *otorga's* rider," he said sighing, "My apologies Lord Breeze. My apologies Lord…?"

"Pablo," Pablo said proudly.

"Pablo. A proud name," the druid said, "And to answer you Shadow Rider, *otorgarash* are the name for the black *otorgas*. They are the kings of the species. Normally otorgas with riders and wild ones to not mix, but the wild and bonded alike will bow to an *otorgarash*. I studied them while I was at the Temple but I never had a chance to meet one of the *otorgarash*. I have long suspected they are magical in nature, like dragon, or unicorns, or *ravastas*."

"*Ravastas?*" Patty asked.

"Forget that, did you say *unicorns*?!" Javier asked.

"Indeed I did. Hello," the druid said to Slappy who had arrived with Lambert, their students, and the rest of the Knight Angels.

Slappy poked at the wound and inspected it closely. The druid grimaced but didn't say anything about it.

"You know of the horse lords?" the druid asked.

"Ya, I think so, are they shiny and white and have horns?" Javier asked excitedly.

"Why ya wanna know Javi? Ya want yourself a cute lil' filly ta keep ya company?" Asha teased.

"I, um, was just wondering," Javier stammered.

"They are some that are white but they only have one horn," the druid said slowly looking between Asha and Javier, "I guess if you were to brush their coats they would be shiny but most are eaten longer before they find out. Ouch, yes that hurts," the druid said to Slappy.

Slappy held his hand out to Patty who glared at him but Slappy stared him down, so with a sigh and a scowl he went over to help.

"What are you doing?" the druid asked.

"Helping," Slappy said curtly, "Don't fight us."

The druid watched him suspiciously but did not resist. Slappy's students crowded around to watch him work. It was hard to tell who was more fascinated, the druid or the students. When the druid prodded the magic gently to see what was going on, he received a slap. He recoiled but otherwise accepted his chastisement and said nothing.

"A truly magnificent display. My arm is perfect," the druid said, "How is it possible?"

"I learned to heal without magic. I know how the body is supposed to be. With Patty's help, I can fix anything the body has wrong. You can now also pee normally again," Slappy replied.

The druid blinked and opened his mouth so say something but found himself without words. Pablo suspected that he wasn't the type to be without words often.

"Thank you. It has been bothersome," the druid said. Slappy only grunted which could have meant anything.

"Yes, yes lovely, back to the unicorns," Javier said impatiently, "Did you say people *eat* them?"

"Oh, Javi. I didn' know ya liked the ponies," Asha teased some more.

"The young ones are the best," Pablo volunteered, "Some keep them as pets. They can be quite adorable and lovable."

The group roared in laughter but neither the druid nor Pablo knew why.

"Yes, well, that's good to know, but why *eat* them?" Javier asked again.

"That is what one does with horses," the druid replied.

"Even the unicorns?" Javier asked incredulous.

"Indeed. I have never tried it, but unicorn meat is said to be superb," the druid said.

"That's…nice. Are they as rare as an *otorga?*" Javier asked.

"They are rare, but not nearly as rare. A few are born every year but by the time you hear about them someone has already turned them into stew," the druid replied.

Javier looked depressed and most of the group sniggered at him. The druid cocked his head trying to understand what was so funny.

"I'm sorry, but why is it so comical that someone would want a unicorn?" the druid asked.

"On Earth, where we come from, unicorns are little more than myths and we make little toys of them for little girls," Patty explained.

"Ah, I see," the druid said. Then he started, "Did you say Earth? Where Merlin the Magnificent and Lancelot the Fallen went?"

"Lancelot the Fallen?" Javier muttered to himself.

"Yes," the Lord Captain answered glancing at Javier.

"Ah, interesting. I don't suppose you know what happened to him do you? Here, we aren't sure what happened. After Merlin cast the Purge, he left this place in the hands of acolytes who had to clean up his mess. I mean, what kind of druid casts something so powerful, leaving countless druids dead and then leaves the mess for someone else to clean up. Then there was that whole Arthur debacle," the druid rambled completely oblivious to the change in attitude around him. "That half dead mess shows up decades later and kills even more druids. It's been centuries and we still aren't back to where we were before the Purge. Ha! We are barely back to where before that Arthur fellow showed up."

"Arthur made it?" the Lord Captain asked.

"Yes. Did you know him? Why didn't Merlin send a yong lad, or someone who would actually survive instead of that old man?" the druid demanded.

"Well, he thought the bloodline was ended. When he sent Arthur, Merlin was dying anyway and sent what he could. It wasn't until after he sent Arthur that he found out that the bloodline hadn't ended," the Lord Captain answered.

"I see. How did you all end up here?" the druid asked.

"We came through my grandfather's portal," Patty said haughtily.

"Your grandfather? Who is he? I must have heard of him," the druid said.

"You have. He's Merlin the Magnificent," Patty said.

The druid threw his head back and laughed, "Right, you're one of Merlin's sons, and this must be Arthur's heir. Ha ha ha!"

When no one laughed or even smiled, the druid's mood changed. His eyes grew large and he cast some sort of spell around Patty. When he did he jumped to his feet startling the *otorgas.*

"By Asha's moon," he whispered, "It's true. You are Merlin's heir. And are you the descendent of Arthur? Or Lancelot?"

"Both," the Lord Captain said.

"The bloodlines mixed?" the druid asked. The Lord Captain nodded. "Well now that's a powerful combination. Strength from one, wisdom from the other, and the right to rule from both. Very nice, brilliant really," the druid muttered to himself.

The Lord Captain shifted nervously but said nothing. The druid muttered to himself too quietly for anyone to hear, and stared at the ground with his eyebrows furrowed. After a few moments he brightened and looked around at them.

"So before me I have the heir of the most powerful druid to grace Avalon, the heir of a fallen kingdom and the promised heir of said druid, and a host of Knight Angels strait from the legends. Do you know what this calls for?" the druid asked.

"Drinks?" Left asked.

"Pizza?" Right asked.

"Unicorn rides?" Asha volunteered.

"Of course not. It is time for a quest worthy of the ancients and I, Xanthamius the Wild, will be your guide."

Chapter

TWENTY

"Why is it that epic quests always have a ridiculous amount of walking involved," Right whined.

"Because it's good for you and it's only been four days. On the bright side, we're making lots of wonderful memories!" Left said cheerfully.

"I would trade these wonderful memories and every last one of my blisters for a cool drink right now," Right grumbled back.

"Look at the grunts," Left said motioning to the small retinue of men leading the pack animals the Captain had brought along, "They march all day, carrying heavy packs, and don't breathe a word of complaint."

"That's because Asha said she hated grumbling and threatened to feed them to Bubbles if they did. Plus, the horses are carrying most of the heavy stuff," Right explained.

"You know she wouldn't do that right? Wait, you don't think she would, do you?" Left asked now not quite so certain.

"Would you risk it?" Right asked

"Hmmm, good point," Left replied.

"Pablo, Contreras, and Lambert have it easy, staying behind and training," Right muttered.

"Hanging out with a bunch of sweaty, smelly, ornery men? Go for it," Left laughed.

"Well, maybe not. I still want a cool drink, though," Right grumbled.

"Allow me, gentleman," Patrick said with a flourish.

He pulled Right's canteen form his gasp and waved his hand

over the canteen mysteriously. He beamed with pleasure as when he handed the canteen back to its owner. Right lifted the canteen to his lips and discovered that no water would come out.

"Yay. I now have an undrinkable block of ice. Not sure how that helped Patty," Right grumbled while watching his twin take a long and luxurious drink of luke-warm water.

"Wha-at? Really? Do you know how hard that was?" Patrick demanded.

"It's just magic Patty, it's not that hard," Right shot back.

"Ya. A wave of your hand and…poof!" Left added.

"Not that hard?! Did he just say not that hard? Do you know how long it took me to figure out how to pull the latent energy out of the water to cool it…?" Patrick sputtered.

Right made a rude noise, while his brother yawned loudly. Patrick's tirade cut off and he walked on grumbling to himself. A little to his side, Xanthamius walked along studying Patrick. After a several minutes of grumbling, he had vented all his frustration out and no longer cared what the twins had said. He started humming to himself, which drew a frown from Xanthamius.

Some people thought that his mood swings were random and strange, and to a point they were, but the truth was much simpler. Patrick just didn't hold grudges. They were counterproductive, so he said what he needed to say and then moved on. He found it odd that people would choose to hold on to those feelings and in some cases let it consume them. No, life was much easier if he didn't let his emotions try to eat him alive.

"How did you do that?" Xanthamius asked.

"A few deep breaths and a calming technique from a yoga

instructor," Patrick replied.

"Not that," Xanthamius laughed, "The ice. The method of turning water in to ice has eluded the druids for many generations. We have tried introducing cold to water but since the Purge, there have been no druids with this knowledge."

"Well, that's because you went at it backwards. You can't introduce 'cold' to anything. There is no such thing. There is only heat and less heat. You have to take the heat away from the water and then it freezes," Patrick explained.

"Ah, I see. That…hmm…I must ponder this. Could you show me the spell again?" Xanthamius asked.

"I'll tell you what. You teach me one of yours and I will teach you mine," Patrick grinned.

A shadow passed over Xanthamius face and Patrick almost missed how sad Xanthamius really was.

"Alas, I cannot. When I was cast from the Temple the archdruids placed a curse on me at the direction of the merlin. I cannot teach magic anymore and all my spells must be cast cloaked so as to not accidently teach an inquisitive young druid. All I can do now is practice and learn," Xanthamius said cheerfully.

Patrick could hear the sorrow hidden in his voice, now that he knew to look for it. He knew that Xanthamius wouldn't want his pity or his comfort, so he decided to give him what he wanted.

"Right," Patrick said pulling up his sleeves.

"Sup?" Right asked.

"Not you," Patrick snapped.

"Me?" Left asked.

Patrick shot them a glare and then ignored them. He spent the next half hour showing Xanthamius how to make ice. By the time they stopped for lunch, Xanthamius treated them all to ice in their drinks. Patrick felt a small twinge of jealousy that Xanthamius was able to control his spell better than he was, but he reminded himself that Xanthamius had decades of experience on him, and had better control of his magic.

"Great ice water Xanthamius!" Travis exclaimed, "Best ice water I've ever had."

"Thank you," Xanthamius replied beaming.

"Where did you find ice at this time of the year?" Rashta asked coming from the bushes.

Xanthamius threw a spell at him that Patrick couldn't see but somehow Rashta avoided it and appeared in Xanthamius' shadow, knife at his throat. Patrick could feel Xanthamius gather mana and just as quickly it evaporated. Xanthamius tried again and once again the mana vanished as fast as he gathered it. Panic crept into his eyes, and Rashta laughed at him.

"You won't be hitting me now druid. Pablo, Contreras, and Lambert warned me about you when I passed through the camp. He seemed to think you may have bewitched my master, is it true?" Rashta asked gently tracing a new knife along Xanthamius' belly.

"You will let me go now, Demon," Xanthamius ordered.

"Oh? And how do you plan on making me?" Rashta teased.

"Rashta!" Patrick snapped.

"That's how," Xanthamius mutter quietly.

"M'Lord?" Rashta asked pointedly ignoring Xanthamius.

"He's a friend, let him go," Patrick order.

"As my Lord requires," Rashta said bowing his head and letting Xanthamius go.

As soon as he was free, Xanthamius lashed out with some spell. Rashta watched him amused but otherwise unharmed. The druid stared unashamed at Rashta with his mouth open. He didn't even seem to notice when a fly wandered in walked around for a bit, found it not to his liking and flew off lazily.

"Where were you?" Patrick demanded.

"Defending our honor," Rashta replied.

"Defending…what?" Patrick asked.

"He killed Rahn," the Captain answered coming up to them.

"You…why?" Patrick asked.

"Because we said we would. Chuffles and Boomer lost their lives, have you forgotten that?" Rashta asked.

"No! I will never forget that but how could you think that killing Rahn was an appropriate reaction?" Patrick growled.

"Because the Knight Angels make no idle threats," the Captain answered for him.

While Patrick turned to look at the Captain, Rashta inclined his head in respect to the Captain. Patrick considered his words carefully.

"You knew, sir?" Patrick asked. The Captain nodded. "I see. Very well Rashta, you did as we promised but next time, you *will* ask me for permission first. That's an order."

"As my Lord wishes," Rashta said bowing.

"Was it…did you…?" Patrick tried to ask.

Rashta held up a hand forestalling him, "It was quick and painless. I didn't torture him nor did I touch his family. His sins were his own. I may not have been your Demon for very long, m'Lord, but I am aware of most of your wishes."

"Thank you," Patrick said sighing with relief.

"You bonded a Demon already? Fascinating. Where did you find him?" Xanthamius wondered.

"In battle. Asha beat him and I broke him. Afterwards he felt like following me so I bonded him," Patrick summarized.

"The woman? Well, that explains why the *otorgarash* bonded her," Xanthamius mused.

"She is quite the warrior," Rashta added.

"I wasn't speaking to you Demon," Xanthamius said haughtily.

Rashta snapped his teeth together and gave him a wicked grin.

"Riiight," Patrick said looking between the two, "Where were you afterwards. You were gone far too long for one mission."

"I was looking for a lake. After I found it I returned to the Kint's fortress and found Pablo and Contreras there and they told me where to look for you. I came across something at Rahn's house that both of you will be interested in," Rashta said motioning to both the Captain and to Patrick.

"Your little toy?" Patrick asked.

"How did…of course, you're Merlin's heir, you would know

such things," Rashta surmised.

"Don't speak of such things," Xanthamius hissed.

Rashta appeared in his shadow and threw the druid in the dirt and had his dagger at the druid's eye, nearly touching it.

"I am Rashta, Demon of the future Archdruid Patrick, and I do *not* answer to a fallen druid," Rashta snarled.

"Rashta," the Captain said wearily.

"With respect, Lord Captain…" Rashta started.

"I am not as weak as Xanthamius. You will do as I say or I will make you," the Captain said quietly yet dangerously.

"You should listen to him, I do," Patrick advised, rubbing the goose bumps from his skin.

"Yes, m'Lord, as you wish," Rashta said as much to Patrick as he did to the Captain, letting Xanthamius up from the dirt and walked back to Patrick.

"Was the big deal if 'e wants ta call 'im Merlin's heir?" Asha asked from above them.

Xanthamius jumped at the sound of her voice and glanced upwards inti the trees.

"Ya lookin' up me skirt Xanny?" she asked.

"No, of course not, I would never…wait, you have no skirts," Xanthamius answered.

"An' how do ya know that I aint got any skirts in my thing?" Asha asked dropping down to the ground and walking seductively toward Xanthamius.

"I did not trust you and I may have accidently seen your belongings," Xanthamius stammered watching Asha's hips sway.

"Oh, he's toast," Patrick muttered to Rashta.

"Indeed," Rashta replied distractedly, eyeing her hips as well.

"Don't look, she'll know," Patrick warned.

Rashta's eyes looked away like they had been burned. Xanthamius on the other hand was not so wise and was unprepared when Asha lunged at him.

"What did you have to show us?" the Captain asked ignoring Xanthamius screams for help. The twins heard the commotion and started placing bets.

"This," Rashta said holding out the dagger.

"Shiny," Patrick commented excitedly.

"So?" the Captain asked impatiently.

"No, sir, shiny in the magical sense. That dagger glows from all the spells on and in it. If I didn't know better, no, it's true, oh wow…" Patrick said.

Patrick was awed by the amount of work and sacrifice used to make the dagger. The Captain stood nearby, his folded arms showing his impatience. Patrick ignored him and gently took the dagger from Rashta and inspected it closely. His behavior captured the Captain attention and his impatience turned to patience while he waited for Patrick to finish his work.

"Sir, this thing is ancient. I mean wicked ancient, as in thousands of years, ancient," Patrick whispered, "What's more, only someone sacrificing their life force could have bound this much magic to this object. Someone, or possibly more than one someone, died making this dagger."

The Captain held out his hand and Patrick handed over the dagger. The Captain held if frowning. He looked at Rashta considering him.

"Do you know what this is?" he asked.

"I do. That is why I went scouting north. Shara gave it to me at the resthouse and told me the dagger had been resting at for some time in a village next to a lake. I found the lake and I have returned to take you there. I believe we will find many of the answers you have been seeking," Rashta assured him.

"What is it, sir?" Patrick asked reaching for the dagger. The Captain pulled it back protectively, then reconsidered and gave it back to Patrick. Patrick raised an eyebrow, repeating the question.

"It's an heirloom. One of many, that belonged to the House of the Sun," the Captain replied hesitantly.

"Who was, or is, the house of the son?" Patrick asked.

"They were the rulers of the light," Xanthamius answered wiping blood from his nose.

"An ancient house an' tha rightful rulers o' this world," Asha added looking at Xanthamius smugly.

"Interesting," Patrick said looking at Xanthamius from the corner of his eye, "So, why is that important? Whose son was he?"

"The House of Sun, as in the Sun," the Captain explained pointing at the sun, "was name of the royal house that ruled from Lancelot the First, to Lancelot the Fallen."

"Technically, Lancelot the Fallen never took the crown," Xanthamius corrected.

"True. Anyway, this dagger was one of their prized possessions that was to be presented to the new king. Merlin took some of them with him when he went to Earth," the Captain continued.

"So it's supposed to be yours?" Travis asked.

"Yes," the Captain said at the same time that Xanthamius said no.

"Well," Xanthamius explained, "it belonged to the House of the Sun but then that Arthur fellow gave it to Nimue as a reward for getting him to the druids alive. Her daughters passed it on from one generation to the next. They tried to enter the temple and claim right as druids with it but they were put to death for their sins and the dagger was lost."

"Sins?" Patrick asked.

"What 'e means is they wouldn't be slaves. 'E thinks they shoulda been nothin' more than brood mares," Asha spat.

"It is rare that a woman is trained and when they are, she must earn the right. Simply claiming the right is blasphemy," Xanthamius shot back.

"Wait, slaves? Like when …" Patrick asked.

"Aye. Just like that. Ya disgust me *druid*," Asha snarled before storming off.

"Such a waste. It doesn't matter if someone is a woman or a man, only if they have the talent. My grandfather would never have approved," Patrick said.

"*Stop* saying that," Xanthamius demanded.

"Well, he wouldn't have," Patrick replied.

"Not that. That Merlin was your grandfather. Those are dangerous words, pup. There are many who would kill you for merely suggesting it," Xanthamius warned.

"What? Why? Because of the Purge thing?" Patrick asked.

"No, well, in part yes, but mostly no," Xanthamius replied.

"Xanthamius, no riddles today," the Captain ordered.

"Of course not, m'Lord," Xanthamius continued hastily, "What I mean is, Merlin the Magnificent was the last in a bloodline that was…unique. The magical world has no kings or royalty, but we did have…something similar."

"Okay, I follow you so far," Patrick said hesitantly.

"You see, there was a bloodline that was unusually powerful. When you gathered the world's strongest mages in one room, chances were, they were all related. As a result, they were the shepherds, of sorts, to the world's mages. The druids in particular, were always jealous of them. Merlin the Magnificent was a legend to men in an age where legends were commonplace," Xanthamius explained.

"So he was a legend to legends?" Patrick asked to clarify.

"Correct," Xanthamius answered.

"And how is this bad?" Patrick asked.

"Many of us believe that if a druid were to arise from that bloodline, we would have to bow to them," Xanthamius explained.

"Oh, so Merlin's line is dead here?" Patrick asked suddenly sad.

"No, not completely. Lesser mages still exist but no druids,"

Xanthamius replied.

"So, why haven't there been any more druids?" Patrick wondered.

"Because," Xanthamius said exasperated, "only druids can father more druids. Lesser mages can father mages, but not druids."

"Oh," Patrick said stunned.

"What about Nimue," the Captain asked, "Both her and her sister were druids. Is her line ended?"

"As far as the Temple knows, yes, but this dagger begs a different answer. It is possible that a few survived their chastisement and hid," Xanthamius answered slowly, "Either way, we should go to this lake and investigate."

"Yes," the Captain said, "We definitely should. Rashta, lead the way, show me this lake."

After Patrick gave him a nod, Rashta bowed and replied, "As you wish m'Lord."

They finished their lunch, gathered their gear and headed north, following Rashta deeper into the wilderness. While they walked, Rashta and Asha started arguing on how to best bend the shadows around them. Xanthamius was drawn to their argument and they grudgingly let him join when he added a few points they hadn't considered. Once they were deep in conversation, the Captain motion Patrick over.

"Sir?" he asked.

"Watch him Patty," the Captain said, "I don't trust him. I think he may have a hidden agenda here and if I am right, we can't trust him."

"But Javier said…"

"That he didn't want to harm us but that doesn't mean that he wants to help us in the way we need him to. If this village is where Nimue's descendants lived and died, it's possible that there are many more treasures to be found in that village. Whatever Xanthamius is, he's a druid first, and given a big enough temptation, he may try to buy his way back into the Temple."

"What kind of treasures?" Patrick asked.

"More of my family's heirlooms," the Captain said.

"Like…?" Patrick asked.

"Excalibur was never found," the Captain replied.

"Whoa, whoa, whoa, like *the* Excalibur? The sword in the stone Excalibur?" Patrick asked, his excitement making his voice shrilly.

"It was a throne but yes, that Excalibur," the Captain explained.

"Was said throne made from stone?" Patrick asked.

"Yes, I suppose it was," the Captain admitted.

"So I was right!" Patrick exclaimed.

"Only by accident."

"Why would he want that?"

"It's the sword of kings and it's magical. Why wouldn't the druids want it? My family may have been light on their teachings of this world but they all agreed the druids meddled in things they didn't need to meddle in."

"Great, more politicians," Patrick grumbled.

"This coming from the strongest druid this world probably has," the Captain smirked.

"Details," Patrick said with a wave of his hand.

"Life is full of them," the Captain laughed then turned serious, "But remember what I said. Don't let him touch any of the relics first. Call me to inspect it."

"Yes, sir. I hate to spy on him. I wish I could at least see his spells. I could learn so much," Patrick grumbled.

"You haven't figured it out yet?" the Captain asked shocked.

"Figured what out?"

"How to look past the cloaking, of course."

"No," Patrick replied grumpily.

"Well then, Patty, it seems I have one more spell to teach you," the Captain said eagerly.

Chapter

TWENTY ONE

Travis stood at the border of the grasslands and looked in at the jungle ahead of him. The line between the two was as obvious as the two side of a coin. On one side was almost desert with sparsely populated prairie landscape that sat quietly. A few inches away a noisy jungle teemed with life. With a slow and deliberate motion, he stuck his hand into the jungle, feeling the humidity and heat on his skin. He pulled his hand back and inspected it for changes.

"This is the area known as Avalon's Eye. It's unique to this world and the people who live here are…different," Xanthamius explained.

"Coming from you, druid, that's hysterical," Rashta said with a smile that conveyed no warmth.

"My name is Xanthamius the Wild. I am normal, while these people tend to be odd," Xanthamius shot back.

"Odd how?" the Captain asked putting an end to their argument.

The two had been picking at each other for the past two days while they traveled north. They had passed out of the forest and into the direct sunlight the first day. The heat and lack of water, along with the freezing nights, had done nothing to improve moods all around, but Knight Angels still held their composure, tolerating the direct sunlight with quiet dignity, even though they hated it just as much.

"They refuse to fight. They are often killed or enslaved but all they do in their defense is try to run away. The survivors rebuild and start over again. So strange," Xanthamius said shaking his head.

"Hmm, that is strange," Rashta mused.

"It's not that strange to want peace," Javier objected. "It's different from the norm perhaps, but not that strange. I have known many pacifists in my day. They can be a bit odd at times but it's not that uncommon."

"Maybe they do things differently on Earth, but here in Avalon the weak die, and those who cannot keep what is theirs don't deserve to have it," Rashta said fiercely.

"On Earth, not every sword is needed," the Captain said quietly. "On Earth, children can laugh and play. They are not always haunted by the wars of their fathers, they do not bathe in blood, and they are safe. Perhaps that is not the way of the world here, but it will be. I will make a place in this world where children can sleep and not fear the night. I will make a land where only a few will hold the sword, not because only a few can, but because a few are needed."

"I hope to live long enough to see it," Rashta said.

"A worthy cause, your highness," Xanthamius added approvingly.

"Thank you. Rashta, where is this village?" the Captain asked.

"About two hours' walk that way," Rashta said pointing, "This jungle isn't very large in any direction."

"Come let us meet the Treehuggers," Xanthamius said stepping forward.

"Wait, what did you say?" Travis asked.

"Yay, hippies are universal," Barry grumbled.

"What are hippies?" Xanthamius asked.

"You know, people with an over attachment to nature, they

like granola, walk around barefoot, ring a bell?" Barry inquired.

"I hear no bells, and what is wrong with liking nature? I like nature," Xanthamius asked.

"Right, Xanthamius the Wild, I forgot. Um, how about this, why do you call them tree huggers?" Barry suggested.

"Because that is what their tribe is named of course," Xanthamius explain puzzled.

"Of course it is," Barry muttered to himself.

"Do they really hug trees?" Patty asked.

"Yes they do. If I recall, they pick a tree on their name day and they live in it," Xanthamius answered.

"When's a name day?" Travis asked curios about a new culture.

"Ugh, for all your knowledge, I forget how uneducated you all are," grumbled to himself, "A name day is the day you leave your parents and pick your own name. It's the day that makes you an adult and you leave your childhood name and life behind."

"Oh, I knew that," Travis said quickly.

"Will we run into these Treehuggers?" the Captain asked rescuing Travis.

"Yes, m'Lord. Their village is found in the Eye," Rashta replied.

"Are you sure?" the Captain pressed.

"I am. As I told you, the jungle is not wide. The magic of the Eye gives life to this jungle, but there is only one settlement of humans here," Rashta assured him.

"What's the other one?" Travis asked.

"Other?" Rashta asked innocently.

"Yes, you specified human. You wouldn't have done that if there wasn't another village here," Travis said.

"There is a small village of elves, but it would be our death to go there. They do not take well to intruders," Rashta said hesitantly.

"Elves? Really?" Travis asked excitedly.

"Do not do so, Sergeant Travis," Xanthamius warned, "The Demon speaks true. Not even the druids enter Elven lands uninvited."

"Bummer," Travis muttered crestfallen.

Of all the things he had seen and heard of in this world, he had hoped to find elves. It was a small hope but he had never voiced his opinion of it. After he heard what the squad had said to Javier, there was no way he was going to let them know how he felt about elves.

He was so caught up in his mix of hope and despair, he didn't realize he was walking forward until he felt the humidity of the jungle assault his nostrils. He took a deep breath, taking in the smell of the moist air. A few vines were in his way, so he drew his sword and hacked his way through them.

"Yay, more jungles," Javier grumbled, "The last one we went into was so fun, what could possibly go wrong?"

"STOP!" Rashta and Xanthamius screamed.

Travis froze. Years of training had engrained in him the reflex to hold still when someone spoke like that. Out of reflex he looked at the ground trying to spot the land mine. A second later he realized there wasn't one, and turned to the Avaloneans to see what was wrong.

"Do on cut the vines of the Eye. Do not burn its green wood. If it is alive, do not harm it. We may eat the fruit, but other than that, do no harm anything," Xanthamius warned ashen faced.

Travis raised an eyebrow at Rashta. In turn, Rashta pointed to the vine that Travis had just cut. The vine oozed a greenish liquid that eerily reminded him of blood seeping from a wound. He bent down and tried some of the liquid. It was surprisingly sweet and rejuvenating.

"Gah!" Xanthamius screamed again.

"It was an honor to know you, Travis," Rashta said solemnly.

"What?!" Travis asked.

"To drink the Eye's blood is death. It's a poison that eats you from the inside. In moments you will bleed from every opening in your body," Xanthamius whispered.

Travis felt the blood drain from his face and his vision swam. Slappy was there in an instant helping him to the ground, and Patty stood next to him. He couldn't see it but he was sure the two were linked and trying to save him.

"Are you sure?" Slappy asked.

"Yes, it is known that any who drink it die horribly," Xanthamius repeated, "The druids have documented this extensively. Only the Elves and Goblins can drink it and live. Why do you ask?"

"I can't find anything wrong with him at all. In fact, he seems healthier than the last time I delved him," Slappy said surprised.

"He must be dying. What did the Eye's blood taste like?"

Xanthamius demanded.

"Sweet, kind of like syrup," Travis said moaning, "How long do I have?"

"Sweet? Are you certain?" Xanthamius asked urgently.

"Yes. Now tell me, how long do I have?" Travis repeated trying to maintain his composure.

"I would say twenty or thirty years," Xanthamius laughed.

"Twenty or thirty…wait, *years?*" Travis asked jumping to his feet.

"Yes," Xanthamius said with a laugh, "It would appear you are a juggernaut."

"Come again?" Travis asked.

"Pardon?" Xanthamius said scrathing his head.

"That's what I said."

"Oh. You are a juggernaut. It's a rare condition that creates a specimen that is far above the others of its species."

"Like unicorns?" Javier asked.

"Correct!" Xanthamius said beaming at him.

"Really, Javi? Ya back ta da unicorns?" Asha teased.

"Hey, shut up, you know you want one too. Don't deny it," Javier shot back. Asha's face flushed red and she looked away. "Holy crap, I was kidding but you really do want one."

"Well, at least I'm a girl," Asha snapped.

"Hey, you two, dead man talking here," Travis growl.

"Oh, don' be so dramatic. Ya heard 'um, yur gonna be just fine," Asha said dismissively still trying to stare down Javier. Barry placed a hand on her shoulder and she calmed down some.

"I'm going to be okay? Tell me I'm not going to die," Travis asked Xanthamius.

"You are a juggernaut. That means Mother Avalon loves you and you are one of the few creatures she doesn't want to die," Xanthamius assured him, "That being said, I wouldn't press your luck. You are one of the few that can drink her blood and live to tell the tale. There are few *ariat* juggernauts, so the details are few, but it would seem consistent with the stories. Her blood will actually make you stronger, give you improved vitality."

"Huh," Travis said thinking. He walked over to a vine and drank from it. "Whoa. I feel great. Maybe too great." His head felt dizzy but then he adjusted. "Ya, differently went overboard, but I feel like I rested a week.

"Let's get a move on," Javier said, "We're wasting daylight."

"Okay, you guys go ahead, I'll catch up," Travis said pulling an empty canteen from his pack.

The group watched silently as he filled his canteen and reverently placed the sealed container back into his pack. When he was done he took the lead again but this time worked his way through the jungle without cutting anything, and avoided stepping on anything that looked green. He didn't have to turn around to know that the others were doing the same thing behind him. This method was harder and longer, but he doubted anyone wanted to rush it.

Two hours later the jungle gave way to a lake in the shape of a perfect circle. At the center of the lake was a small circular island dominated by an imposing oak tree. Even at a distance Travis still had to look up to see the top. Its shadow reached them at the shore, and it actually felt peaceful to Travis. The other side of the lake had a small village with people milling around. They hadn't spotted them yet, so they melded back into the jungle before they did.

"Well, what do we do now?" Travis asked the Captain.

The Captain wasn't paying attention to him in the least. He had his eyes fixed on the island, a faraway look in his eye. He turned slowly to them, his eyes golden and glowing. Tears streamed down his face before he was able to compose himself.

"It still remembers," the Captain said with a little awe in his voice.

"It remembers what?" Patty asked him.

The Captain blinked the gold light from his eyes, "It remembers Arthur. It remembers Merlin asking it to bring him here alive. It normally requires two lives to move between worlds, but it felt Arthur's heart and decided to bring him anyway."

"What?" the twins said echoing each other.

"The island is a natural portal between worlds. It can be used to transfer things between worlds, but it requires two life forces as payment. Nimue was willing to be the second life, but it knew how important Arthur was and it brought him here while only taking Merlin's life. That let her keep Arthur alive long enough to be healed by the druids. It brought the heirlooms with it too, but Nimue came for those later," the Captain explained.

"I wonder if the people in the village know anything," Barry wondered.

"They know," the Captain said firmly.

"How can you be sure?" Barry asked.

"Because, they are its caretakers. That's why they don't fight. They have to remain pure so they can care for the island. They know everything. The only question is if they will help us," the Captain replied.

"How do you know that?" Barry asked.

"It told me so. I asked it if it knew of Arthur, and it showed me everything. That island is here and in all the other worlds, if you know how to find it. Here is where its heart is, and the only place it can be reached on foot. In the rest it must be summoned," the Captain explained.

"So, a tree told you all of that?" Barry asked.

"Don't be crazy, the tree said no such thing. It couldn't care less about Arthur. The island told me," the Captain said as if it explained everything.

"Right, the island, of course," Barry said warily.

"So the mystical island of Avalon in the stories is..." Travis prompted.

"This island, yes. It's a portal *to* Avalon," the Captain clarified.

"Well, time to go meet the neighbors," Barry said cheerfully leading the way.

They reached the village a few moments later and were greeted at the border by a small envoy. The party consisted of two women and one man, all of which were smiling pleasantly. They made no move to stop them but they did plant themselves firmly in their way.

"Hello travelers," the man said pleasantly, "I am sorry but the village is closed to outsiders today. We would thank you to come another day."

"We are very weary," Barry said pleasantly meeting smile with smile, "We merely wish to rest a moment and maybe share a story or two before moving on."

"We know why you are here, Barry Silvertounge. You have charmed many people out of their secrets, but the Island's secrets are its own. Yours however are not," the man said smoothly.

Barry's smile wavered but didn't come off, "Surely you are mistaken. We bare you no ill will. We merely wish to talk."

"There is nothing for you here, Silvertounge. Turn back," the man replied.

"Back? Where would we go? It is not the nature of man to go back but to go forward," Barry said as sagely as possible.

The man cocked his head considering the words. "What you say is true, the only path *is* forward, but why do you look back?"

"Those who do not study the past are, of themselves, doomed to repeat it and while the past had its bright spots, the tomorrow is so much brighter, and can be brighter still if there are none of yesterday's shadows," Barry reasoned.

The man considered his words again, "Twice you have spoken truth and wisdom, but fail to capture any of it for yourself. Why do you use the truth to blind others in your deceptions?"

"Are mine any worse than yours?" Barry asked.

"I have told no lies, there is nothing for you here," the man said.

"Barry, he's telling the truth," Javier said from behind.

"True, I suspect there isn't anything for me here, but there is something for him here," Barry said pointing to the Captain.

"Is truth from lying lips, any cleaner than pure water from a soiled cup?" the man asked.

"Any water to a dying man is sustenance. Even the worst directions give a lost man a course," Barry replied. "Perhaps my lips are not the purest vessel, but my heart is pure in its intentions. Can you claim the same?"

The man maintained eye contact for a while and then inclined his head in respect to Barry and bowed slightly. The women behind him bowed deeper.

"You would be welcome another time, but the village is closed for now. We are still rebuilding from the last attack. If you would come back later we would appreciate it," the man said regretfully.

"It is never closed to me," the Captain said stepping forward.

"Who might you be?" the man asked politely.

"Ask your Elven friends hiding from us. They know who I am," the Captain said nodding toward the nearest hut.

A figure emerged from the hut covered in a robe. It walked over to them so gracefully it seemed to be floating across the air. When it reached them it pulled back the hood, taking care to avoid touching the ears, and gently placed it on her shoulders. A bulkier elf came out behind her, forgoing the robe. This elf was dressed in full mail and walked like he didn't notice the weight. Considering his size, Travis figured he didn't feel it.

"Greeting, traveler," the female elf said with a slight bow.

"Tell them who I am," the Captain demanded.

"Who are you to command such as I?" she asked.

"The heir of the Rising Sun," the Captain declared meeting her eye.

She backed up a step, and the male elf rushed to her side his blade half drawn. She placed a hand on his arm stopping him.

"Peace, brother, he is of no threat to us. Are you the heir of the Rising Sun? Or are you more like the Bleeding Sun?" she asked.

"I am the best of both. I will take the best parts of their legacies, but I follow the path of my other fathers," the Captain said.

"I see. Then you are the Setting Sun as was promised so long ago. We have come as covenanted, and so have you. Will our reparations be met?" she asked delicately.

"In time, for now, I have nothing to offer you," the Captain said sadly, and since Travis knew him so well, he heard the embarrassment hidden in his voice.

"Then how can we trust your word? The Bleeding Sun gave us his word, and it nearly killed us. Your family has not been the most trustworthy. Not even to their allies," she replied.

"Sadly, this is so, but as I said, I am the best of both," the Captain assured her.

"I wish I could believe it," she said sadly turning away.

"Will you take the word of a juggernaut?" Travis called to her.

She started and turned to him, her mouth slightly open. She eyed him and held her hand out to him. Travis's legs felt like jelly but he kept his pace steady and his footing firm. He stopped before he got to her and kneeled down reaching up to grasp her hand. Her other hand wrapped around his and he felt the calluses on her warm hands. A tingle went up her arms as she looked into his eyes.

"Are you lying to me?" she asked.

Travis shook his head and slowly reached into his pack. Her brother was at her side again, this time with his sword fully drawn and she didn't tell him to put it away. Travis pulled out his canteen and extracted his hand regretfully from hers to open the top of his canteen.

He poured a small amount of the vine syrup into the lid and raised it to his lips. He drank the capful and replaced the cap. The elf watched him curiously, waiting for him to collapse. A few minutes later, he remained unchanged, and she sighed and motioned for him to stand.

"I will accept him as one testimony, but I will need more than the word of one man," she said to the Captain.

Bubbles came from the shadows grumbling to himself and came and sat in front of her. She reeled in surprise, bringing her hand to her mouth.

"Hello little brother, you would speak on this man's behalf?" she asked him.

Bubbles grumbled something Travis was sure wasn't the most flattering. The elf found something he said funny because she giggled. The tinkling sound made Travis's skin tingle and his blood rush through his veins. Arete, not to be outdone came to up to her as well and added her two cents.

"Well, that is odd, but I see your point. Very well, Setting Sun, I accept these testimonies for now. Have you anyone of note that will speak for you? Keep in mind I see you fallen druid, and I do not count you among those of note," she asked.

"I will," Javier said stepping forward shooting Xanthamius a look but otherwise didn't acknowledge her comment.

"Who are you?" she asked looking him up and down.

Javier pulled his sword from his back and placed it point down in front of him. He flexed his shoulders sprouting his wings and looked her in the eye and said, "I am Javier, High Commander of the Night Angels."

The male elf knelt down at the sight and then stood to lift his own sword in a salute. Javier nodded at him acknowledging the salute but kept his attention on the female, who was clearly the leader between the two.

"So you are. Do you vouch for this man?" she asked.

"I have never liked the idea of one man ruling the word, or having as much power as he will undoubtedly claim, but if there was ever a man born to wield such a burden, it's him. He will make us all proud and he is a living legend that makes his legend pale to the truth of what he is," Javier replied.

She stood motionless with no sign of what she thought of what Javier said, but Travis could tell it wasn't what she wanted to hear. The Captain's birthright was going to be fulfilled, so why would she fight it? This was a good thing.

"Excuse me, your elfness," Right asked, "but what more do you want? The Captain is…"

"The best kind of man you'd want," Left finished.

The elf looked at them and screamed. Her brother rushed forward again but she was already gone and standing between the twins. She held a face in each hand looking at them alternately. She whispered to herself and then walked around them eyeing them.

"Would you like us to drop trousers?" Right asked.

"So you can see how identical we really are?" Left asked.

"Would you?" she asked with bright eyes.

The twins both turned bright red, "No!"

"Oh," she said disappointedly. She turned to the Captain, "Where did you find these two? It has been generations since two that shared one soul have been born. Do they follow you as well?"

"I found them in an orphanage and I knew what they were. They had no parents, so I looked after them and sent them to be trained and cared for. They found their way back to me on their own," the Captain said.

"I see. A rare gift. I cannot deny you gather to you the best that the world has to offer. You have master liar, a champion, a thief, an assassin, a general, a druid, and one who would save the whole world. Did you know who and what they were when you gathered them?" she asked looking the Captain over again.

"I did, but for everyone you see here, there are ten more that were cast aside. I have never been one to settle for half measures or men of shaky resolve. They will forge their own destinies but for now, they are bound to me as well," he said.

She turned and looked into the forest considering what he had said, and didn't notice one of her locks fall free from her braid and caress her cheek. Travis considered tucking it behind her ear for her, but she did it herself before he got the courage up. She glance at her brother who nodded to her and she threw him a dirty look not knowing Travis could still see her. When she turned back to the Captain, her composure was back in place like a mask.

"Very well, Setting Sun, I approve of you. I only pray to the stars that my decision does not curse my people again," she said softly.

She turned back to the hut and played with the cloak resting around her shoulders, motioning to her brother. He sheathed his sword and fell into place beside her.

"Wait!" Travis called out.

She stopped and half turned to him and he took that as an invitation to join her. He came up to her and reached back into his pack. Travis didn't miss the tightening of her brother's grip on his sword. He threw him a wink, which drew a frown, but pulled a present from his pack for her.

"What is this?" she asked feeling the shiny plastic wrap.

"It is a delicacy we eat from the land of my fathers. It is known as chocolate," he grinned.

"Chocolate? Is it made from animals?"

"No, it's made from beans. Try it. It's delicious."

She bit down on the wrapper and made a face. She looked at him clearly upset, "I do not see the appeal."

Travis laughed and gently took the chocolate from her and unwrapped it, "It has a cover to protect it."

He saw the pink at the tip of her ears but didn't say anything to draw attention to it. She took the chocolate from his hand and took a hesitant bite. She chewed twice and then stopped. Her eyes grew wide and she dropped the chocolate in surprise. Travis reached out to snatch the chocolate from the air and froze at he caught it.

Her brother had closed the small gap between them and had a sword at his throat. The Captain had seen the move coming and had appeared in time to stop the blade. The two warriors locked eyes and strained at each other. Travis felt sorry for the elf until he realized that neither was gaining ground. They stood with silent snarls on their faces as they struggle for dominance. At some unseen cue they broke apart but kept each other in view.

The elf moved first trying to surprise him, but the Captain flipped over him and kicked him between the shoulders throwing him off balance. When he spun to face the Captain, the Captain hit his arm numbing the hand and then knocked the blade from his hand. It flew end over end at the stunned female elf. Travis didn't think as he threw himself at her and bore her to the ground out of harm's way. The blade flew past his shoulder grazing him but causing no real damage.

Travis spared a glance at the Captain and saw that he was holding the elf down while making sure that Travis was okay. Travis gave him a small nod and then checked on his elf. She was looking up at him, watching him carefully. Her face still gave no idea of what she was thinking, but somehow he got the distinct impression that she did not approve of him touching her. He hastily stood up and helped her to her feet. He was lost in her eyes with a stupid grin and didn't even notice Slappy looking at his shoulder. The male elf struggled momentarily, but the Captain held him fast.

"How are you Travis?" the Captain asked.

"Good, sir," Travis replied, still looking into the elf's eyes, "Just a scratch, nothing to be worried about."

The male elf struggled against the Captain again. The Captain kicked the elf's sword to Javier and then let him go.

"All you alright?" Barry asked.

The elf's eyes narrowed at Barry and her emotionless mask broke slightly. She regarded him carefully before answering, "Yes, I am unharmed. I was merely startled by the taste of this 'chocolate'. It is not anything I have ever tasted before. Are you able to make more?"

"I don't …" Barry started.

"Not you, Silvertounge. I was speaking to Travis," she snapped.

"Sorry, I never was much of a cook. I just bought the stuff and was saving it for a special occasion. I figured if a beautiful woman such as yourself isn't special enough then nothing is," Travis replied.

She raised an eyebrow at him, "Bold, but this chocolate is worth the insolence."

"Well, it ain't insolence if it's truth, ma'am," he said with a grin, pressing the chocolate into her hand.

"Perhaps," she said with a slight smile, "Come Azruf. We are leaving."

Azruf went to his sister's side and wrapped an arm around her protectively as they walked into the jungle.

"You forgot your sword!" Javier called out.

"Keep it," Azruf called back gruffly, "The High Commander of the Knight Angels needs a proper sword. If we meet again, you may return it if you wish."

"Thank you," Javier shouted at them.

"Take care and farewell your highness!" Barry called to her.

She spun glaring at him, her emotionless mask abandoned. She started to say something, but Azruf pulled her into the jungle, and they didn't hear what she said. The group looked at Barry who shrugged.

"She was too arrogant, even for a woman," Barry explained dodging Asha playful swing.

"I don't know if I've ever been in a more…interesting group," Xanthamius hesitantly.

"Aww do ya mean it or are ya just bein' nice ta meh?" Asha asked with a wink.

"Welcome travelers to the village in the Eye," the old man said interrupting, "Come, join us for our evening meal and rest."

"Thank you," Barry said brushing past him.

The group filed in past him eager to rest and eat.

Chapter

TWENTY TWO

They rested at the Eye for two weeks while they waited for their hosts to prepare the island. They refused to speak about what was needed or how much longer it was going to be. They had tried to stop the Captain and his men from training, but snarl from the *otorgas* cut their arguments short. They bowed and retreated back to their preparations.

After the morning's training, Javier pulled the Captain to the side to talk to him. "Sir, I don't mind the free food and the R and R, but we are on a timeline that we don't quite know here."

"Are you referring to Aster?" the Captain asked.

"I am, sir," Javier replied.

"Don't worry about that just yet, Javi, Xanthamius and I have been keeping an eye on it," the Captain assured him.

"How?" Javier asked.

"According to our friendly neighborhood exile, there are two locations where the Temple rests. It shifts randomly between the two. It will stay at either one for at least six months, but it could stay there years," the Captain explained, "They were getting close to the Temple and then it shifted. Aster had to turn his camp around and go back the way they came. At the rate that they travel, it should be about two months before they get there now. The temple's current location is less than a week away from us now."

"Oh, well, if that's the case, what's the rush?" Javier laughed.

The watched some of the other sparing and honing their skills. Asha went thundering by on top of Bubbles waving a sword that was clearly too large for her, yet she had insisted on carrying it. As far as they knew the *otorgas* were roughly six months old, and were approaching full size. Xanthamius explained that the animals were quick to grow but not so quick to mature. While they might be big enough to ride now, they would need a lot of training to become suitable mounts.

Bubbles was the largest of the three *otorgas* and Xanthamius had declared him ready to ride and begin learning how to fight with Asha. When she heard the news, Asha immediately went to Travis and explained to him that it would be beneficial to his health to give her his spare sword. He didn't argue with her, he just handed it over and laughed while she tried to handle the large sword. Javier considered putting a stop to it, but decided against it. While considered the oversized sword ridiculous, he didn't have the courage or desire to tell Asha that.

Javier watched them stumble through maneuver after maneuver, failing at each one, yet enjoying themselves immensely. Javier could squash the feelings of envy. A furry head bumped against his hand, and Javier didn't need to turn to know that Arete was standing next to him now. He rubbed her ear just how she liked it. It made him feel better having her close to him and to be able to touch her. She was almost shoulder height, the size Xanthamius said she needed to be before he started riding her.

"Don't worry Arete; we will be doing that soon too. Only we'll do it better," Javier whispered to her.

Arete gave him a look that said she already knew they were going to do better, so why was he bringing it up. Javier chuckled to himself, the last of his resentment and envy evaporating faster than that morning's mist. There was always mist in the mornings, but this morning's mist was stubbornly refusing to burn off. Javier took a moment to look at it but gave it a mental shrug, accepting it as part of phenomenon that was Avalon.

This morning, Asha had also convinced or threatened the twins into helping her train Bubbles. The twins would "ambush" Asha and Bubbles, and who would then fight themselves free. It wasn't hard to beat such odds, but it was hard to do it together, as partners. Javier decided they needed more of an opposition so he motioned to Arete and they went over to help with the train as well. This would help the twins escape injury while helping Asha and Bubbles face a worthy foe.

Their involvement extended the morning's usual training session but they finished satisfied with their work. To cool down before breakfast, they all went for a quick swim in the lake. They *otorgas* enjoyed the swimming session more than their riders and would often stay in the water longer, splashing and playing. Most mornings it took a while to coax them out of the water but today they left them to their games and got ready for breakfast.

They walked toward the center of the camp where their hosts had left out a breakfast out for them as was usual. This time it was different. They were surprised to find the old man waiting for them with his pleasant smile. They hadn't seen him since their arrival at the camp. He wasn't sure but Javier believed he was the leader here or something along those lines.

"What are you doing here?" Javier asked.

"I am waiting," the old man replied.

"What's your name?" Javier asked pleasantly.

The old man didn't respond to the question. He merely continued smiling and motioned to the meal in front of them. Javier hadn't really expected him to answer the question, after all no one else would tell them their names.

The rest of the squad trickled in and dug into the food. This morning's breakfast held a special treat, meat. Their hosts refused to kill anything so the only time they had meat available was one the animals died from old age or some other injury.

"So, my old friend," Barry asked with his mouth full, "How long 'till that tree of yours lets us over?"

"I am trying to decide if you are talking about the amount of time we have been friends, or if you are poking fun of my age," the old man answered.

"Does it matter?" Barry asked.

"No I suppose not," the old man decided, "How is your meal, Captain? This particular pig wandered in last night and died from her wounds. It may have been wounded by one of your *otorgas.*"

"Are ya gonna ask us ta not let 'um hunt? 'Cus if that's the case, imma tell ya now the answer is no. They gonna be the way nature intended an' yur not gonna change that," Asha snapped.

The old man laughed softly, "I think we would have better luck asking the clouds to not rain. No, they are acting as they were intended and the Eye is tolerant of animals, you have no need to fear for them. Have you any plans for the day?"

"Stop changing the topic, old man," Barry said around a fruit he was eating.

"She asked a question, I answered it," the old man said.

"A question you baited. You changed the topic three times already which means you really don't want to talk about it. That only makes me more curious. There are only so many secrets a man can keep before others start to notice. The fact that you don't want to tell us, makes me think it's something we really need to know," Barry countered.

"And if I am?" the old man asked.

"Then we will have problems, I suspect," Barry countered.

"Well that's strange, I thought you were here to bring peace and hope," the old man mused.

"Peace is bought by blood," the Captain answered.

"Is that so?" the old man asked.

"It is," the Captain affirmed, "Your cooperation would be preferred but not required. You have something that I need and I will not let you keep it from me. It was never yours to keep nor to protect, so I have no obligation to play your little games or pass your tests."

"My, aren't you a fountain of knowledge?" the old man smirked.

"*I* am the Guardian of Avalon, heir to the thrones of mankind and of the light," the Captain growled, "Who are you to deny me my birthright?"

"Correction," the old man said raising a finger, "You are *one* of the Guardians of Avalon. I will not give you the tool you will use to destroy this world again. You are not worthy of your title nor are you worthy of your heritage. The swords and the daggers will not be yours, go back to where you came from, pretender."

The Captain stared at the old man expressionless for several seconds across his breakfast. The squad had stopped eating, some with mouthfuls had stopped chewing, watching the exchange to see what would happen.

Javier wasn't sure what the Captain was going to do to this affront, but he was sure that he wouldn't let it stand. He knew the Captain was an honorable man, and there wasn't a person alive he respected more, but he also knew that disrespect was the Captain's one weakness. He never overreacted, but he did respond or react in some way when he was being blatantly disrespected.

So he watched the Captain curiously to see what he would do. During the few tense minutes while they studied each other, a few more of the village's elders came and sat with them. The Captain took a deep breath and asked the old man again.

"Reconsider. These are my heirlooms, they belong to me, and I will have them," he said.

"No," the old man flatly refused.

"Last chance," the Captain warned.

"You are merely Lancelot the Fallen, born again, come to destroy this world. I judge you and find you wanting," the old man spat.

"So be it, I judge you as well, old man," the Captain snarled.

The Captain lunged across the narrow space between then and grabbed the old man by the neck, squeezing hard enough to make his muscles bulge and the veins to stand out. The brittle bones crackled as they succumbed to the Captain's tremendous strength. Javier jumped to his feet incredulous.

"Captain! What have you done? This is *not* the way we do things. I can't let this slide, sir. Why did you do that?" Javier screamed.

The Captain ignored him and the crumpled body of the old man. He was too busy considering the women carefully, "What about you? Will you bar me from what is mine by right?"

The women trembled, but nodded together. Javier was suddenly afraid for the women's lives. He recognized the bunching of shoulder muscles that told him the Captain was preparing to lunge again. Javier leapt across the gap between them and threw his smaller bulk at the Captain, using his momentum, along with his new magic, to throw the Captain across the clearing and into a tree.

"RUN!" Javier bellowed.

The women needed no second prompting. They fled, leaving Javier between them and the man who wanted to kill them. The Captain raised his sword and Javier drew his elven sword in response.

"Move, Lieutenant," the Captain ordered.

"No," Javier said.

"Move. Now," the Captain ordered again.

"You asked me once to keep an eye on you, so that you would know if you ever got out of hand. This is it," Javier informed it.

"This is not it Lieutenant, now move or I will make you," the Captain warned.

"I am not a Lieutenant anymore. I am Rider Javier, High Captain of the Knight Angels, and I say you will not have them," Javier vowed planting his feet.

"Javi, you can't take him," Travis warned.

"No, I can't," Javier admitted, "But what I can do, is buy you time. Go. Have Patty hide your trail. I'll buy you all the time I can."

The Captain howled in fury and charged him. Javier felt, rather and saw his fellow Knights run after the women, to protect them or flee he didn't care. The only thing he could care about right now was his one-time friend coming at him with blood in his eyes.

They clashed, sending sparks flying with every blow. The

Captain's fury fueled him, sending increasingly harder and harder strikes. Javier met him stroke for stroke, not giving any ground to the Captain, not really believing that he was pulling it off. The tempo changed and Javier flowed to the new one flawlessly. Their foot work entered into the battle making them dance around each other, rendering the Captain unable to follow after his quarry. They battled unfettered for several minutes, and Javier knew he had given the squad enough time to get away, so he let the worry go and immersed himself into the fight, hoping to calm the Captain down, or let him vent all his frustration out.

"I am death incarnate, Javier," the Captain grunted between swings.

The words caught Javier off guard and he staggered momentarily. The Captain exploited the lapse and stabbed Javier in his left arm, rendering it useless. The pain coursed down his arm, and he stumbled back holding his sword up in his one good hand hoping to fend the Captain off. The expected attack didn't come. He looked up to see the Captain's eyes still filled with bloodlust and he was only giving Javier the time he needed to set himself to embrace death.

"So, this is it then?" Javier asked.

"You shouldn't have opposed me, you knew that I would kill you," the Captain replied.

"Only if we fought," Javier laughed in spite of himself, "But that's what is required of me."

"How so?" the Captain inquired.

"I am a Knight Angel. It may not have been the life I was born to follow, but it is the destiny I have chosen. I will stop injustice or die trying, no matter who it is," Javier answered.

"Even if it's me? Your Captain and king?" the Captain asked.

"Especially if it's you," Javier said resolutely, "Do you remember the words you taught me? '*I am a child of the light sworn to fight in the night. I am the bane of darkness. Vengeance is my calling, justice is my charge, and mercy is my guide. As darkness gathers, I stand firm, the last shield of the light, the shining bastion of strength against the darkness. By blood and honor I fight and by blood and honor I die. The Sons of darkness fear the Night, for Justice is come.*'"

"You could still let me pass and live. You should do that. Move aside and choose life," the Captain advised.

"I was never one to die old and in my sleep," Javier chuckled, "Now is as good a time as any to embrace death."

"Move aside and choose life," the Captain repeated.

"I choose glory," Javier countered.

The Captain raised his sword in salute and Javier saluted back. While the Captain charged Javier extended his wings and faced the Captain's charge with his feet set and his face toward the sun. Javier absorbed the clash and embraced the darkness. He smiled, knowing that even while he sacrificed his life, he scored a hit on the Captain's leg, slowing him down. Then he knew nothing.

Slappy went to the breakfast fire and wolfed down the portion of pork he had carved off for himself. It tasted so much better than he had been expecting. The quality of meat that he had subjected his stomach to lately had been a disappointment at best and nauseating at their worst. This particular pork chop would have put any four-star restaurant to shame. He wiped his hands on his pants before digging into his fruit and another pork chop. His pleasant feeling evaporated when he bit down on the other pork chop. He turned his attention to the conversation that had sprung up next to him.

"So, my old friend," Barry asked grinning, "How long till that tree of yours lets us over?"

"I am trying to decide if you are talking about the amount of time we have been friends, or if you are poking fun of my age," the old man answered.

Normally he would have groaned inwardly very loudly and maybe sighed outwardly at their display of one-upmanship, but he understood the undercurrents going on here. The two of them were feeling each other out and playing out the time-honored tradition of negotiating.

"Does it matter?" Barry asked.

"No, I suppose not," the old man admitted grudgingly. Point for Barry, "How is your meal, Captain? This particular pig wandered in last night and died from her wounds. It may have been from one of your *otorgas*."

"Are ya gonna ask us ta not let 'um hunt? 'Cus if that's the case, imma tell ya now the answer is no. They gonna be the way nature intended an' nothing' ya say is gonna change that," Asha snapped, her hands reaching for her favorite dagger.

For a woman that seemed to have no loyalty to anyone or anything the first time he ran into her, she had come along way. Of course, she was more of an animal back then, only listening to Patty, and occasionally the Captain.

The old man laughed softly, "I think we would have better luck asking the clouds to not rain. No, they are acting as they were intended and the Eye is tolerant of animals, you have no need to fear for them."

True. Point to the old man.

"Stop changing the topic, old man," Barry said around a fruit he was eating.

Odd, not the normal response, but then again the villagers and Barry had been having this verbal sparring for the better part of two weeks, so maybe even Barry had his limits.

"She asked a question, I answered it," the old man said.

Slappy smelled a set up. That comment was a little too prepared.

"A question you baited. You changed the topic three times already which means you really don't want to talk about it. That only makes me more curious. There are only so many secrets a man can keep before others start to notice. The fact that you don't want to tell us, make me think it's something we really need to know," Barry snapped.

Well, set and match to the old man. Barry didn't seem too concerned about winning this time. It appeared to him that the time for games had passed and Barry was after results now.

"And if I am?" the old man asked.

"Then we will have problems," Barry warned.

"Well, that's strange, I thought you were here to bring peace and hope," the old man mused.

"Peace is only bought by the blood of those strong enough to strive for it," the Captain answered.

"Is that so?" the old man asked.

"It is," the Captain affirmed, "Your cooperation would be preferred but it is not required. You have something that I need and I will not let you keep it from me. It was never yours to keep or to protect, so I have no obligation to play your little games or pass your tests."

"My, aren't you a fountain of wisdom?" the old man smirked.

Slappy's veteran nerves started tingling, violence was about to erupt. He casually set his plate down and wiped any traces of grease from his fingers.

"*I* am the Guardian of Avalon, heir to the thrones of mankind and of the light," the Captain growled, "Who are you to deny me my birthright?"

"Correction," the old man said raising a finger, "You are *one* of the Guardians of Avalon. I will not give you the tool you will use to destroy this world again. You are not worthy of your title nor are you worthy of your heritage. The swords and the daggers will not be yours, go back to where you came from, pretender."

The words shocked Slappy, but he didn't let the shock show on his face. His uncle had trained him well enough to allow him near perfect control of his facial expressions. He gauged the silence between the Captain and the old man and decided that their tension was only rising. While a few more village elders gathered, Slappy eased himself out of a lounging position and into a comfortable sitting position that he could jump from at a moment's notice.

"Reconsider. These are my heirlooms, they belong to me, and I will stop at nothing to have them. You cannot stop me, so reconsider," the Captain said carefully.

"No," the old man flatly refused.

"Last chance," the Captain warned.

"You are merely Lancelot the Fallen, born again, come to

destroy this world. I Judge you and find you wanting," the old man spat.

"So be it, I judge you as well, old man," the Captain snarled.

Even though he was tensed and prepared for action, he was not ready when the Captain lunged across the fire and snapped the old man's neck. Slappy heard the pop and was across the fire to the old man's side before he fell to the ground. When he reached the old man's side, he was surprised to find that the life had left his body. He looked up and met Javier's eyes. He gave him a small shake of his head, and then they both turned back to the Captain.

"Captain! What have you done? This is *not* the way we do things. Why did you do that?" Javier demanded.

The Captain ignored him and spoke to the women instead, "What about you? Will you bar me from what is mine by right?"

The women trembled, but nodded together. They were clearly scared but were obviously determined to follow their leader's example.

"So be it, which of you will die first?" the Captain asked looking from one to the other.

"Sir, no, don't do this," Javier begged.

Slappy cocked his head slightly and saw that none of the squad would meet Javier's pleading eyes. They tried looking anywhere but where the body was or where Javier was standing.

The Captain ignored him and spoke to the women instead, "Are you certain you do not wish to reconsider?"

The women trembled, but nodded together. They were clearly scared out of their minds, and Slappy admired their commitment to their cause. He walked over so he could stand just behind the Captain.

"So be it, which of you will die first?" the Captain asked looking from one to the other.

"Sir, no, don't do this," Javier begged.

"He's right, Captain, don't do this," Slappy added.

The Captain lifted his sword prepared for a devastating attack on the women and Slappy could take no more of it. He weighed his options and did what he knew the whole squad knew needed to be done. He calmly took his own dagger and plunged it deep into the Captain's right eye. Slappy considered the body while it thrashed and then fall over, creating a puddle of blood and other fluids.

Slappy watched the great warrior die and pursed his lips in disgust. No, this was all wrong, this was not how it was supposed to be. There was no movement from the squad, just looks of disbelief, and he hated them for it. He kicked at the dead body and grunted to himself nodding. He knew what this was and why they did it, but he still hated them for it.

Even though his muscles still burned from the work out, Travis felt refreshed, and ready for action. Ever since he had become a Knight Angel, he had felt the energy traveling from the ground to fill his frame. He supposed the magic of the binding had other properties to go along with it, but he didn't realize that this level of recuperation was possible. It was so much different than a couple of weeks ago, but the training in the Eye had been different. Before it had still taken him an hour to get his energy back up, but here he was mere minutes from one of the most intense workouts of his life, and he was back to fighting shape.

He wasn't the first one to breakfast, so he waited his turn while he took in the conversation. The fruit looked fresh and delicious, but the roasted pig looked sublime and its scent was intoxicating.

"So, my old friend," Barry said with a full mouth, "How long till that tree of yours lets us over?"

Travis wasn't surprised that Barry was here with a plateful of food already. That one always seemed to know when there was free food to be had and how to be first in line. To be fair to him, after the squad was done with any spread, there wasn't much left, so it might be best for him to get there first. There were too many that wouldn't mind seeing him miss a meal or two.

"I am trying to decide if you are talking about the amount of time we have been friends, or if you are poking fun of my age," the old man answered.

Travis snorted at the joke. He had been carving at the pig and felt his knife slip. He jerked his other hand back but was too slow pulling back. He inspected his hand and found no wound. Huh. Lucky break for him. Still, Barry had a fair point. The old man looked like a piece of worn leather. The kind of old that told you he had been around the block once or twice or fifty times but still had that timeless look that seemed like he would outlive them all.

"Does it matter?" Barry asked.

Another fair point.

"No, I suppose not," the old man decided, "How is your meal, Captain? This particular pig wandered in last night and died from her wounds. It may have been from one of your *otorgas*."

"Are ya gonna ask us ta not let 'um hunt? 'Cus if that's the case, imma tell ya now the answer is no. They gonna be the way nature intended an' yur not gonna change that," Asha snapped.

When her hands dropped to her dagger, it drew Travis's attention, but he decided that it was more for show than for action. He turned his attention to his meal instead. Important things first, homicidal femme fatales could wait until after breakfast.

The old man laughed softly, "I think we would have better luck asking the clouds to not rain. No, they are acting as they were intended and the Eye is tolerant of animals, you have no need to fear for them. What are your plans for today?"

"Stop changing the topic, old man," Barry said around a fruit he was eating.

Travis looked up from his breakfast, unable to ignore the sudden hostility in Barry's voice.

"She asked a question, I answered it," the old man said innocently.

"A question you baited. You changed the topic three times already which means you really don't want to talk about it. That only makes me more curious. There are only so many secrets a man can keep before others start to notice. The fact that you don't want to tell us, make me think it's something we really need to know," Barry countered.

Travis frowned at Barry, who as usual, ignored him completely. Once he realized that his frown was not having the desired result, he regretfully set his plate to the side.

"And if I am?" the old man asked.

"Then we will have problems, I suspect," Barry countered.

Now things were heating up quickly. He eased himself in his seat, and check to make sure his sword was close by. He figured it would only be a moment before he would have to stop these idiots from killing each other.

"Well, that's strange, I thought you were here to bring peace and hope," the old man mused.

"Peace is never bought, except by blood," the Captain answered.

"Is that so?" the old man asked turning to the Captain.

"It is," the Captain said smiling without mirth, "Your cooperation would be preferred but not required. You have something that I need, and I will not let you keep it from me. It was never yours to keep nor to protect, so I have no obligation to play your little games or pass your tests."

"My, aren't you a fountain of knowledge today?" the old man smirked.

"*I* am the Guardian of Avalon, heir to the thrones of mankind and of the light. I will not be dissuaded," the Captain snarled, "Who are you to deny me my birthright?"

The hair on the back of his neck stood up at the heated words. Something important was about to happen, he could feel it in his bones.

"Correction," the old man said haughtily raising a finger, "You are *one* of the Guardians of Avalon. I will not give you the tool you will use to destroy this world again. You are not worthy of your nor are you worthy of your heritage. The swords and the daggers will not be yours, go back to where you came from, pretender."

Travis looked between the old man and the Captain trying to decide what the Captain was thinking. The only thing that Travis knew for certain was that he hadn't seen the Captain this furious in a long time. The deathly silence coming from him only meant that he was planning something violent soon.

While the Captain took time to take a few calming breaths, the village's other elders came to sit with old man. The women were staring down their nose at them like women were prone to do when they felt the men were doing something incredibly stupid. While Travis would never doubt the fairer sex, his experience had taught him that they were just as capable and prone to monumentally stupid actions as men were.

"Reconsider, these are my heirlooms, they belong to me, it is my birthright to have them," he demanded.

"No," the old man said stubbornly.

"Last chance," the Captain warned. Travis blinked at the forwardness but the Captain wasn't finished, "You would be wise to take this offer. No one knows who else might suffer from your foolish pride."

The Captain's eyes flickered to the women seated on either side of the old man. Travis considered them as well.

"You are merely Lancelot the Fallen, born again, come to destroy this world. I judge you and find you wanting," the old man declared spitting at the Captain's feet.

"So be it, old man, I judge you as well," the Captain snarled.

The Captain lunged across the narrow space between then and grabbed the old man by the neck, squeezing with all his considerable strength. The frail neck bones popped as they snapped. Travis jumped to his feet in shock and horror, going to stop the Captain but it was too late. The old man's lifeless body fell to the ground in a rumpled heap. The Captain didn't even look at Travis while he considered the other women nearby.

"Sir! What have you done?" Travis demanded.

The Captain ignored him and spoke to the women instead, "What about you? Will you bar me from what is mine by right?"

The women trembled, but nodded together. They were clearly scared but were obviously determined to follow their leader's example.

"So be it, which of you will die first?" the Captain asked looking from one to the other.

"Sir, no, don't do this," Travis begged.

He cast glances around to the rest of the squad, but they wouldn't meet his eyes, and they held their seats resolutely. He turned back to the Captain in time to see him slide his sword from the chest of the oldest of the women.

"NO!" Travis screamed.

The Captain continued to ignore him, "Which of you is next? The youngest perhaps?"

The remaining women clung to each other sobbing. The squad looked upset, but instead of doing anything, they just averted their eyes. Travis cried out as he watched the Captain raise his sword for another thrust. Travis threw himself at the Captain, but got casually back handed and sent flying for his trouble. He painfully picked himself up as the Captain dispatched another.

"Who's next?" the Captain asked.

Only sobs answered him. The Captain drew his sword back to swing at the women again. Travis cried out as he tried to close the gap between them. His wings exploded from his back and magical flames coated his sword. He drove the sword through the

Captain's back and then back out again. Travis's hands fell numbly to his side and he didn't hear his own sword clatter to the ground. He closed his eyes momentarily but eventually looked down at the Captain in horror, barely able to make eye contact. His sword's path left a gaping hole in the Captain's back. He hadn't been sure how to stop the Captain, so he did the only thing he could. He stopped him permanently.

The Captain's face was in the dirt and the hole in his back sluggishly pumped his blood out. The Captain turned his head enough to look Travis in the eye. They stared into each other's eyes until the life drain from them. Travis let himself go and fell to his knees weeping. He heart felt torn to pieces, while whole world crumbled around him.

Chapter

TWENTY THREE

Asha felt Bubbles muscles ripple under her, and it thrilled her beyond words. Among all of the Captain's team, she was the one who knew the true value of freedom, and relished the extra freedom that her *otorga* was able offer her now. She pulled up next to the lake and got off of his back so that he could drink and rest in the shade of one of the nearby trees.

Even though he was trying to be tough for her, she could feel the slight trembling in his muscles that signaled just how tired he was getting. Xanthamius might be right that Bubbles was near full grown, but he still had to fill out. Apparently, it was good for him to constantly carry her, but she didn't want to push him too far. The benefits of the development in their relationship were already beginning to show. The men might be too heavy for their *otorga* to carry them, but Asha was noticing how much stronger her bond with Bubbles was was. At times she could almost feel his mind.

She saw the squad gathering for breakfast but didn't move to join to them at the fire. She and Bubbles had shared a wild boar that had wandered close to the camp the night before. The squealing had drawn the old man to them to see if he could help the poor creature, but the sight of Bubbles glowing red eyes and dripping fangs had changed his mind. She was so proud of her little Bubbles. He had learned how to scare people half to death with just a look. As if reading her thoughts, he gave her his best kitty grin, showing off his sparkling white fangs. Asha grinned back showing off her own fangs.

A movement to her left in her peripherals drew her attention, and she turn to face it. The Captain came towards her with the old man in tow. She nodded in respect to the Captain, but hid none of her distain for the old man. Bubbles jumped into the lake to swim a little and maybe catch a fish. She had noticed that a light swim after one of their training sessions helped his muscles relax. The mist from the lake was creeping onto the shore, so she had a hard time seeing where Bubbles was.

"Hello, Asha, how fairs your morning," the old man asked.

"Well enough, thank ya," she replied.

"Good, good, we wanted to speak to you concerning your Captain's request to approach and supplicate the Eye for the return of the heirlooms of the house of the Sun," the old man said nervously.

She picked up on the scent of his fear readily enough, and tried to fuel it by grinning at him in her most dangerous smile, seductive yet deadly. The Captain shifted, so Asha knew that he was annoyed but she didn't care in the least. Off by the shore, a couple of the village members brought Bubbles some treats. She ignored them. Such occurrences were common.

"Asha," the Captain sighed wearily

"Sir?" she asked sweetly.

"These men have something in mind. Something that will help us get what we need," the Captain informed her.

"Wat do ya need from meh?" she asked.

"Come, walk with us," the Captain insisted, walking away.

Asha shrugged and followed after him. Bubbles was still being entertained by the villagers so she didn't want to tear him away from them. He liked their fawning and she didn't mind it. The Captain and the old man led her through the village and Asha trailed behind them humming a little ditty to herself, not really paying attention to where they were going. They eventually came to a hut that had been built recently on the edge of the village. The Captain stopped short of the door and looked back at her before following the old man in, with Asha right behind him.

Inside the hut sat a cage with gold chains attached to the stone ground surrounded by several men from the village. The sight of the cage with its special chains froze her blood in her veins. She reached out with her mind towards Bubbles, but only got a fuzzy reply in return. She turned horrified eyes toward the Captain, who now blocked her exit from the hut.

"Bubbles won't be coming," the Captain informed her, "The kind village people drugged his food, so he'll sleep instead of us having to kill him."

"Sir, no, not this," Asha begged starting to freak out.

"Asha," he said gently.

"I got outta these once, an' I will again!" she screamed.

"Not this time," the Captain said apologetically, "I sent Patty away already. I'll tell him you died, and he will never come looking for you."

"NO! I don't believe this. Please, ya can't be tellin' me what I think yur about ta tell meh," Asha begged.

"These men needed something in return for their help. This is the only way I will get my crown," the Captain explained, "I need this to happen. I made promises to this world and I won't be stopped short of my goal."

"Ya made promises ta me, too, sir," Asha reminded him.

"I did indeed. I gave you your freedom and now I need it back. I never promised to keep you free. Your sacrifice will be remembered," the Captain assured her heading for the door.

Strong arms grabbed her from behind, catching her off guard. Her shock at seeing the cage prevented her from checking the corners and shadows of the hut like she normally would. They dragged her back towards the cage, but she fought them as she went.

"This ain't the Knight Angel way!" she cried out.

"I know," the Captain replied turning his back to her, "But it's the way it has to be. I am a king, and I can't let petty relationships come between me and my throne."

"Would ya really let yur lust fer power drive ya ta betray those closest to ya an' abandon all the things ya held dear?" she asked grunting with the effort of fighting off two men.

"I will not lose my crown like my fathers did. I was born to rule and come hell or high water I will do just that!" he shouted at her still not turning.

"If ya truly believe that then yur nothin' more than a fallen tyrant, an' are no better than yur uncle!" she threw at his back.

The Captain snorted at the comment. "Typical words from those too weak to understand what needs doing. See the bigger picture Asha, the ends justify the means, and right now you are the means I must use to secure my birthright."

"Then ya have truly let yur power twist an' corrupt ya," she decided.

She felt one of the cool chains brush against her arm and it felt like fire was branding her skin again. She felt her rage and desperation building again but his time she knew what to do, she knew how to defend herself. Her roar of defiance was loud and feral. The rage came bursting forward and her bloodrage activated.

She ripped her arms out of her captor's hands. She spun on them and snapped their necks before they even knew she was attacking them. She felt the air rippling behind her, giving her enough time to dodge the Captain's initial assault. He stumbled slightly, not expecting her to dodge. She spun, bringing her heel to his side with bone crushing force. She felt at least one rib break before she sent him flying through the hut wall. She jumped through the gap after him, continuing her attack before he could recover. He tried to fend her off, but with her bloodrage going, and his still dormant, there was no real fight.

Moments later, she was on top of his bleeding body, dagger poised, waiting to plunge into his body. He didn't beg or ask her to stop. His eyes just searched hers, trying to decide what she was going to do.

"Are you going to kill me?" he asked.

"You fell," she said, "Ya were willin' ta sell me for yur throne. I was da blood money you were goin' ta pay for your power."

"Will. You're the price I will pay," he smirked.

"You can't kill him," the old man warned from the door of the hut.

"Silence ya old goat. Yur next," she snarled.

"If you kill him you will be cursed. You are his demon, you know what will be required of you if you do that," he reminded her.

"I know what will be required of meh. I've always known. If that's what's waitin' fer meh, I will bear the curse, as me fathers have done through the centuries," she whispered.

"Your fathers are the ones who locked you away the first time, and you would still honor their wishes?" the Captain asked.

"This ain't got nothin' ta do with 'em. This is the promise made ta you, the real you. Not this shadow of a man that ya 'ave become. Ya taught meh honor, I suppose I best teach ya tha same. We do what needs doin'. If that mean's cursin' meself, then that's what I'll do," she replied.

"Asha…" the Captain started.

"Ya know what has ta happen now," Asha whispered slipping out a special knife, "Ya rembemer what ya told meh when ya gave meh this? Ya know wat it was meant fer. What it 'as ta do now."

"It doesn't have to. We can't still live," he told her.

"It was made fer this, as was I. I am a Demon Blades. I am the knife that keeps the good things of da world from turnin' ta the dark. It's what ya taught meh when I was just startin' out. Everythin' you taught me, everythin' ya stood for, tells meh now what ta do," she murmured tears streaming down her face.

"You hate me so much you would betray me? ME?!" he demanded.

"No, my king, I don' 'ate ya, not even a little. It's because I luv ya this much that I will do this ta ya," she answered through her tears.

"Ha! Love me. You don't even know the meaning of the word," he spat at her. "You will forever be remembered as the one who betrayed the Guardian of the Light!"

"Ya are no longer the Guardian. Goodbye, shadow of a former king," she sobbed.

"You dare…" he started.

He never got to finish. Asha's blade pierced his heart, stilling it. She pulled the dagger from his chest and placed against her own breast.

"I am the shield of the light…" she whispered before stilling her own heart.

Patrick hummed to himself while he whittled a statue. He was using minute streams of highly pressurized air to slice flakes off of the piece of wood he was carving. The effort of maintaining the wood while delicately shaving the block of wood was strenuous but it helped him focus his magic. So far, the feathers he was carving on his wooden duck looked perfect. A few delicate wooden feathers were sticking up like they would on a real duck.

The villagers didn't like him practicing his magic inside the village limits, so he had found himself a small boulder on the outskirts of the village to perch on while he practiced magic and explored new spells. He had discovered many new ones and was working on so many more.

He caught sight of Xanthamius wandering by, prompting him to set down the duck and jump up to go chase him down. He caught up to him before the druid reached the village proper.

"Xanthamius!" he shouted.

Xanthamius turned to him and raised an eyebrow in inquiry.

"Xanthamius the Wild! I challenge you to a duel!" Patrick shouted at him.

"Again?" Xanthamius sighed.

"I declare you to be an old raisin of a man, and to be unworthy of the title of druid," Patrick taunted.

"Careful boy, you may not like it when you wake up this bear,"

Xanthamius growled.

"I like it well enough," Patrick smiled, "So do you accept?"

"No," Xanthamius replied turning.

"Then a bet!" Patrick called out trying to stall him.

"A bet?" Xanthamius asked half turning.

"Yes, I bet I beat you today," Patrick replied.

"Pup, you haven't come close to beating me these past two weeks, and you've goaded me into a fight every day," Xanthamius said wearily.

"Ah, but today is different," Patrick smiled.

"Why is that?" Xanthamius asked.

"Today, chocolate is on the line," Patrick teased while pulling out a bar of chocolate.

"Chocolate?" Xanthamius gasped eagerly, "You would place that light blessed morsel as your wager?"

"I would," Patrick smirked.

"And in return?" Xanthamius asked.

"If I win you will declare me superior druid to our entire group and will spend the rest of the day trying to kiss Asha," Patrick said wickedly.

"That would be suicide," Xanthamius said nervously, "I agree to the first condition, but the second will never happen. Not even chocolate will tempt me."

"Ha ha! All too true," Patrick laughed, "I accept your

challenge!"

"My challenge…" Xanthamius sputtered but was cut off when Patrick launched his offensive.

He started with a rapid flurry of fire needles. Xanthamius waved the attack off with almost no effort. He launched an attack at Patrick, a massive fireball shaped like a fist. Patrick skipped to the side instead of blocking the blow. The first turned around and came at the back of his head but he skipped to the side again and pushed the fist at Xanthamius. Xanthamius was forced to destroy his own attack before it hit him.

When the smoke cleared, he was nodding to Patrick in respect when Patrick's next attack came at him. He had used the cover of the smoke to pull water from the lake and freeze it into spears. He launched the spears in waves with flame spears in between. He finished with a twin dragon's breath. He waited before attacking again to make sure the druid was okay. The attacks had driven Xanthamius to his knees, but the old druid seemed to be unshaken.

"Well done, pup, you may amount to something yet," he said softly, "but it will take more than that to bring down a trained Brother."

Xanthamius stood and faced Patrick, his eyes flowing golden, with arms crackling with power. He launched his own attacks at Patrick. Blizzards of tiny icicles launched themselves at Patrick, with torrents of flames following. Plants erupted from the ground grabbing his limbs, limiting his movements, while hordes of small bugs appeared form the forest to attack him and filling his nose.

Xanthamius kept sending wave after wave of attacks, popping Patrick's carefully constructed layers of protection, one by one. He could hear Xanthamius laughing at him. He knew he couldn't match Xanthamius on his best day yet, but having the druid rub his face in it like that was infuriating. His rage built and the made his blood boil. He went cold and felt something in himself change again. If he had been able to see himself he would have seen his eyes go golden and start blazing with power.

Patrick roared in primal rage and unleashed a wave of raw power. The ground around his was swept bare, while walls of air smashed into the bugs flinging them backwards, killing most of them. Xanthamius felt his weave tear apart and rebound onto him while he was thrown into the dirt.

"Yield," Patrick rumbled from above him.

Xanthamius considered pushing it, but decided against it. He nodded to Patrick, and slowly stood up. Patrick watched him to make sure that he didn't change his mind and suddenly attack him again.

"I yield," Xanthamius said, bowing his head.

Patrick felt himself relax, and the primal power leave his system. Xanthamius grinned at him and they walked back into the camp together. The lake's mist pooled around his feet as they made their way back to the camp, swirling and spinning in their wake. Patrick felt his head spin a little bit, and his vision swim.

"I must gather something from my hut," Xanthamius grumbled, "I will meet you at the morning's meal to fulfill the agreement."

"Can't wait to see you there," Patrick grinned.

He walked toward the breakfast spread, humming to himself and immensely proud that he had beaten the druid. The more important part of the duel, was that he had seen the spells that Xanthamius had used against him, and was certain that he would be not only be able to replicate it, but expand and improve them.

He was so lost in his thoughts that he didn't see the Captain standing in his way. He walked head long into him and bounced off into the dirt. He stood and dusted himself off while he apologized to him.

"Sorry, sir, I didn't see you there," Patrick apologized.

"Patty," the Captain said gently, "We need to talk."

"Sure what's up Captain?" Patrick asked.

"How is you gift coming along?" the Captain inquired.

"Great!"

"Good, good. I'm glad to hear that."

"Why do you ask, sir?"

"As you know, Patty, I am in need of certain things before I can assume the throne."

"Okay…"

"The druids of the Temple are vital to my plans, and on top of that they have some of the heirlooms I will need."

"Do you want me to beat them into submission for you?"

"No," the Captain chuckled, "Nothing so crass. What I need from you is going to be hard to accept but I need it all the same."

"What is it, sir," Patrick asked concerned.

"I need you to give me your Talent."

"My Talent, sir? If I do that, I won't be a druid. I'll lose part of my soul. I won't be myself anymore," Patrick replied panicking a little.

"I must have it Patty, if you don't give it up, the druids at the Temple will not join me nor will they help me. In fact, I would expect them to actively oppose me," the Captain explained.

"Sir, what you are asking is worse than death. Why not just kill me instead?" Patrick asked.

"They want to send a message. They will not let your line rise up again. They require this of me, so I will give it to them, one way or another," the Captain hissed dangerously.

"Sir, I won't let you," Patrick replied backing up.

"You have no choice in this Patty, it *will* happen," the Captain snarled keeping step with him.

"I do have a choice, sir, and I choose freedom, I choose life," Patrick spat, "There is always a choice, sir, and even if there wasn't, I would fight anyway, just like you taught me."

"This isn't the time or place Patty. This is for the greater good. You're a soldier, Patty, you know what it means to sacrifice," the Captain shot back.

"A soldier…" Patrick echoed softly.

"Yes, Patty, we know the meaning of sacrifice."

"A soldier…"

"Our lot is to suffer so that others don't have to. We shoulder the burden for those who never could," the Captain said gently.

"That is true, sir," Patrick responded, "but we are not soldiers."

"What do you mean?" the Captain asked confused.

"We are Marines," Patrick replied, his eyes flaring.

"That's what I meant," the Captain stammered.

"I'm sure you did, but you are not the man you are pretending to be. The Captain would never call me a soldier," Patrick grinned toothily, with no mirth in his smile.

He gathered energy to himself, as much as he had ever dared. He felt his vitality fill, but surprisingly it wasn't full yet. He gathered more mana, opening his fortitude completely. His frame glowed, and vibrated from the raw power.

"Patty! What do you think you're doing?" the Captain asked.

"What I must," Patrick answered.

"Stop it!" the Captain demanded.

"Even if you were my C.O., I still wouldn't follow that order," Patrick responded still gathering more and more mana.

"Patty…" the Captain said beginning to sweat.

"Not…now," Patrick grunted.

He felt his vitality stretching now. He knew that if he took in any more power, he would cause damage to himself. He took the mana he had gathered and wove a spell by instinct. He wasn't sure what it was going to do, but he could feel the rightness of it.

He *pushed* against the wrongness. It resisted his attack but he kept at it, pushing harder, making it bend to his will. It pushed even harder back driving him to his knees with the effort of keeping the spell up. His breath became raged and sweat ran freely down his face, but he wove on doggedly.

"Patty, what are you doing," the Captain slurred, his voice drawn out and warped.

Patrick ignored him pushing even harder. He roared in effort, his eye blazing in golden light. The Wrongness was trying hard to maintain itself but Patrick could feel it starting to crack. With a mighty push, he swept it to the side, shattering the hold it had on him. Patrick looked around and saw that he was alone. He felt around himself magically, making sure the wrongness was gone. When he was satisfied that it was, he laid his head down and went to sleep.

The tree where Barry had decided to rest this morning was a perfect place to carry a small breeze by him. He had trained with the twins earlier that morning. They tended not to inflict unnecessary damage when "helping" him hone his fighting skills. Thanks to their relatively gently training session, he wasn't as sore. If he had to venture a guess, he would actually be able to move normally today.

A sweet aroma reached his nose, making his eyes fly open. He sniffed the air again and sprang to his feet, making his way to where the smell was coming from. If his nose was correct, someone was cooking bacon. With the amount of red meat the Captain's squad was used to eating, there was no chance he would get any meat if he didn't get there first. He didn't blame them for hating him. It was the way he wanted it, but sometimes he wished that they didn't have to hate him so much. It was normal for him to get that kind of treatment for doing what he needed to do, but he did it anyway. The rewards far outweighed the repercussions.

He reached the breakfast spread late. To his dismay, most of the squad was already there and eating breakfast. To his surprise, there was still a large amount of meat left. He hurried and gathered a plate full of food, then sat down listening to the conversation.

"What are you doing here?" Javier asked.

"I am waiting," the old man replied.

"What's your name?" Javier asked using the smile Barry recognized. It was the one he used himself.

The old man didn't respond to the question. He merely continued smiling and motioned to the meal in front of them. Barry wasn't surprised that the old man didn't answer him. There was much more to the art of negotiating than asking questions.

"So, my old friend," Javier said with a full mouth, "How long 'till that tree of yours lets us over?"

Barry frowned at him. As far as he could remember, Javier never talked with a mouthful. The lieutenant had such good manners, it was infuriating at times.

"I am trying to decide if you are talking about the amount of time we have been friends, or if you are poking fun of my age," the old man answered.

"Does it matter?" Javier countered. Barry kept his face carefully blank. This wasn't right.

"No, I suppose not," the old man decided, "How is your meal, Captain? This particular pig wandered in last night and died from her wounds. It may have been from one of your *otorgas.*"

"Are ya gonna ask us ta not let 'um hunt? 'Cus if that's the case, imma tell ya now the answer is no. They gonna be the way nature intended an' yur not gonna change that," Asha snapped.

The old man laughed softly, "I think we would have better luck …"

"Stop changing the topic, old man," Barry snapped.

"She asked a question, I answered it," the old man replied innocently.

"Hmmm," Barry replied.

"Are you avoiding our questions?" the Captain asked.

"And if I am?" the old man asked.

"Then we will have problems, I suspect," the Captain growled.

"Well, that's strange, I thought you were here to bring peace and hope," the old man mused.

"Peace is never bought, except by blood," the Captain answered.

Barry laughed softly to himself.

"Is that so?" the old man asked glancing over at Barry.

"It is," the Captain affirmed, "Your cooperation would be preferred but not required. You have something that I need and I will not let you keep it from me. It was never yours to keep nor to protect, so I have no obligation to play your little games or pass your tests."

"My, aren't you a fountain of knowledge?" the old man smirked.

"Wow I think I just grew a third nipple!" Barry exclaimed looking down his shirt.

"*I* am the Guardian of Avalon, heir to the thrones of mankind and of the light," the Captain growled, completely ignoring Barry, "Who are you to deny me my birthright?"

"Correction," the old man said raising a finger, "You are *one* of the Guardians of Avalon. I will not give you the tool you will use to destroy this world again. You are not worthy of your title nor are you worthy of your heritage. The swords and the daggers will not be yours, go back to where you came from, pretender."

"Ah, snap. Big man is throwin' down," Barry drawled.

Barry was surprised when he felt the tension in the group rise. The Captain didn't even look his way when Barry let loose a giant belch.

"Reconsider, these are my heirlooms, they belong to me, and I will have them," he said.

"No," the old man flatly refused.

"Last chance," the Captain warned.

"Ohhhhh…now you done it old man. You done poked the bear," Barry taunted.

"You are merely Lancelot the Fallen, born again, come to destroy this world. I Judge you and find you wanting," the old man spat.

"Ouch, I felt that from here," Barry winced.

"So be it, I judge you as well, old man," the Captain snarled.

While the Captain lunged across the space between him and the old man, Barry yawned loudly. He smirked at the old man's corpse on the ground. He was aware that the Captain was now threatening the ladies that had come to the breakfast as well, but he walked over to the old man casually. He looked down at the old man studying the rumpled form on the ground.

"Get up," Barry demanded while the Captain ran the first woman through.

There was no response, so Barry nudged him with his foot.

"I'm bored with this, old man, get up," Barry ordered. The Captain ran the second woman through. The remaining women scattered into the village and the Captain gave chase while the squad sat stunned and immobile.

Barry glanced around and snorted in disgust, "Get up old man, I know you're not dead. I have spent my whole life getting into other people's heads. I know when someone is tinkering around in mine. You can stop pretending, I'm not buying what you're peddling."

He gave the old man's copse a healthy kick and the body dissolved. The Captain and his squad also faded away. The only thing Barry was disappointed about was the bacon fading too. His stomach rumbled in protest that his breakfast had been nothing more than an illusion.

Once the scene finished fading away, the old man stood a little ways away glaring at Barry. They locked eyes for a while, but Barry grinned at him winningly. The old man held his frown for a little while before cracking and smiling back at Barry.

"Well, you are the third one in the Lord Captain's army to break the spell," the old man mused, "I can count on one hand the amount of people who have previously broken this spell."

"Me, Patty, and Xanthamius?" Barry asked.

"No, we did not test the fallen druid, but the untrained druid was tested and shattered the spell. The only other person to do that was his grandfather," the old man corrected.

"Merlin? Merlin was here?" Barry asked.

"Of course. Nearly every druid comes here seeking wisdom. Merlin the Magnificent was the only one in recent memory to break the spell on him. The island tests you by showing you some of what it most fears is the greatest threat to Avalon. In this case, it wants to make sure there is someone to stop this Guardian in case he turns. It also tests against possible shadows in your heart," the old man informed him.

"So, what's that mean for me? I figured it out, so I don't think the test had the desired results when it comes to me," Barry mused.

"No, it did not, but you did impress the island somehow," the old man replied.

"So, the island, is it alive?" Barry wanted to know.

"Of course it is. It is alive as Avalon is. Every world is alive, you and I are the proof of it. The difference is that this island holds an energy unlike most. It has developed a conciseness that allows it to make decisions," the old man answered.

"Interesting. Where are my comrades?" Barry asked.

"They are not here," the old man smiled.

"Really? I hadn't noticed," Barry said drily.

The old man laughed softly before replying, "Well, then your powers of observation seem to be diminishing." He held up a hand to forestall Barry's argument. "I am certain that you are as sharp as you always were. To answer your question, they are still with the island."

"We...went there together, right?" Barry asked touching his head, shaking it a little.

"Yes," the old man replied.

"We exercised and then you came for us at breakfast, telling us it was time. The others insisted on going right away, so I didn't get my bacon because of you," Barry moped.

The old man grinned and handed Barry a small cloth. When he unwrapped it, Barry found four pieces of prime bacon. He inhaled three pieced and nibbled on the fourth, savoring the flavor.

"So, the others haven't returned yet?" he asked.

"No, you are the first, I am not sure why, but the island has decided to trust you," the old man replied.

"I am almost offended by that," Barry muttered.

"Well, you do have a reputation to uphold," the old man agreed.

"Yes, well, I *am* trustworthy, just not in the way people always think. I see the world differently, but I have always strived for the greater good," Barry explained.

"Of that I have no doubt. You always think with your mind, but before this is said and done, you will have to learn to think with your heart as well, Mr. *Green*," the old man said with a knowing smile.

"How…bah! Never mind. You wouldn't tell me even if you could. When can I expect the others?" Barry inquired.

"The island told me. As for your friends, it depends on them. They will return as the finish, that is all I know," the old man replied.

"Why the sudden openness? Don't get me wrong, I'm loving the ease of it, but it's such a departure from the norm," Barry asked skeptically.

"The island trusts you, that is good enough for me," the old man replied, "Don't worry about your comrades, they will return soon."

No sooner had he spoken than Slappy appeared, looking at something on the ground in disgust. His boot knife was out, held in his hand like he had just used it. He blinked a couple of times, like a man waking up from sleep walking. After shaking his head a few times, his eyes fell on the old man. Impassive as always, he walked up to the old man, considered him carefully, and then delivered a thundering slap on the cheek. The old man spun once before falling to the ground, clutching his face.

"If you wanted to know what I would do, you could have asked me, instead of playing some pathetic little side show," Slappy murmured in a tone Barry had come to recognize as his angry voice.

"It was not me, it was the island," the old man protested.

"If that makes you feel better," Slappy shot back.

"How did you know?" the old man asked.

"The bodies, they were dead before they should have been," Slappy replied.

A moment later Asha appeared on the ground with a gaping hole in her chest. Slappy flew to her side to see what he could do, while Barry turned steely eyes to the old man.

"Peace, warriors, this will pass, what the island does to its visitors, it repairs," the old man soothed, taking a few calculated steps back.

Even as he spoke, mist snaked its way up from the lake and filled the hole in Asha chest, sealing it and leaving only smooth skin. The armor was slower to close. Slappy glanced at the old man, a warning hidden in his eyes. The old man only motioned him back towards Asha. She groaned softly drawing everyone's attention. Quick as a wink, she disappeared from under Slappy's shadow and appeared a few feet away. She frowned and disappeared again, only to reappear in the same place again.

"You can't get to him that way, Shadow Rider," the old man informed her, "He is in the grip of the island, and it will not let him go just yet."

Asha snarled once, and appeared behind the old man in his shadow, atop Bubbles. Steel rasped softly as she slid her sword from its sheath, resting it on the old man's shoulder. Dark clouds boiled out from her, partially cloaking parts of her and Bubbles. Three glowing red eyes stared out from the shadows at the old man.

"If ya hurt 'im, or if 'e don' come back, imma kill ya slowly old man. Wat's more, imma like it," she smiled dangerously.

The old man giggled nervously as he nodded his acknowledgement, but was unable to meet her blood red eye.

TWENTY FOUR

As night fell, the group returned one by one. Their gruesome wounds were the only indication that something horrible had happened to them. By unspoken consent, no one spoke about what they saw, or what happened to them. This suited Asha just fine. Her story would just ask more questions than it answered and she was not prepared to answer any of them.

She didn't worry overly about the Captain or Patty until night truly fell and the moon she was named after was high in the sky above her. She didn't voice her concerns to anyone, mostly because she knew they were having the same ones.

The village people were extremely nice to them, bringing them food and blankets, along with whatever meager supplies they could offer. The squad thanked them but like Asha, they had no appetite, preferring to wait for the Captain and Patty in silence. Well, almost everyone.

Barry sat to one side, goring himself on the roast pig, starting with the bacon. He shared his meal with the *otorgas*, but no one else seemed inclined to eat. After a particularly large belch, Asha faded into the shadows slowly, so she wouldn't draw attention to herself. She appeared in Barry's blind spot, slipping a dagger into his mouth when he wasn't paying attention.

"Barry, why ya gotta be a lil' piggy when there are some of us missin'?" she asked sweetly.

Barry tried saying something, but the dagger limited his ability to actually talk.

"Now Barry, if ya don' give me a strait answer, I might just have ta hurt ya," she whispered nipping an ear with her fangs.

"I wa ho huh I hawh," he warbled sweating buckets.

"I'm glad ya like my delicates but what did I tell ya 'bout

lookin' at 'em?" she asked.

Barry made a lot of shocked and protesting noises.

"Oh, I see, ya weren't sayin' that," she reasoned.

He made a noise she figured meant yes.

"So yur, sayin' I'm ugly now are ya?" She asked.

Even louder protests followed this time but were cut short when she added a little pressure to his tongue with her dagger.

"So ya were lookin' at meh like ya weren't suppose ta?" she demanded.

A small noise between a protest and a sob came out this time.

"Asha!" Javier's voiced cracked from across the fire.

"Yessum Javi?" she asked innocently.

"Let him go," Javier ordered angrily, "You had your fun and so did we all watching you, but that is enough. You *will* let him go now."

"Oh, just a lil' bit more, Javi," she begged seductively.

"I said let him go," Javier repeated standing up.

"Oh, ya think I should?" She asked.

Javier advanced slowly, his wing unfurling behind him, "I am the High Commander of the Knight Angels, and I say, leave him be. Will you defy the light Shadow Rider?"

Asha blinked at him in surprise, not expecting such a harsh response. She let Barry go, not noticing he slumped to the ground. She watched Javier warily, feeling just a little scared of what he could do.

"Are ya okay, Javi? This ain't new to us," she asked, motioning to Barry.

"I'm fine," Javier snapped.

"Ya sure? This ain't like you," she replied.

"I…" Javier started, looking around at the rest of the squad. They all had concerned looks mixed with fear on their faces. "I may have overreacted a tad, but I think it's safe to say we all are a bit wound-up."

"He's so wound up, if ya took a lump of coal and stuck it…" Right started.

"I know, you'd get a diamond in no time," Left finished.

While Asha giggled at their joke, Javier shot them a withering look, but soon flashed a grin of his own.

"Think I may be bleeding over here," Barry called out, "Anyone going to care about that?"

"No!" they all replied in unison.

"Figures," Barry muttered.

"Ya talkin' 'bout me delicates again Barry?" Asha asked walking around him, hip swaying.

"Nooo…" he said, hypnotized by her walk.

"Here it comes…" Right and Left whispered with anticipation.

Before Asha could pounce, a bolt of lightning hit the ground, sending a column of fire into the air thirty feet high. As the flames came down, a beam of moonlight fell from the sky landing in the ground bathing a figure with pure white light. Small birds burst from the light singing as they circled the figure. The ground at his feet sprouted grass and fragrant wildflowers.

The figure raised a staff above its head and slammed it into the ground with a resonating sound silencing the birds, and the jungle around him. The light flashed making them all cover their eyes. A voice of thunder rumbled out calling to them.

"Have no fear, Knight Angels, your anointed druid has returned!" the voice cried out.

The man in the middle resolved himself into Patty, who stood looking extremely pleased. The twins jumped to their feet clapping wildly, making Patty beam even more. Asha growled softly freezing the look on his face. She tackled him, slamming him to the ground. Patty's wide eyes only went wider after she slapped him full force across the face.

"That's fer makin' me worry," she hissed.

"I'm sor…" Patty tried to apologize.

She smothered his protest with a violent kiss. His surprised cry was muffled by her lips. She kept her lips on his until his arms started to wrap around her. She let his strong arms hold her for a moment, before jumping off of him and retreating into the trees. Patty called after her, and tried to follow, but Bubbles blocked his path with dangerous looking red eyes. On her way out, she blew past Rashta, who was still trying to decide if she was a threat to Patty and if he dared try to stop her. Patty stopped, scratching his headin confusion, watching after her.

Asha stopped a few trees over, willing her heart to stop racing, unable to sort out the feelings in her heart. She heard rustling in the foliage beneath her, so she quickly wiped the tears that had appeared on her face. On the ground, it wasn't Patty like she had expected, but a pair of the men sent with the Captain.

She fell from her branch, landing on the balls of her feet, making no noise. She shadowed the two for a few steps before noisily drawing her daggers. They spun, only one swinging at her. She blocked the blade, burying her knee into his groin.

"Didn' yur muther ever teach ya not ta hit a gurl?" she sniggered.

"Yer…not…a girl," he gasped clutching his manhood.

"Mistress Asha," the other one said trying to distract her.

"Hmmm?" she asked, holding the unfortunate one's hair, trying to decide how to punish him.

"What he meant was, you are not merely a woman, you are a warrior, and his attacking you was merely his way of showing you that he sees you as an equal, or even a superior in the arts of war," he explained adding, "Ma'am."

"Hmmm," she purred considering them both, "I think that yur full of crap, but I think I like the crap ya be givin' me. Wat's yur name cutie."

"I am Cricket, mistress," Cricket answer.

"Sing fer me Cricket, wat's 'is name?" Asha asked.

"Sing?" Cricket repeated looking very confused, "I don't know many songs but if you wish I…" He cut off when Asha held up a finger.

"Wat's his name?" Asha asked again pointing at the other man on the ground.

"I… I'm sorry, I don't actually know, mistress Asha," Cricket apologized.

"I am…" the other man started.

"Gonna be really really quiet," Asha finish for him softly.

The men shared a glance and then kept their eye glued to the ground, not daring to antagonize Asha any more than they already had.

"Now, Cricket, yur gonna tell meh every thin' that happened ta ya," Asha smiled toying with her gutting dagger.

"So, the Captain went into the tree alone?" Javier asked Asha.

Asha sigh loudly, like a teen annoyed at her father. For good measure she rolled her eyes and tossed her hair back, knowing that it would at the very least annoy him.

"Again, what the lil' bug told me was, we was all walkin' ta da tree, when the mist comes up and snatches us all up. We disappeared an' left the Cap'in alone with nuthin' but 'is lil' minions wif 'im," she explained, "When we was gone they kept goin' and found a big ol' chair…"

"Throne," Cricket corrected but hastily realized his mistake.

Asha gave him a pointed warning look before continuing, "Throne, with fancy lookin' swords stabbed in tha middle of it. The Cap'in fell to 'is knees in front of it an' call it Scalibur or somthin' like that."

"Excalibur?!" Patty cried leaping to his feet, "He said Excalibur?!" he repeated shaking Cricket senseless.

"Ain't that wat I jus' said?" Asha pouted.

"Yes but, it's *Excalibur,*" Patty explained excitedly.

"An'…" Asha promted.

"The legendary sword of kings? Blade of Arthur? The sword that grants its wielder victory on every battlefield? Ring a bell?" Patty asked impatiently.

"Nope. I don' think I've hearda that one," Asha replied.

Patty groaned and covered his face. Xanthamius looked at him amused and then turned to Asha, "It is the Holy Blade of the Sun."

"Oooooh," Asha exclaimed in realization, "Why didn' ya say that?"

"Never mind that," Javier interjected impatiently, "What happened next."

"Then the ghost of kings past showed up an' scared the lot of 'em all out of their wee britches," Asha giggled.

"It was Merlin's essence that he tied to the tree when he sent Arthur over," Cricket explained.

Asha sent him a withering glare that had him flinching and cowering in place.

"As, I was sayin', Merlin's ghost popped up an' scared 'em. He told the Cap'in that if 'e was really the heir 'e could pull da sword from da throne. 'E pulls the big pigsticker from da throne an' starts bein' all glowy an' what not an' then da ghost tries ta kill 'um and they have this big fight an' the Cap'in wins. So now 'e's got hisself a shiny new sword an' wants ta talk ta us in da tree. 'E sent this chuckle 'ead ta get us," Asha continued.

"Interesting," Javier replied.

"Let's go see it! Can you believe it? Ex-freaking-calibur. Wow," Patty jabbered excitedly.

"Not yet," Javier said.

"Why not?" Patty demanded to know.

"Because, we haven't verified this man's story," Javier warned.

"But I jus' told ya…" Asha protested.

"What he told you," Javier finished for her. He turned to Patty, "Can you do some sort of truth spell? See if he's telling the truth?"

"I can," Xanthamius volunteered.

"I don't trust you, druid. You may have been a friend, but druids are notorious for meddling in things that are not theirs to meddle in," Javier responded.

"For someone not of this world, you have some strong opinions," Xanthamius observed.

"Yes. People with power are universal. You have some so you think it's your place to 'shepherd' everyone else," Javier shot back. He unfurled his wings, "You forget, we have our own power, and I, as High Commander, outrank you."

Xanthamius bowed his head to Javier in acknowledgement.

"Yes…I can do that spell, too," Patty answered hesitantly, looking between Javier and Xanthamius nervously.

Even though none of them could see it, everyone with a magical gift felt the druid's attack. Javier didn't move a muscle even though he knew it was coming at him. Xanthamius's spell raced toward him, roaring with power, and splitting around him as it went. It slammed into the trees behind him with devastating force.

"That is the only test you get, druid," Javier warned, "The next time you attack me, it will be an attack on the Knight Angels, and we do not tolerate acts of unprovoked aggression."

"As you say, High Commander," Xanthamius replied bowing low.

"Patty?" Javier called out.

"Sir?" Patty answered.

"Your spell, if you would," Javier ordered.

"Yes, sir," Patty said, already casting the truth spell.

"You, Cricket, is the story you told Asha, the truth? Did the events in the tree happen as you reported?" Javier asked.

"They did, High Commander," Cricket responded not looking up.

Javier glanced at Patty who confirmed that it was indeed the truth.

"Are you attempting to deceive us in any way?" Javier asked.

"No, m'lord," Cricket murmered.

"Very well. Let's go find the Captain," Javier decided.

The walk there had Asha grinding her teeth. She still couldn't Shadow Walk to where the Captain was, which made her fret more than usual. Patty kept babbling about the sword, explaining how he thought all the spells on it must work. The *otorgas* didn't know what was going on, but now that their riders were back, they were staying as close as possible to them.

"Patty!" Asha scream, "No one bloody cares! Jus' shuddup!"

While Patty's words cut short, the group looked at her, trying to decide what to say.

"It will be fine, Asha," Barry soothed.

"Ya can't know that! 'E was attacked an' I was suppose ta have 'is back," she snarled.

"Asha, the Captain can handle himself," Barry assured her, "I have known every assassin and warrior imaginable and have never met anyone equal to the Captain."

"I know that," Asha snapped, "It doesn't mean anythin'. I was suppose ta be there for 'im and I got sent away an' thought I ki… thought I had ta…"

Asha gave a strangled sob, before jumping on Bubble's back and leaving them all behind. She raced to the edge of the water, not slowing Bubbles down before jumping him into the lake. She ignored the boats on the shore, knowing that Bubbles could swim to the island faster than she could row a boat.

On the opposite shore, she quickly found the tunnel leading into the bowels of the tree, and entered, ignoring the calls to wait for them. The tunnel was drier and more bug free than she had expected. The path went down for a while before leveling out and meandering between the roots of the tree above her.

At what must have been the center of the island, a large chamber opened up before her. Judging from the size of the island above, magic was distorting the space here, making a larger space than could actually exist there.

The center of the room was dominated by a large stone throne; it was a masterpiece of workmanship. The arms of the throne had twin dragons carved into it. The seat of the throne was carved to look like a crouching wolf, its snarling face looking at you. The back of the throne was carved into half of a blazing sun.

Asha found the Captain sitting on the throne, with a naked blade on his lap, not paying attention to her, or anyone in the room for that matter. The blade itself was a mirror that seemed to shine light rather than reflect it. The cross guard and pommel of the sword appeared to be made of gold with intricate patterns etched on the surface. The grip peeking out from under the Captain's hand appeared to be made of wood wrapped in leather.

The Captain's left hand clutched the grip furiously. His knuckles had turned white but he seemed oblivious to it. His right hand held the sword's scabbard. Gold and glittering gems adorned the full length of the scabbard.

Resting on the Captain's back was a twin sword and scabbard except for the precious medal of choice was silver. Asha looked between the blades, trying to make sense of it. She knelt down in front of the throne, bowing her head to the Captain.

"My king," she whispered.

The Captain blinked out of his revere and noticed her for the first time. He smiled at her peacefully.

"Asha, rise, you have no need to kneel," the Captain told her.

"Ya are my king, from this day until the day I die, an' I will serve ya until the last breathe leaves my body," she vowed.

"Asha, you are my demon, and I will not have you kneel before me like some whipped dog," the Captain said gently.

Asha whipped her head up, shock written on her every feature, "Ya think me a whipped dog?"

"No, not since I met you," the Captain replied truthfully.

"The only other time I ever kneeled in front of ya was the night we first met. If Patty hadn't found me, and ya hadn't stood with 'im then, today, I would be worse than dead, sir, far worse," she reminded him.

"I know, and I saved you, not so that you could kneel, but so that you could soar. I need a fierce warrior to watch my back, not another subject to kneel before me," the Captain told her.

"So, I will never kneel ta ya?" she asked.

"Only this once," the Captain assured her.

"Then I swear myself ta ya again," she replied cutting her hand, letting the blood fall to the floor, "I swear ta always watch yer back, ta stand guard over yer honor, yer blood, an' yer dreams. I will hold myself above mere mortals an' stand a giant in the land o' men so that I can stand with ya, no matter how glorious yer life becomes."

"I accept your oath. I can only stand in anticipation of the warrior you will have to become to keep up with me," the Captain grinned.

Asha wrapped a bandage around her hand before inspecting the chamber around her. She noticed small doors around the edges, some of which were open.

"Where's yer minions?" she asked.

"Checking the other rooms for hidden treasures. I'm not sure which relics were left by Nimue and which she took," the Captain replied.

"I see taday is an important day," she said solemnly.

"How so?" the Captain asked frowning slightly

"Today, ya 'old the swords of kings, the Blessed Sword and Blade of the House of the Sun," She replied.

"A blade of battle and a blade of blood," Xanthamius commented from behind her.

Asha turned enough to see that the group had caught up to her and entered into the chamber. Patty raised an eyebrow at her and he winked in return. Slappy grabbed her hand to inspect her wound but she brushed him off. He wisely didn't push the subject.

"Indeed, they are," the Captain said, "They are mine, druid. These heirlooms were meant to be used by me and not held by some self-important druid."

"Are you referring to me?" Xanthamius asked bemused.

"Yes," the Captain growled.

"Why would you think I would want either of those swords?" Xanthamius asked.

"Because you aren't sure if I am who I say I am. I have only this to tell you, you are not among those to test me. I have already passed the test set by those much stronger and wiser than you and they approved of me, so there is no need for you to attempt to take them. They wouldn't answer to you anyway. I've already bound them to me," the Captain explained.

"Tradition states that the king gives one of the swords to his champion and the other to his general," Xanthamius reminded him.

"For weak kings, yes. Unfortunately, this world has seen too many of those. Like Lancelot the First, I will not have others fight my battles for me, nor will I let unworthy men lead my people. I will give power to those who are ready for it, but I will be a king, a true king, in both name and in deed," the Captain declared.

They locked eyes for a several seconds but Xanthamius was unable to maintain the eye contact. He looked away, looking ashamed.

"So Captain, is that Excalibur?" Patty asked excitedly.

The Captain hefted the sword admiring it, "Yes, this is Excalibur. It's everything I expected from a sword."

"The famous sword in the stone," Travis murmured.

"No. That was Caliburn," the Captain corrected, "That's the sword Merlin originally gave him hoping that it would be enough."

"It wasn't?" Travis asked.

"It was, at first, but then Arthur started leading more and fighting less. As his kingdom grew and the battles became larger, he started leading less from the front and more from the back. Both Merlin and Arthur realized he needed more help than Merlin could give him. Small scale battles and skirmishes are different than wars and an entire kingdom's army. The answer was Excalibur," the Captain replied.

"So what's difference between them?" Patty asked excitedly.

"Caliburn is the sword of battle. It is always razor sharp, and next to impossible to break. If it somehow does break, it heals itself," the Captain explained.

"Heals itself?" Slappy asked, his interest peaked.

"Yes. Any cracks disappear and chunks that break off are regrown," the Captain said.

"Wicked," the twins echoed.

"Indeed," the Captain agreed, "Excalibur on the other hand is special, too. It remembers every battle it's ever been used in. It contains every tactic used, every order given. Generations of battles and strategies used by kings and generals alike," the Captain said excitedly.

"It remembers all the blood," Xanthamius commented drily.

"Yes," the Captain replied, "but not how you imagine it I'm sure."

"Blood and battle," Patty mused, "The complexity of the spells required would be astronomical. Even Merlin would have been hard pressed to fashion better. What about the scabbards? Are they magic too?"

The Captain nodded, "Yes, Excalibur's scabbard grants stamina. With it, I could fight most of every day and not tire. Caliburn grants me…"

The Captain cut off as a blade tip appeared poking out from his belly. He looked at it curiously, watching the sparks of magic as the blade's spell battled with the Captain's magical skin. He traced the tip of the sword, not seeming to care that steel had sprouted from his body. Asha leapt into action, pummeling the assailant with her bare hands, too furious to draw her blades.

"Asha stop!" the Captain ordered.

She ignored him and continued to pound her fists into the traitor.

"Asha!" the Captain thundered.

She turned and faltered at the sight of him skewered by a

sword. The Captain moved toward her, not seeming to feel the wound. When he reached her, he casually pulled the blade from his body and handed it to her. While she reached for the blade, he suddenly lunged forward. He grabbed the assasin's hand but he was too late. What ever the would-be assassin had, he swallowed it. The Captain knelt down so he could put his face close to the would-be assassin, not seeming to care that he was now kneeling in a pool of his own blood.

"You should have let me finish," the Captain told him, "Caliburn's scabbard allows me to withstand nearly any attack on my body. My body can bleed endlessly while I hold it."

"Well, that makes more sense," Xanthamius muttered to himself.

Slappy stepped up to the Captain, linked with Patty so they could heal the wound.

"I hope…it hurts," the assassin managed to gasp out.

"Oh it does, but it doesn't matter. You're clever to wait this long to betray me. Are you Aster's creature?" the Captain asked.

The only response he got was a face full of blood the assassin spit at him.

"The hard way then," the Captain decided.

His purple eyes went golden as he placed a hand on the assassin's chest. A moment later, the Captain looked at the assassin with pity.

"I will do what I can for your wife, and while I cannot guarantee that I will save her, I swear I will do my best," the Captain promised.

The assassin nodded his thanks. The Captain slipped a slim blade from behind his bracer.

"You're on your way out; there is nothing we can do to save you now. I offer you the only comfort I can," the Captain said sadly.

The assassin nodded and the Captain buried the blade in his heart, ending his suffering. Asha stood a little to the side, looking down at the man lacking the Captain's pity but still full of understanding.

"So, my Knights, shall get to the next part?" the Captain asked gently closing the eyes of the dead assassin.

"What's that?" the twins asked excitedly.

"My soldiers," the Captain said motioning to the men filing in holding armfuls of weapons, "have found the cache of weapons hidden here. They are the pride of the House of the Sun, the Unbroken Blades."

Xanthamius gasped at the name not believing his ears. Asha rushed to the men eagerly, instantly rummaging for daggers and smaller blades.

"Asha," the Captain said gently.

She stopped long enough to turn to him to see what he wanted.

"You need a real sword, you're a Shadow Rider now," he reminded her.

She nodded and picked up an enormous double handed broadsword that she could barely lift. She tried to cover her mistake by taking it over to Travis. He took it from her, wisely not smiling. She returned to the selection, the rest closely behind her, to find the perfect weapon. She found a slim blade with a hand and a half hilt. The blade was as graceful as a feather, with minute etchings down the whole length of it. The sword had only one edge, but as soon as she held it, she knew, it was the one meant for her.

Once they had their weapons they chosen, they assembled in front of the Captain. Asha glanced over at Javier and saw that he had kept the elf's blade and found a twin among the blades offered. They now rested on either hip.

"Now that we have passed our tests and armed in the weapons of destiny, we have one thing left to do," the Captain said dramatically.

"What's that, sir?" Slappy asked.

"Ya haven't figured it out yet Slappy?" Asha teased.

"You have?" Slappy asked.

"Aye, we got ta go save the world, silly," she replied.

Slappy grinned wolfishly at her, and she returned it. The Travis laughed at their eagerness and the whole group joined him.

"That's right, Asha," the Captain confirmed with equal eagerness, "Time to save the world."

"Again," Patty added.

Chapter
TWENTY FIVE

They piled out of the tree, the regular soldiers panting with the exertion of carrying so much weight. It took a few trips to take all of the weaponry and armor across the lake to the village. The villager's supplied them with hand carts to load the weapons into. From there, Javier and Travis rigged harnesses for the horses.

Patrick studied the wagons for a little while and smiled to himself. He brought Xanthamius to confirm his theory. The druid did what he could to walk Patrick through the spell. It helped that he didn't know one himself, so theorizing was not prohibited by his curse. Once he was sure the spell was right, he gathered mana and cast the spell.

It worked as intended. The wagons could now carry more weight that would not affect horses. As far as the horses were concerned, their load just got a lot lighter.

"Well, that will make their job easier. Well done Patty," Javier praised.

Patrick beamed at the complement. Before he left he adjusted the grip on his new staff and walked away humming to himself.

"Patty?" Javier called out.

Patrick spun with a flourish to look Javier in the eye. He raised an eyebrow at him.

"Why didn't you get anything from the tree?" Javier asked.

"I did," He replied lifting his shirt, showing off the chain mail shirt, "This baby is made of some kind of metal that will stop any blade and all but the strongest spells."

"And the staff? Going for the whole wizard look? If you want, I think we can find you a robe and a pointy had," Javier smirked.

"Hey," Patrick protested, "This is a very special staff."

"Ya? How do you figure that?" Javier asked.

"It was Merlin's," Patrick smirked knowing it would surprise Javier. Javier's eyebrows did indeed fly up into his hair line at the comment, "Ya, that's right, *the* Merlin. He gave me his staff."

"Wha…how?"

"After my…test, I took a small nap and we had a chat while I slept. He had used the staff to power his essence and tie some of his conciseness to the tree. He figured Arthur wouldn't make it, so just in case some other king rose up; he wanted to be able to test them before they took the swords and claimed the throne. By the time we talked he had already tested the Captain, and found him worthy. This conciousness didn't know Arthur's line hadn't ended so he was really excited and emotional."

"I can imagine,"

"Ya! He found out he wasn't a complete failure. Anyway, he gave the king his second blessing, and let him into the throne room. Afterwards he gave me his staff."

"What good is his staff?"

"Well, it's kind of like Excalibur."

"It remembers the spells?"

"Eh, kinda. It remembers echoes, so I can piece together a lot of them. Mostly it works as an amplifier. This is one of three magic enhancers in the world. It took Merlin almost a decade to make this one."

"How much does it boost your power?"

"About double. The best thing is, if someone tries to use it, it turns their magic on them, burning them up."

"Ouch."

"Yup."

"Well, grats man."

"Thanks!"

"How's Xanthamius taking it?"

"Oh, he grumbled a bit," Patrick laughed, "But he got over it fast enough. How do you like your swords?"

"They're awesome. They're sharper than any other blade I've ever known, and they are just the right weight," Javier replied.

"So, when does the convoy leave?"

"Tonight, as soon as it's all secured and they have provisions."

"Ah, I see. Why aren't we taking them with us?"

"The Captain wants to arm the men back at the camp. He says Contreras and Pablo will know who to give the weapons and armor to. We will push on to the temple in the meantime, so we can set up some defenses."

"What about the men at camp? They gonna lend a hand?"

"They sure are. The Captain's sending orders to prepare the men as much as they can and then force march to the temple so they arrive two or three days before Aster's force gets there."

"Risky," Patrick commented.

"Yes," Javier agreed, "but they need the extra time to train."

"Well, let's get going, we're wasting time," Patrick said firmly.

That night the group split into two parts. The weapons guarded by twins and the most of regulars left, heading back to the fort, while the Captain led the remaining group towards the temple. The village people gave them all the supplies they could carry, wishing them luck and health at the edge of the jungle.

Xanthamius led them in a northeastern direction, toward the temple. As they got closer, they spotted more and more groups in the distance, most traveling parallel to their group. On their sixth day, the temple came into view. The groups that had kept their distance now converged into a stream of people headed to a temporary camp at the base of the hill that held the druid temple.

It was obvious to Patrick that the hill was anything but natural. The sides were all sheer, perfectly smooth cliffs, except for a spot at the front where a narrow trail went up the side to the temple. A small amount of people could be seen climbing up and down the path.

The temple it's self was an imposing structure. It was black at the bottom and slowly faded into brilliant white at the top. Patrick sharpened his eyesight so that he could see the murals of the figures on the outside of the temple. Wise looking men were depicted all along it exterior. Some were facing orcish hordes, others mesmerizing dragons, and still others wielding magic while crowds looked on in admiration or perhaps fear. It was hard to tell the difference.

"What do you think of our humble abode?" Xanthamius asked.

"It's breath taking," Patrick admitted, "Who are the people on the outside?"

"They are druids of particular note. The greatest wish and

desire of any druid who studies here is to be immortalized on the walls of the temple. The ones who have been exceptional are on the outside. Merlin the Magnificent is on the outside, of course, about halfway up," Xanthamius replied, "I had a little spot on the inside but I wouldn't put it past my Brothers to have scrubbed me off the walls by now."

"Really?" Patrick asked eagerly.

"Yes, he's on the other side though, you can't see it from here unfortunately," Xanthamius apologized.

The walked along in silence for most of the rest of that day. As they approached the camp of people waiting to go up to the temple, the Captain pulled them to a stop. They gathered around him to see what he wanted.

"This is it, men," the Captain said solemnly, "This is where we will have to make our stand. I'm not sure how many people Aster has for certain but there's enough that he thinks he can take this temple by force if he needs to."

"Didn't Pablo say he had five thousand with him and only a fraction of them were actually soldiers?" Javier asked.

"He did. What he didn't know was that Aster broke up his forces so they could be supported in different parts of the wilderness. When I was in Kint's mind, he showed me that there were many groups composed of five thousand. I think that Aster has about six thousand trained soldiers but that's not his only force," the Captain explained grimly.

Patrick felt an uneasiness fill the pit of his stomach. He shared a glance with Asha and knew she was feeling the same way. She gave him a small smile, squeezed his hand quickly.

"Why do I have a feeling I'm not gonna like what you have to say, sir?" Patrick asked him.

"Because I don't like it," the Captain replied.

"What is it, sir?" Patrick pressed.

"Aster's plan is to send in the untrained men and women as cannon fodder against the druids. When they are exhausted from blasting all the people rushing them, he will send in his real troops, armed with magic resistant armor, to gain entrance to the temple. If they breach the doors, Aster wins," the Captain answered grimly.

"Not to rain on the parade, but that seems like a really simple plan," Travis chimed in.

"I thought it was brilliant," Xanthamius, "My brothers will never see it coming."

"Really?" Travis asked.

"Travis, ever since the Purge, tactics and war have been… simple," the Captain explained, "There's not much imagination on that front here."

"Fair enough," Travis replied, "What are you thinking? Full enclosure or just a palisade along the entrance to path?"

"The back side is not passible so we only have to defend the path. Patty do you think you could build a…what are you doing?" the Captain asked.

Patrick froze with the second handful of dirt halfway to his mouth. He looked around at his comrades. They were all looking at him with a mixture of horror and mirth. Barry in particular looked like he was almost unable to hold back of his laughter.

"I…uh…I'm testing dirt. If I eat it, I can sense the trace elements better," Patrick explained.

"I see," the Captain mused, "Anything useful?"

"Yes, sir. There's some sulfur, phosphorus, and magnesium. Somewhere in this area there is an iron deposit. Also, sir," Patrick added lowering his voice, "There's gold too. Traces, but if we want it, I think I can gather together a fair amount."

"I'll keep that in mind. We may need it later on, but for now, keep the gold where it is. What can you do with the rest?" the Captain asked.

Patrick didn't answer. He just grinned and gave him the crazy eyes.

"Roger that," the Captain chuckled.

"How are you able to gather so much from the earth?" Xanthamius asked.

"I studied the geography in college for a couple years," Patrick replied absently around another mouthful of dirt.

"College?" Xanthamius asked.

"A place of learning, full of masters. You can study whatever you want there, if you are willing to pay the price," Patrick explained, "Don't you have those kinds of place here? Where you can study?"

"There were such things before the Purge, but those, like so much else, were lost," Xanthamius replied sadly.

"Okay, what the hell is this Purge?" Peters demanded.

Xanthamius shook his head in mock sorrow, "So much to learn, it is almost sad."

"Care to explain?" Javier asked without really asking.

Xanthamius sighed but obliged them, "In the time of Merlin the Magnificent, the armies of the Light went to war with the armies of the Dark. They were led by Lancelot the Betrayer, then known as Lancelot the Invincible. He was the last confirmed Guardian to grace Avalon. He convinced the other races to attack the Dark in a preemptive strike, before they could finish gathering their armies and flooding over to the lands of the Light again. In all the years that the eternal struggle had existed, the armies of the Light had never attacked the Dark.

"In all the wars that were fought between the Light and the Dark, the Light had always followed the practice of only protecting their lands. They had never been the aggressors, only responding to the attacks, of the Dark. To do otherwise was and still is a foreign concept. When Lancelot discovered they were amassing an army, he suggested they attack first. At first the leaders resisted, but eventually he convinced them that it was better to bring the inevitable war to the enemy.

"The armies of the Dark were not prepared for an offensive and they were crushed thoroughly, unable to mount an effective resistance. The armies of the Light rejoiced that their lands had been spared and the loss of life had been much lower this time. Their joy was short lived though.

"The Betrayer became drunk with power and battle and ordered the armies forward deeper into the enemy lands to push the Dark back even farther. At first the other monarchs thought that he knew of more armies, so they followed. It didn't take long for them to realize he was after blood and vengeance. Only when he started putting whole villages to the sword, did they try to leave his army.

"They tried to assure him that they were his allies but this was not the way of the Light. The Betrayer was furious with them. He had destroyed every army the Dark he could find and much of the population of the Dark. He had secretly hoped to destroy them once and for all.

"The other races knew that it was folly so they returned with their armies to their own lands. For the Betrayer, this was the last straw. Once he had destroyed all of the large populations of Dark he could find, he also returned to the land of the Light with his armies but not in peace. He turned on his allies, determined to punish them for their perceived betrayal. The armies of the Dwarves and Elves offered little resistance at first; not willing to believe their allies would turn on them. This was the start of the end for them."

Xanthamius voice cracked at this point and he tried to compose himself. The Captain was staring off into the distance, not looking at any of them. The group didn't notice him. They were too busy hanging on Xanthamius's every word.

Xanthamius cleared his throat and continued, "The Dwarven armies fell first, its remnants scattering along with the rest of their people. They retreated into their mountains, collapsing their tunnels behind them. The Betrayer left part of his army there to pin them in and pulled the rest out to deal with elves.

"As you saw, male elves are imposing creatures. The average male elf is almost twice as strong as a human. They females are not nearly as strong but they make up for that with speed. They are quicker than the average human. Combined they make daunting armies. Their greatest weakness is their longevity. Humans and dwarves breed like rats while elves will only have two or three children per family, and those are normally spaced out over a couple decades.

"The elves are almost all magically talented which allowed them to stand against the human armies longer than the dwarves. Once the dwarves fell, the majority of the Betrayers armies fell on them, grinding down the elven armies.

"While the Betrayer was distracted, the armies of the Dark gathered one last army, composed of every able body they could muster to protect themselves. What they didn't know was the Betrayer anticipated this move and left an army to deal with them. The Dark's army was larger, but they were no match for the Betrayer's battle hardened army. This army also fell to human swords.

"The druids had refused to follow the Betrayer into enemy lands and had sealed off the temple. Once the last Dark army fell they knew the elves would be obliterated as well. Unlike the dwarves, the elves would not hide, not while their forests were in danger.

"Merlin reached out to Lancelot the Fallen, son of the Betrayer, to plead on behalf of the entire world. Lancelot the Fallen was no Guardian but he was a Champion. It was widely believed he had sworn to his father but he did not. Together, Merlin, Lancelot the Fallen, and the Betrayer's Demon…"

"Wat was 'is name?" Asha interrupted.

"It is not known. She was bonded in secret and her name was never spoken," Xanthamius replied, "What *is* known is that she agreed to end the Betrayer, even though it meant her death. It took all three of them to bring him down. Their battle lasted three days and laid waste to the human capital. Thousands died in the wake of their fighting.

"Merlin returned to the temple and informed the druids that Lancelot the Fallen had rejected the crown, and would not assume the throne. They had thought the Betrayer's death would end the fighting but it did not. He had poisoned the minds of his generals and they continued their master's monstrous war.

"The druids knew that all the races of Avalon were on the brink of destruction, and not even the centaurs could rein it in. The Betrayer had beaten them back too."

"Wait," Javier said holding up a hand, "Centaurs? Where did they come in?"

"They are creatures of balance," Xanthamius explained impatiently, "They came to the aid of the Dark when they thought the Light was tipping the balance, but they couldn't stop the Betrayer's advance. They pulled out their armies so they wouldn't be destroyed.

"Back to my story. The druids knew they had to do something drastic. Merlin proposed the Purge of Light. The counsel was so desperate they took his advice, even though it would take near unfathomable power.

"The world's druids gathered in once spot and all linked. Merlin used all their power and their life forces to cast a spell that wiped war from the mind of nearly every living soul and from most of the manuscripts in Avalon. The only ones spared were the Centaurs, Lancelot the Fallen and Merlin.

"The spell killed every druid linked, which also happened to be every fully trained druid in the world, along with a few other powerful mages. All but Merlin. The spell made every person in Avalon fall asleep as the spell worked on their minds.

"In the morning, the human armies returned home, not sure why they were in elven lands. Most left their weapons of war, not knowing what they were for, only finding them heavy chunks of metal.

"Merlin left soon after, promising the acolytes left in the temple that he would return with a new king from another world. He said that this world had no one to offer, and we needed someone new, someone who knew what honor was, and could lead us back to where we were supposed to be. He never returned."

"That's…" Patrick said unable to fully gasp the story.

"Horrible," Travis volunteered.

"Gruesome," Javier supplied.

"Heart breakin'," Asha added.

"Truly a tragedy," Barry concerned, "But a question if may, if war was wiped from your memories, how do you know this?"

"The druids kept meticulous records. Before Merlin disappeared he raised the three strongest acolytes to full druids and left them in charge. He had sealed all the records in a special room, sheltering them from the Purge and when it was over, he showed the room to the new druids. He told them to open it if he didn't return in twenty years. When he didn't, they read the records but kept the most of the information and the specifics to the Master Archdruids," Xanthamius explained.

"My how the mighty have fallen," Barry said.

"What?" Patrick asked trying to catch Xanthamius's eye but he wouldn't look at him.

"That explains why you're so bitter. You read it all and interpreted it correctly and were right. We're proof of that. Now you're here on the outside while they stay on the inside, stealing your job from under you," Barry continued.

"Your job?" Patrick asked again.

"He was the Master Archdruid," the Captain explained.

"Why would they kick you out though?" Patrick asked.

"Because he supported the man who destroyed their world," Barry clarified.

"The Betrayer?" Patrick asked.

"No, Merlin," Barry corrected.

"Merlin? But he saved them," Patrick protested.

Barry shook his head, "Merlin saved Avalon, but he destroyed the druids in order to do it."

"Oh," Patrick exclaimed suddenly getting it.

"That's what I have to overcome," the Captain said softly.

"How are we going to do it, sir?" Javier asked.

"You don't have to do anything," the Captain assured him.

"Sir, we're in this with you," Javier replied.

"That's not what I mean, Javi. The Knight Angels stood with the elves and the dwarves. They were swept aside as well. You already have the respect and confidence of Avalon. The heir of the Betrayer has no such confidence," the Captain said sadly.

"Well, we've never run from a good fight," Patrick said cheerfully, "I don't think we should break with tradition."

"I have no plans of that, Patty," the Captain replied stretching, "It's a beautiful day. We have some defenses to build."

The group moved to the front of the temple. Over the centuries, a small town had sprung up in front of the temple to service those who had come to seek help from the druids. The Captain decided to build the fortifications not only around the town but also around the camp that had sprung up next to the town now that the temple was here.

The Captain set Patrick to blasting a trench in front temple. Patrick responded by challenging Xanthamius to a contest, but the old druid flatly refused. Not really caring too much, Patrick started in on his project and created a semi-circle around the town and camp throwing the dirt on the camp side of the trench so they could build a rampart on top of it.

Thanks to his new staff the project was done much faster and easily than he had expected. He had originally expected to spend several days on the project but it turned out he only needed one. The staff allowed him to work at twice his capacity and do twice as long before he got tired.

Patrick had just finished digging the trench when he was attacked from behind. The attack was weak, so the shield he perpetually wore since meeting Xanthamius, blocked the attack. He turned slowly to he who was annoying him. A bald man in a brown robe stood on top of his newly built rampart. The man held a surprising amount of contempt for someone so weak. Patrick raised an eyebrow at him so he could change his mind before Patrick pummeled him

The bald man didn't seem to get the hint because he gathered a fireball and threw it at Patrick. Instead of trying to dodge or deflect it, Patrick caught it. He studied the construction of the fireball. When he figured out how the man had built his ball, he crushed it between two hands. The bald man reached back to throw another fireball but Patrick waved his hand and wrapped him up in vines he had caused to come bursting out from the ground.

The bald man's eyes widened at the vines while he used his fireball to burn through the vines. Patrick was getting annoyed so he wove three Dragon's breath spells simultaneously. They flew over his head creating quite the stir in the town. Some of the villagers run while others were mesmerized into immobility.

The bald man licked his lips nervously but doggedly wove another fireball. He was trembling while he cast it. Xanthamius appeared between them, intercepting the ball.

"Enough, acolyte," Xanthamius growled at him.

"Master! I mean, um…" the acolyte stammered.

"The proper term for a cursed druid is Fallen," Xanthamius supplied.

"Yes, Ma…Fallen," the acolyte said bowing.

"Why are you here assaulting my recruit?" Xanthamius demanded.

"I was sent to test him to see who he was. The Brothers asked me to see if he was a warlock or a druid. Either way I was relieve him of his staff and bring it back to the temple where it belongs," the acolyte answered.

"The staff is mine, and it wouldn't work for them anyway," Patrick snapped.

"Silence," Xanthamius ordered.

Patrick started to protest but he caught the look in Xanthamius eye and held his peace. He wasn't sure what Xanthamius had planned but whatever he had planned he was desperate to have Patrick go along with it. The Captain might not trust Xanthamius but Patrick had spent enough time with him to grant him some leeway.

"Your recruit?" the acolyte asked.

"Yes I found him in the wilderness and brought him here to

be trained," Xanthamius explained impatiently, "I may be cursed, but I was never banished boy. Now run along and tell the Brothers I have brought a recruit. They cannot cast him aside, regardless of who brings him. Make sure you tell them that he was casting Dragon's breath. Also remind them that I am unable to teach him."

"Yes, Fallen, right away," the acolyte said bowing and scurrying away.

"Okay, you need to explain that," Patrick demanded as soon as the acolyte was out of earshot.

"I have just guaranteed you an interview at the temple," Xanthamius explained, "The acolyte will make enough fuss to make sure they can't bury this in their politics."

"Well, this is unexpected," Patrick muttered to himself, "Real teachers. Too bad Aster is so close, or I would go."

"Do you know how much I just put on the line for you pup?" Xanthamius thundered.

"Not as much as *my* brothers are counting on. They need me here to help them a lot more than a stuck-up temple needs another acolyte," Patrick shot back.

"Bah!" Xanthamius said in exasperation.

Patrick watched him walk away with a twinge of regret. He wanted to go desperately, but he knew that the squad needed him, and he would not let them down.

"What was that about Patty," the Captain asked from his shoulder.

"He wants me to enter the temple. Apparently, he got me in and now I have some interview with them," Patrick answered.

"Then what the hell are you doing here?" the Captain demanded angrily.

"Sir?" Patrick asked thoroughly shocked and a little scared.

"If you won't better yourself, then I have no use for you," the Captain snapped.

"But you need me here," Patrick stammer.

"Patty," the Captain sighed rubbing his head, "I could use you if you stayed here, but every day you spend up there is a day you learn some new spell that could save us. The way you make intuitive leaps, you will put them to shame in days. Go, Patty. Be bold, be great, be the man we both know you are."

"Sir!" Patrick said saluting.

The Captain saluted back sharply. Patrick turned on his heel and went looking for Xanthamius. He found the old druid sitting on a stump near the trail that went up the trail. Behind him, at the head of the trail, two acolytes stood letting people up or turning them away.

Xanthamius raised an eyebrow at him in question. Patrick grinned impishly at him in return and nodded. Xanthamius matched his grin. Together they went up the hill ingnoring the acolytes that moved to stop them. They brushed past them boldly, ignoring their calls to stop.

Patrick felt them try to stop him but his defenses made their spells slide right off. He felt them gathering energy to try again. Xanthamius whipped around and blasted them off the trail, growling at them. Rashta appeared behind a third coming down the hill to help. He hit the acolyte behind the head, letting his unconscious body hit the ground.

"Thanks," Patrick said.

"Ha! I hated those two when I was here, and it wasn't until now that I finally had a good excuse to thump them like they deserved," Xanthamius chuckled. Rashta just shrugged.

The climb up the hill was one of the longest in Patrick's life. The anticipation of entering the temple was getting to him. When they crested the last switch back, the doors of the temple were firmly shut. Xanthamius muttered to himself, while Patrick walked up to the doors. He knocked on them but no answer came.

"They won't open, pup," Xanthamius grumbled.

"But you said…" Patrick protested.

"Oh, they'll talk to you if you go in, but this is your first test. It's part of an old tradition, a law really, that if a druid can open these doors alone and unaided, then they cannot deny him anything. I'm sorry lad I didn't think that they would go this far," Xanthamius apologized.

"This is perfect!" Patrick exclaimed, "Why would you be sorry?"

"The doors have to be opened by force, and even in my prime, I didn't have the power to do it," Xanthamius explained.

"Well, that just means they'll love me even more when I throw this in their face," Patrick giggled.

He handed Xanthamius his staff, while he prepared himself. He opened his vitality wide open and filled his fortitude to the brim. He forced a little more in, stretching it to its max. He took his time weaving four hands, two to stabilize himself and two to pull on the door.

Sweat beaded on his forehead from the strain, but he ignored the nuisance. Grimacing from the pain he pushed onward. He heaved against the doors, feeling them give slightly. He wedged on of the hands into the crack and used that to lever his way in. Once the door was open a crack he could see the spells on the other side trying to hold the door shut.

Patrick let go of the door and fell to his knees panting from the exhaustion. Xanthamius came up behind him to pat him sympathetically on the back.

"I told you it was impossible, pup," Xanthamius reminded him.

"You didn't tell me they would try to hold it shut too," Patrick hissed.

"What?!" Xanthamius shouted in indignation, "They held the door from the other side? That is beyond breaking customs and rules…wait, you opened it that far even when they held it shut?"

"Yes. Say, what does the rule say anyway?" Patrick inquired.

"It says 'To him who passes the doors unaided upon his own power, will be admitted and all the secrets of the temple shall be his, with nothing and no one barred from him.' Why do you ask?" Xanthamius wanted to know.

"Hmm…'Passes the doors…' yes…I can see…hmmm," Patrick muttered considering the doors.

Patrick stood again and placed his hands on the doors, feeling out the spells woven into them and the material used to construct them. He glanced up and caught a glimpse of head ducking back into the windows.

"This is how you will stop me is it?!" Patrick shouted at them,

"You're going to cheat? Well guess what, that won't stop me, I will not stop here so close to what is mine!" He looked over his shoulder at Xanthamius. "You may want to back up."

Xanthamius and Rashta dove behind a rock, not sure what Patrick was up to, be given that look in his eye, they would want the protection. Patrick filled his fortitude to the brim again and summoned his hands. This time he could feel the subtle spells on the other side of the door holding the door shut. He pulled on the doors again, pretending to strain. When he thought they were pulling as hard as they could as well, he dismissed the hands holding the doors and channeled their energy into a fist, bringing it to bear on the door, smashing it to splinters.

The doors shattered inwards, spraying bits on the acolytes inside. Patrick reached back toward Xanthamius, who threw him Merlin's staff. Patrick caught in and strode forward. As soon as he was across the threshold, he wove a shield against the attacks thrown at him. He tied up all the acolytes in weaves of air. Rashta strode forward with a deadly grace, openly carrying his daggers.

"Stop intruder!" a druid in voluminous robes ordered. The robes billowed around his plump frame as he waddled down the hall, "Who are you do defile our halls?!"

"I am he who has passed the doors unaided upon my own power," Patrick answered calmly, still holding the acolytes captive.

"Liar, you wield a staff of power!" the fat druid protested.

"Indeed, I do, but I did not use it until I cleared the door. If you are half the druid you are pretending to be, you already knew that," Patrick smirked.

"I..." the fat druid stammered, clearly fishing for ideas.

"...Am trying to cheat?" Patrick volunteered.

"I did no such thing!" the druid protested.

"You violated the spirit of the rule," Patrick pointed out.

"Who are you?" the druid asked changing the subject.

"This is my student," Xanthamius said striding up to the druid grinning wolfishly.

"You…you were cursed," the druid stammered trembling, "You can't teach anymore."

"How little you know Mathias. How many times did I tell you that if you have the desire, the way will come?" Xanthamius asked him.

"I was just doing what the Brothers Council ordered," Mathias whined.

"You are good at doing what your told," Xanthamius spat, "Now be a good little butter ball and take my student to his rooms."

"Who is he?" Mathias whispered.

"Who am I?" Patrick repeated, "I am Patrick O'Leary, great son and heir of Merlin the Magnificent, and I have come to claim my birthright."

All around him the acolytes whispered excitedly. Mathias looked at him with his eye bulging from their sockets, and his mouth working like a fish. Xanthamius buried his head in his hands and moaned.

"Acolyte Patrick," a wizened druid called from a side room, "I am the Intaker, come with me please."

Patrick looked to Xanthamius who nodded to him, "Go, this is start of you training."

So Patrick went.

Chapter

TWENTY SIX

Javier sagged in exhaustion against the timber pile they had stockpiled. It had been a long day and at the end of it, he still wasn't sure what he was going to do. Patty had left without a word, and the only clue was the Captain assuring him that Patty was doing what he was supposed to be doing. Javier closed his eyes considering taking a nap before eating dinner and then going to bed.

"Hey! You!" a voice called.

Javier opened one eye to glance at richly dressed man, guard by several burly, hairy men standing in front of him. Javier had met dozens of self-important wealthy men, and this one seemed to be as much of a tool as the next one. He ignored him and closed his eye again. He knew that the man would assume him an easy target, so he kept his ears open.

Sure enough, he heard one trying to sneak up on him. Javier timed it so that just as a meaty hand reached him, he twisted out of the grip and used his momentum to snap his assailant's wrist. While the man was too busy howling and mourning his wrist, Javier kicked him full in the chest, sending him crashing into his buddies who had come to help. The remainder refrained from attacking him, too afraid of getting hurt.

"Just who do you think you are?" the rich man asked.

"A better question is who are you?" Javier demanded.

"I am Creeve, Resthouse Keeper and mayor of this proud city. Now, who are you and what makes you think you can build this wall here?" Creeve replied.

"Judging from your gaudy clothes and excessive rings, you over charge the people just wanting help," Javier said in disgust.

"I am an honest merchant," Creeve replied in an oily voice,

"But you still haven't answered my questions and these good people," Creeve motioned to the crowd gathering, "would like to know as well. You are limiting access to this humble town."

"I have a friend that may agree with your version of 'honest' but I do not. What I think you meant was you were happy to let someone build your town a defensive wall until you realized that it was restricting the amount of people staying at your resthouse. With a wall like this, people feel safe in a field and no longer pay your outrageous fees to sleep in safety under your roof," Javier spat.

"Now that's entirely untrue," Creeve protested with exaggerated innocence, "I am simply conveying the concerns of the people."

"Doubtful," Javier said.

"Will you tell me who you are, or will my men have to throw you out? They are very good at it," Creeve warned.

"It would be their death if they tried. As for you, you have no authority over me, while I have every right to judge you," Javier replied steely eyed.

"Very well, kill him," Creeve ordered feigning boredom.

The goons charged up the embankment toward Javier, who set his feet and waited for them. Before they reached him, Arete jumped over the logs, screaming her angry war cry. The goons fell over themselves to get away from her.

"That's right boys, this is my *otorga*," he said grinning evilly at the goons.

Javier looked at the crowd that had gathered. Most of the town was now gathered looking at Javier's *otorga*. He considered them carefully. He noticed the Creeve was about to ask him something again.

"Arete," Javier said cutting him off, "If Creeve says anything else, please kindly eat him."

Arete turned her golden eyes to Creeve and took her time licking her lips. Creeve tried to stay calm but Javier could see him starting to sweat and edge behind a goon. A large portion of the crowd laughed, with a few even cheering. Javier smiled at him wickedly knowing he had severely limited his power.

"Children of Avalon!" Javier cried out, "Brothers, sister, friends, I am Javier Botto, High Commander of the Knight Angels!"

"The Knight Angels all died long ago!" a voice called out from the back.

"We were killed off, but things born of the Light do not die," Javier called back, "I know this is hard for you to understand or even believe but I am here to show you that you are not alone. In this world so dark and full of sorrow, you can once again rejoice, the Knight Angels have returned and brought with them the Light!"

Javier hadn't planned it, but Avalon seemed to be helping him. As he flared his wings to show the people, the setting sun flared, surrounding him with light, making him seem like figure made of pure light. The crowd responded with awe. Most of them fell to their knees weeping with joy. Javier had expected some sort of response but this was more than he had dreamed of.

"You sided with the Betrayer," Creeve spat, "Everyone knows that."

"We fought the armies of the Dark, but when the betrayer turned on the Armies of the Light, we were the first to stand against him. That is our nature. No matter where the threat is, we fight against it whether it is a goblin army or an unjust mayor, it makes no difference to us, we stand and protect those in need of protecting. We guard them from harm or die trying. I come with a warning. A great evil comes this way. He seeks to subvert the temple and twist its treasures for his own use.

"The druids are men of learning and healing but of a necessity they have learn to fight as well. This is a sad state for them to be in. We should not hide behind them, as Creeve plans to do, but stand with them against this threat. The Knight Angles have come to protect this land." The squad climbed to the top of the embankment to stand behind Javier. "We are here to protect Avalon again against a man that would enslave you all and turn this world to ash with his love of war."

"How can we stand against such a powerful man?" Creeve asked.

"With courage, Housemaster. Do you remember the meaning of the word?" Javier shot back.

"I choose life," Creeve sneered.

"And I choose glory," Javier declared, "I ask you now, fellow children of Avalon, will you cower like children, as Creeve has opted to or will you rise up, and answer my call? I call upon you to stand firm against this evil. I ask you lay your lives on the line, not for just for yourselves, but for your children and the hope of a better tomorrow. Stand with me so that your children and your children's children can play in green fields. Stand with me so that they can live in a land without fear, a land where they grow old not knowing the constant shadow of war. Children of the Light! Stand with me and discover the strength that I know that is in you, the strength that will give you life, light and freedom."

"We are mere *ariats* not Sons of Lancelot, like you. What good are we in a fight?" came a concerned cry.

"I am no Son of Lancelot, yet I have fought them. Together we are stronger than any army this evil can throw at up. I do not march off to my death, I march towards victory. I would not waste your lives as so many other would, rather I will cherish them and protect them as much as I can. It is true that war brings death with it, but it also brings opportunity. I give you two promises. First, I promise you victory. Second, I promise you that if you do die, your sacrifice will bring about a better tomorrow," Javier promised solemnly.

"Yet we will still be dead," Creeve laughed, "What good is that?"

"Death comes to us all, my friend, regardless of what you do. I ask you, my friends, would you rather die, screaming in defiance in face evil, or would you rather die old and worn out, having spent your whole lives beneath the boot of one tyrant or another?" Javier asked them.

An old, wizened man limped to the front. The crowd parted to let him pass.

"Grandfather?" Javier asked.

"Let's say we join you, who will lead us. You may be a Knight Angel, but you are no king. What you promise is beautiful but without a true leader it will never last. I have searched for it all my life, but without someone to lead us, this struggle is for not," he rasped.

"Exactly!" Creeve shouted pointing.

"Arete," Javier murmured.

His cat jumped a short way toward Creeve who gave a shrilly

scream before passing out on his face. Again, the crowd cheered and laughed.

"Knight, I would have my answer," the old man said.

"No, it will not be me who leads you. I will lead the Knight Angels and anyone that will fight with us but I will not rule over you. I am not the type to rule. In you are looking for someone to guide you, lead you and rule over you, then you need someone else. There is one person that can. Next to him, I am a pale comparison," Javier admitted.

"Then who will lead us?" he asked.

"The new Guardian of Avalon," Javier said with a smile.

Again, the crowd gasped. The Captain crested the embankment and stood with blazing purple eyes looking down at them. The old man knelt on creaky knees and the rest followed suit. Javier looked back at the Captain, smiling.

"Now, who will stand with us? Who will fight for a better tomorrow? Who will seize this opportunity? Who will claim their freedom?!" Javier cried.

To the man, the crowd jumped to their feet roaring their commitment. Creeve's goons stepped over his limp form and joined the crowd pledging their assistance.

"Welcome my brothers," Javier grinned, "Welcome to the armies of the Light."

The crowd rushed forward eager to show him their resolve. Javier shook all the hands he could reach. He kept his wings out to remind them of who he was. Many of them stretched their hands out to reverently stroke the feathers. The old man came up to Javier with tears in his eyes.

"The Knight Angles have returned as you promised and you have brought us the man who will save us," he said through tears.

"We have," Javier said smiling and hugging the old man.

A young lithe boy came and helped the old man off the embankment and off into the village. Javier watched him leave feeling happy. He felt a tug on the bottom of his shirt and look down to see a pair of large emerald green eyes. He squatted down to look her in the eye. Arete came over and licked her gently.

"Are you gonna save us?" she asked in her sweet small voice.

"I will do everything that I can, little one," Javier promised.

"So, you're gonna keep us safe?" she asked twirling an ebony curl.

"As long as I'm here, nothing will harm you. I am Knight Angel, the shield of the Light against the Darkness of the night," he assured her.

"Good," she said reaching out for a hug.

Javier embraced her and found himself standing somewhere else. He looked around and saw that he was on top of a tower made of light, situated at the peak of a mountain. He did a full turn, taking in the view of the landscape far below him.

"This is the Bastion of Light," a woman said from slightly behind him.

Javier jumped in surprise and spun to see who it was. A woman with flowing black hair and emerald green eyes looked out on the horizon.

"Who…" Javier started.

"Am I?" she finished, "I am Jona. I was the High Commander of the Knight Angels when we stood against the Betrayer."

"How…?"

"Am I alive? I'm not. I died centuries ago. I was last Knight to fall. The Betrayer killed me himself. Apparently, I was important enough to kill personally."

"I'm sorry."

"Why? It wasn't your fault. Like I said it was centuries ago, I got over it."

"Liar."

"True but today I was reminded of hope. Today I saw the Knight Angels rise again."

"So, if you're dead, then how are you here? Are you a ghost?"

"Of sorts, but you already know the answer."

"I do?"

"'Things born of the light do not die'. Those were your words."

"I said them because they felt right," Javier said. Something tickled him at the back of his mind. "Hey, I know you!"

"Yes, we met briefly, but I was more interested in your *otorga*. When I was alive, I rode her ancestor."

"What was her name?"

Jona made a strange hissing noise.

"What was that?"

"Her name. As you bond with your *otorga* more, you will be able to understand their speech. Enough of that for now. I brought you here for a reason. This is the tower where one High Commander passes on the mantle to their successor. My soul was sustained by the tower so that I could help the Knight Angels when they rose again. I was afraid it would never happen and I would spend an eternity wandering Avalon, unable to rest. You won't believe how happy I was to find you."

"What do we do?" Javier asked.

"Kneel, for starters," she laughed. Javier knelt. "Now you swear the oath."

"I already have."

"To the Guardian, yes but not to me. He did not found the Knight Angels, we exist seperatly, independent of any Guardian, yet symbiotic. All he did was activate a dormant bond that was already in place. Because he is a Guardian, he has a certain connection to Avalon. This allows him to help her reestablish the bonds that were broken but we have our own authority that must be followed, that does not pertain to him. We exist outside his authority, always remember that. If he is a friend of the Light, and this one appears to be, you will often fight alongside him but there will be times where Knight Angel business does not follow Guardian business."

"I was afraid of that," Javier whispered.

"I know. I know better than anyone how far apart the Knight Angels and the Guardian can drift. But enough of that. Speak the oath."

Javier nodded bracing himself for the next step. "I am a child of the light sworn to fight in the night. I am the bane of darkness. Vengeance is my calling, justice is my charge, and mercy is my guide. As darkness gathers, I stand firm, the last shield of the light, the shining bastion of strength against the darkness. By blood and honor I fight and by blood and honor I die. The Sons of darkness fear the Night, for Justice is come."

Jona bent down and kissed him on the forehead. Javier felt enormous power fill his frame. He knew that it would take him a while to fully adjust to the amount of power that now coursed through his body. He flexed experimentally, feeling out the new strength and power.

"Is this how the Captain feels all the time?" Javier wondered.

"I suspect so. That blessing will allow you to stand an equal to any Son of Lancelot, though the training you had under this 'Captain' will make you their superior," she answered.

"So, just a question here, will I have to kiss the next guy too?"

She laughed at him. "No not necessarily. That is merely how I chose to pass on my blessing."

"Oh good," Javier said letting out a sigh of relief.

"Good luck, High Commander, I think your job will be harder than mine."

"You had to fight against a Guardian, I won't have to."

"Time will tell," she said mysteriously, "Besides, that was just a tyrant. Those are commonplace for us. You will have to rebuild the entire Knight Angels from nothing."

"I have captains already."

She gave him a flat look.

"I have to make them revow wont I?"

"Hmmm." She hummed clearly insinuating that she found the question dumb.

"Well, how will I know if I'm doing my job right? I mean beyond my gut feelings?" Javier asked.

"Follow you heart, High Commander. You have a good one, molded by your service to others and the teaching of your grandfather."

"Yes, I suppose I do. I just wish there was a manual or something."

"Well, there is our archive. You could always read about the past adventures of our order," she mused.

"Perfect!" Javier exclaimed eagerly, "Where is it?"

"Here, of course. This is more than a fancy view," she giggled, "We keep our own records safe from prying eyes and corrupting spells."

"They were safe from the Purge?"

"Yes, both of them."

"Wait what?" Javier asked.

"Nevermind that," she replied impatiently, "There's too much for you to do now. You made some promises and the High Commander does not break them."

"Right. How do I get back?"

"You just leave. Will yourself back."

"Will you be alright?"

"Always the hero," she murmured to herself, "Yes, Javi, I will be alright."

"How did you know my…"

"Arete told me."

"Chatter box."

"May your blade find glory and your soul find peace."

"And may your soul find peace."

Javier willed himself back. A few of the people gasped when he reappeared but he ignored them. He went and found the Captain and told him everything that had happened. The Captain only nodded and told him to follow the advice that Jona had given him. They agreed that it would be to best to do it that night.

In the meantime, Javier organized his new army into work groups, getting the defenses ready. Now that he had excessive manpower, he was able to properly begin creating defenses. The Captain divided up their new recruits into three different groups. The groups rotated between building defenses, combat training, and resting. He placed Javier in charge of the defenses and Travis over the training. At first the recruits were confused that they would have a day off, but the rigor of their training soon showed them how important it was to rest.

During the first few days, the children and older townsfolk were a nuisance rather than a resource. They had plenty of enthusiasm but little to offer in the way of physical labor and military strength. It was Barry that came up with tasks for them to do that were both helpful and kept them from getting under foot. He gathered the smaller children and set to work gathering feathers and the straightest sticks they could find. The older men were handy with their knives, so he taught them how to properly carve bows and fletch arrows.

As the camp morphed from a refugee camp into a war camp, the townsfolk took notice as well, joining them in their efforts. The Captain cheerfully accepted every offer to help. When Creeve came around asking for compensation for the lost men and occupants, he went straight to Javier, thinking him more levelheaded and less threatening than the Captain. When he complained to Javier, Javier didn't even have to say anything. His army carted Creeve off and dumped him back on his doorstep and informed him that he was not to bother the High Commander again.

The next five weeks flew by while Javier attempted to get the fortifications in place. The wall on top of the ramparts was as strong as they could make it. He wasn't sure how well it would hold against the warlock, but it would do just fine against regular troops. Right and Left returned and wasted no time upgrading the defenses Javier had in place. The engineers they had brought with them slaved night and day on the siege machines. Most of the laborers didn't know or really understant what the twins were asking them to make so they had to make small scale machines first so their new engineering teams would understand.

The townsfolk provided ideal labor for the construction of arrows and bows. It had taken them two precious weeks to find the right material for the bow strings and another week to make enough. Once they got that all taken care of, they got their archers training. A few showed real skill and were pulled out for special instruction. Travis was covered in bruises from all the training sessions he was leading. He knew the others weren't fairing much better but he couldn't afford to tell them to take it easy. Besides, his bruises faded more quickly than others.

People continued to trickle in, coming to ask for help at the temple. They would more often than not stay afterwards and help with the defense of the temple. Javier lost count of how many times he gave his speech over those weeks. It didn't take long before his army reached a respectable size. If the Captain estimates on Aster's army were correct, they wouldn't have enough people to stop them. Their plan banked on Pablo and Contreras reaching them on time, and the war machines being enough to force the enemy back.

The last day of the fifth week they finished the wall and Javier got his first full night's sleep. When he woke the Captain was waiting outside his tent with a grim look.

"Javi, I've got bad news," the Captain told him solemnly.

"What's that, sir?" Javier asked.

"Aster is moving faster than we thought. He'll be here in two days," the Captain informed him.

Javier felt the blood drain from his face. A cold panic gripped his heart. "That's almost a week early. Pablo and Contreras won't be here in time."

"I already sent a rider to get them, but it looks like they won't," the Captain concurred.

"What are we going to do? Any brilliant back up plans?"

"What have we always done my friend? What would you have the Knight Angels do?"

"We fight on."

"And that what we'll do. We have prepared this place as best we can with the time and materials we have at hand. It will have to be enough."

"Sir, what about the druids? Have they responded to our request for help?"

The Captain snorted in disgust. "They said they don't interfere with the petty squabbles between clans."

"Don't they know what's going on? They do realize that we're risking *everything* to help them, right?"

"I'm sure that they do but they just don't care."

"What about Patty? Any word from him?"

"No, they are keeping him, Rashta and Xanthamius cut off from us. Still nothing from any of them."

"Is there any good news today?" Javier grumbled.

"High Commander," the Captain said sharply, "There is no time for that. Time to step up and lead. Like me, you are a symbol now. What you are is more than a man, you have to be, that's what the people need."

"Yes, sir."

Javier quickly washed his face and followed the Captain throughout the camp getting them ready for the upcoming battle. The day was a frenzy of people getting supplies gathered in the right places, and people readying for a fight. Javier knew that the wilderness fort was at least four days away, and it would take any army at least that long to get back. That meant they were going to have to stall Aster for week until their reinforcements came, or crush Aster's army. Neither scenario seemed likely to him. He let none of the anxiety he felt reach his face. His people needed him to be strong and he would be the rock they could count on.

The morning of the second day he awoke to whiskers in his face. He pushed Arete to the side and dressed slowly. He knew what the day would bring and he wasn't sure if he was up to the task. He joined a group of recruits for breakfast, forcing himself to eat and joke with them. The playful attitude helped them relax, and Javier found that it helped him as well.

When he had finished breakfast, he went to find the Captain. He rode Arete through the camp, he wasn't sure if she was full grown yet, but she held his weight, so he rode her. The army always drew strength from the sight of him riding her. He knew she wasn't strong enough to ride into battle yet, but the small rides were good for moral, and both he and Arete enjoyed them.

He found the Captain on the ramparts giving orders to nervous recruits. He spoke to them calmly, sometimes explaining his instructions several times. His calm voice eased their fears, and they all left him standing taller.

"Morning, sir," Javier said when he reached him.

The Captain sent his last recruit scurrying away and then came over to talk to Javier.

"Good morning, Javi," the Captain said with nod, "What's eating at you."

Javier wasn't surprised that Captain had read him so easily. He leaned against the ramparts considering his words carefully. "I'm scared, sir. I got over combat jitters years ago. I've lost count how many times we went into battle, not believing we were going to live. What makes this so different?"

"You're more than a simple leader this time, Javi. You have never had this many lives looking to you for protection. You promised them victory, and now we have to deliver," the Captain explained.

"I've led penty of men before, sir, I don't know why this is so different," Javier pressed.

"You've led soldiers, Javi, not farmers. These aren't men trained and ready for war like you're used to. These are just simple folk that want to live. They want to stay free and keep what is theirs. These are the type of people you risked your life for."

"The salt of the earth."

"Exactly. No some pompous politician or an entitled heiress." Javier blushed at that one. "These are simple folk that just want something better than mud and fear. You can see their hope and I for one know I don't want to betray that hope."

"I guess that's true, I don't know if I'm ready though, sir," Javier sighed.

"Well, that's a moot point now," the Captain replied.

"How do you figure that?" Javier asked.

"Because the party has arrived," the Captain grinned.

"Party…?" Javier asked confused.

Javier spun around and saw Aster's army on the horizon. The teaming mass filled it, exceeding the numbers they had originally thought. There were more than the five thousand they had estimated. Javier put the number closer to ten or twelve thousand. Now that he could see his enemy, Javier felt his anxiety melt away.

"A party indeed," he grinned back.

Chapter

TWENTY SEVEN

"Oh light, look at them all, how can we beat that?" a recruit moaned.

Travis slapped him gently in the back of the head before answering, "Easy."

"How? Tell us," another begged.

"All we have to do is kill them all," he answered cheerfully.

They looked at him like he was crazy, drawing a laugh from him, which did nothing to ease their fears. He patted a few of them on the back while he watched the army draw closer. He knew they wouldn't be close enough to attack for a couple more hours and at least as long before they were in formation to attack, so he left his squad to look for the Captain.

He passed Slappy, still with his group of midwives and new recruits he had commandeered to teach the basics of field medicine. The first week had tested the lieutenant. Most of his students were woman and Travis knew his uncle had drilled into him that he was to never hit a woman. After the first week they started shaping up. The midwives stopped second guessing him every chance they got, and the recruits started remembering their lessons, so his hand had finally stopped twitching. Travis nodded to him and continued on.

The Captain wasn't hard to find. He just looked for the busiest part of the rampart. The Captain was at the epicenter of the activity. He dismissed the runners as Travis approached.

"What do you think?" the Captain asked.

"Well, seems simple from here," Travis replied knowing the Captain was asking for ideas.

"How do you figure?" the Captain asked.

"Well, there's some bad guys over there that need killing and an army full of people willing to help you do that," Travis answered.

"Thanks," the Captain drawled.

"My pleasure," Travis smiled, "Besides, you have the twin swords of destiny."

"That I do," the Captain replied absently. His hand drifted up to touch Excalibur.

"Any similarities?" Travis asked.

"Too many," the Captain responded, "This is a lot like every time the Dark armies come flooding into the lands held by the Light."

"Well, that's horrifying," Travis muttered.

"What's your assessment of the army?"

"We couldn't be more ready," Travis lied.

The Captain's lips twitch, letting Travis know that his lie had been caught but the Captain wasn't going to call him on it.

"It will do nicely. It has to," the Captain replied absently, gripping the rampart with white knuckles.

The army behind them grew restless. Their soldiers talked quietly to each other, but their anxiety was palpable. Both Travis and the Captain turned to them trying to determine how nervous their army was.

"Captain, you need to say something. If you don't, this battle may be over before it starts," Travis warned.

"You're right," the Captain agreed. He turned to the crowd

clearing his voice and holding up his hand for silence.

"SILENCE!" Travis roared, "Lock it up! Eyes forward!"

The part of the army within earshot quieted instantly. Those farther back nudged their neighbors so that they could hear what was going to be said. The Captain spared him a grateful nod before opening his mouth.

"Brother, comrades, sons of Avalon and the Light, my friends," the Captain started. His voice was amplified by a spell Travis assumed he added right before speaking. "I am the promised Guardian of the Light. I am a lord of victory. A lord of light and life. I stand before you this day and tell you to rise. Rise up sons of the Light, and seize this day. This day is a day that comes only once a generation. On this field of battle, there is a chance for glory and brave few will be immortalized in story and song. Will that be you? Will your grandchildren, years from now, tell their children and grandchildren stories of this day? That when the Light called on you to stand with your brothers, you stood firm?

"Rise up my brothers. This is the day Avalon will remember forever. Rise up and fight! Rise with all your fury and might. Let us make the mountains tremble at our awesome strength. Let the winds carry forth the tales of our deeds. Rise to the challenge my brothers, and stand with me against this evil.

"I look at you, and I do not see *ariats*. I do not see inferior beings. I see heroes. I see champions. I see men thirsty for justice and on this day you shall have it. So rise, my brothers. Rise above your squalor. Rise above your presumed fate. Rise above the other mere mortal men. Rise above the despair I see in your hearts."

He paused briefly before continuing. "If today is your day to die, then so be it. Death comes for us all, but if it comes for you today, meet it with a smile, knowing you are already heroes. So rise with me brothers! Rise up and fight! For Avalon and the Light!" he roared drawing Caliburn from its scabbard.

"For Avalon and the Light!" they roared back at him.

Travis joined them in their cheers, feeling the goose bumps play along his arms. He drew his enormous blade in salute to the Captain. He heard a rush of steel as others joined him, still cheering. The Captain stood tall absorbing their cheers, his back to the rays of the rising sun.

"To your places!" he ordered.

There was an instant rush of eager faces scrambling to reach their designated posts. Travis smiled to himself in satisfaction. What they lacked in skill they now made up for in eagerness. Travis followed them to his own section of the wall, preparing his men for the inevitable attack. Farther back from the wall was a group of their largest and strongest men. When the wall was breached, their job was to rush their and plug the hole.

Travis stood side by side with his men, waiting impatiently for the enemy army to arrange into battle lines. He spoke continuously, doling out as much last-minute advice as he could, knowing every little bit of advice he could cram in would help them in the long run.

Below him a smaller man struggled with a large clay jar. Travis jumped down to give him a hand and realized the man was actually a boy twelve or thirteen years old. The grimy face glared at him, daring him to say something.

"What are you doing, son?" Travis asked.

"I'm not your son," the boy snapped.

"Fine. What are you doing, boy?" Travis asked again.

"Helping defeat this monster," the boy grunted, still trying to move the jar to where the others were being piled.

"We can't have boys messing up our lines," Travis told him.

The boy stopped dragging his pot to give Travis a pointed and cold stare.

"I stopped being a boy last year when Aster killed my mother, kidnapped my sisters and left me to care for my little brothers. Two of them starved to death, another died on the way here and the last brother I have left alive is with me in the village. If Aster makes it past this wall, he will die," the boy informed him.

"Why not leave? There are many places that Aster hasn't touched yet," Travis said.

"My brother is sick. Only the druids can save him now. Like I said, if Aster breaks through, we die," the boy replied, resuming his attempt to drag the pot to the wall.

Travis watched him work for a bit. He started to walk back to his post when he heard the boy call out again.

"You're not going to make me go?" the boy asked.

"As you said, you're not a boy, you're a man," Travis replied, "Around here men are free to choose their own fate. If this is what you want, then I could always use another brave warrior."

The boy flashed him a quick grin before scampering off after another pot. Travis watched him grinning to himself. A moment later the grin faded from his face. It hurt him that children so small had to be adults so early.

"For a better tomorrow," Travis muttered.

"Sir?" a soldier asked.

"To your post," Travis replied turning back to the enemy army.

While the enemy lines finished assembling themselves, a small contingent of five men broke off from the main army and walked towards the center of the field. The Captain had anticipated this, so Travis was ready to go. He dropped over the wall, right where he was and jogged toward the center and the Captain. He spotted Slappy, Peters, and Javier, riding Arete, walking toward the Captain as well. By agreement, Asha was staying behind, out of sight. She and Bubbles were to be their ace in the hole when the situation required one. They fell in step, slightly behind him, walking to meet the enemy representatives.

"What do you suppose they want?" Peters asked.

"Terms most likely," the Captain replied.

"What are the odds they want to surrender?" Travis asked.

"I'll tell you what, if that's what this meeting is about, I'll give you every coin I have," Javier laughed.

"I'll take that action," Travis said instantly.

"Deal," Javier answered, "Wait, how many coins do you have left?"

"None," Travis said with a smile.

"Ha! Me either!" Javier roared with laughter.

The Captain snorted before he shut them down, "Let's get our game faces on people."

"Yes, sir, applying game face now," Travis replied solemnly.

The Captain gave him a flat, sideways look.

"I know, sir, I can't pull off snarky, but Patty isn't here, and someone needs you to keep you humble," Travis tease.

The Captain only grunted.

"Really?" Javier asked.

"I am only a man, Javi. True I was born with special gifts and abilities, not to mention the enormous amount of responsibility, but I am still a man. I, like everyone else, am defined more by the choices I make than by the products of my birth. Most may go along with the hand they were dealt, but I strive to rise above that. I want to be more than what life says I should be. Having Patty remind me that I am only a man and not an omnipotent god helps," the Captain answered.

"Fair enough," Javier agreed.

True to his word, Travis put on his game face. The men in front of them were deadly. Their gait, posture, and eyes told him that. Before they were anything else, these men were killers, and they had grown to like killing. More than ever, he was glad they had decided to take a stand here.

"Hello," their leader said pleasantly still walking forward.

"Hello," the Captain echoed back.

They stopped a few feet away, closer than decorum dictated. This close he could tell that they were each slightly larger than he was. This was a very strange feeling for Travis. He had been in too many fights to give height too much of an advantage, but being the smaller guy in the fight was not something he had experienced since middle school. He figured they were still the better fighters, but having this many large men in close proximity, did not help his anxiety.

"I am Aster. Are you the legendary Lord Captain? Master of the Wilderness Fort?" Aster asked politely.

"I am. I see my reputation proceeds me," the Captain replied.

"I take note when someone makes wild claims that they are a Guardian of the Light," Aster smiled.

"I merely state facts. Whatever rumors fly are not my problem," the Captain countered.

Aster's smile flickered, "Ah, so you actually believe you are a Guardian. Well, it would not be the first time a Champion was mistaken. I have met a few in my days, but I put them all in their place since then."

"I glad your heart is in the right place," the Captain smiled.

Aster's smile remained plastered on his face but his eyes turned deadly. "It is. Shall we get down to business?"

"If you would like to. I would hate to keep you from moving on," the Captain answered pleasantly.

"That will be... difficult," Aster said, "I simply *must* speak to the druids."

"I doubt that. There is nothing for you here," the Captain assured him.

"Oh, I think there is. I am here for my birthright. Unlike you, I really am a Guardian, and I need what the druids have stolen from me," Aster countered.

"Perhaps you are a Guardian, but you lack everything that would make you a king," the Captain replied.

"I have the will and the strength to lead. That is all I need to rule. What do you have?" Aster demanded.

"I have the blessing of Merlin the Magnificient. I have the backing of the Knight Angels. I have a Demon that guards my back," the Captain shot back.

"Do you now?" Aster asked curiously, "How can the Knights support you, when they are with me?"

On cue, one of them behind him sprouted wings. Travis stared in surprise at the golden wings. He tried to say something but Javier kicked him gently. He looked over and caught the subtle shake of his head.

"An interesting display," the Captain mused.

"And your Knights? Where are they?" Aster asked.

"Like all Knights of old, they are not at my beck and call. The Knights stand outside kingdoms and bow to no king. Surely your Knights told you that," the Captain smiled.

While fury bloomed on Aster's face, a glimmer of doubt passed along the face of the mysterious Knight. "Enough of this chatter. Move your pathetic little army and dismantle those walls, or I will do it for you and slaughter every last one of you!" Aster ordered.

"No, I think we won't. The forces of the Light do not bow to the wishes of a mad man," the Captain replied.

"So, you presume yourselves my betters," Aster snarled.

"Well let's face it," Travis cut in, "You're setting a pretty low standard. It's really not that hard to be better."

Javier laughed softly. Aster's eyes turned to him.

"Nice cat. Before we are through I will ride that beast while I drink from your skull," Aster snarled.

"I wouldn't recommend it, the taste is horrible. Not as bad as your breath, but still quite unpleasant," Javier smirked.

"You allow you men to speak to their betters in such tones?" Aster hissed at the Captain, his eyes narrowed.

"Respect is earned. You have yet to earn any," the Captain replied, "Now, remove your army, leave in peace, and we shall let you live. Press the attack, and you will die."

"So, to battle then," Aster smiled, "I look forward to it. Just remember this, that you had a chance to bow to a true Guardian, you chose to fight instead. Later, when you lay on the ground choking on your own blood, look to me, so that I can laugh while the light fades from your eyes."

"Only if you promise to do the same for me," Travis grinned.

Aster stared at him, not moving. Abruptly, he turned on his heels and headed back to his army, flanked by his warriors. The Captain watched him walk away for a moment before returning to his own army.

"Are we ready Javi?" the Captain asked urgently.

"We are, sir," Javier replied.

"Good, ride ahead and prepare the archers. The attack will come as soon as Aster reaches his army," the Captain ordered.

"Sir, I don't know if Arete will be in shape to fight if I do that," Javier protested.

"Don't worry, the hand-to-hand combat won't start yet. She'll have time to rest," the Captain assured him.

Javier urged Arete into a sprint, leaving them behind.

"Sir?" Peter's asked.

"What is it?" the Captain asked.

"Are we sure that there was only one spy?" he asked uneasily.

"Yes, there is no one else. I looked at them all and he was the only one with betrayal in his heart," the Captain answered.

"So, we let him sneak through tonight?" Travis asked.

"Yes. We have him so full of false information that he will help us more than he will hurt us giving away any real intel," the Captain assured them.

They jogged back to the wall, seeking its shelter. They were fifty yards from the wall when he saw men on the wall. Turning back, Travis saw the first lines of men start marching forward. He could just make out the beat of war drums. Without speaking, the men broke into a sprint heading back into the fort.

Chapter

TWENTY EIGHT

"*Ready archers,*" the Captain's voice crackled over the coms. Patty's spell still held, making it easy for the Captain's orders to be heard by his squad.

"Ready archers!" Javier roared.

Lines of swords and axemen stepped back making room for the archers. They lined up waiting with an arrow nocked, just like he had trained them. In the field in front of them the first waves of men were trotting at them. Everything they had learned so far still suggested that Avaloneans really didn't know what bows were anymore.

"*Draw,*" the Captain ordered.

"Draw!" Javier echoed.

Wooden arrow shafts rasped against the grain of the bows. Creaks could be heard coming from the wood, as the bow limbs bent.

"*Hold.*"

"Hold!"

The Aster's army marched silently, and the Captain's army watched them just as silently. The only sound was the raged breath of men, a few hushed prayers, and the rhythmic pounding of feet from the marching army. The cloudless sky shined cheerily on the field were the carnage was about to begin. A gently breeze blew across the field gently playing with the beads of sweat on the men's forheads and arms.

They were assembled in neat blocks ten across and ten deep. Advancing towards him, there were seven blocks.

Travis could see the officers wave their swords even though

he was too far away to hear the orders. Aster's first wave rushed forward screaming at the top of their lungs.

"Hold!" Javier ordered again. Thankfully none of the archers had panicked and let loose. He took pride in their disciple. They stood still as statues waiting for the order to loose. He knew the weight of the bowstrings made it difficult, but they still held.

"*Loose!*"

"Loose!" Javier roared.

The archer let their arrows fly. They had been given strict orders to make no sound while the arrow fell. Javier was able to hear the gentle whisper of hundreds of arrows falling toward the enemy lines.

"Nock arrows!" he ordered before the first ones had begun to fall on the enemy.

"Draw!" The arrows started to fall among the running bodies. They still didn't know what was happening, only that some of their number were down and screaming.

"*Loose!*" the Captain ordered.

"Loose!" Javier shouted.

A second wave flew out across the field.

"Nock arrows!" The charging army had skipped a beat.

"Draw!" The second wave fell, kill and wounding more of the enemy.

"*Hold,*" came the order.

"Hold," Javier repeated. The enemy charge had mostly ground

to a halt. The survivors looked at one another in confusion. A couple of stragglers at the front hadn't seen their comrades fall. The Captain's elite archers picked a few of them off, sending the rest scrambling back.

Javier hoped that they would all retreat, but they didn't. The remaining officers were screaming and cursing them. They used their whips liberally, getting their troops back into formation. Javier shook his head. Even though they didn't know it yet, he knew that they were doomed already. The army started forward again at a slow trot.

"*Loose.*"

"Loose!" Again a wave of death flew.

"Nock arrows!" Death rained down a third time. Now there were no war cries. There was only screams of fear and pain.

"Draw!" The officers pushed them forward. They were close now. A hundred yards at most. Close enough he could almost make out the orders.

"Aim!" Javier prayed this wave would break them.

"*Loose!*"

"Loose!" This time most of the arrows found their mark. Hundreds fell to the arrows. Javier wasn't sure how many were dead, but there wasn't enough left of this first wave to ever dream of breaching their walls.

The elites had targeted the officers, with orders to kill them. Judging by how many arrows decorated their corpses, more of his archers had also decided to target them. Without the officers to hold them in place, what remained of the wave broke and ran back towards Aster's main army. Javier estimated that there was only three or four hundred left.

As they reached their comrades, large figures, Javier was certain were Sons of Lancelot, step forward and slaughtered them. They scrambled, trying to hide among the army, but the other soldiers betrayed them and threw them out where the Sons could find them. Aster's message was clear. Yes, you might die attacking the wall, but you *will* die if you retreat.

"Get ready. The next wave will be much larger and this one we won't be able to break."

Apparently, the Captain had reached the same conclusion that he had. Javier readied himself. Runners ran up to the archers topping off their supply of arrows. More than one archer limbered up their arms readying for the next wave.

It didn't take long for the drums to change their beat. The army responded. This time twenty blocks lined themselves up for the march across the field. A group of officers scattered from where they were talking to Aster, and went to their respective units. Amid the thunderous pounding drums, the army lurched forward. They walked slowly at first, no doubt conserving their energy for a last minute burst to the wall.

"Nock arrows!" Javier ordered.

The archers rustled as they complied, still not making a sound. The field was still full of groaning men, trying to crawl back to their army while others lay where they fell, moaning and waiting for death to come take them.

"Draw."

"Draw arrows!" The enemy army was still trotting at them, maintaining formation. Javier watched them enter ranged, trampling their comrades under foot.

"*Loose!*"

"Loose!" Once again arrows arched out seeking targets. A shout went up from the enemy officers. Shields rose from the ranks and sheltered them. Many of the arrows still found targets but the majority bounced harmlessly off of shields.

"Sir, that was faster than we anticipated," Javier said over the coms.

"*Yes it was, but that changes nothing. We proceed as planned.*"

Javier could do nothing but agree with the Captain. "Nock arrows!"

"*Fire at will!*"

"Fire at will! Loose! Loose! Loose!" Javier roared.

The archers responded, sending every arrow in their quiver at the attackers. The arrows started having more and more effect as they ripped holes in the army's defenses. Even with as many of the army as they dropped, there were still too many coming at them.

"Archers, fall back! Infantry, forward!" Javier ordered.

The archer slipped in between the armor bodies of the infantry and dropped down to the dirt, forming up again behind the wall. Runners appeared again bring a fresh supply of arrows. In the village, Javier new every able hand was churning out more arrows. If there was a chicken with a feather left, Javier would pay its weight in gold for it.

The Aster's army realized there were no more arrow dropping and that the archers had retreated so the broke into a full run. They screamed defiance at the Captain's army, but no one from the Captain's army shouted back. Ladders were passed forward while they ran in preparation for the assault. The first lines came up to the wall screaming. Spears meant to be thrown at the defenders went awry when the ground disappeared beneath them. The trench that Patty had dug, had been filled with sharpened stakes, and then carefully covered. Since the trench had been dug deeper than a man with his arms stretched up, there was plenty of room for a few more lines to fall in. The army was unable to stop their momentum and pushed some of their comrades into the trench.

The Captain's army finally roared at them, heaving large jugs filled with oil and tar into the pit. The jars shattered, spilling their contents on the bodies below. Torches followed into the trench, lighting a roaring fire. There would be no assaulting the wall anytime soon. Javier nodded to the teams dedicated to throwing the occasional jar into the pit to make sure the fire stay going.

Most of the infantry melted off the walls, headed for the gates into the camp. Aster's army also pushed toward that area, now that it was the only accessible point. Javier was considering going with them, when a portion of the wall near him was ripped into pieces. Parts of the trench near the breaches also exploded, showing dirt and burning oil everywhere. He looked out into the field and saw little groups of men with large shields, protecting figures at their center. Aster's warlocks had entered the fight.

They threw fireballs at groups of men and at the wall. Whole sections of wall flew into the air, landing on friend and foe alike. At one breach enemy forces rushed the gap while a warlock blew apart the trench in front of it. Their timing was off and he ended up killing most of that squad.

Javier drew his swords calling for Arete and his squad to form up. They jogged towards the nearest gap, ready to stop the enemy there. Fireballs arched towards him, but the aim was off, so they fell harmlessly to the side.

From the hill above him, he heard the crack of a sniper rifle. Around the field, warlocks fell, with each crack of the sniper rifle. It didn't take long for the guards to realize their warlocks were in danger. They tightened the rings, using their own bodies to shelter the mages. The cracks of the sniper rifle came less frequently, since Porter had to take more time aiming. Weeks was with him, acting as a spotter. When the last warlock fell, the Captain's army let out a cheer.

"That's the last of my ammo, sir, not a bullet to spare," Porter reported.

"Copy that," the Captain sighed.

"Any chance one of them was Meem?" Travis asked.

"Negative, he won't commit his good troops yet. Not until we're weakened," the Captain replied, *"That should make Meem keep his head down though."*

Javier hurried with his men to the gap, throwing in with the defenders already there. The teeming masses on the other side threatened to overwhelm them but he stood firm. Arete tore into enemy soldiers that got near her. He could feel his blood pounding and his pulse race while he cut through them. His body responded faster than it ever had. He turned blows he had never been able to before. Whatever Jona had done to his body, he liked it.

"Sir, we're getting hammered on the west gate. Requesting archer support," Peters said.

Strings thrummed behind him. The archer resumed dropping death from above. The attack was focused mostly on the west gate and at Javier's gap. Aster's army seemed to respond instantly. The front line fought on, but those farther back panicked as arrows fell among them.

The Captain's training was apparent all around. Aster's men fell much faster than the Captain's, boosting moral. The panicked troops in the back failed to fill the gaps opened by the Captain's men. Enemy lines crumbled and they started to retreat.

"M'Lord, you must pull back," a voice at his elbow said.

"What?" Javier asked whipping his head back.

"You must pull back," he repeated.

"I need to hold this gap. I'm not pulling my men out," Javier said defiantly.

"M'Lord, you have been at the front for over an hour, you need to pull back and rest," the man said cringing.

"Oh. Really?" Javier asked bewildered.

He looked up and saw that the sun had moved significantly in the sky. Arete limped up to him panting. He wasn't sure when she had taken her wound. He stooped down to inspect it and his own leg gave out.

"Let me see," another forceful voice order.

"I'm fine," Javier insisted pushing him away.

A powerful slap whipped his head to the side, making him see stars. He wasn't sure, because he was a little loopy, but he was certain he heard Arete laugh. Javier looked up with blurry eyes at Slappy's stern eyes.

"Let. Me. See," Slappy repeated firmly.

Javier moved his leg closer, letting Slappy look at it. A runner brought Javier water and food, which he inhaled while Slappy stitched up the wound. From his pouch, Slappy pulled some leaves and stuck them in his mouth. From another pouch he pulled a length of cloth. Javier was afraid of where this was going. He tried to worm away, but a look from Slappy stilled him. Sure enough, Slappy spit the gooey mess on his leg and then wrapped it tight. Despite his reservations, the pain in his leg faded almost instantly.

"Ooooh, that's nice," Javier moaned.

"I hear it is. One of the midwives showed me it. It works wonders so far," Slappy commented.

Javier stood testing the leg and found it solid and pain-free.

"Don't strain it," Slappy warned, "It may not hurt but you're still injured."

Javier tried to nod but was distracted by the shouting coming from the walls. He ran to the top to see what was so important. When he looked, his heart fell down to his toes. The rest of Aster's army was marching across the field at them.

"Push men!" Javier roared, "Finish these ones off!"

As he shouted he lobbed a grenade into a group of heavily armed men advancing with shields locked. The grenade exploded sending shrapnel flying though out the entire formation. Javier men fell on the survivors, cutting them down. With the last of the attackers down his men let out a ragged cheer. He looked at them and saw a disturbing portion of them dead or injured.

"Well done men, you've made me proud. You've done everything I have asked of you, and I have asked everything from you. Now I must ask for even more," Javier said regretfully. Their cheers died down. "That was the first wave of men. They were Aster's weakest, meant to break our defenses so his real army could march in and destroy us. I will stand here, as long as I can, but you have earned the right to know the truth. Any of you who stand with me, will give their lives to this cause. I will stand as long as I can, but I will fall here. If you stay with me, we will share the same fate. If you leave now, I won't think any less of you, you've done enough."

The men's weapons were held loosely in weak grips. They watched him not accepting what their ears had heard.

"M'Lord, I didn't follow this far to give up so close to glory," one of his archers called out, "If the Knight Angles are fighting here than so will I. As long as you fight here, I will fight as well."

Javier nodded to him.

"I stand with the Knights as well!" another shouted.

"Darkness take it," Another cursed, "death comes for us all. Why not grab a little glory on the way out?"

"We are with you!"

"For Avalon and the Light!"

"The Knight Angels!"

The shouts kept coming. Javier nodded to them and went down to the gap. They cleared the bodies and waited for the army to arrive. Javier looked to his left and saw an archer with his sword drawn. When Javier raised an eyebrow at him, the man shrugged and raised an empty quiver at him. Javier nodded in understanding, and then turned attention back to the field.

Another block of heavily armed soldier marched for them. Javier pulled his side arm and emptied the clip. He loaded a new clip and aimed for the gaps left by the last volley of bullets. He threw his last grenade in the middle of the survivors and droped the grenade pin on the ground.

His eyes followed the pin to the ground, and he saw himself surrounded by the shinning brass cases of the spent ammunition poking out of the mud. He looked at them and then at his empty gun smiling.

"Fix bayonets," he whispered.

"M'Lord?" one of the men asked.

"Prepare for combat," Javier ordered.

The opposing army marched slowly, taking their time crossing the field. No arrows fell among them. While they marched, the Captain's army finished off their opponents and filed to the wall getting ready for the next wave.

A small group of men charged ahead headed straight for Javier's gap. Javier charged out to meet them, his men a step behind him. The front runner was the same enormous Son who had claimed to be a Knight Angel. He locked eyes with Javier, and they ran straight at each other. Before they clashed, the Son flared his wings again. Javier felt his men hesitate. As their swords clashed, Javier flared his wings. Unlike the Son, Javier now had four wings sprouting from his back. Both sides stopped in their tracks not quite understanding what was going on.

"What are you?" the Son demanded locking hilts with Javier.

"I am Javier, High Commander of the Knight Angels. Who are you to perverse the name of the Knight Angels?" Javier shot back.

"That cannot be true! I was given that rank by Aster, the Guardian of Avalon!" he grunted.

"Aster can't give you that rank. Only the previous High Commander can give the rank," Javier grunted back.

"How are you so strong?" the Son gasped.

"I am the High Commander," Javier repeated, "It comes with the job."

He pushed the Son away. He stumbled for back, then setting his feet glaring at Javier. Javier met him glare for glare.

"I am the High Commander, and I am giving you an order, turn from Aster. He is not the chosen Guardian. I fight with the chosen Guardian and so should you," Javier ordered.

"No," the Son spat.

"So be it, Fallen Angel," Javier said.

He made a snatching motion with his hand, weaving a spell he instinctively knew. The Son gasped in shock and pain as his wings rumpled and disappeared. The wings appeared miniaturized in Javier's hand. He looked at them sadly, before crushing them. The Son gasped again and fell to his knees. Javier walked up to him and looked down into his eyes.

"Goodbye brother," he whispered before stabbing him through the chest.

While the body slipped of the blade, he looked out at Aster's army that was still watching him. The Captain had finally ordered the catapults to start firing. Fist size rocks rained down in the middle of their army, ripping giant holes in their lines. Despite this, they were oddly calm.

"Will you defy the Knight Angels?" Javier asked.

"To defy Aster is death, and I only see one Knight here," an officer said.

"Then come, I will grant you your deaths," Javier smiled.

Travis watched the army approach. Javier's duel was brief, then he was swamped by bodies rushing forward. From here, it looked like he and his men were holding their own, so he didn't worry about it. He turned to his own fight. A group of Sons was headed straight for them. His group was the best in the Captain's army, so they placed themselves in their path. The largest of them charged out ahead of the others.

"I am Nord, chief of this clan! Send your pitiful champion forward!" the giant screamed.

Travis didn't hesitate rushing forward to meet him. Their blades flashed in the sunlight. Sparks flew in all directions. Others from both sides tried to edge in on their duel but were killed as quickly as they approached.

"Who are you?" Nord panted when they separated briefly.

"I am Travis, of the Knight Angels," he replied.

Nord's eyes widened slightly when Travis flared his wings, but it was clear to him, that Nord was not impressed. A few heartbeats later Nord attacked again, pressing Travis. They danced around each other trying to get around the other's blade.

Travis stumbled first taking a blade to the leg. He went down hard onto his back. Nord looked down from above smiling evilly.

"You're mine Knight," he cackled kicking Travis sword away.

Travis reached down to his hip and whipped his glock out. He fired both of his bullets into Nord's chest.

"Oof," Nord grunted feeling the holes in his chest.

Travis pulled his legs out from where Nord was falling. The giant's breath became labored as he fell to his knees. Travis rose to his knees meeting Nord face to face. He drew Nord's knife from its sheath and placed it against Nord chest, above his heart.

"You should not have fought against the Knights," Travis told him.

He buried the blade into Nord's chest up to the hilt. Blood welled up around the blade and covered Travis's hand. Nord held a small grin, as he died. Travis felt his veins ice up. Something was wrong, something was very wrong. He looked down and saw Nord's other knife deep in his own gut.

Gritting his teeth against the pain he rose to his feet, leaving the blade where it was. He remembered Slappy telling him once to keep the blade in wounds like this one until a surgeon could take it out or would cause more harm than good. The Sons who had come with Nord stood in a circle around him, creating a bubble of calm.

"Well, that was fun," Travis muttered retreaving his sword, "Which one of you is next?"

"Chief?" one of the Sons asked.

"Me? Chief?" Travis asked a little dazed.

"That is the law. Only the strong may lead and you are the strongest," he replied.

"So why don't you just kill me then? I couldn't stop you," Travis grumbled.

"That is against our laws. A chief may only be challenged once a week," he answered.

"Well then, shall we get back into the fight?" Travis asked.

The Sons shuffled, not sure what to do.

"Against Aster, we are fighting against him," Travis clarified.

"You heard him!" the Son shouted.

As one the twenty odd Sons turned and stood shoulder to shoulder against the onslaught. At first, Aster's army didn't respond to the sudden change of allegiance. The officers adjusted quickly enough. Travis's troops took the change in stride, standing with their new allies but not too close.

Travis watched from one knee trying to see what would happen. His new Sons fought with incredible skill and strength, but Aster's superior numbers were being brought to bear. Even as skilled at they were, that were no match for the thousands still at Aster's disposal.

It doesn't matter, Travis thought spitting up blood, *We can't turn this away. Even with these new Sons and the catapults ripping into them, Javier will go down any minute now and I'm done.*

"M'Lord!" a little voice cried.

Travis turned to see the boy standing behind him.

"How are you lad?" he asked numbly.

"M'Lord, you're mortally wounded," the boy sobbed, tears leaking from his eyes.

"I am," Travis admitted.

"I will seek the healer, the one you call Slappy," the boy chattered.

"Don't bother," Travis muttered but the boy was already gone.

Travis felt himself fall to the ground. It was seeped in blood. The scuffling of boots and men had churned the blood and dirt together, making a sticky, reeking mud. Travis landed sideways onto it glad he couldn't smell it. The boy rushed to his side placing Travis head on his lap.

"Drink, m'Lord," the boy pleaded bringing Travis's canteen to his lips.

Travis only drank a mouthful before sputtering and spraying more blood into the air. He nodded his thanks to the boy and closed his eyes.

"I did it Captain," he murmured into the coms, "I was the last shield of the light. I stood against evil men with everything I had. I think you would be proud."

The Captain said something, but Travis was too far gone to understand or care.

Chapter

TWENTY NINE

Javier panted in exhaustion, feeling his lungs burn, and his limbs begging for a break, but he kept on fighting. He was the only thing keeping the line from collapsing. Every time someone fell another stepped up and he knew it was because this was where the Knight Angels were. His strokes were coming slower now. He had sent Arete back, knowing she wouldn't be able to fight properly with her injured leg.

It was only a matter of time before he ran out of men and Aster's army broke through. If he gave in here, the army would pour through. The Captain was at the west gate holding them there, so he was counting on Javier to hold his side of the line.

Javier whipped his blade in a desperate move that left him exposed, but it succeeded in beheading the two men he was fighting. A spear snaked in from behind them and grazed his ribs. He hissed at the pain, but it was just one of many small wounds he now bore. He killed the spearman and looked for another enemy. There wasn't one.

Javier blinked weary eyes, looking around the field. The enemy was still there but they weren't attacking anymore. They were more interested in something coming from behind them. Now that he had attention to spare, Javier could hear horns sounding.

Aster didn't use horns before; he thought thickly, *I wonder what he's brought now.*

The horns continued to sound in the distance. From the tree line, a group of horses stepped out in formation. They trotted forward under the coaxing of the horns. They sped up to a canter, still in formation. Armored infantry flowed out behind them jogging out across the field.

The cavalry sped up to a full charge, slamming into the new front lines of Aster's army, trampling them beneath their feet. The charge flagged and the cavalry disengaged. Aster's troops tried to follow but they were met by the infantry, which had finally arrived. The cavalry split into two groups and slammed into the flanks of the army.

Ragged cheers rose form his men, who were as exhausted as Javier was. He tried to cheer with them but between his wounds and his fatigue, he just couldn't muster up the energy. He contented himself with watching in admiration.

A small contingent of horses came towards them, led by a black beast of a horse Javier had noticed in the initial charge. His men parted, letting them pass. As they drew closer Javier noticed a horn growing from the head of the black horse. This creature was nothing like the delicate beauties he had grown up with. This beast was anything but delicate. Even as tired as he was, he could feel the fiery spirit, and pride.

He reached a hand hesitantly toward its nose, and the stallion let him stroke its snout. Javier blew in his nostrils gently, letting the horse take in his scent. The stallion snorted and reared, throwing its rider. He settled down on all four, calming under Javier's voice.

"Pablo sent you this gift to apologize for being so late," the rider said dusting himself off.

"Lambert, I didn't know you could ride," Javier laughed which morphed into a cough.

Lambert was there in a flash with another figure next to him. Javier felt magic course through his body, healing his wounds. Energy filled his limbs again, bolstering his thoughts and spirits.

"Did you hide my exhaustion? And who is this?" Javier asked.

"This is Yender, a Healer mage," Lambert replied, "We're supposed to heal you and Arete, infuse you with energy and then send you back into the field."

"And you?" Javier asked mentally summoning Arete.

"I have to meet up with Lieutenant Roberts," he informed him.

Arete limped up to the mage to receive her healing. The mage was extremely efficient and had her on her feet on a flash.

"I have worked with them before," he explained moving on to the men nearby. He healed them quickly.

"You'll need a horse, time is of the essence," Javier said.

"Take mine, sir," a soldier volunteered.

"Thank you Cricket," Lamberts said accepting the reins.

"Good luck," Javier said mounting up.

"Good luck to you too," Lambert wished back.

They parted ways; Lamberts went farther into the camp while Javier turned towards the battle. Arete hissed at the unicorn who stomped his hoof at her, not wanting her to think she had the upper hand.

"Easy Arete, this is just for now," Javier promised climbing up on to the unicorn's back. He turned to his men, "So, who's got room for just a little more glory?"

They roared rushing forward not waiting for him to order the charge.

"Alrighty then, I guess we go now," he muttered to himself.

Javier kicked the horse forward, feeling the muscles ripple

under him with powerful legs eating up the ground. Arete streaked next to them. They hit the enemy line destroying any semblance of a front line. His line filed in behind them. Javier felt a smile rise to his lips, and he didn't stop it. His line was the anvil that their reinforcements break this army on.

Asha sat in her hut grinding her teeth. Bubbles feeling her anxiety, had worn a tract in the dirt around the inside edge of the hut. The wizened old crones and toddlers she shared the hut with sat in a tight circle in the middle of the hut, being very careful to stay out of their paths. The whisper quietly to each other or sang softly to the children to comfort them.

She could hear the fighting going on all day, the screams of the men giving their lives, while she hid. Every time she tried to leave, she felt the Captain order to stay again. She had almost lost it when she felt the Captain take a wound to his flank. Bubbles gripped her arm and growled at her.

When she could stand the anxiouty no longer, she screamed in frustration, venting her fury on the wall. Her hand went through it creating a small window for her to watch the battle unfold. The women and children were deathly silent and still. One little boy clapped his hands and smiled at her. She gave him an evil smile in return before focusing her attention back to her improvised window.

It looked like that were losing terribly to her, but still the Captain held her back. She watched Travis fall with tears in her eyes, and still she held. She watched Javier's position get overwhelmed and still she held. She was losing friends while she sat in relative comfort and safety.

When she decided that she was going whether the Captain liked it or not, she heard the horns. She pressed her eye to the hole watching them charge. The sun glinted off the horses' armor. She spotted Pablo on Breeze easily, holding the center. They would have smashed into the front line, but the line was already running from them.

She breathed a sigh of relief when the smaller contingent got to Javier, relieving him. She felt an enormous amount of pride when he climbed up on the horse and charged back in. Her feelings were short lived since she was *still* in the hut.

She was moping and once again considering breaking orders, when the largest explosion yet rocked the wall. An enormous chunk of the wall flew into the air, landing in the town, flattening two buildings. A group from Aster's army raced through the hole and made their way to the path toward the temple.

Asha saw the Captain running up the hill towards them. Asha had enough of waiting. She wrapped herself into Shadow Cloak and Stepped into the Captain's shadow. She knew that he knew she was there but chose to not say anything. Peters, Porter and Weeks met them on the trail up. Together they reached the top, Asha still hiding in the shadows.

They crested the top of the trail. Before them the great doors of the Temple were firmly shut, blocking all access to the temple. The building cast a shadow in the courtyard, shading Aster with a group of soldiers. Aster was pounding on the door, which held off his attacks without so much as a shudder.

"Aster!" the Captain roared.

"You!" Aster snarled abandoning the door.

"This is enough. Your army is beaten. I have won. Back down now!" the Captain ordered.

"I am a Guardian, and I will not bow down to you!" Aster screamed, "Behold the terrible might of a Guardian!"

Aster slammed his fists together bearing down. Asha wasn't sure if he was gathering energy or trying to pass a stool, but either way it wasn't going to be good. Aster opened his eyes and Asha saw they were blood red. Bloodrage. It was worse than she had expected.

"Do you see your mistake yet?" Aster smirked.

"Do you see yours?" the Captain asked him back.

The Captain's own eyes also showed his Bloodrage.

"NO!" Aster cried, "That's impossible. *I am the Guardian!*"

"As am I," the Captain said gently, "The difference is, I passed the tests, I was chosen, and I will be king. Not you."

"You lied to me!" Aster snarled at a woman next to him.

"I was mistaken, but I did not lie to you," she replied calmly.

"Meem! Do not test me," Aster warned.

"We can still kill him. Together, he is no match for us," Meem urged.

Asha Stepped into Aster's shadow, her dagger raised, ready for the kill. A figure Stepped out of the shadows as well, blocking her blade. Of course, Aster would have a demon. They spun around each other trying to end the other.

"You would send your assassin?" Aster asked in contempt.

"You weren't thinking the same thing?" the Captain asked back.

"I suppose I was," Aster smiled.

Asha could feel Meem gather energy for a blast. She let loose an incredible force of fire, lightning, and ice at the Captain. She knew the Captain's shields were not strong enough to stop them all. She was too skilled for him.

Before they struck, a figure dropped from the tower with an insane amount of force. His landing cracked the stone and sent a cloud of dust flying through the air. With casual ease he slapped the attacks to the side.

"You will need more than that to best Merlin's heir," Patty smirked.

"Yur late!" Asha screamed dodging a throwing dart.

"I know, they tried to hide the battle from me, but a little bird told me what was happening," Patty explained.

"Good, we can kill you too," Meem purred.

"You can try, but killing a brother of the temple is much harder than it seems," Patty grinned.

"Oye, Patty, ya best not be flirtin' with that hussy!" Asha warned.

"I wouldn't dream of it," Patty called back.

Without warning Aster streaked forward at the Captain, the Captain met him and together they dance their deadly dance. They both fought with two swords which blurred too fast for even her to follow. Their kicks and punches were faster than any she had ever thrown. On the other side, Patty and Meem stood face to face, trading earth shattering blows. Fireballs in varying sizes and shapes flashed in and out of existence. Meem drew a slim sword and attacked. Patty's staff blurred, fending off the physical attacks.

Asha was too distracted by their fight and missed a parry. She felt the blade slip past her guard. She twisted enough that it didn't hit her heart but it did get stuck between two ribs. Aster's demon pounced on her. He tried to end the fight, but he was thrown to the side. Bubbles stood over Asha, his sides heaving and slathered in sweat from the exertion getting to the top of the hill. He ignored the knife stabbing him in the gut so he could try to get his jaws around the demon's neck. His claws tore chunks out of the demon's arms. With a mighty heave he threw Bubbles to the side. While his arms were extended, Asha threw a knife trying to bury it in chest, but the Demon twisted out of the way.

Asha crawled over to Bubbles and laid her head on his limp body. He whimpered, and she whimpered with him. Together, they watched the Demon slink toward them. She glared at him while licked his dagger and raised it for the final blow. The blade came flashing down but she didn't blink.

"No, you don't!" A figure screamed at it dove between her and the Demon.

The Demon tried to redirect the blade. His strike swiped Asha's rescuer's face and blocked his blade as well.

"Gaaah!" Barry screamed while holding the ruined mess where his eye had been.

The Demon tried to take a step forward, but stumbled. He plucked a small needle from his arm and looked at it in disbelief.

"Poison?" he asked in disbelief, "Poison is a coward's weapon…"

"Perhaps," Barry grunted, straightening and walking towards him, "But I won't let you hurt her. And this," he said motioning to his own dagger, "This is what I will use on you."

The Demon tried to fend him off, but the poison was in his

blood, slowing him. Barry pushed his hands down and calmly stabbed him through the eye.

"An eye for an eye," Barry grunted. He unceremoniously heaved the body off the edge of the cliff and returned to Asha.

He placed his hands on her wound, stemming the flow of blood. Asha clutched his hands in one of hers. Her other held Bubbles' wound. She looked into Barry's good eye, a question in her own eyes.

"It's a scratch, beautiful. Besides, like I told him, I couldn't let him kill you. The world is dark enough with the light of my life in it. With out you…," Barry answered clearing his throat. "We can talk about it later. There's still lots of battle left."

Asha turned her attention back to the fights raging around her. There was a scuffle at the top of the path as the Captain's men kept Aster's men from interfering in the fight. She couldn't tell who all was fighting there but it appeared that the Captain's men were winning. She turned to see how Patty was doing.

Patty had Meem from behind and was driving a knife slowly toward her eye. He was so intent he didn't notice the figure forming behind him. Asha recognized the rippling patterns of a Shadow Step. Someone as strong and important as Meem would have her own Demon too. Asha tried to call out, but her throat wouldn't work.

She didn't have to worry though; another figure appeared behind the Demon. Meem's Demon didn't have time to react before Rashta's blade enter entered the base of his skull. Meem felt her Demon die and screamed in shock. She knew she was done. Lightning crackled down her arms as she used her life-force to create one last spell, a self-destruct.

Patty dropped her so he could clutch his staff with both hands.

Meem's explosion went upwards and out away from the temple. The last part of Meem's explosion shattered the spell Patty had constructed to funnel the explosion harmlessly upwards. The shockwave of his own shattered spell threw him in the air. His limp body hit the ground with a sickening thud. Asha felt tears spring to her eyes. She watched his chest rise and fall. His face was grey, but he was alive. For now, he was live. She sobbed in relief and buried her face in Barry's chest. She composed herself and turned her attention to the Captain.

Aster and the Captain picked themselves off the ground and resumed their fight. Asha watched, barely able to follow their flashing blades. Aster swung his blade in with reckless strength. The Captain's right sword shattered under the blow. Aster laughed and brought his swords down on a double over head strike. The Captain used his left sword to block both blades.

"It's over *Captain,*" Aster sneered pressing down.

"You poor fool, these are the Blessed Swords of the Sun," the Captain grunted back.

Aster realized what the Captain had said, just as he was stabbed in the heart by the newly regrown blade. His mouth flopped up and down, but no sounds came out. The Captain grabbed him before he fell to the ground. He held his head with one and his hand with the other cradling him tenderly like a child.

"Sleep, brother. Sleep," the Captain soothed.

Aster's eyes fluttered gently. As the light slowly faded from his eyes, the bloodrage faded as well. Even through this, the rage and hate burned there, bright as ever. Even when he died, his eyes stared on in angry accusation. The Captain closed them gently before retrieving his sword from the body. Asha tried to move again, but her body was even weaker. The Captain came over to her, tears in his eyes. His Bloodrage had cleared. Tears streamed down her face as well.

He glanced at her wounds, sizing them up. His hands started to glow with a healing spell but the light winked out before he could bring it to her. He took a deep breath and tried again. Small sparks play along his arms. Asha and Barry both reached out to stop him before he could channel the spell.

"No, not like that, sir. I'm dyin' an' that's okay. Ya need ta live more'n I do, sir. It was an honor ta have served ya as long as I did," Asha smiled.

"Asha, I'm so sorry, this isn't what I wanted for you," he whispered holding her hand.

"Not my plan either," Slappy growled.

Asha peeked over the Captain's shoulder and saw the blood-streaked sweaty, man grinning at them. He knelt down next to her, and the Captain placed a hand on his shoulder. A grumpy looking man walked up to Slappy's side.

"Yender, I'll need your magic, come here," Slappy ordered.

"She's too far gone, that one, m'Lord," Yender protested.

Slappy spun and slapped him in one fluid motion snarling, "I'm no lord. If I think I can save her than I can. Maybe you can't but I can."

Yander bowed his head in deference and placed a hand on Slappy's back. She felt the spells inflate her lungs, and knit her bones together.

"Thank you," she gasped when her vision cleared.

Slappy grunted but he was too busy healing Bubbles to

respond properly. When he finished with him, they moved on to Patty. Patty only needed little healing before he was sitting up rubbing his head quickly.

"Sir, let's not do that again," Patty suggested.

"I second that motion," Slappy griped squatting down, holding his head between his hands.

"Motion carries," the Captain laughed, but then turned serious. "Let's end this. The battle is all but over, and the druids have far too much to answer for. Now that Aster is dealt with, I will deal with them. How do we get in?"

"You have to get past the doors," Patty explained, "Careful they cheat."

"So do I," the Captain said with a grin.

"Sir, we need ta rest. This was a bad day, an' we can't rush inta dis one. Them lil' buggers are not ta be messed with," Asha warned.

"They are more off balanced then they will ever be. We put everything on the line for them and they didn't even have the decency to say thank you," the Captain growled.

"Well, now, we wouldn't want them to miss out on the opportunity to have good manners," Slappy said with a grin.

"Aye, I suppose not," Asha agreed.

He summoned his Bloodrage again and wrenched on the doors ripping chunks out them until he was able to step through.

"Interesting," Patty mused.

"What?" Asha asked.

"Well to get in I had to destroy the old doors. My graduation project was to rebuild them. Merlin built the originals, so I used my staff to rebuild them again. They hated me for my perfection," he said dramatically, "I made the doors so that they would resist just about any magical attack, but the Captain ripped the doors apart with brute strength. I didn't think that was possible. He's probably the only one in the world that can do that."

"Maybe we should follow him in?" Slappy asked.

"Aye," Asha agreed.

Inside they found an angry fat druid blocking the Captains path.

"Now just who do you think you are?" he asked.

The Captain waved his sword under his nose and smiled evilly.

"I am the Guardian of the Light, I am here by right of conquest and I have come for what is mine," he said pleasantly.

"So you are. May I have your name Guardian? For the records?" A wizened old druid asked from a side room.

"I am Lancelot Arturius Pendragon, heir to the throne of the Sun, and rightful king of mankind."

"This way your majesty. If you will follow me, I will add your name to the records."

"I have no interest in your petty formalities. I have wasted enough time waiting on you."

"Sir, Arthur did it too," Patty interjected.

"Really?"

"Yes, sir. It's just how you start. From there you can go anywhere in the temple. Mathis is a good man, one of the few in this snake pit," Patty assured him.

Once he followed Mathis into the records room, the rest of the group looked around awkwardly.

"Whose hungry?" Patty asked.

Epilogue

"Are you sure about this?" Patty asked.

"I am," Barry replied.

"You know she will most like kill you if she finds out you lied to her. You could tell her you got it fixed," Patty reasoned.

"No. It's my best feature right now, and the fewer people that know about it the better off I will be," Barry replied, "Everyone heard you say that you couldn't heal it so no one will doubt that."

"I hope you know how much it kills me to this and not be able to tell people that I pulled off the impossible," Patty pouted.

"Then why help me?" Barry asked.

"Because, for now she's happy, and that's all that matters. Just…don't come to me when she comes after you."

Barry nodded as he placed an eye patch over his restored eye.

"You're okay with this?" Barry asked.

"I'm not her father. If you're what she wants, then that's what I want for her too. I gave her the freedom to choose her own destiny. She knows what she wants," Patty assured him.

"But you and her…?"

"What? No! Dude, she the little sister I never had and always wanted."

"Oh. Good."

"Did you find out who took the body?" Patty asked changing the subject.

"How would I know?" Barry asked.

"You're always looking into everything. If anyone knows, you do," Patty countered.

Barry chuckled. He nodded to Patty with a crooked smile, "You're right of course. Best I can tell a few of the goons weren't as dead as we thought they were, and they snuck off with the body before we came back out."

"He's not going to like that. I think he wanted to burn the body himself, or maybe make me do it," Patty grumbled.

"He was a worthy opponent. I think that was his last rights, you know the acknowledgement of a worthy foe, someone he could respect, maybe not like, but definitely respect."

"I suppose that's true. What about Javi?" Patty wondered.

"The High Commander," Barry reminded him, "went to the Bastion of the Light. Apparently, he was over eager to read the documents hidden in the tower."

"Jealous?" Patty tease.

"Maybe. Aren't you?" Barry asked.

"A little. The druids still won't let me in to their libraries. I may be a full brother, but they still don't like me."

"I can't say that I blame them."

"Ouch."

Barry roared in laughter. "Oh, Patty my lad, this isn't a

military institution. They don't just have to take it like they do in the military. This is a political playground. If you want to rise and not get killed, you're going to have to play the game."

"That sounds…horrible," Patty moaned.

"Well, that's your lot in life I guess," Barry grinned, "Don't worry I know how to play the game better than anyone."

Asha stood on the road into the village. The walls were in shambles, the gate was missing and people were still looking through the bodies for loved ones. Her boots sank a little into the mud. It was still wet from the blood of the previous day's battle.

She reached down and scooped up a handful of the saturated soil. She confirmed Travis's blood but the trail was too contaminated to follow. The villagers had told her that the strange Sons had gathered up Travis's corpse and taken it with them. She was furious with them, but without a trail there was no way for her to follow them.

"Now why would they wanna take 'is body fer I wonder," Asha mumbled.

"I dunno m'Lady, but I gave him a drink and they took him south," a grimy little lad informed her.

Asha shot him a glare, but the boy didn't flinch. His little brother, the resemblance was obvious, hid behind him.

"Who are ya boy?" she asked.

"I am not a boy. General Travis named me a man," the boy said furiously.

Asha laughed softly. "Alright, I'll give ya that. Why did they take 'im that way?"

"He told them to, m'Lady. He said there was someone he wanted to see before he died. Some princess or somethin'."

Asha gave him a small smile, and nodded. Now she realized why they had carted him off. She figured he had probably lasted long enough to see that done.

He felt the stiffness in his limbs and knew what it meant before he opened his eyes. He shoved the corpses off of himself and pulled the golden blade from his chest. His skin crackled as the magic healed the wound. His own magic filled his body, banishing the stiffness from his body.

He looked around but couldn't find a weapon besides the golden blade, but he would never use that. He dusted himself off and headed into the woods. That pretender may have won this first round, but a Guardian is never so easily bested. Next time it wouldn't be him that found himself among the corpses.

He stood on top of the cliff looking down at the plains below him. The sides were perfectly smooth, and the raised land held a perfect vantage point. The road to the top was narrow but perfect. The climb up hadn't been taxing for him but for the druids that had brought him here, the climb had been exhausting. He could hear their ragged breath. He was tempted to laugh at the fat ones weezing but he squashed the desire as soon as it surfaced.

"Lord Captain," Pablo whispered from behind him, "The druids are asking again why we had to come here."

"You can use my name now, Pablo" he replied, "I had to see it. This spot, right here, this is where Arthur died. He planned to build his city here, and I think it's perfect as well. This will be my seat of power."

"It will require a lot of work, and many years to establish it," Pablo observed.

He nodded in agreement. It would take a lot of manpower, but it would be worth it. It would be perfect. From here he would save mankind.

A warm breeze, blew into the cave carrying a leaf straight on to his nose. He snorted blowing the leaf away. He opened the outer lid to make sure the leaf actually blew away. He sighed to himself in sleepy boredom. A scent in the wind brought something to his attention. The winds were wrong. No, not wrong, they had been wrong for as long as he could remember, and now they were right again. Almost. It was time for him to leave the cave. At last, he was free. He stretched and headed out into the world. Men had forgot him, but they would remember him soon enough.

www.ingramcontent.com/pod-product-compliance
Lightning Source LLC
Chambersburg PA
CBHW021239200726
48288CB00014B/52